PRAISE FOR K.J.
SWORN

"*Fortuna Sworn* is a lush, action-packed fantasy with an ending you won't see coming!" —Jessi Elliott, author of *Twisted Fate*

"K.J. Sutton has created a world that is equal parts mesmerizing and terrifying… for fantasy readers who are looking for a little fresh and a lot fantastic!" —Tome Tender Book Blog

"I absolutely adored this book." —SnoopyDoo's Book Reviews

"Prepare to delve into a dark and twisted world!" —Perspective of a Writer

"[K.J. Sutton] has got me hooked." —Mindy Lou's Book Review

"Sutton… managed to create a spin on not only the fae but other supernatural creatures that will fascinate you [and] leave you turning the pages as fast as you possibly can!" —My Guilty Obsession

"The romance tantalizes and teases… leaving the reader begging for more." —This Girl Reads a Lot

"A captivating, fast-paced paranormal fantasy that is sure to sweep you away to a world unlike any other." —Lovely Loveday

"*Fortuna Sworn* created a die-hard fan in me." —BookedMercy

FORTUNA SWORN

K.J. SUTTON

ONCE UPON A TIME
books

ISBN 978-1-087-92183-9 (hardback)

ISBN 978-0-578-48967-4 (paperback)

ISBN 978-0-578-52101-5 (e-book)

This is a work of fiction. Names, characters, places, and incidents either are the products of the author's imagination or are used fictitiously. Any resemblance to actual persons, living or dead, businesses, companies, events, or locales is entirely coincidental.

Front cover image by Gwenn Danae

Typography by Jesse Green

Published in the United States of America

ALSO BY K.J. SUTTON

The *Fortuna Sworn* Saga

Fortuna Sworn

Restless Slumber

Deadly Dreams

Beautiful Nightmares

The *Charlie Travesty* Serial

with Jessi Elliott

A Whisper in the Dark

A Light in the Dusk

A Memory in the Flame

A Sacrifice in the Smoke

Standalones

Straight on 'Til Morning

Novellas

Summer in the Elevator

Please be aware this novel contains scenes or themes of slavery, profanity, spiders, an eating disorder, sexual harassment, an abusive relationship, violence, cannibalism, an animal death, sex, and murder.

I hold a beast, an angel, and a madman in me.

—Dylan Thomas

PREFACE

The room was warm and inviting. A cheery fire burned, the bed was made, and a bath awaited. Nothing had changed since I left hours ago. It seemed bizarre, even wrong, because everything had changed.

Feeling hollow, I walked to the water basin and put my hands inside. Red instantly bloomed across the clear surface. As I watched it, a whimper escaped me. Suddenly I was frantic. I rubbed at my skin so violently that water sloshed over the sides of the bowl. Within seconds all the blood was off, but it wasn't enough. I kept rubbing, scraping, splashing. I needed to feel clean.

Only when my hands were pink and stinging did I realize the truth; I would never be clean again.

Breathing hard, I backed away from the basin. The room was too quiet, too still. Water dripped onto the dirt floor. Seconds or minutes ticked by; I wasn't certain which. Eventually I drifted to the fire, drawn to the life emanating from those bright flames. Slowly, I dropped to my knees. The warmth comforting, almost a presence of its own. But, inevitably, the events that had just transpired came creeping back. What I had seen. What I had done.

Quietly, so no one would hear, I pressed my face against my hands and wept.

CHAPTER ONE

ONE WEEK EARLIER

*T*hey put me in a cage.

After that, they loaded it into the back of a van. I tilted with the container and slammed hard onto my elbow, but I didn't give them the satisfaction of crying out. The doors closed, leaving me in darkness. I sat there and shook with rage as the engine rumbled to life. I could hear my captors talking and laughing. One made a lewd joke.

I didn't bother demanding to know our destination; they had been talking about the market for the three days I'd been in their grasp. More often than not, it was a place Fallen went to die.

Fallen. I hadn't had to use that term in ages. Every species— faeries, werewolves, shapeshifters, nymphs—were descended from angels. No one knew whether it was mutation or evolution that had separated us.

My captors thought I was a werewolf or a faerie, both of which would fetch a high price. Some buyers would pay even more if they intended to kill the creature and sell its parts. It was well-known that the muscles of a werewolf gave you unparalleled strength. The hands of a faerie lent you their magic. The lungs of a nymph brought the ability to breathe underwater.

The heart of my kind would eliminate all the eater's fears.

I didn't allow myself to wonder what would happen if I caught the attention of a buyer; I'd find a way to escape before then.

It was still hard to believe this was happening. I kept replaying the kidnapping in my head, cursing my own recklessness. A few nights ago, I'd been in the woods. During my exploration of those hills, a splash of color had caught my notice. A flower, nestled in the grass, beneath the sky's luminous glow. As I'd knelt to admire it, something struck me from behind.

And here I was.

Hours later, my muscles were screaming. Just when I thought I would finally open my mouth and give the pain a voice, the van lurched to a halt. The engine died again. My captors got out, still talking, and the doors opened. Brightness poured inside. I squinted, so disoriented that I forgot to curse at them as they took hold of the cage.

The selling hadn't begun yet. It was mid-morning and everything was awash in soft, yellow light. Dew still clung to the grass. Every time someone spoke, white puffs of air accompanied the words. The men—although I suspected they were goblins, based on the greed that shone from their dark eyes—carried me along a row of stalls, platforms, and cages. Vendors and merchants unpacked their wares or lined up their prisoners. Chains clinked, undoubtedly dipped in holy water. The stories of iron or silver holding us had been fabricated for humans.

The holy water also made it difficult to maintain any glamour —a powerful but subtle magic that disguised a Fallen's true form. In passing, I caught a glimpse of wings. Those were worth a fortune, as well.

As my captors found a place for their prize, I couldn't resist looking at the rest of those for sale. A boy stared back at me with his watery blue gaze. He stood on a small, wooden platform, a sign around his neck that displayed his species and price. Vampire. They could be out in the sun, of course; they simply preferred the night. He looked like a boy of twelve or thirteen. If he was lucky, he'd be sold to a family that wanted someone in their kitchen. If he was unlucky, he'd be sold for his incisors—their teeth were useful for witch spells and poisons. But a vampire without his fangs would soon die of starvation.

Within seconds, we were out of each other's line of sight. My captors had found an open spot toward the end of the row, and as they set the cage down, it brought me within reach of them. But even if my powers weren't dormant in the daylight, my bound hands prevented me from touching anyone through the bars. I leaned back to wait for another opportunity. With every second that passed, one thought screamed louder than the rest. Torturing me, taunting me.

Is this what happened to Damon?

"I smell coffee," one of the men said, rubbing his hands together for warmth. "Want to find it?"

The other nodded, and they walked away, leaving me there. The cage was so small that I could only stand bent over or remain seated. I chose the latter. A lovely smell teased my senses, and I saw that an old woman selling herbs and flowers had set up nearby. She noticed me and bared pointed, yellow teeth. I quickly looked away.

While the market filled, I took stock of what I had in my possession for the umpteenth time. Jeans, a plaid button-up, and hiking boots. The men had taken the laces, though, and the rest of my gear. They'd also found Dad's pocket knife after I'd been knocked unconscious.

I began searching the ground for a rock, but my skin prickled in that way it did when someone was watching. Tensing, I lifted my head. There was a male standing in front of me. Not a man, for I knew instantly this was no human.

"Hello there," he said the moment our eyes met.

His hair rested against the back of his neck in soft, brown curls. His cheekbones were sharp and his jawline defined. His irises were gray, or hazel, I couldn't tell from a distance. He wore a wool coat to ward off the chill in the air. He appeared human, but that was the work of a glamour—power rolled off him like perfume. I studied his ears, his eyes, his fingers. Nothing gave him away. He was appealing, yet not so much that he attracted attention.

"What is your name?" the stranger asked. I realized I'd been staring. His voice was crisp and unhurried, like a dead leaf falling from a tree.

"Fuck," I answered, hiding my embarrassment. "Would you like to guess my last name? I'll give you a hint. It rhymes with 'shoe.'"

To my surprise, a faint smile curved his lips. "How refreshing. A slave with spirit left in her."

Though there was no point in engaging with him, the word made my stomach churn with fury. I longed to be free of the rusty bars. "I'm not a slave," I hissed.

He tilted his head. "You're in a cage. You can be purchased. Isn't this the definition of a slave?"

"I'll show you the definition," I purred. "Find the key and let me out."

"Something tells me it's in my best interest to leave you there," the stranger remarked. His tone was dry but his eyes twinkled merrily.

Just I started to respond, my captors returned, cups of coffee in hand. The stranger slipped away soundlessly. I watched him go, noting that he walked as though his feet didn't quite touch the ground. *Faerie*, I thought darkly. Of course, there were any number of things he could be, but my gut told me I was right.

So far, I had yet to meet a faerie I could trust. Once, one came into the bar where I worked and stole tips from my apron while I wasn't looking. Another tried to sexually assault me in the street after a closing shift.

And then there had been Sorcha. Vivacious, lovely, intriguing Sorcha. We'd sensed each other at the movie theatre one night, during my freshman year of high school. Our friendship had been immediate and all-consuming. For me, someone who didn't make friends easily, it had been everything. Then Sorcha seemed to fall off the face of the earth. She stopped texting, stopped coming by, stopped showing up at the local haunts. My theories had ranged from her being killed by a faerie hunter to something with her parents' jobs going wrong.

Weeks later, though, I saw her again at a pool party.

The image was still vivid in my mind. Her laying there on that lounge chair, wearing a neon orange bikini. My stricken face reflecting in the darkness of her sunglasses. When I asked her why she hadn't called me back, she said in a bored tone, "Oh, you didn't know? I'm done with you now."

It had been years since that conversation, but the effect of it hadn't faded.

"...so beautiful. But what is it?" a woman was asking. I tore my focus away from the faerie's retreating back. A couple now stood before the cage. It seemed my captors had found some prospective buyers. The woman studied me like I was a side of meat or a charmed necklace. Insults and taunts rose to my lips.

"Not entirely sure," one of the men replied, giving me a warning glare. His fingers idly brushed against the cattle prod at his hip. I ground my teeth together and stayed silent. "We found it on a mountain, kneeling in some moonlight. It has a lot of power, though. Makes my hair stand on end."

I had never bothered telling these morons the truth; I'd been on the mountain for a purpose, yes, but not to change form or draw power from the moon.

5

That night, I'd been looking for my brother.

There was still some small, unconquerable part of me that couldn't accept he was gone. Really, though, going into the woods had been more for myself than Damon. Two years had passed since I'd come home from work and found his note on the kitchen table. *Went out to check the garden,* it said in my brother's nearly illegible handwriting. It wasn't out of the usual for him to go out in the middle of the night; I felt the restlessness, too, when the moon was bright and high. His vegetable patch was in the backyard, visible through the kitchen window, but I'd been so tired from a shift at Bea's that I didn't even look out the glass before heading to bed.

When I woke up the next morning, his room was still empty.

The sheriff's department went through all the motions. Search parties, missing posters, phone calls to hospitals. Eventually, everyone reached the same conclusion.

Damon Sworn was dead.

The night my captors found me was the anniversary of his disappearance.

Unsurprisingly, the two of them had trouble selling something they couldn't advertise. Guess that hadn't occurred to them in all the excitement of discovering me. The couple moved on, and farther along the row, a young shapeshifter caught their interest. She was so frightened that she couldn't keep hold of one skin, switching from girl to cougar to bird between one breath and the next. She was in a glass box so she couldn't fly away. Anyone who bought her would have to know a spell or possess a bespelled item to keep her from escaping. I watched the couple negotiate with a black-haired woman standing beside the box, but couldn't stomach seeing how it ended. I leaned my temple against the bars and closed my eyes.

More time went by. Mist retreated and sunlight crept forward. The fools trying to sell me grew bored. They got lawn chairs out of the van and started playing a game of cards. Somewhere in the market, an auction began, and the auctioneer was louder than the crowds. I'd barely slept in three days, and I began to drift off, his bellowing voice a bizarre lullaby. "Ten thousand dollar bid! Do I hear fifteen thousand? Now fifteen thousand, will you give me twenty thousand?"

Suddenly there was a clinking sound near my head. I jerked upright so quickly, I nearly collided with the bars. Something glittered on the metal floor, and the breath caught in my throat when I saw what it was.

Keys.

I snatched them up, terrified that my captors had noticed. But they'd started drinking hours earlier, and they saw nothing but their bottles and cards. I looked around for whoever had left this unexpected gift. There were only merchants, buyers, and slaves. No one looked in my direction.

I'd asked one person for a key—the faerie. Why would he help me? What did he stand to gain from my escape?

Questions that I would ask myself later. I tucked the keys into my pocket and waited. Everything inside of me longed to take action, but sunlight still touched the market, keeping my abilities dormant. Any escape attempt would fail.

Night was slow in coming. Though I continually started to tap and fidget, I forced myself to be still again. Eventually the sky darkened and part of the moon turned its face toward us. Feeling its effects, some of the other captives began to whine and pull at their chains. Fortunately for the slavers, it wasn't a full moon. While werewolves weren't forced to change, as the humans believed, they were stronger then. We all were.

My captors had been careful to avoid physical contact these past three days. It was the only intelligence they'd displayed. At their cabin, they'd kept me tied up in a storage room, with just a bucket for company. I'd had to eat food from a bowl like a dog. When they decided to switch to the cage, they'd used tranquilizer darts. Several, in fact, since they weren't certain what I was.

And if I happened to be allergic or have a bad reaction to the drugs, well, too bad.

I remembered all of this as dusk faded, and the fire crackling within me climbed higher and hotter. Starlight shone serenely upon the market. My captors put away their chairs, talking about possibilities for tomorrow. The small-eyed one suggested using torture to find out what I was. The other mentioned displaying me naked. Every word only stoked the flames.

Luck was finally on my side. Slavers and vendors were so preoccupied packing up their wares, no one saw me use the key and slip out of the cage. Well, no one but the shapeshifter, whose eyes met mine for a brief moment before she fixed hers pointedly on her feet. She'd been sold earlier, so I had no idea why she was still here. Maybe her new owners had gone to get another vehicle. Couldn't have a dirty slave on their sleek leather upholstery, now, could they?

Like the rest of my kind, I moved silently, creeping upon the kidnappers like a dream. My heart pounded harder as I edged around the van. I would only have one chance to do this right; goblins possessed enhanced speed, strength, and healing abilities. The men were lifting the empty cooler inside when my time came. Quickly, giving them no chance to react, I opened the door on the other side. They were just lifting their heads when I reached across and grasped their wrists—no easy task with my own hands tied. That was all it took. I had hold of their minds now, and before they could seize me or shout an alarm, I disappeared in a burst of black smoke. To them, anyway. Anyone else would still see me, standing there, smiling like a cat with its paw in a bowl of dead mice.

I allowed my voice to slither around them, echo a thousand times, as though I were a legion instead of one. "You will regret the night you took me. You will repent for these last three days."

"What are you?" the small-eyed goblin whimpered. For goblins they were. A single touch had told me so much.

It wasn't enough to answer. Instead, I let go of their wrists and circled the van—Nightmares don't sit on our victims' chests as they sleep, like it describes on Wikipedia or in books; once I touch someone, there's no need to maintain physical contact—until I was right behind them. I leaned close and pressed the side of my chin against the trembling goblin's temple. I stroked the back of his head with my still-bound hands. He probably would've bolted right then, but I'd made them believe they couldn't move. "I am the last of my kind," I whispered. "Does that mean anything to you?"

His breathing was ragged. There were only a few deadly possibilities, and everyone paid attention to endangered species. Especially slavers. Better selling value, of course. The thought made my nails dig into his scalp. The goblin made another sound, deep in his throat. Now that I had finally touched him, I could taste his terror. Everyone's had a unique flavor and most were decidedly unpleasant. This one had the tang of chicken fat, and it coated my tongue.

I hardly noticed, however, as images flickered across my closed eyelids; I'd found his fears. Not all of them, not the ones that kept him awake at night. But the phobias that hovered just beneath his skin, ready to come out at a moment's notice, those were mine. The small-eyed goblin had typical ones. Spiders, heights, death.

His companion was a bit more interesting. Above all, he dreaded being alone.

Now that's exactly what he was.

All the goblin saw was whiteness. There was no ground and no sky, no walls and no surroundings. He wrapped his arms around his knobby knees—no glamour, because this was his own mind, after all—and began to rock back and forth. His pointed teeth flashed as he sang a song his mother had taught him. Meanwhile, the other was slapping at his own arms and legs, believing himself to be covered in spiders. Cliché, maybe, but there was no time for ingenuity.

I held out my wrists, making the goblin believe they were his. He couldn't very well slap at any spiders if his hands were tied, so he desperately yanked Dad's knife out of his boot and hacked at the ropes. I tried to jerk back, but he was too fast. The blade nicked my arm. I hissed at the pain. The ropes fell away, though, and I ended the illusion before the goblin could cut my entire hand off. He returned to slapping at the spiders, dropping Dad's knife, and I bent to retrieve it. It was a welcome weight in my hand.

He'd loved this thing. The blade was Damascus steel, made by a hand-forged process of folding and refolding layers of hot high-carbon steel and iron. There were beautiful swirls and contours along its length. The handle was made of dyed wood, which I rubbed affectionately with my thumb before tucking the knife away.

Despite an ever-increasing sense of urgency, I lingered to observe my handiwork. The other goblin was already soaked in his own urine. Satisfaction curled around my heart. Smirking, I climbed into the van to reclaim my belongings. Everything was scattered, presumably from when they'd dug through everything on the day of my capture. They must have gotten rid of my phone—no doubt it was back at the cabin. I didn't know where that was, and not even an expensive iPhone could tempt me to find the place again. Seething, I slung my bag on and got out of the van. I planned on driving it back home, but I couldn't leave. Not yet.

Outside, the goblins were both crying now. I still put more power into their visions. More spiders, more echoes. They wouldn't be free of me until dawn, if the terror didn't kill them before then.

I hurried into the aisle of crushed grass and straggling

buyers. Using my power after so long—I hadn't touched it even before the goblins took me, so it had been a few weeks since the last time, probably—made the blood in my veins feel like champagne. My head felt fuzzy, too. It was better than any drink or drug. Striding through the market, I cracked my neck in an effort to stay alert. At the same time, I noticed someone standing a few yards away. My steps slowed.

The faerie stood in a slant of moonlight, and in that moment, he truly looked like the angels we were all descended from. The corners of his mouth tilted up in a half-smile. I scowled in return, still distrustful, regardless of the fact that he'd aided my escape. Was he coming to collect a debt? Did he want me for his own?

Apparently not, because once again, he turned and walked away.

I suspected it wasn't the last I'd see him. Shaking myself, I continued on through the market. My progress didn't go unnoticed; Nightmares always drew stares. Whenever someone looked at me, they saw whatever face they believed the most beautiful. Like the nightmares that came at night, we were meant to be seductive. We were designed to lure our victims in. Then, when it was too late to draw back, we struck.

I couldn't find the keys for each and every cage. I also couldn't take on all the slavers here. But there was one thing I could do.

The woman who had sold the shapeshifter was preoccupied with a game on her phone. It was impressive she even got a signal up here. I knelt in front of her. "Hello."

"What do you want?" she asked without looking up. She looked entirely human and there was no trace of glamour. Her hair was gray at the roots. The rest was an unnatural, black dye.

I wrapped my fingers around her ankle, the closest patch of bare skin within reach. The woman's head snapped up, but it was too late. She was afraid of small spaces, shrinking walls, being locked in the dark. With another wicked grin, I made her believe she was the one in a glass box. The woman jumped up, gasping, and fumbled with a chain hanging around her neck. A key appeared at the end of it. She fit it into the lock, and the door swung open. The shapeshifter scrambled out so quickly that she tripped on her skirt. She took a few steps, paused, and faced me again.

"Thank you," she whispered. Hair hung over her eyes, hiding them from view, but there was gratitude in her voice.

Before I could reply, she transformed into an owl and flew away.

CHAPTER TWO

*B*y the time I got home, dawn shone over the horizon.
I parked the van and heaved a sigh. Seconds ticked by, but I made no move to get out. Instead I sat there and stared at the house. All the windows were dark and it radiated emptiness. Even my truck was absent, which was probably still parked at the base of the mountain. Tears blurred my vision, but I wiped them away roughly.

The clock read 6:36 a.m. I stared at the green, glowing numbers. They would be starting breakfast at Bea's. If I closed my eyes, I could hear the quiet chatter and smell the frying bacon. My grip tightened on the steering wheel. Part of me was tempted to go straight there, avoid the inevitable silence of those rooms in front of me. But the customers probably wouldn't appreciate the layer of grime and sweat on my skin. The employees, either.

So I got out and went inside.

First, I took a long shower. As the hot water pounded down on me, I finally took stock of the wounds I'd been trying to ignore. Bruises, scrapes, burns. The adrenaline had drained from my veins, leaving exhaustion in its wake. I'd only been gone three days, but it felt like three years. I moved like the old woman from the market, as though my very bones hurt.

My room was exactly as I'd left it. I pulled a pair of sweatpants from the dresser, along with a huge t-shirt. Then I curled onto the bed and stared at the flowered wallpaper.

I'd rented this house for me and Damon at eighteen—the previous owner had died and her family lived hours away in Denver. Therefore, as long as I paid the rent on time, no one bothered me.

Hoping to silence the thoughts in my head, I burrowed beneath the ancient quilt and waited for sleep to take me.

Instead, I tossed and turned for two hours. In doing so, I kept catching glimpses of the clock on the nightstand. Magic still stirred inside me, eager for an outlet. Usually I had pills in the medicine cabinet, but I'd run out a week before my trip to the mountain. It was why I'd been there in the middle of the night, restlessness driving me, despite the darkness and danger.

Now every time I closed my eyes, I was back in that cabin. Rope rubbing my wrists raw. Laughter drifting through the wall. For a while, I let myself cry. Mom always said there was no shame in it, but usually I refused to. It either drew attention or made me feel vulnerable, two things I loathed.

At last, when my eyes were puffy, I gave up on sleeping. I tossed the blankets aside and yanked on some jeans. It was only 8:47 a.m. I opened the cupboard beneath the kitchen sink, where we kept the cleaning supplies.

I spent the day taking my frustrations out on the house.

By 5:27 p.m., my skin was bright red from scrubbing. The carpet was vacuumed, the floors gleamed, the dishes were neatly stacked, the sheets were washed. I'd hauled everything out of the van, and the goblins' belongings were either in the trash bin or on a shelf in the garage. Most of it had been wrappers and crumpled beer cans. There were a couple interesting items, though. A jar full of flesh-eating pixies—most people mistook their bites for mosquitos—and a clunky ring. Power radiated from the stones and I didn't dare put it on.

With nothing else to do, I got back in the van and drove to town. It took an hour to buy and set up a new cell phone. Then I finally headed to Bea's.

Granby, Colorado, boasted a population of 1,864 people. The bar I'd been working at for the past six years was a run-down building on Main Street. It was tucked between the post office and an antique shop. I found a parking space one block away and caught my reflection in the rearview mirror. I wished I'd thought to bring some concealer. It wouldn't completely hide the smudges beneath my eyes, but at least I'd look tired instead of haunted. Well, there was nothing to do about it now. Sighing some more, I opened the door and got out.

I'd arrived just before the dinner rush. There were six or seven people filling the booths when I walked in, and I recognized almost every face. That didn't stop them from gaping, and it wasn't because of my obvious exhaustion. Though my power worked on most creatures, it was particularly influential on humans.

I ignored them all and went to the back. The floorboards moaned with every step. It brought me past the order window, where Cyrus was cooking at the stove. As I watched, he wiped an arm across his forehead. I reached over the metal shelf to turn on the fan for him—sometimes he forgot, if he was feeling particularly agitated—and headed down the hall. The familiarity of it all was even more comforting than being home.

My boss was in her office. She was on the phone, and when I tapped on the door, it creaked open. Wearing an annoyed expression, Bea glanced up. "Not a good..." She trailed off at the sight of me.

"Should I come back later?"

She hung up on whoever was still talking on the other end. Then she shoved the chair back so roughly the legs screeched. In three long-legged strides, Bea was there. Though she knew I avoided physical contact, she yanked me to her in a gruff hug. Somehow I'd forgotten how tall she was. "Jesus Christ, where have you been?" her voice rumbled against my ear.

I swallowed. Bea had no idea what I was or what other secrets the world hid, so she wouldn't believe the truth. Any other version of it would lead to calling the police. And if officers went to that market, they would only find an empty clearing. "Out of town," was all I said, pulling away.

"And you couldn't let me know?" Bea demanded, holding my elbows in her rough palms. "We've been worried sick around here—you haven't missed a shift since the day you started. We even filed a missing persons report."

Her fears were sweeping through me, no matter how hard I tried to fight it; Bea was terrified of flying and public speaking. Some of her memories came along with them, like bits of skin on a bandage. I saw Bea as a child, standing in a brightly-lit auditorium. A man asked her to spell something, and she just stared back at the crowd, silent and frozen.

Invading the privacy of someone I respected made my head hurt. When I spoke, my voice was sharper than I meant it to be. "Do I still have a job here, or not?"

She frowned. Between her and Gretchen, Bea was the one who was always worried, and her face settled into the familiar wrinkles. "Is this about Damon, honey?"

Hearing his name spoken out loud only made the pain in my skull worse. I didn't want to talk about my brother. "No," I managed. "Look, I know I should've told you before I left. I'm sorry."

Bea let out a breath. She pulled her long ponytail over her shoulder. "Promise me it won't happen again."

At this, I hesitated. Dad's lessons were never far from my mind, no matter how long ago they'd occurred. *Fortuna, never make a promise that you can't keep. Nightmares may be lies, but we don't have to be liars.* "I'll do my best," I said.

She didn't seem to notice the evasion. Bea squeezed my arm, smiling warmly, and someone called her name. Her attention moved toward the hallway. She sighed and focused on me again. "Duty calls. Of course you still have a job here, Fortuna. There's an extra shirt in your locker, right? We didn't touch a thing."

The same voice called again, a bit more urgently this time. Bea hurried out, closing the door behind her. I went to my locker and changed into my uniform. It hadn't been washed recently; the cotton smelled like grease and coffee. I secured the apron with a loose knot, put on my tennis shoes, and clocked in for the night.

The bar was already getting busy. "Order up," Cyrus said, ringing the bell. A server I didn't recognize hurried to take the plates. She turned, holding the edge carefully, but the tip of her finger had still touched some gravy.

"Damn it," I heard her mutter. The voice was familiar; she was the one who'd called for Bea earlier. My natural distrust kicked in. I appraised the beautiful girl while she adjusted her hold on the plate. She was black and petite, her hair wild and shoulder-length. Dark lashes fringed brown eyes and her eyebrows were enviously thick. Freckles dotted her nose and cheeks.

I sensed no power around her.

Just then, the girl spotted me, and a wide smile stretched across her face. "You must be Fortuna! Everyone has been talking about you."

"Well, here I am," I said. "Fortuna Sworn. I'd shake your hand, but..."

She lifted a plate slightly, as if to try it anyway, and laughed a little. "Oh, right. My name is Ariel. It's nice to meet you. In advance, I'm sorry if I spill or drop something. I started last night, and they really just throw you in, huh?"

I gave her a rueful smile. "Bea has a firm belief in her 'sink or swim' teaching method."

"No kidding. Well, I better bring these to table nine. He gets a little handsy if I make him wait."

I looked over her shoulder, toward the customer she was talking about. Ian O'Connell, one of the local deputies. He was watching the two of us with a rapt, hungry expression. Our eyes met, and his burned with desire. No girl should have to deal with him on her first day. I turned back to Ariel. "I can take this one, if you want. I'll make sure you get the tip."

"If you're sure," she replied uncertainly, but she relinquished the plates easily enough.

"It's not a problem."

People pretended not to watch as I walked toward Ian with his food. His smile grew with every step. I'd known the round-faced deputy for years now, and he hadn't improved from our first meeting. He'd slapped my ass and I'd punched him in the face. Though he had never tried to touch me again, Ian O'Connell knew how to hold a grudge.

I set his steak and potatoes down, along with a piece of pie. Before I could speak, he said in a low voice, "We have a pot going, you know."

The badge pinned to his uniform gleamed, and I resisted the urge to rip it off. "What are you talking about?"

"Well, everyone has theories about where you disappeared to. Mine was that you finally got your cherry popped and were off on a three-day sex bender. Was I right? Did I win?"

God, give me patience or an untraceable handgun, I thought.

My virginity was a popular topic in Granby, which had become public knowledge when I'd made the mistake of confiding in Angela during my early days at Bea's. Contrary to what people believed—which wildly varied from me being a lesbian, or a prude, or a closet transgender person—the reason was very simple. While any partner I had would be focused on the sex, all I would able to feel were the fears emanating from his skin. It was also perturbing that, when they looked at me, they saw a face that wasn't truly mine. Once, I'd almost gone through with it just to have the experience. Something stopped me, though. Maybe some misplaced sense of nostalgia. My parents had been deeply in love, and I couldn't help wanting the same.

"Watch yourself, Ian," I growled now, glaring down at him. "You may have your daddy's money to protect you, but someday even that might not be enough."

"Come on, Fortuna! Help a guy out," he pleaded, completely disregarding this. I gritted my teeth and walked away, feeling his eyes on me the entire time.

Growing up, one of my parents' strictest rules was restraint. To not use our powers unless we had to. But Dad wasn't around to see all the perverts and assholes I dealt with on a daily basis. Sometimes restraint was overrated.

The instant Ian lowered his head to cut the steak, my power surrounded him. It wasn't night, but it must've been close enough. At first, he only felt a slight throb behind his eye. Ian faltered, but went on cutting after a moment. The throb became a full-blown pounding. I could practically hear his thoughts. Could this be the tumor he had feared of getting all his life?

I leaned against the counter, unable to hold back a smirk. For years I'd resisted using this knowledge. But the result was so worth the wait.

"It's good to see you, Fortuna."

I turned to find Gretchen Nelson standing behind me. She was Bea's partner in business and life. Where Bea was tall and heavyset, Gretchen was short and thin. For as long as I had known her, Gretchen had struggled with an eating disorder. But this was not what I usually thought of whenever I was near her —it was Gretchen's unwavering kindness. It was she who'd convinced Bea to give me a chance, six years ago.

I wrapped my arms around her brittle shoulders; Gretchen was the only human that was an exception to my no-touching rule. Her fear shuddered through me. Finding cellulite on her thighs, being unable to button her pants, scornful stares from strangers. There were anxieties that went much, much deeper. But that wasn't how my power worked.

A sudden cry shot through the room, and we quickly parted. At his table, Ian threw down some bills and rushed past. He didn't even pause to offer a final leer or insult. "Oh, dear. I hope there's not an emergency," Gretchen murmured. We watched him practically run through the door.

I hid a smile. "Me, too."

Gretchen gave me her full attention again, and I steeled myself. But she didn't lecture or ask for promises, as Bea had. "Would you talk to Cyrus? He's been pretty rattled since you left," she said softly.

Remorse filled my throat, and I was only capable of nodding. The staff at Bea's had always looked out for our autistic fry cook. He'd seemed fine when I walked by earlier, but it made sense that my absence would be a change in routine for him. Not that I'd had any choice in the matter. Oblivious to my dark thoughts, Gretchen smiled and returned to her place behind the bar.

One of the other servers passed with a full tray balanced on her hand. "You're welcome, by the way, for covering your ass this week," Angela muttered under her breath. "Are you actually going to take a table tonight?"

She bailed her boyfriend out of jail at least once a month, and I'd covered her shifts so many times, I'd lost count. It was hard to summon any guilt. I smiled sweetly. "Nice to see you too, Angie."

"Oh, my God, it's *Angela*. How many times do—"

Cyrus's voice sliced between us, shouting out another order. The bell rang, a high, pure sound. It was a jarring reminder of what I'd been on my way to do. Leaving Angela to her string of complaints, I hurried into the back hallway. Scents poured from the open doorway of Cyrus's domain. Grease spat and sizzled. I rapped on the wall and poked my head in. "Hey, Cyrus. I'm back. How have you been?"

Unlike most bars, the kitchen at Bea's was immaculate. The tiled floor was freshly mopped, the sink empty, the shelves organized. I'd sensed power rising off Cyrus the first time I met him, but whatever he was, it was an aura I had never encountered before. Eventually I concluded that he must be an elf of some kind, one that possessed particular gifts of cleanliness and productivity. If there were such a thing as elves.

It wasn't surprising that he gave no answer. "Order up," Cyrus called again, keeping his back to me. *Ding.*

I hadn't been around then, but Bea told me he used to have anxiety attacks when the servers asked him to say those two words. The phrase didn't seem to cause him trouble anymore, but it was all the customers heard out of his mouth. When I was hired at eighteen, it had taken him six months to utter a word in my own presence. Another six for a sentence. Consistency and patience were the keys to Cyrus Lavender's heart.

Tentatively, I stepped over the threshold. "Listen... I'm really sorry that I took off like that. It wasn't cool."

Silence settled over the small room. One thing I'd learned about Cyrus over the years was that he wouldn't lie. Responses people usually gave because it was expected or normal didn't occur to him. "You worried us," he said finally.

"I know. I would never make you guys feel that way on purpose." But apparently my friend was finished speaking, because his only response was to throw some eggshells into a bin next to the deep fryer. It was almost overflowing, and I frowned at the sight. Replacing bags was the servers' job, and Bea had once given Cyrus stern instructions to never do it for us. It must've been driving him insane since his shift started at noon. No wonder he was in such a bad mood. "Did Angela forget to take the trash out last night?"

"There was a man here asking about you," Cyrus said abruptly, as if I hadn't spoken. "I didn't recognize his face, but I think he was talking to Regina a while before someone told him to leave."

Regina Hart was the local gossip. It seemed every town had one, and she was ours. Her husband had died a few years ago, leaving behind a sizeable life insurance policy, so she spent most of her time eavesdropping at Bea's. But strangers asking about me wasn't out of the ordinary; both men and women often took it upon themselves to find out who I was. Many left phone numbers. Once or twice, talent agents left cards. To them, I was the next Marilyn Monroe, Audrey Hepburn, or Kate Winslet.

I was about to answer when some oil slid down the side of a hot pan. Before I could warn Cyrus, it plopped onto the burner. A flame burst from the stovetop. It died a second later, but that was all it took. Cyrus recoiled. I was already in motion when he hit the opposite wall, shielding his head with his arms. He slid down so he was pressed into a corner. "Cyrus, it's gone, it's over," I said, kneeling beside him. His entire body trembled.

Soothing sounds and meaningless croons left my mouth. Slowly, I dared to touch his hand. Freckles covered every inch of it, and I concentrated on that instead of Cyrus's terror. It spread through me anyway, images of a roaring inferno. I studied the top of his head, thinking of how women envied his hair. In certain lighting, it looked like fire, too. If that wasn't irony, I didn't know what was.

Cyrus was beginning to calm. The tremors weren't so violent, and his ragged gasps had gone quiet. Food continued cooking on the burners; already there was a faint smell of something burning. Gently I said, "If you need a break from the kitchen tonight, no one would be upset if you washed dishes or cleared tables. Gretchen can cook."

He lifted his head and stared at the stove for a moment. Then he pulled his hand away, avoiding my eyes. "No. I'm fine."

After a beat of hesitation, I nodded. Cyrus began to stand, and I moved toward the garbage bin to pull the bag out. Liquid dripped out of the bottom. As I adjusted my grip, I noticed a second bag, tucked behind the bin. It was so full, old food was about to topple onto the tiles. *Damn it, Angela.* "Cy, I'm going to take these out, okay? If you need anything, let me know."

He nodded. I hated to leave Cyrus like that, but I suspected he wanted to be alone. It was a feeling we often shared. So I rushed out of the kitchen, trying to keep the bags from dripping on his clean floor, and pushed the back door open with my shoulder. The hinges squealed.

Moonlight shone into the alley, bouncing off Bea's truck. The dumpster waited in the shadows, tucked against the building. I blew some stray hairs out of my eye and hauled the bags down the stairs. Someone had thrown a knife away in one of them, and the tip was poking out. The plastic was going to tear any second. Grunting, I used all my strength and tossed it in. A piece of bacon landed on my shoulder.

"Shit," I muttered, flicking it off.

"You escape a black market full of slavers and the first thing you do is go back to work?" a familiar voice asked.

I stiffened. Part of me insisted that it was a hallucination or an illusion—there was no way he'd found me here. When I turned, however, there he was. The faerie from the black market. And faerie he was, because I could see those telltale ears now, poking out from beneath his silky-looking hair.

He stood next to Bea's truck, hands shoved in his coat pockets. He looked different from our first meeting. The glamour was still there, but it had altered. The features that had been nondescript during our first encounter were sharper and brighter. The most notable variation, however, was a long scar along one side of his face. It dragged the corner of his left eye down. Somehow it didn't detract from his allure.

"Those goblins won't be coming back. I made sure of it. Plus, no one else is going to pay the bills," I added. My cheeks felt hot. "How did you find me? Are you stalking me now?"

"Hardly. I simply wanted to speak again. Would you like some help with that?"

In response, I lifted the second garbage bag and threw that one into the dumpster, too. I smacked my hands together, then faced him squarely. I didn't miss that he hadn't offered an explanation on how he knew where I worked. "Why were you talking to Regina about me?" I demanded next, putting two and two together. Cyrus had mentioned a man asking questions. "Not sure if you know this, but it's considered creepy when you try to learn things about someone without talking to them directly."

He gave an elegant shrug of his shoulders. Laughter drifted in from the street. "Actually, she volunteered that information. I said I was there to see you. She started talking and couldn't seem to stop."

Everything about his demeanor was nonthreatening, but the power emanating from him was even stronger now. It felt like sparks. This creature didn't come to Bea's for conversation.

"Listen closely, because I'm only going to say this once." I spoke as though there was a razor in my mouth, slicing and cutting with every word. "I'm not a faerie groupie, and I don't like people that come on strong. Whatever you want, you won't get. So go away and leave me alone."

The faerie appraised me. "I'll respect your wishes. But first, I'd like to give you something."

Alarm bells went off in my head, and every muscle in my body went rigid. If he reached for a weapon or used magic, I would fight. No one was going to take me again. "You have no idea what I'm capable of," I warned, readying myself.

"Of course I do," he replied affably, giving me that faint half-smile again. "You're a Nightmare. Your kind has been feared for so long, you've been hunted nearly to extinction. Your hearts are coveted like the fountain of youth. It's been a long time since I've encountered power like yours, but I recognized it instantly."

Hearing the truth out loud, as if he were talking about the weather, made my breath catch. If he had already figured out what I was, nothing I said would deter him. But that didn't stop me from trying. "If I see you again, I'll kill you," I managed. My eyes searched the alley around us, hoping to spot something I could use against him. Then I remembered the knife in the trash bag.

My threat rolled off the faerie like rain down a roof. He inclined his head, looking thoughtful. "I don't make such statements lightly, Fortuna Sworn, but I swear that I intend you no harm," he told me. I remained silent, still considering the time it would take to dive into the dumpster and get that knife.

He waited for a moment or two. When it became evident I wouldn't respond, the faerie bowed. He strolled away without further comment. *So much for that gift*, I thought. A car drove past the mouth of the alley, a flash of lights and metal. Though I jumped, the faerie didn't falter. His movements were graceful and leisurely, which only rankled more; clearly nothing posed a threat to him.

That would have to change.

After he'd rounded the corner and disappeared from sight, I lingered next to the dumpster to make sure he was really gone. The fresh surge of adrenaline coursing through me slowly faded. Its absence made me sag against the dumpster. I hardly noticed the smell. God, I was tired. But there was still a long night ahead of me and I'd committed to a shift. I never broke a promise.

So I straightened, tightened my ponytail, and went back inside.

The hours crawled by. Faces and words blended together. I

smiled, I nodded, I moved. Orders materialized in my notepad and plates appeared in my hands. By closing time, around one a.m., I was nearly delirious. Music played from the jukebox, and the lyrics sounded like they were being sung underwater. I bent to scrub a booth, and someone took the rag out of my hand. "Go home, Fortuna," Bea ordered. Normally I would protest, but this time, I could only manage a bleary nod.

Once again, I got into the goblins' van and drove home.

It occurred to me that the faerie could be following, but if he'd already found where I worked, there was no point in trying to hide. Even so, I glanced in the rearview mirror now and then. There was nothing behind me but trees and a dirt road. Did faeries drive?

Concentrating on the road drained whatever endurance I had left. The moment I put the gear into park and killed the engine, I wanted to close my eyes and fall asleep right there. But the air reeked of stale beer and unwashed bodies, bringing unwanted memories along with it. I forced myself to get out and trudge up the sidewalk. At the front door, I struggled to fit the key in. Darkness hovered at the edges of my vision, and I stumbled in an effort to remain standing.

My foot landed on something hard and raised. Swaying, I looked down. Moonlight reflected off a gilt-edged mirror someone had left on the welcome mat. *What the hell?* I thought wearily. Any other night, I wouldn't have touched or looked at the thing without knowing exactly where it had come from. But caution had disintegrated, along with any of my usual instincts. I leaned over to peer in the glass, expecting to see my own face.

There was something else in the mirror.

Not my face, not the sky above. The haze of exhaustion began to clear as I frowned, picked it up, and brought it closer. Part of me had thought I was imagining the image, but it still depicted a man. He rested on his side, back turned to me. There were scars covering his skin. Not from a whip; these were too short and deep.

As if he could feel me watching him, the man glanced over his broad shoulder. I gasped and almost dropped the mirror.

It was my brother.

CHAPTER THREE

I opened my eyes to rolling hills and pink skies.

Everything I'd fallen asleep to—the ceiling of my bedroom, the image of my brother's ruined back, the faerie's taunting smile—was nowhere to be seen. The only sign of life was a small and solitary house nearby, and I'd been inside many times over the years. If I'd had my way, though, I wouldn't be here right now.

After seeing Damon in the glass, I'd immediately begun packing.

It had taken several minutes to realize that I had no idea where I intended to go. There was no one to torture answers from. No one to tell me who had left the mirror, though I certainly had a theory. *I'd like to give you something.* Savannah, my brother's girlfriend and the only witch I knew, lived hours away. I was in no condition to drive, anyway.

I'd had no choice but to go to bed. I would've thought sleep would be impossible, but it had been disturbingly easy. However much my mind roiled, my body was eager for respite. For once, it won their eternal war.

Now, the familiarity of this place eased the tightness in my chest. The sensation had lingered there since the goblins took me, and I'd grown accustomed to its presence. Now my breath came easier, and for a minute I could only stand there, inhaling and exhaling. When I felt like myself again, I looked around. My lips curved into a smile, which was a sensation I hadn't felt in a long time.

In the distance, there was a figure. He stood with his back to me, a breeze tousling his golden hair. Still in my pajamas, I rushed toward him. My best friend.

Too bad he wasn't real.

Oliver didn't hear me approach. As I got closer, I moved more quietly through the long grass. He continued watching the sunset intently. The line of his shoulders was taut. I settled my hands over his eyes and felt him start. He snatched my wrists in his large hands and whirled. Instantly his warm, brown gaze examined me for wounds or marks. Sometimes I carried them with me into these dreams. "Are you all right?" Oliver asked without preamble, a muscle bulging in his jaw.

As I pondered the answer to this, I couldn't help but admire him for what felt like the millionth time. His hair was thick and swept across his forehead in a perfect, golden wave. His cheekbones were so sculpted that, if he was turned just right, the curves of his face looked like a distant horizon. All of this was topped off with a full, sensuous mouth that was quick to smile.

But there, across the bridge of his nose, was the faintest sprinkling of freckles. That was my favorite part of his face. It was so perfect, so humanizing, so... Oliver.

Instead of responding to the question still hovering between us, I went straight into his arms. For a moment, he was tense and unyielding. As always, though, he relented and held me tight against him. "I am now," I whispered.

For as long as I could remember, Oliver had been waiting the moment I fell asleep. At some point I named him, though I couldn't remember how I'd chosen it now. Maybe it was from a movie or a book. He'd grown up with me, inch by inch, year by year. Eventually our friendship turned into something more. He was the only person I trusted, the only one I could be myself with. Logically, I knew I had created him, either with my power or my mind. He was a coping mechanism for a girl who'd lost her parents. Every night we spent together, a niggling voice insisted that it was time to let go and grow up. *Someday*, I told it.

But that day hadn't come yet.

I made a sound of protest when Oliver pulled back to peer into my face. "You've gone too long without sleep. Is everything all right?" he pressed.

If it were anyone else, I would have a lie perched on the tip of my tongue. But with Oliver, I just mutely shook my head. I tucked myself back into the hollow between his arm and shoulder. He was wearing a t-shirt, and our skin brushed. Even then, it stayed blissfully silent in my head. I had never asked Oliver what he was afraid of, not in all our time together. I didn't want to know. I liked that I couldn't.

Too much time had passed. When I gave no answer, Oliver opened his mouth to ask more questions. Reluctantly I told him, "I was taken by slavers. They tried to sell me at one of the black markets."

Before he could react, I also told him about the faerie and the mirror, which I suspected was the gift he'd mentioned in the alley. The timing of it was too coincidental otherwise. By the time I'd finished, rage smoldered in Oliver's eyes. He made a visible effort to suppress it, but the sight was startling. Oliver was the calmest, most level-headed person I knew. "I assume the slavers are dead by now?" he asked evenly.

"If not, they're wishing they were."

"I should've been there," he said through his teeth. "To protect you. To stop it from happening."

"Do you have any new paintings?" I asked suddenly, a none-too-subtle way of changing the subject. I didn't want to keep reliving the past three days.

"No. I couldn't concentrate," Oliver said pointedly.

When we were teenagers, he had asked for a picture of me. Though I couldn't seem to bring anything into the dreams but clothes, it didn't stop him. The next time I visited, he'd managed to conjure paintbrushes and canvases. He began with my portrait. Next he painted the hills, the clouds, the sea. His skill improved with each project. Secretly I was glad he'd discovered something to be passionate about. Oliver didn't vanish once I was awake; he was always here, day or night. It pained me to think about what a lonely existence I'd created for him.

"Well, why don't we go inside? You can paint, I can watch," I suggested hopefully. It was my favorite way to pass the time. The only smattering of minutes or hours that I felt something like peace.

"Fortuna, you can't pretend this isn't happening," Oliver insisted, his tone at odds with the serenity of the pink sky. "You should leave town. Don't confront the faerie. The mirror was nothing but a trick, and he's counting on your desperation to find Damon."

My patience snapped. "So you do remember his name. He's the reason I can't just leave, okay? Trick or not, it's the first clue of my brother's whereabouts in two years. This faerie must know where he is."

"Exactly, Fortuna. Damon has been gone for *two years*. I'm sorry, but he isn't coming back. You're the one that told me what faeries are like—this one probably learned about your missing brother and is using that to get what he wants. Whatever the hell that may be."

A sharp retort rose to my lips, but I swallowed it. Oliver was a dream. There was no point arguing with a dream. Besides that, he was all I had left, and I didn't want to fight anymore.

Catching Oliver by surprise, I cupped the back of his neck

and kissed him. I channeled all my pain and fear into it, almost rough in my need. He responded instantly. The tension around us dissipated and became something else entirely. He gripped my waist and urged me even closer. I jumped up, wrapping my legs around him, grinding instinctively.

Just like that, the kiss changed. Oliver lowered us to the ground and put me on my back. His mouth became more demanding, more intense. I couldn't get enough of his tongue—he tasted like honey and ambrosia. I buried both my hands in his hair, but he laced his fingers through mine and pinned them to the ground. The length of his body settled on top of me. He gripped my wrists in one hand, while the other hand went under my shirt. It skimmed up my torso, to my breast, leaving a trail of heat in its wake. Our kiss never broke.

Already I could feel Oliver between my thighs, hard and ready. My first instinct was to yank his pants off, beg him to push inside me, where I was hot and throbbing. But, right on cue, another instinct whispered past. A faint sense this wasn't right. Whether it was the place or the person, I didn't know. Shouldn't I be ready by now? Should it matter this much? I wasn't entirely sure having sex in a dream counted, anyway.

Despite these thoughts, the feeling wouldn't go away. I knew it would stay there, hovering like a poisonous fog. Oliver finally pulled back, breathing heavily. His eyes asked the question. I bit my lip, guilt pushing out the pleasure. "I'm sorry," I said in a small voice. "Not yet."

Every time I rejected him, I expected hurt or anger. Instead, Oliver grinned, revealing his dimples. A breeze stirred his hair. He had never looked more beautiful. "At least let me satisfy you."

I hesitated. "That wouldn't exactly be fair to—"

"I get my satisfaction from watching you," he said firmly. With deft fingers, he slid my underwear down. My feeble protests quieted. First, he rubbed slow circles with the ball of his thumb, until I was squirming and whimpering. Then, without warning, Oliver dipped his head and licked me. I gasped. A low growl rumbled through him. His mouth claimed me completely, sucking and teasing. Moaning, I opened my legs wider and arched my back. The world narrowed down to him and the sensation building within. Higher and higher, hotter and hotter.

The orgasm left me weak and shaking. Afterward I could only lay there, breathing hard. Oliver returned to my side and stretched out on the grass. Once I could move, I curled against him. My eyelids fluttered. Oliver cupped my head, as gently as if it were breakable. "Go ahead," he urged tenderly. "Rest. I'll be right here. You're safe."

I was reluctant to close my eyes, though. I gazed up at him, thinking that he was the most beautiful creature I knew. Perhaps I had drawn inspiration from my mom's Greek artwork when I'd dreamed him up.

The object of my adoration glanced down and caught me staring. His eyebrow arched. "Sleep," he repeated, more sternly this time. The world was coming in and out of focus. I nodded against him. Oliver looked upward again and I followed his gaze. The sky glittered with scattered stars. My mother's stories echoed in my head, Greek legends that ended in constellations and silenced gods.

For the first time in days, I fell into a deep and dreamless sleep.

Birdsong eventually drew me out of the darkness. For a minute or two, I struggled to stay there. But sunlight streamed through the window, making the insides of my eyelids bright red. Reluctantly I opened them, half-hoping to see Oliver and rolling hills. The four walls of my room stared back. Sighing, I focused drowsily on the alarm clock. It was six o'clock in the afternoon; my shift started in an hour. I resisted the urge to bury my head under the covers and return to Oliver.

Forty-five minutes later, Bea smiled as I walked through the front door. She and Gretchen stood behind the counter, their arms lightly touching. "Look at you, all bright-eyed and bushy-tailed," Bea said by way of greeting. The drawer to the register was open, and she held a wad of cash in her hand. "It's a nice change from yesterday. You had us worried."

Beside her, Gretchen was cutting a lime into small, precise pieces. Without looking up, she inclined her head and told me, "There's someone here to see you. New boyfriend?"

Angela snorted as she walked past with a tray full of salt and pepper shakers. Everyone ignored her. I turned to see who Gretchen was talking about, but part of me already knew from the prickling sensation over my skin.

The faerie stood by the bar.

At the sight of him, my first instinct was to do something violent—the image of my brother's ruined back was still fresh and vivid. But there were too many witnesses here, too many who would intervene if I tried to beat the answers out of him. I smiled at Gretchen in reassurance, who was watching us closely. Satisfied, she turned away to give us a semblance of privacy. She spoke to Bea in a low voice.

Wearing a guise of calm, I walked toward the faerie. Though he must've felt the storm of power around me, his stance didn't change. He leaned his forearms on the back of a chair and watched me approach. "Did you like my gift?" he asked once I was within earshot.

The words confirmed my suspicions and my control snapped. I launched at the faerie so quickly, he had no time to defend himself. In a flash, I had him against the counter and the edge of a steak knife at his throat, which I'd snatched from the silver-ware tray behind him. "What have you done to my brother, you son of a bitch?" I hissed, forgetting about witnesses or appearances.

The faerie didn't look afraid, and the absence of such a familiar reaction made me pause. My palm pressed down on his collarbone, where the skin was smooth and unexpectedly cold. But there was no flavor on my tongue, no images in my head. I was so shocked at the realization, I nearly dropped the knife.

No one seemed to notice or care about the commotion—the faerie must've cast a glamour over us. Gretchen was still talking quietly and Angela had finished putting the shakers back. She was now preoccupied with adjusting her breasts, trying to fit them in a bra two sizes too small. Frowning, I faced the faerie again. He hadn't taken his eyes off me. A burst of fury whirled through me like a hurricane, and I buried my nails into his flesh. Small, dark bloodstains spread through the material of his shirt. Still no flavor or visions.

Noting my bewilderment, the faerie murmured, "I'm not so transparent, Fortuna Sworn. You must dig a little deeper to discover *my* fears."

"What are you?" I whispered, standing so close, his breath tickled my cheek. It was an odd but pleasant smell, like spices and freshly-churned soil. Something stirred inside me, low and hot.

The faerie sensed it, too. When he spoke again, his voice was thicker, his eyes darker. "I'm exactly what you think I am."

"Angela, one of your kids is on the phone!" Gretchen called, startling me.

The redhead hurried over. She didn't even glance our way as she took the landline out of its cradle. "Yeah?" Angela sighed. She raked her greasy hair back. "No, Noah, I've told you this a million times. I put the parental control on there for a reason. Please trust me, okay? It's for your own good."

I returned my attention to the faerie. The sudden rush of lust faded as, once again, the image of Damon's destroyed back came to me. Now guilt and disgust shot through my veins, more powerful than attraction, and I jerked away. The knife stayed at the faerie's throat, though. "Where is Damon?" I asked through my teeth.

Seemingly unperturbed, he continued examining every facet and curve of my face. "Your brother is alive, but you will find him much altered."

"I asked you *where* he is, you piece of shit, not *how*—"

"Powerful you may be, but I'm not a goblin." In the space of a blink, the faerie vanished. He reappeared a few feet away, and the blood on his shirt was gone. It was obvious now he'd been toying with me, allowing me to hold him against the bar. Still, he was careful not to reveal the full extent of his abilities. Unease rippled through my mind, a faint whisper that I couldn't win against this creature. He wasn't an ordinary faerie, that was obvious. I took a step toward him. My grip was even tighter on the knife.

"Before you make any rash decisions, I should mention that I'm not the one who took him," the faerie added casually. His gaze didn't move from mine.

At this, I paused. Faeries couldn't lie, after all. I searched his eyes, but they didn't give anything away. "Fine, I'll bite," I snapped. My heart felt like a frantic animal trying to break free of its cage; for the first time in two years, I was close to finding out where Damon was. "If you didn't take him, who did?"

"All in good time."

My nostrils flared at the dismissal, and I fought the urge to dive at him again. "Do you get punched a lot? You seem like the kind of faerie who gets punched a lot."

The corners of his mouths twitched. "Not necessarily. That would require actually catching me."

"Noted. Now what do you want?" I asked again, somehow knowing that this time, I would get an answer.

"You."

Of course I had been expecting it, but his response was so unabashed that, at first, I could only blink. Just as I started to speak—still uncertain what would come out—the front door squeaked open and Regina Hart lumbered in. The glamour must've been still intact, because she didn't gasp at the sight of me brandishing a knife. She did, however, give the faerie a long, appreciative look.

I rolled my eyes. When I faced forward again, the faerie plucked the knife away and put it on the counter behind us. It brought him in such close proximity that his neck was inches from my mouth. Wintry air rolled off him. He stepped back again, smiling slightly. The asshole knew exactly what kind of effect he'd had on me. "I wish to make a bargain, Fortuna Sworn," he declared.

Suddenly every instinct I had screamed to *run*. That alone should've been enough to have me packing a bag and driving far, far away from Granby. But then I remembered the mirror, the scars, the emptiness in my brother's eyes. Tightly I asked, "What kind of bargain?"

"I will bring you to Damon Sworn. In return, I ask for one thing."

"Enough with the dramatics," I hissed. "In return for what?"

Once again, the faerie looked me in the eye. In this light, they looked more black than gray or hazel. Still beautiful, whatever the color. Feeling like a coward, I focused on his eyelids instead. But his next words made me forget all that, and my shocked gaze snapped back to his.

"Marry me," he said.

CHAPTER FOUR

*D*uring our conversation, two men had begun a game of pool. As I gaped at the faerie, I was dimly aware of two balls clinking together. In my mind's eye I saw them flying across the green felt and falling into opposite pockets. "You're insane," I managed at last. "Either that or there's something you're not telling me. Which, judging from my experience with your species, is just as likely. Why me? Why marriage?"

The faerie ignored this. He tilted his head in a way that was already becoming familiar. "I knew the moment I laid eyes on you."

Panic was expanding in my chest, making it feel tight. Heedless of whether or not the glamour was still in place, or that I still had a shift to finish, I shoved past and ran toward the door. Within seconds the faerie materialized in front of me. I jerked to a halt, breathing hard. The people around us still didn't seem to notice anything amiss. "Tell me what you think you know," I snarled. I was more frightened than I'd ever been—even more than the night I'd been taken by goblins—and that baffled me.

"What we could do together."

I sneered. "Such a faerie. You thought the best way to have

me was through manipulation and talk of power? You don't know me at all. Guess you didn't learn enough from Regina."

Once again, I darted around him. Though the faerie didn't interfere this time, he still followed. "Regardless, I need your answer," he said.

In my haste, the door slammed violently against the bricks. I hurried down the sidewalk, remembering too late that the van keys were in my locker. I also couldn't leave Bea short-staffed. But I kept going, stopping only when the sidewalk did. My shoes peeked over the edge of the curb. Thankfully, there weren't many people to witness my wild flight; businesses closed early around here.

The sun was nearly gone now. Faint, pinkish light touched upon the shabby storefronts of Granby. I squinted at the horizon, hoping to catch the moment day gave way to night. It always felt calming, somehow. The faerie moved to stand beside me. I spoke without looking at him. "You want my answer? Here it is. Go fuck yourself. I won't be making any bargains today."

"Even at your brother's expense?" he asked, although he sounded unsurprised.

"I'll find him on my own."

He gave no reply. A breeze stirred tendrils of my hair and the distant treetops. The movement drew my attention to them, and I thought about how much those woods had taken from me. My freedom, my brother. I'd fought and regained one. Would I sacrifice everything for the other, as well?

One winter evening, when I was seven, Mom had to teach a class and Dad ran into traffic. They asked me to watch Damon for an hour or two, just until he got home. But a friend had invited me to a sleepover. Though I was supposed to be babysitting Damon, I went anyway. He woke up and found himself alone. Terrified, my six-year-old brother left the house to search for me, clad in only his pajamas. One of our neighbors picked him up from the side of the road. The next day, my parents brought him to the hospital, where he was treated for a severe case of pneumonia. As he lay in that bed, I never left his side. That was when my mother said the words I would live by from that moment on.

You need to take care of each other, she had whispered. I felt her finger on my cheek, saw her round face in a slant of moonlight.

During my descent into memory, the faerie had remained silent. I came back to reality, blinking rapidly at the sun, which was a sliver now. There was a lump in my throat. I swallowed it, knowing that the dinner rush had started. Bea would be wondering where I was.

I was about to turn away when the faerie's voice drifted to me like a spirit. "I'm not trying to be cruel, Fortuna, but finding him on your own is impossible."

I whirled to face him, brows raised in challenge. "Why? Because he's in Faerie?"

"Faerie is another human myth. Such a place doesn't exist." He looked amused at the thought. I started to brush past him, and the light in his eyes went out. The faerie grasped my shoulder to stop me, his expression sober, and I wrenched away. "I apologize. I wasn't mocking you."

"Can I get back to work now?"

"I'm not the sort of creature who takes a female against her wishes," he said as though I hadn't spoken. I let out an impatient sigh. "To claim a mate unwillingly will not be pleasant for either of us. So if you change your mind, know that your end of the bargain is not just standing in a ceremony. I would expect you to be a participant in our life together."

My face warmed. "P-participant?"

"Indeed. However, I won't expect to share a bed until you're ready," he added. His eyes crinkled at the corners, the beginnings of another smile, but not quite.

"And if that never happens?" Thankfully, my voice didn't betray the heat spreading through me.

Now he did smile, slow and sensual. As if he knew anyway, the arrogant bastard. "I suspect a celibate existence is not for either of us, but if that's the case, there are other ways to enjoy each other's company."

For a third time, I pushed by the faerie. Finally, he let me go. The sun had moved on, leaving darkness and monsters to rule this half of the planet. Streetlights guided the way back to Bea's. At the door, I paused and looked back. He still stood there, watching, waiting. I raised my voice so he could hear. "I meant what I said. No bargain. Not ever!"

Though the faerie didn't move, his words came to me clearly. They caressed the tender skin just below my ear. "If a time comes that you should feel differently, all you must do is say my name."

"That's going to be hard to do, considering you haven't told me what it is," I shouted back. There was a challenge in the words; I knew a faerie's name was sacred.

Another pause. It was difficult to see him now, but there was the slightest sensation of ghostly fingertips trailing over my skin. Then, a moment later, his reply came. "It's Collith," he breathed. A shock went through me, driven by the fact that he'd given it so freely. Before I could speak, the faerie became a swirl of dead leaves, and a breeze carried them away.

Dramatic… but it had the effect he'd probably intended. I couldn't help the awe I felt at his display of power. This was more than glamour. Who *was* he? One of the first faeries, maybe? But that would make him thousands of years old. The prospect was too frightening to accept.

Once Collith was gone, I allowed myself another moment or two. Closing my eyes, breathing deeply, digging for any veins of untapped strength. Then I tightened my ponytail and went back inside, where impatient customers and concerned employers were waiting.

Unlike the night before, I was aware of every minute and hour that passed. Ian O'Connell was back, a bit more subdued this time. Even so, his eyes followed me all night—I could feel them between my shoulder blades, on my ass, up and down my legs. Yet every time I turned his way, he was looking elsewhere. He couldn't possibly suspect I had something to do with his meltdown, but my instincts stood on end. I tried not to hunch my shoulders or show that I was affected by the intensity of his focus.

The dinner shift wore on, and Bea's got busier. So busy I forgot about Ian, the faerie, the goblins, Oliver, and Damon. There was only hurrying back and forth between the order window and the booths, counting change from my apron, and keeping a smile pasted on my face. It was different from last night, when I'd been sleep deprived and raw. Now there was something comforting about the familiar motions and the monotony of serving. By one a.m., I felt more like myself than I had in days. Like maybe the slavers hadn't completely broken me.

Since my parents died, I had never been truly happy. After Damon disappeared, this became even more true. But before being taken by those slavers, I'd been able to find moments of something similar. Contentedness, perhaps, or hope. Tonight I felt the stirrings of it again, and my feet didn't feel so heavy. Screw that self-assured faerie; he wasn't going to win. So far, I'd survived everything thrown my way. This wouldn't be any different.

"Good night," I called to Cyrus, who gave no indication that he'd heard. Bea and Gretchen waved from where they slow-danced in front of the jukebox. Angela deliberately turned her back. Ariel, who'd already shown signs of improvement, called a chipper goodbye.

I exited Bea's once again, holding keys and mace at the ready. There was no sign of Ian or Collith, though. Granby felt... calm. Normal. The moon had emerged and shone unhindered by clouds. A strong wind sent leaves flying through the air like birds. They made me think of the lovely flocks in Oliver's world —I'd get to see them soon. With the barest beginnings of a smile, I got into the van and shut the door, locking it to be safe.

My smile died when I saw Collith's mirror. It glinted in the passenger seat, where I'd left it at the start of my shift. Part of me yearned to get another glimpse of Damon, part of me was terrified to. I clenched my hands into fists. Told myself to turn the keys and go home. Fall asleep in Oliver's arms again. *Choose happiness, Fortuna.*

It felt like I was watching someone else's hand reach for the mirror.

At first, there was nothing to see. Just my own pale, pinched face. But then the glass clouded, as though I'd breathed on it too hard. Now there were movements and vague shapes. My heart hammered as I waited for the image to become clear.

This time, Damon was crying.

He was sitting in the middle of an enormous bed, holding his knees against a pale and bony chest. He was completely naked, from what I could tell. He didn't sob, or speak, or move. Instead, his tears were silent. The sort of grief that couldn't be given a voice, or it would become so big, so loud, that it ripped you apart from the inside. He stared straight ahead, as though he were waiting for something.

Underground, I thought dimly. *He's underground.*

Tears were running down my own face. I thought about that cage the slavers had put me in, the sense of powerlessness I'd felt. Seeing someone I loved in such pain was far worse.

Except this time, there was something I could do.

Seconds later, the image faded. Even when it was gone, though, I sat there and stared at the glass. A strange, cold calm

K.J. SUTTON

stole over me. Any thoughts about happiness or choices were long gone. With a shuddering breath, I set the mirror back in the passenger seat, like it was a child.

Suddenly the door to Bea's opened. A laugh rang out, and I caught sight of Ariel. Cyrus appeared next to her. Then came Angela, followed by Bea and Gretchen, whose arms were wrapped around each other. My makeshift family. Someone played music from their phone as they started down the sidewalk. A lump swelled in my throat. Before any of them could notice me, I turned the key in the ignition, listened to the engine roll over, switched gears, and drove home.

Trees and stars blurred past. I focused on that, on trying to memorize this—my last night of freedom. Already I could feel a cage closing in. Soon enough the van was rolling and bumping up the driveway. I parked and resisted the temptation to sit there; Damon couldn't wait.

Moving quickly, as if to outrun second thoughts, I got out and shut the door. The sound echoed through the stillness. But inside me, it felt like there was a nest of hornets, swarming and buzzing. For a minute I paced back and forth, trying to think of another way. Even if Savannah did manage to locate Damon with a spell—which she'd already attempted countless times—it wasn't realistic to think I could go up against his captor alone. My power had its limits.

Finally I stopped and faced the trees; it seemed logical the faerie would come from that direction. I gritted my teeth and forced myself to say it. "Collith."

"A little louder, please."

His voice came from behind. I whirled toward him, an instant scowl twisting my face. The faerie leaned against the van, arms crossed. I searched for any trace of smugness in his expression, but it was either well-hidden or he truly took no enjoyment from this. "Just take me to my brother," I snapped.

"That wasn't our bargain. Ceremony first, then Damon

44

Sworn."

The faerie moved closer and held out his hand. I stared down at it, willing myself to reach back. His fingers were so pale, so elegant. Beautiful. But my own face was proof that beauty couldn't be trusted. As the seconds stretched to minutes, I forced myself to picture Damon. He needed me now. There was no time for hesitation or cowardice. Still, I didn't take the faerie's proffered hand.

"What makes you so special?" I blurted. The faerie tilted his head, brow furrowing in confusion. I made a vague gesture that was meant to encompass the world. Crickets continued their tranquil serenade, oblivious to the tension. "Out of all the men who have pawed at me, been kind to me, or interested me. Out of all the men who have been attractive, intelligent, or decent. What makes you the one I should bind myself to forever?"

The faerie lowered his hand and shoved it into his coat pocket. A breeze whistled between us as he considered my question. I liked that. Most people listened, but they didn't hear. At last he answered, "The first thing you should understand is that I am not a man. Let there be no illusions about that. I don't have human instincts or desires."

I frowned. "What does that mean?"

"It means that I have killed," he replied matter-of-factly. "It means that I am constantly torn between civility and ferocity. It means that I do not want you for a wife, but a mate. As to why you should accept me, above all others, consider this. I know exactly what you are... and I think it's magnificent. Your enemies are my enemies. My power is your power. If nothing else, let that be the reason."

Apparently the faerie was finished. He tilted his head again and studied me. His words had caused both intrigue and fear. But he was right that it would be a huge advantage having him for an ally. I was also curious what it would be like to be with a man who wasn't Oliver or whose fears careened through my head like an out-of-control car. Ultimately, though, I knew that I didn't want this. There was no love between me and this creature, and if I went with him, I was choosing a life utterly different from the one my parents had wanted for me. From the one I had once envisioned for myself.

You need to take care of each other, Mom's voice whispered. Her face filled my mind, sad and worried. I would've done anything to make that look disappear. I still would.

"Fine," I heard myself say. The word was barely audible, but the faerie heard it anyway; he put his hand out again. This time, before I could reconsider, I took it.

Part of me had expected the faerie's grip to instantly tighten. Instead, it remained loose and gentle, as though he were still giving me a chance to change my mind. His skin was as freezing as I remembered. There was still no hint of fear, no flavors on my tongue, and I wasn't sure whether I still found this infuriating. I waited for the faerie to move—lift into the air like a great bird, or use magic to make us both vanish—but he paused again.

"Honesty isn't in my nature, but before we proceed, you should know what you're risking," he said.

"What am I risking?"

"Your life," he told me bluntly. "It won't be easy, retrieving your brother. There are limits to how much I can do. If we enter the place where your brother is being held, there's a possibility you won't leave."

I met his gaze. "Do we need anyone else for this ceremony? We should get started."

My simple response made it clear how much I cared about any potential danger. The faerie turned away, but I still caught the tiny smile on his lips. Once again, I shoved down a sense of unease. My brother's tear-streaked face loomed before me. We left the van and walked through the yard. I'd let the grass go this summer, and dry, brittle strands tickled my legs. The faerie led me into the trees. In just a few steps, it seemed like we'd gone into another world. This one was made of darkness and moon-light. An owl hooted in the distance. Save for that, everything was silent and still. Even the wind had quieted. Bare branches stretched and tangled overhead, casting intricate shadows on the leaf-covered ground.

"Why are we out here? Is there more power in nature, or something?" I asked. My voice felt loud and abrasive.

The faerie faced me. We stood in the smallest of clearings, an audience of stars watching from above. "Yes, but that's not why we're here. I just didn't want to marry you on a driveway," he said dryly.

He held out his other hand now. Waited. Wanting this to be over with, I took it without hesitation. The faerie continued, his words soft yet brisk. "The ceremony is only effective if you're sincere, which is why I'll make my vows in another tongue. You should make yours in the language that feels truest to you."

Before I could respond, a sound came from the woods. The faerie frowned and twisted slightly, probably using his height-ened senses. The moment his back was turned I pulled out my cell phone, hurried to find the video app, and hit the red dot that would start recording. Then I shoved it back into my pocket.

The faerie refocused on me. He didn't seem to notice anything amiss. When I said nothing, he began his vows. It was so startling that I gave a little jump. This was it? The magical ceremony that would permanently tie us together? I had no idea what he was saying, which seemed strange, considering this was essentially a wedding. The words he used were musical and complex. But there was no mistaking the tenderness and inti-macy with which he spoke them. Gradually I pieced together that he was speaking Enochian—the language of angels.

As he spoke, my strongest instinct was to look away. Some-how, though, I managed to keep my eyes on his. For the first time, I noticed flecks of gold in his eyes, vivid in the moonlight.

Like pieces of hardened sap trapped within a tree. After another moment, the faerie stopped talking. My turn, then. I licked my lips. Even as a girl, I'd never given thought to what I'd say in this moment. What could I offer that wasn't a lie?

"I promise to... be faithful," I said haltingly. "To always tell you the truth. To keep you from harm to the best of my ability."

The vows felt inadequate. I faltered, searching for something else to add. But I couldn't promise to be passionate, or loving, or kind. I couldn't even say that I would stay with him for the rest of our lives. The reality was that I didn't know this creature; he could reveal violence or cruelty. However unhappy I was now, I refused to be miserable.

My obvious struggle didn't seem to bother the faerie. Instead, his eyes were brighter than I'd ever seen them. My husband—no, my mate—smiled again. There was nothing amused or secret about this one. He looked younger, like a boy that had just been given a long-awaited gift. It made me wonder if, just maybe, this wouldn't turn out to be a huge mistake. When I didn't go on, he murmured, "I've chosen well."

Trying to hide any discomfort, I cleared my throat. Fought the urge to pull free of his touch. "Is that it, then? Now what?"

"We kiss, of course. Shouldn't you know this part? Haven't you been living among humans?"

Somehow, I wasn't surprised. For once, though, I wanted to have the upper hand with this faerie. So I ignored my trepidation and reached up to pull his face to mine. The faerie made a sound of surprise deep in his throat.

He recovered quickly. Within seconds one of his hands cupped the back of my neck, while the other traveled down to the small of my back, pulling me closer, until every part of me was pressed against him. His body was lean and hard, but the faerie was gentler than I expected; he teased and explored the inside of my mouth as though we had all the time in the world. I couldn't deny the heat that spread through me, and my usual instincts were silent. I didn't push away or pull free. Instead, I demanded more. A small, niggling voice in my head worried I was being weak, but I ignored this, too.

Then, without warning, the intensity heightened. It had nothing to do with attraction—this was pure, unadulterated magic. The secret parts of me came alive, tingling, and I gasped against the faerie's mouth. He hadn't been hard a moment ago, but now he was, poking my hip. It felt like we were feeling what the other was feeling, seeing what the other was seeing. His desire swept through me. The sensation was heady and disorienting. Soon, though, I sensed something else at the back of Collith's mind. Not fear, I realized. This was revealed from the mating bond. I suspected he hadn't intended for me to discover it.

Hope.

As the magic lingered, I became blind with need, and suddenly there was a tree at my back. Part of me knew it was my doing, that I'd yanked the faerie toward it so I could use the trunk as leverage. The bark scraped my spine as I hopped up and wrapped my legs around his slim waist. I wanted him inside me, moving in me. My fingers fumbled for a zipper while his fingers made swift work of my shirt buttons.

"No," he said.

I barely heard him—the fog of lust thickened and clung. Finally the faerie's zipper cooperated. Just as I reached within, eager to grip the length of him, Collith was gone. My feet hit the ground and cold air rushed in the space between us. I made a pathetic sound and opened my eyes.

The faerie stood in the center of the clearing, his chest heaving. The distance felt vast and deliberate. "W-what's wrong?" I managed.

His lips were deliciously swollen. I couldn't help but watch them as he said, "I want you to have a clear mind when we consummate this."

A few seconds ticked past. Now that we were no longer touching, I was able to fight the magic; it was like nothing I'd ever encountered before. My own abilities felt natural, part of me, a heartbeat or an exhale. This force was undeniably summoned, and it was as inevitable as a thunderstorm. Now I knew what we'd done was more binding than marriage. We were two beings again, but also not. There was a sense of… fullness that hadn't been there minutes ago.

Thinking about anything besides the faerie helped me regain control. Little by little, I separated from the magic. Once it had completely retreated, leaving an ache in its place, the kiss replayed in my head. A mortified flush spread through my face. Belatedly I realized that my shirt had come undone. I fumbled for the buttons and muttered, "Don't worry, it won't happen again. Now where is my brother? And what did you say during your vows, by the way?"

"Yes, you're right. We'd better get started. It's already dark, and despite my formidable mate, I'd prefer to avoid the other things that come out around this time." The faerie didn't acknowledge my question about the vows. Good thing I had the recording on my phone, then.

Seemingly unaware of my scowl, Collith glanced toward the waxing moon. In its pale light, he was even lovelier. But his scar was deeper and darker. What creature had been strong enough to harm him in such a way?

I tried to smother my curiosity. "Where are we going? You still haven't said."

"You should probably pack some belongings," he added as though I hadn't spoken. "There's no telling how long we'll be—"

"Collith. I fulfilled my end of the bargain. It's your turn. Where the hell are you taking me?"

At the use of his name, the faerie smiled. And at last, he gave me the truth. "To the Unseelie Court, of course."

CHAPTER FIVE

*A*ccording to Collith, there were entries to his Court all over the world. One existed in the very woods we'd married in. He informed me there weren't any roads or sidewalks leading to it, so when I went inside to pack, I pulled on a pair of hiking boots, as well. Next, I went to my nightstand. Where most women kept lotion, vibrators, or a trashy romance novel, I had a small weapons cache. I regularly doused everything in holy water. Now I pulled out Dad's knife, along with a sheath to hold it in. It settled around my waist more loosely than normal—I must've lost some weight during my time with the goblins.

In the entryway, I hesitated. Should I turn off the water? Lower the heat? Pack some food? Ideally, rescuing Damon wouldn't take as long as that, but I had no idea what to expect from the Unseelie Court. What if some of the old wives' tales were true, and time worked differently there? What if something went wrong?

I'd never been the optimistic sort. Two minutes later, the water was off and the thermostat had been adjusted. My backpack bulged with energy bars and stale chips. As an afterthought, I used the bathroom, too. Then, at the door, I pulled out my phone. It was still recording, since I'd never pressed the button again. I did so now, then opened a new text. I selected Bea and Cyrus from the contact list. For a brief moment, I considered adding Savannah, Damon's girlfriend. It seemed cruel, though, to give her hope when I had no idea how this rescue attempt would go. Leaving her name untouched, I switched back to the new text screen and typed quickly.

Got a lead on Damon. Not sure how long I'll be gone. I'm sorry.

My thumb hovered over the arrow that would send it. Guilt pricked my heart as I imagined what this text would do to them. But there was no other option. If I called, Bea would try to talk me out of it. If I delayed going, Damon would endure even more torment. So I clenched my jaw and sent the text. It was too quick, too easy.

After that, I didn't let myself look around or say a silent farewell; I just left. The key—never used, since there was no need to lock the door out here—was hidden under a miniature David statue. I took it out and put it in the lock.

"We need to hurry," Collith called.

Pocketing the key, along with my phone, I began to rush toward him. Gravel crunched with every step. I paused beside the van and glanced at the passenger seat. After a moment of consideration, I opened the door and retrieved the mirror. I didn't know what it did, or whether Collith wanted it back, but I'd seen Damon in it. That meant it was staying with me. I ran the rest of the way to Collith. There was a sense of urgency around him now, and it only increased my agitation. Without another word, he turned and plunged back into the thicket. *We're coming, Damon*, I thought as I followed.

Moonlight filtered through the canopy overhead, shining a spotlight on the place we'd made our vows. My gaze found the tree we'd kissed against and skittered away. Oblivious, Collith shortened his strides to walk beside me. He didn't speak. It seemed strange that he should be wary of the night; to me it felt safer. The incident with the slavers notwithstanding, the darkness had always been a refuge. A haven. A time when misunderstood creatures could creep from their hiding places and stand out in the open. Even now, I felt my powers stirring. Stretching and cracking like a joint too long unused.

"How did you know about Damon?" I asked abruptly, stepping over a fallen tree. I thought about digging a flashlight out of my bag, but that would only draw attention to us. "What he was, or that he was my brother?"

Collith scanned the shadows around us. His reply was distracted. "I've noticed him before. A Nightmare's essence is unique, even one that isn't particularly strong, like him. When I came across you at the market, I saw the physical resemblance immediately. Undoubtedly siblings. Twins, perhaps."

"No. I'm a little older. Where did you see Damon?" I frowned. "Wait. What do I look like to you?"

At this, Collith focused on me. Despite the dimness, the force of his attention was almost tangible. "Dark hair. More red than brown, I think, in a certain light. Brown eyes and fair skin. There's the slightest bump in your nose. Was it broken in your childhood, perhaps? I'd heard that Nightmares appear differently to every individual, but I suppose I thought it was another myth, like vampires and sunlight or werewolves and a full moon. So it's true?"

I was too stunned to answer. Too dazed by a single, impossible realization.

Collith could see my real face.

"Now it's my turn," I heard him say. "What's the story behind your name?"

Still shaken, I stared at Collith blankly. I would have to think about his ability to see my true face later. "My *name*? Why?"

He gave an elegant shrug, barely perceptible in the faint

starlight. "We're mated. I'd like to know more about the one I'll be spending my life with."

His words created a flutter of panic in my chest—I tried not to consider the length of a life or the magnitude of what we'd just done. Even if I were to leave him, he'd always be there. A presence in the back of my head and in my veins. *No, don't think about it.* "Well, Mom was a professor of ancient religions. In Rome, Fortuna was the goddess of chance, luck, and fate. My parents figured our lives would be difficult enough, being what we are, and I could use all the help I could get. Also, they just thought the name was beautiful."

"It is."

Thinking Collith was making fun of me, I turned to glare at him. There was nothing but sincerity in those eyes, though. I looked away and cleared my throat. The ground was beginning to slope upward; I chose where to step more carefully. One slip and I'd be tumbling. "She named Damon after a story," I added. I had never been prone to revealing details of the past, or even talking, but right now it was better than silence. It felt like Collith was using the stillness to pry through my thoughts. Could faeries read minds? "He was a character known for friendship and loyalty. They taught us to look out for each other. Always. The name suits him, too. He's one of the best people I know."

Collith was silent, but I was thinking of Damon again, remembering that terrible image in the mirror. Guilt gripped my stomach like food poisoning. All this time, I'd been living up here, while he was being tormented down there.

"It's your turn," Collith said abruptly.

"What?"

"To ask a question," he clarified.

"Oh." The ground had leveled out now. The trees around us were more bare, like starved soldiers lined up in tidy rows. Collith stepped in front of me to lead the way. I studied the back of his silky head, my thoughts turning to our destination and how little I'd learned about the fae. The ones I'd met hadn't exactly been forthcoming, and Mom admitted during our lessons that most of what she knew came from folklore. According to the stories, they had an aversion to iron, couldn't tell a lie, and were immortal. While many castes of Fallen had lives much longer than the average human's, we still died eventually.

There was a tinge of desperation in my voice as I blurted, "I need to know more about the Unseelie Court. Is there a… hierarchy? Is the faerie imprisoning Damon powerful? Who are you to them? How will they react to me? How—"

"Breathe, Fortuna. I know you're eager to save your brother, and I'll tell you what I can." Collith was about to continue when a sound reached both our ears. It was faint, barely louder than the rustling leaves, but something about it made my heart quicken. We stopped at the same time, straining to peer into the darkness.

"There," I whispered.

Through the trees, something moved. A tall, reedy shape, rapidly coming toward us. In that moment, I realized what I was hearing.

Panting.

The sound was excited, ragged, and hungry. I knew my eyes were huge as I turned to Collith. He was already looking back at me, his expression grim.

"Run," he said.

We burst into motion. Suddenly the moonlight and shadows seemed sinister, and I kept my eyes trained on Collith to block out the fear. Every breath felt too loud. The backpack thumped against me, a steady rhythm in contrast to my wild pulse. Whatever the creature was, it was faster, and I could sense it getting closer. The sounds it made echoed all around us. "I've seen you vanish into thin air," I managed to say, my lungs burning. "Just go. I'll be fine."

"'Til death do us part, remember?" Collith gasped back.

"Looks like that's going to be a lot sooner than either of us expected." But his words reminded me of the vows we'd just made. Reminded me of the ones I had chosen with the intention to keep. *I promise to keep you from harm to the best of my ability.* I had only myself to blame, really.

I steeled myself for what was about to come next. "Fine. Let's kill this thing together, then."

Without waiting for Collith to respond, I spun to face the creature. My fingers reached for the knife at my hip, grasped the hilt, and pulled it out of the sheath. Within seconds Collith was to my left—I didn't turn to look, but I felt him there, a spot of cold. No, it was more than that. Like we were connected by a string, and it tugged within me each time he moved or inhaled.

The creature attacked in a burst of clacking teeth and swiping claws. My father had taught me self-defense as a child, and since then I'd practiced the movements so often they were embedded in my bones. I reacted on instinct, throwing out the heel of my hand. The execution was perfect, and the creature's momentum was so forceful that my strike sent it reeling. It shrieked—more in surprise than pain, I thought—and recovered quickly.

When it came at me again, I retreated hastily, waiting for a good opening to bring the knife up and into its gut. At this proximity, I could make out the details of what I was fighting. This thing had been human once; I could see every rib, every ridge along its spine. A white film covered its pupils. Tattered clothing clung to those emaciated limbs and strands of long, dark hair tickled my cheek.

Just as I was about to make my move, Collith was there. He had no weapons, but he fought like he'd been born doing it. I watched with raised brows as he dodged the creature's swipe and gracefully swung his leg up. His foot connected with its chest, and once again, it went flying. I didn't give the creature a chance to stand; I darted forward and shoved my knee against its narrow chest.

It screamed with rage and tried to sit upright. Gritting my teeth, I slammed the knife through its eye socket. But... nothing happened. Just a slight waft of steam from contact with the holy water. The thing was stronger than I anticipated, and when it shot up again, I fell backward. Something in the backpack shattered. Suddenly I was the one trapped against the ground. The creature's weight made my arms tremble as it lunged again and again, trying to bite and rip. It moved so quickly I had trouble tracking it. "Intervene at any time!" I shouted to Collith. A glob of drool landed on my forehead.

Then the weight on top of me was gone, landing hard a few feet away. This time it had no opportunity to stand. With an expression of intense concentration, Collith held up his hands. Light and heat burst forth, burning the creature and everything else around it.

"Heavenly fire," I breathed. My mother used to tell me stories about Prometheus giving humankind the gift of fire, or God crafting his angels a weapon of flames, but I'd never seen it with my own eyes. Not even pictures. It was nothing like I imagined; not a blaze of orange and red, but an explosion of blue, green, and white. Lightning.

The creature released one more scream, but the sound quickly subsided. It slumped, reduced to a black skeleton. Once it was completely still, Collith lowered his hands. The fire died, but moonlight shone through the treetops, allowing me to examine my mate. He was pale and trembling. "I'm no dragon," Collith murmured, referring to a species talked about even more than Nightmares, "but I'll be damned again if I let my mate get killed so soon after finding her."

"There's no such thing as dragons," I said automatically, moving to support his weight. He looked ready to collapse.

Collith apparently didn't have the strength to argue. He leaned on me, breathing hard. No wonder he'd taken so long to get that thing off me—apparently he'd been summoning every drop of strength and power he had. "The door isn't far. Half a mile," he said.

"Well, if we meet another one of those things, we probably won't survive another yard, much less half a mile."

With visible effort, he shook his head. "It takes an extraordinary amount of energy and personal sacrifice to harness that kind of power. Whoever was responsible won't be able to repeat the spell. Do you have enemies, Fortuna? A witch, maybe?"

"I only know one witch, and she wouldn't do this." The knife was still in my other hand, but I didn't put it away. Every sound and shadow felt threatening now.

The rest of the journey to the door was slow going. We shuffled along, the bats above us the only sign of life. Now and then Collith muttered guidance, but beyond that, we didn't speak. At last he lifted his head and said, "There."

I followed his gaze. I didn't know what I'd been imagining, but it looked like nothing to me. Just a cave—a word that would be generous, in my opinion, as it was more an opening in the rocks—without any sense of power emanating from it. "The trick is to expect more," Collith whispered. His lips brushed the tender skin below my ear, and I couldn't suppress a shiver. Though I didn't look at him, I felt Collith smile.

Together, we moved toward the entrance. It was too small for both of us, so once we reached the outer edges, I finally released him. The sense of anxiety surrounding Collith had vanished, replaced by a seemingly impenetrable calm. Without any parting comments or words of wisdom, he put his hand against the rock and stepped into the yawning darkness.

But I lingered in the open air. All my instincts writhed and roiled, insistent that I belonged up here. Beneath those voices of reason, like an ancient beast at the bottom of the sea, was a feeling that if I followed Collith into the Unseelie Court, I would never walk out again.

Picturing my brother's face for the thousandth time, I forced myself to go in.

My outstretched hand collided with Collith's chest; he'd waited for me. He captured it against him and pressed a fleeting kiss to my fingers before letting go again. I was so startled that I froze for an instant. Collith was already moving again, making his way through the cave. The sound of his footsteps grew fainter, and after a moment, I hurried to follow. The dark had never unnerved me before, but now every line of my body was tense. I blinked rapidly, straining to see something. Anything. I kept expecting to hit a wall or to reach the end. Instead, it kept going, and going, and going.

Eventually the path slanted downward. The air cooled with every step, but thankfully, low temperatures didn't really bother my kind. Several times I started to ask Collith how much farther, or what awaited us below, but the words stuck in my throat. Though there still wasn't any detectable power in the air, it felt like we were being watched. I held the knife tighter.

Flickers of light appeared ahead. My heartbeat was a drum, echoing all around. I strained to hear voices or footsteps. Were they waiting for us? Was there a guard? We drew closer, though, and I saw they were just torches. In her lessons, Mom told me faeries avoided technology, but I was still surprised at the sight of them. The flames were small enough that they left no smoke in the air. Faint shadows quivered on the walls. We kept going.

Now the cave widened, and Collith dropped back to walk beside me. His arm brushed against mine, a shock of arctic skin. Suddenly he straightened. His stride became swift and confident. All traces of exhaustion vanished from his face. He was the faerie I'd met at the slave market, collected and formidable. That familiar half-smile curved his lips.

"Were you faking the whole time?" I hissed.

Collith glanced at me sidelong. "I suppose you'll never know. But please, try not to speak. I'd like to avoid drawing attention to us."

I fumed silently. Then doors began to appear on either side, unevenly spaced apart. Slowly, my rage was overpowered by curiosity. I took the opportunity to study this place, the center of countless fairy tales and horror stories. Within those pages, the Unseelie Court had been entirely glass chandeliers and grandeur. Reality was slightly disappointing. The walls and ground were rough, made of earth and roots. The ornate doors were an oddity. Someone had taken the time to carve intricate designs into the wood. No two were the same. I saw vines, faces, mountains, rivers, figures. I resisted the urge to ask Collith about them.

Gradually, the dirt around us became rock. Again, it seemed that someone had taken the time to lay down individual stones and give this place a semblance of elegance. The tunnels broke apart, becoming a maze of choices and turns. I'd never been good at puzzles, but I did my best to memorize our route.

Despite Collith's words, we saw nothing and no one. When he finally halted in front of a door—this one covered in carved flowers—I was beginning to suspect his warning was just an attempt to avoid my questions.

"For however long you're at Court, these will be your rooms," he said, pushing the door open. It had no knob. "Should you need anything, there's a rope here. It's attached to a bell. Someone will hear it ring and come."

"Wait, so you live here?" I blurted. "In the same place Damon has been held prisoner? Why haven't you—"

The sight of another faerie inside the room made me forget the rest. Collith didn't acknowledge him, but the stranger cowered as we drew near. He was fine-boned and shorter than my mate. Still taller than me, though. His hair was silky and light. Not red, exactly, but like the color of the sun's outer edges, when you look toward it a moment too long. Almost silver. Despite the appearance of fragility, he had a strong face, made of decisive features. Full lips, square jaw, thick brows. Similar to his hair, his eyes were silvery. Sharp and detailed, like the cut of a diamond. He wore tired-looking jeans and a white t-shirt with a stain on the collar.

I waited for Collith to make an introduction to the bright-haired faerie, but he just stared back at me, a slight furrow between his brows. "Are you going somewhere?" I asked finally.

He hesitated. The torchlight made his scar an ominous slash. "I have obligations that are unavoidable. I'll be back by this evening. I won't bother telling you to stay put, but I would strongly advise it. Faeries are ruled by their baser instincts. Should you encounter one in the passageways, I can't promise—"

"I came here for Damon," I cut in, feeling the stranger's eyes on me. "Hiding would accomplish nothing. And don't forget, we had a deal."

Frustration flitted across Collith's lovely face. "I haven't forgotten anything. There's a gathering tomorrow; doubtless your brother will attend."

"If I wait until then, that forces Damon to spend another night here. I don't know what's being done to him or what kind of condition he's in. Why did you bring me here today if you didn't intend to reunite us right away? Do you even have a plan?"

In the stillness, my voice felt harsh and biting. Collith faltered again, and this was unlike the faerie I'd known so far. It was more than the fact we currently had an audience; he was different here. There was something I didn't know, something I was missing.

Yet again, it was as though Collith could hear my thoughts. "There's still much you don't know, Fortuna," he said.

"And whose fault is that?"

But it seemed he was finished. Collith simply promised to return soon, bowed, and left. I clenched my fists, feeling furious and helpless. Once again, he'd managed to avoid most of my questions. It hadn't escaped me that Collith apparently lived in the same place my brother had been held for two years. Anyone capable of standing by while that was happening wasn't worth my trust. I was done listening to him.

All at once, I remembered that I wasn't alone. I turned toward the faerie still in the room. Now that Collith was gone, he had straightened. He spoke before I could. "Welcome to the Court of Shadows, my lady," he said, eyes twinkling. His countenance was utterly changed, as though his terror earlier was a cloak and now it had fallen away. "I would advise you sleep with one eye open."

It seemed a strange thing to say upon first meeting someone. "Why did Collith act like you don't exist?" I asked, swinging my backpack to the ground. I'd been so distracted by the faerie and my conversation with Collith that I hadn't examined the room. I did so now.

"To them, we don't," I heard the faerie say. Like the rest of what I'd seen, everything was simple. A bed frame had been put together out of tree branches. In one corner, there was a bucket, which made me glad I'd used the bathroom at home and dread when I'd need to go next. More torches lit the space, along with a fireplace dug into the far wall. There were no rugs or paintings, no dressers or closets.

"Them?" I asked absently, testing the mattress. Hard and lumpy—they'd probably filled it with grass or straw. Just another reason to get the hell out of here tonight.

"The blue bloods."

"Didn't expect the fae to use such human phrases," I

muttered. It was so cold down here, I could see my breath with every exhale. I focused on the faerie again. It crossed my mind that he was here to watch me, and I wanted to be alone to check the mirror. Maybe this time, there'd be something in the background to reveal where Damon was. How to get rid of him, though?

"Where do you think the humans got them? Or most of their cultural influences?" the faerie asked with a grin, referring to my offhand comment. "You might be interested to know that we use the phrase very literally. Should you ever see Collith's blood, it spills blue as a berry."

That actually was interesting. I'd learned more about faeries in one day than I had in one lifetime. "Well, I don't need anything right now," I chirped. The smile I gave him felt tight and unnatural. "Thanks anyway. Enjoy an afternoon off or something."

The faerie didn't move. Something in his demeanor shifted. "You should know, my lady, that I am loyal to Collith."

At this, I studied him. His expression was open and sincere. Was he trying to tell me that I could trust him because of his devotion to my mate? Or was it a warning? My instincts shrieked at me to shut down, distrust, deceive. I'd never really been proven wrong about a person, simply because I didn't bother trusting anyone in the first place. Much less a faerie. But there was something about this one I was drawn to. The usual revulsion I felt around his kind was... absent. "What's your name?" I asked. *Faeries can't lie*, I reminded myself.

"I am Laurie," he replied without an instant of hesitation. He swept into a bow far more dramatic than Collith's had been. "And I can take you to your brother."

Never had eight words made my heart pound so hard... but it seemed too easy. This faerie had literally just told me he was loyal to Collith, who had advised I stay in this room. Was it a test of some kind? A trap? More importantly, was I going to let fear of that turn down an offer to see the brother who had vanished two years ago? "Then let's go. Now," I added. A challenge.

Laurie's smile returned. I almost smiled, too, and caught myself just in time. The faerie didn't seem bothered by this; he took a step back and surveyed me from head to toe. "First, we should change your appearance. Word of your presence has already spread—however resistant we are to technology, one of the old kings had cameras installed in dozens of the passages—but it will increase your chances of survival as we're roaming the passages."

I had so many questions about this, but getting to Damon was more important. "Fine. Do whatever you want. Just hurry, please."

He nodded briskly. With graceful movements, Laurie grasped my shoulders and guided me to the bed. Then he went to a rope in the corner. A few seconds after he pulled it, there was a knock at the door. Since there was no latch, it opened slightly at the contact. Laurie poked his head out and murmured in the language Collith had spoken his vows in. Another second, and he was pulling back again. There were several wooden bowls clustered in his palm. In his other hand were brushes.

Laurie perched on the edge of the bed. "Close your eyes," he instructed.

It was a knee-jerk reaction to do the exact opposite. I caught myself, though, and forced them shut. I felt Laurie lean closer and his breath touched my cheek. It had a pleasant smell, one I couldn't put a name to. Sunlight? Spring? There was a tickling sensation on my eyelids—the tip of the brush. As Laurie worked, he didn't speak. Though a thousand questions were buzzing around inside me, it seemed like I shouldn't move or say anything, either.

Then his warmth and slight weight on the bed were gone. I opened my eyes. Once again, Laurie went to the rope. Once again, someone tapped at the door. But when he reemerged this time, he held a gown. It was a bizarre and rough material. Curious, I peered closer. There were spiderwebs and sticks tangled within it, along with what appeared to be tiny bones. An incredulous laugh escaped me. "Uh, sorry to disappoint, but I'm not wearing that."

Laurie raised his pale eyebrows. "Do you want to find your brother or not?"

The reckless part of me—the part that felt like a wild animal, cornered and surrounded by enemies—wanted to defy him. Leap up and battle my way through the passages. Find Damon with nothing but my own power and determination. I pictured every moment, knowing even as I did so that it was a childish fantasy.

The faerie still waited for my response. I studied his patient expression and the angelic way firelight quivered over his skin. Was he toying with me? Was this a game to him? If that was the case, I was losing. Laurie knew what I wanted, while all I knew about him was a name. But without this faerie's help, finding Damon would be far more complicated. The thought made me scowl. "Turn around," I said, snatching the dress. Laurie spun in a fluid motion.

Knowing he could hear every sound in the too-quiet room, I yanked off my coat, t-shirt, and jeans. Cold air rushed over me. I hurried to pull the cumbersome dress over my head. It settled into place with a few wriggles and tugs. The waist was tight, almost like a corset, and the skirt was fuller than I expected. The sleeves were like a second skin and ended at my wrists, while the front exposed so much that no one would need to use their imagination. "Okay, done," I said, pretending that my cheeks weren't on fire. "But if you're lying to me about Damon, I'll make you wish you were never born. Or however faeries come into the world."

Laurie turned again, and his silver eyes took me in. I forced myself not to fidget or look away; it was one of Mom's fiercest beliefs that women should never allow themselves to experience shame or self-deprecation. "You are a queen, Fortuna Sworn," Laurie murmured. He held out a pair of slippers.

How did he know my name? My stomach fluttered. "Thank you," I managed, taking them. I wanted to see what he'd done with the makeup, but there was no glass or reflective surfaces. My thoughts returned to the mirror in my bag. All at once, I remembered the confrontation in the forest, the sound of something breaking. Suddenly it didn't matter that Laurie was watching—I rushed to the backpack and fumbled with the zipper. "No, no, no."

It *was* the mirror I'd heard. A crack traveled down the middle of it, and there was no sign of Damon. Whatever power or spell it had possessed was gone. I sank onto the bed, willing an image to appear, but the glass remained still. What if these faeries were lying to me? How would I find Damon without the mirror?

Laurie's voice drifted through the fog around me. "You don't need it anymore. I'll take you to him."

I lifted my head, seized by an abrupt and overwhelming desperation. "Let's go, then. Please."

"Don't you want to see my handiwork first?" Before I could form a response, Laurie held up the broken mirror. Just as snakes are immune to their own venom, so are Nightmares to their own abilities. When I looked at the face in the glass, she was not overwhelmingly beautiful or a combination of what I considered to be ideal features. She had my mother's chestnut hair and brown eyes. There was even the same beauty mark below her right eye. The dramatic eyebrows, however, were all my father's. The girl's skin was pale, like someone who was still recovering from an illness. Somehow, though, she still looked strong. Laurie's makeup was strange and jarring—glittering swoops of orange, red, and black—which highlighted my cheekbones and dark eyes.

I didn't know what to say. Thankfully, Laurie's attention wandered upward. "We should do something about your hair," he said. He handed the mirror back to me, and with those deft fingers, he began plucking and arranging. I sat down again to give him better access. I remembered the slippers as I did so. Laurie continued his task while I kicked off my boots and tucked my feet into the delicate fae-made shoes. Perfect fit.

"Do you know anything about Collith's 'obligations'?" I asked without preamble. "Does he have an overbearing mother?"

Laurie's reply was distracted. I could feel him braiding. Out of the corner of my eye, I saw him take some pins from his pocket. "Collith doesn't have any family at Court; he wasn't raised among us. Normally, he would be considered a lesser faerie. Somewhere on the level of a guard or just another member of Court."

"But he's not?"

At this, his eyes met mine. They were so bright, it seemed impossible that he wasn't wearing colored contacts. "No. Because no other faerie matches his power," he answered.

There was a warning in his voice. In my mind's eye, I saw that blast of heavenly fire pouring from Collith's hands. "Because he has more of it, or because it's different?" I asked now, my own voice faint.

"Both."

I took a moment to absorb the revelation. From the very start, my instincts had been telling me there was more to this marriage; Collith's reasons were careful and vague. And however sincere his vows had sounded, the truth was that I had no idea what he'd promised me. If things took a turn, I had to know what I was up against. I focused on Laurie again, whose attention didn't waver from what his fingers were doing. "What makes his power so special?"

"That I cannot tell you."

I frowned. "Why not?"

"Because Collith wouldn't appreciate his darkest secrets being revealed. Not for free, at least."

"I'm not going to tell anyone."

"It's not you I'm worried about. Nothing said in the Court of Shadows goes unheard, my lady. Shall we go?" he added. He moved back a few steps, every movement fluid. Like a dance. I considered pressing the issue, but something told me Laurie would evade and dodge any efforts.

Well, if we were going out there, I wanted to be prepared. My pile of clothing was still in the corner, looking dull and forlorn. The backpack rested beside it. If we were trying to avoid attention, it would have to stay here. I went to retrieve Dad's knife, hefted the dress up, and wrapped the sheath belt around my thigh twice. Laurie stood very still, his expression openly admiring, which I ignored. With a little adjusting, the skirt settled back into place. I took a breath and faced Laurie again. "Okay. Let's go."

He nodded, flashing another grin, as if this was all a play and we were about to go onstage. "After you, my lady."

I pushed the door, and it opened with a long whine. The passage was even colder than before. It was so quiet, so still. The torches seemed to line the walls for miles. Where was everyone? Laurie slipped past me to lead the way, causing my skirt to rustle. Where Collith was a rush of frigid air, he was a subtle warm breeze. I caught myself staring at the back of his head, the line of his slender shoulders, his tight backside. The fae were directly descended from fallen angels, while the rest of us were several generations further removed, so it stood to reason that they should be beautiful. But I'd grown accustomed to the men of Granby, to Oliver, and I couldn't deny something awakening inside me.

Thankfully, a few seconds later, the dress took up the whole of my concentration; it felt like I was going to trip with each step. Though I wanted to pay attention to the passages—I didn't trust Collith or Laurie to show the way out—it was too much. The thought of seeing Damon, the damn dress, my anxiety surrounding Collith. I trailed after Laurie, distracted and agitated. We turned left, then right, then left. The Unseelie Court was a maze and I felt like a tiny mouse.

You're not helpless, I reminded myself. Power tingled under my skin like stoked coals. Collith might be impenetrable, but not all faeries were as strong as him. If one of them got in our way, they'd regret it. Just like the goblins had.

Suddenly Laurie's arm flew out to stop me. "That's the one," he whispered, inclining his head. I followed his gaze to yet another door. Like the others, there was a design carved into the old wood. A great tree, with numerous branches reaching upward and outward, like a many-armed goddess. Damon was in there, I could feel it. My stomach quaked.

"What do we—" I started.

The door opened. Laurie yanked me back, out of sight, and pressed a finger to his lips. Slowly, we both peered around the corner again. It felt like my heart was exploding. A tall faerie emerged.

In that moment, I knew I was probably looking at the creature responsible for Damon's disappearance.

He had waist-length hair the color of copper. Were he human, I would put his age in mid to late twenties. His clothing was elegant and old-fashioned, with tight pants, a billowing white shirt, and a long coat. Porcelain skin was visible through the open collar. Shining, black boots covered his feet. In one hand, he held the end of a strange-looking cane, and his fingernails were long.

"Until this evening," we heard him say. The sensual suggestion in those words was unmistakable. His voice was crisp and detached. I tried to launch myself at him, but at some point, Laurie had wrapped his arms around my shoulders. His grip was like steel. I opened my mouth to shout, but his arm clapped over it. The sleeve of his shirt was between our skin, so I couldn't use my powers on him.

Oblivious to the silent struggle a few feet away, the faerie left. His departure revealed a shorter figure in the doorway, and I went still at the sight of him. A strangled sound left me, something halfway between a gasp and a sigh. Slowly, Laurie released his hold. I didn't even notice.

For the first time in over two years, I was looking at my brother. He still hadn't seen us. His gaze lingered on the dim passageway, watching the faerie go with obvious fear. The last time I saw him, Damon was nineteen. Now, at twenty-one, he was the spitting image of our father—there was even the overly large ears. All that was missing were the glasses. His sandy hair was too long, his Adam's apple pronounced. Were he a healthy weight, I surmised he'd be as gangly as Dad, too.

"Not yet," Laurie hissed. But it had already been two years, and I couldn't wait one second longer. I stepped into the open, hardly daring to breathe. Startled, Damon's gaze snapped to me.

There was an instant of silence. Damon and I stared at each other, our identical brown eyes unblinking. My heart pounded so hard, it felt like it was about to burst from my chest. I searched Damon's for disbelief or joy. I expected him to shout my name and rush to me with open arms.

Instead, my brother began to scream.

CHAPTER SIX

The sound was so piercing that the air itself seemed to shatter. My first reaction was panic—there was no possibility that the copper-haired faerie couldn't hear it—but then Damon fell to his knees. He was still screaming. Now I rushed forward without hesitation. My brother shied away from me, and I merely knelt and wrapped my arms around him. After another moment of resistance, the strength seemed to go out of him and he went silent. Damon slumped, tremors wracking his body. I rocked him back and forth, making meaningless noises as I'd done for Cyrus. I was dimly aware of Laurie saying something, probably a warning. It didn't matter.

"Oh, Damon," I whispered. He had always been thin, but the person resting against me was so gaunt, one gust of wind could blow him away. I glanced at the passageway, terrified that the copper-haired faerie was coming. Somehow, though, he must not have heard the commotion; he would've been here by now.

"Do whatever you want to me," Damon moaned. Tears streamed from his eyes and left gleaming rivers. One fell into my skirt and lingered on a strand of web. "Feast on my pain.

Bathe in it. I'm yours. Do you want me to beg? Would you like that?"

Every word felt like a knife going into my stomach. I leaned back so Damon could see me—silently I cursed Laurie for talking me into this ridiculous makeup—and cupped his damp cheeks. I spoke firmly. "He isn't here, Damon. It's only me. I'm real."

Just as quickly as he'd succumbed to despair, rage overtook him. Damon shoved at my shoulders. He was stronger than he looked, and my spine hit the wall. I winced. "Prove it, then!" he spat. "Show me you're not just another trick or illusion. That I'm not losing my mind."

His narrow chest heaved. For the first time, I realized I no longer knew what my brother was capable of. Two years would change any person. Two years enduring what Damon had... I'd been a fool to think that he would come easily or be excited to see me.

Hoping Laurie would have an idea, I searched the darkness. There was no sign of him. I was on my own, then. Fine. What would convince me a long-lost sibling was real, if I were in Damon's position?

Nothing. Absolutely nothing. This was why I hated faeries. Mom and Dad may have taught us to accept every kind of creature, but I knew better. My hands became fists, and I forced myself to quell the anger rising within me. Damon was more important, and I needed to be level-headed for him. We were also sitting ducks in the open like this.

"He's made you see things? Showed you horrible things?" I asked evenly.

Damon had one hand on the door, as though he was about to dart back inside. His eyes looked bottomless in the flickering light. "I saw you dying," he told me in a voice twisted with anguish. "I saw Mom getting... assaulted. I saw Dad being torn apart by wolves. Every time I tried to leave or whenever I talked about going home, the images filled my head. It was as real as any nightmare we could inflict."

At his words, unwelcome visions forced their way into my own head. I blinked rapidly and made an effort to focus. It wasn't much better; the tortured man was such a contrast from the boy I used to know. I swallowed a lump in my throat before continuing. "So this could be another game. A way to give you hope and take it away again. I get why you don't want to let yourself believe, and I'm proud of you for surviving this long."

Silence hovered around us. But there was a spark in his gaze, a glimpse of the old Damon. Maybe the fae hadn't completely broken him. Encouraged, I pressed on.

"What did Dad teach us, huh? Never make a promise that you can't keep. Nightmares may be lies, but we don't have to be liars. That's what he always said." I held out my hand. Never mind that we'd already touched; somehow, this was the one that mattered. "I promise that this won't turn out to be a trick. I promise that if you take my hand, it'll be solid. And not just in your mind. You need to be brave one more time, little brother. Take one more chance."

Damon appraised me. Years went by in the shadowy passageway. Finally he drew nearer, keeping his gaze on my face. His bare feet made soft sounds on the stones. As though he were a wounded animal, I stayed very still. Damon reached out, and there was a visible tremor in his fingers. Twice he stopped. His breath came in short gasps and a fine sheen of sweat dotted his forehead. At last, his fingertips settled on the center of my palm. I didn't dare move or speak.

When nothing happened—I didn't vanish into a puff of smoke or transform into his captor—Damon looked at me with wonder. "Fortuna? You're really here?" he breathed.

Words were impossible; I could only nod. Damon's grip tightened, like someone taking hold as they dangled off an impossibly high edge. We met halfway and embraced fiercely.

Hot tears sprang to my eyes. I buried my face in Damon's neck to hide them. I'd forgotten what this felt like. Being touched, being held. My brother's smell surrounded me, so familiar and dear. A thousand memories slammed into me. So many Christmases, countless arguments, laugh-filled games. *Never again*, I thought. *I'm never going to lose you again.*

"I'm getting you out of here," I said through my teeth.

Slowly, Damon pulled away. I released him with obvious reluctance, knowing it was for the best. We'd already wasted too much time. But Damon didn't ask me about an escape plan or any of the other questions I would've expected out of his mouth. "You shouldn't have come, Fortuna," he said instead. The torchlight cast half of Damon's features into shadow. In the half I could see, the earlier wariness in his expression had returned.

I squeezed his hands in reassurance, thinking of how much he'd been through. "Don't worry, I have friends in high places. That's where I got this ridiculous getup. So nothing will happen to us, okay?"

Damon's throat bobbed as he swallowed. "That's not what I meant."

"Then what do you..." I trailed off as comprehension began to dawn.

I'm yours. That's what Damon had said when he believed I was his captor, his voice ringing with a truth that I'd been too distracted to hear. In a burst of awful clarity, I understood. It hadn't been fear in his eyes as he watched the copper-haired faerie depart; it was awe. My mind went even further back to the awful scene I'd witnessed in the mirror. Now the tears that I'd thought were pain had a sense of longing. He'd been staring at the door. Waiting, I had thought, in fear of his tormentor's return. But what if it had been in anticipation?

Something sour and acrid rose in my throat. This was Stockholm syndrome, it had to be. I focused on Damon again and tried to sound logical, despite the panic shredding my insides to ribbons. "Damon, he's a faerie of the Unseelie Court. You're under his influence. You may not want to leave now, but once you've spent a few days at home, you'll start to—"

"His name is Jassin," Damon interrupted.

I couldn't bear to put a name to the creature that had imprisoned and broken my brother. "What about Savannah?" I demanded. There was an edge of desperation in my voice now, impossible to conceal. "That kind of love doesn't just go away, I know it doesn't. When you disappeared, she did everything to find you. Spells, posters, radio interviews, search parties. She needs you to come home just as much as I do."

I'd been so certain the mention of his girlfriend would bring reason back to Damon's clouded eyes. But he just shook his head and whispered, "I'm sorry."

In all my imaginings of how this would go, it never occurred to me that Damon would be unwilling to leave. If logic had no effect, then manipulation and force were the only options. I thought of the bargain between me and Collith. However trapped and resentful it made me feel, it had worked. "Fine," I said. "It's your turn to prove something. If you're not being manipulated by his power, you'll come home. Tonight. Then, if you still want to return to the Unseelie Court after a week or so, I won't stop you."

Saying the words made me feel dirty, as though a layer of grime covered my skin. I'd only been married to Collith a few hours and I was already acting more like him. Was it the result of the bond between us, or my own doing?

Damon didn't even react. "I love him, Fortuna," he said simply, as if anything were that simple. "I'm not going anywhere."

Words failed me again. I stood there, searching Damon's expression for any sign or tell. Maybe this was all a lie; he could be trying to communicate in some other way. But nothing moved or changed in his face, and all I could see was regret shining from his eyes. Not regret for his choice—just for hurting me.

The only sound between us came from a nearby torch. Its flame wavered and sputtered. It didn't go out, though. I looked away from the soft light to meet Damon's gaze again. My resolve hardened. Self-loathing rolled in my stomach as I played the last card I had. "What about your promise to Mom?"

Damon blanched.

So much changed for both of us that day. Despite how much time had passed, every moment was still vivid. All I had to do was close my eyes, and I was back there, sitting in that dim room. The faint smell of medicine in the air and the barest beginnings of morning filtering through the curtains. When young Damon had woken up in the hospital bed, and I saw that he would truly be all right, sobs racked my body. I buried my face in the covers and cried. After a few minutes I lifted my face, took Damon's small hand in mine, and made a watery vow. "From now on, I'll be a better sister. I'll take care of you. Promise."

"I'll take care of you, too," my brother had rasped. There was no hesitation in his reply. He turned to Mom, who knelt on his other side. Somehow he understood, even then, that saying the words to her had more weight. "Promise."

Three weeks later, she was dead.

Though I'd never asked, I knew it was probably one of Damon's last memories of her. And here I was exploiting it, something that should've been sacred and untouched forever.

But my brother didn't let his pain become anger, as I would have. Instead, Damon Sworn touched my cheek. There was infinite tenderness in the gesture, and it was just more proof that he was indisputably a better person than I would ever be—something I'd accepted long ago. "You're right. We did promise," he murmured. A sad smile curved his lips.

"So let me keep it," I begged, trapping his hand against my face.

"Don't you see? This is a blessing. You're *free*, big sister," Damon insisted. "There's someone else to look after me now. You don't have to worry anymore."

"No, that's not how a promise works." There was a tremor in my voice and I faltered. There in the lovely darkness, which guarded so many secrets and fears, another truth emerged. "And who's going to look after *me*?"

"Oh, Fortuna. Do I really need to tell you how resilient you are? How brave and strong? I was so jealous of that when we were growing up. But regardless of you or Jassin, I can't go back. We just don't belong up there. We never did." Suddenly Damon's eyes lit up. He grabbed the back of my neck with his free hand. "You should stay! No more hiding. No more shame. In the Unseelie Court, we can be a family again!"

Speechless, I could only stare at him. It was like arguing with a madman. I'd tried reasoning and manipulation—it was time to resort to other methods. In a burst of frustration, I yanked away and searched the dark again. "Collith?" I muttered. "Can you hear me?"

Nothing happened.

I repeated his name, more forcefully this time, despite the risk of someone else hearing it instead. Damon's brow wrinkled in bewilderment. Then his eyes shifted slightly. They widened. In an instant, he prostrated himself in the dirt. Exasperated, I turned to face Collith, whose presence I'd already felt. It filled the passageway like water. His face was hidden in shadow and he was oddly silent. Aggravated by Damon's reaction—clearly the faeries had warped his mind so much that he now believed they were gods—I raised my brows at Collith. "Took you long enough," I snapped. "Will you please help me get Damon to the surface?"

Just as I started to face my brother again, ready for his resistance, Collith spoke. "I can't do that, Fortuna."

I paused. Damon still hadn't moved, and my instincts came
alive, speculating and urging in a burst of whispers. Slowly, I
turned again. Collith didn't step forward, but apparently I didn't
need to see his expression to sense what he was feeling. It was
there, alongside my own, like two veins running through the
same arm. He was experiencing... guilt. "I beg your pardon?" I
asked, trying to hide my dread. *Don't make me regret trusting you.
Don't play me for a fool. Don't betray me.*

"He said he can't help you, my dear."

The voice was coldly amused, and I went rigid. My fear filled
the air, stronger than any perfume. Even before I saw him, I
knew who it was. Jassin leaned against the wall like a languid
cat. Maybe it was his smile or how still he stood, but in that
instant, I knew he'd been watching us the entire time. "I'm
taking my brother home," I snarled, finding my own voice again.

Jassin straightened and brushed imaginary specks of dirt off
his coat. He sauntered closer. "Unfortunately, I'm not feeling
generous today. Although I may be willing to give you a good
fuck, since it seems Collith hasn't gotten around to it yet."

I felt my lip curl with disgust. I looked down at Damon,
wondering what he thought of his lover's comments. My
brother remained on the ground, silent and trembling. *This is the
one you love?* I wanted to ask him. Instead I lifted my chin and
met the faerie's gaze. His eyes had a distinctly feline tilt to
them, and they shone gold in the torchlight. "Go to hell."

"Haven't you heard?" Jassin leaned close. He smelled like
everything tempting and addictive. Like chocolate. Like sex.
"Hell is empty, and all the devils are here."

Though he didn't touch me, it felt like someone had run
their finger along the ridges of my spine. He had power, there
was no denying it. I retaliated with false bravado. "Satan came

to my christening, little boy. Stay out of my way, or I'll make you piss in your fancy clothes."

The faerie made a sound deep in his throat, almost like a purr. He glanced toward my mate. "She's exquisite, Collith, I'll give you that. And you've even dressed her for the part."

"What's going on here? Why aren't you doing anything?" I demanded, also focusing on the other faerie in the passageway. Throughout our exchange, he hadn't said a word. Was he that weak? Had his display of power been an illusion? *At least it's finally clear why he married you*, a cruel voice whispered.

"You didn't know?" Jassin asked incredulously. Apparently it was a rhetorical question, because he threw his head back and laughed.

Once again, I looked to Collith. Confusion and fear warred inside me, and I resisted reaching for Dad's knife. "What is he talking about?"

Before he could reply, Jassin wiped his tears away and said, "They will write songs about you, Fortuna Sworn. Oh, how they'll laugh and sing. You'll be a legend. The female who married the King of the Unseelie Court and didn't even know it."

CHAPTER SEVEN

*J*assin's mocking laughter rang in my ears, but I hardly heard it now. My mind spun like a colorful carousel. Collith had finally stepped forward, into the light, but his expression was neutral. I grasped at stray memories, hoping for any mention of the Unseelie King. Mom had focused more on lore and mythology, though. Dad on his beliefs of acceptance and equality. What did this really mean? Why had Collith kept who he was a secret?

He didn't acknowledge us as he stooped to say something in Damon's ear, and at last my frail brother stood up. Maybe it was the angle of firelight, or just my own mind fracturing, but for a wild instant I found myself looking at Dad. His dear, familiar face stared back. I blinked, dazed and overwhelmed. Hope tore through me. Had it been a bad dream? All of it?

A moment later, Damon's features came into focus. His hair was a bit lighter than Dad's, his mouth a bit fuller. The carousel in my head jerked to a screeching halt. I experienced a sharp pain, like Dad had died all over again, and reality returned. It was exactly what I needed—a jarring reminder that none of this mattered. Not Collith, not Jassin, not my questions. I'd come here for Damon. *From now on, I'll be a better sister. I'll take care of you. Promise.*

"You're right," I blurted. Jassin cocked his head. The movement made me think of a cat again, its eyes bright and unblinking as it watched a bird outside the window. I swallowed and forced myself to continue. "Collith hasn't touched me. No one has."

"What are you getting at?" Jassin asked, his expression more entertained than intrigued. Damon looked ill. I tried to get a read of Collith's emotions through our mating bond, but he was a curious blank.

My mind worked quickly. Jassin knew we were Nightmares, of course. There would be no element of surprise there. But I'd always been stronger than my brother; the faerie wouldn't expect that. I took a breath.

"I'm a virgin. Fresh and ripe for the picking. Take me in Damon's place."

Part of me expected Collith to intervene or protest. Anything but his continued silence. Damon, however, didn't remain silent. "Fortuna, stop this," he spat. "It's not necessary. I already told you—"

"Shut up," Jassin said. Damon obeyed instantly, and his mouth closed with an audible snap. I kept my eyes on Jassin, because I worried if I didn't, the others would guess my intentions. The copper-haired faerie regarded me for a long, long moment. My heart thundered in my chest. Then, in a gesture eerily similar to Collith's just before our mating ceremony, Jassin offered his hand.

His fingers were decorated with silver rings. One of them had scales and glittering rubies for eyes. Those long nails looked like they could slice my skin with a single twitch. Suddenly I remembered the scars I had seen on Damon's back—I'd stood there wondering what could've made such small, deep wounds. *Mystery solved*, I thought numbly.

Jassin waited patiently for my decision. He didn't say the words, but the implication was clear; if I took it, a bargain was struck. Damon leaned forward, probably to get my attention, but I didn't look away from Jassin's hand. I steeled myself and reached out.

My fingers curled around his.

I didn't give him a chance to react—a second was all I needed. I clawed through Jassin's mind without mercy. It was far more complex than anything I'd encountered. His thoughts and memories were a maze of twists and turns, endings and beginnings. There was violence and blood around every corner. It was like walking through a funhouse of horrors. At some point, I stumbled across the realization that Jassin could hear or insert thoughts into others' heads, which was how he'd tormented Damon with visions of his dying family. Fury blackened my heart, but I forced myself to keep going.

Eventually I found it. On the outer edges, cowering in the darkness, a secret hid. I seized it, ignoring the lightning bolts of pain that shot through me from the contact.

Jassin of the Unseelie Court, a creature who had taken my brother from me for two years, was afraid of light. Blinding, incandescent light. A triumphant smile stretched across my face.

"I see you," I crooned. Suddenly the passageway was full of sunlight, lamp posts, fire, flashlights. Nowhere to hide. Damon and Collith couldn't see my illusion, but they knew something had changed—both of them went stiff. I waited and watched, expecting Jassin to whimper or crumble as all the rest had.

With his eyes still closed, he yanked me close. I was so surprised that I lost my footing and fell against him. Jassin dug his fingers into my ass and pressed us together, showing me how aroused he was. The damn skirt tore and I felt cool air on my bare leg.

"Oh, how you've miscalculated," the faerie breathed. Now he opened his eyes and looked at me with pure, unadulterated glee.

At this proximity, I could see that his irises were gold. "I was among the soldiers when the Dark Prince gathered his army. I followed him into the throne room when he marched against God. Few things give me pleasure or reprieve from this endless *boredom*. Fear is one of them. Why else do you think I've kept your pretty brother alive?"

He was telling the truth. I could feel his terror, taste it like all the others. It had a tangy flavor this time, like an apple plucked from the tree too soon. But rather than cripple him, the sensation gave Jassin a high. Never in my life had I met a creature that thrived on my power. *New plan*, I thought in a haze of panic. The brilliant light around us faded as I withdrew from Jassin's mind.

I didn't pause to reconsider as I acted on instinct and desperation. Between one breath and the next, Dad's knife was in my hand, easily accessible through the tear in the dress. I pressed my hand against Jassin's chest to put some distance between us and raised the other. He anticipated the move—it was so sloppy, Dad would've been appalled—and my wrist slammed into his waiting hand. Jassin's grip tightened painfully. I cried out, and the knife hit the earth with a dull thud.

Damon was pale. "Jassin, please, she didn't—"

This time Jassin didn't bother with a command—he just backhanded my brother with the full force of his strength. Damon slammed into the wall. I shrieked with fury and reached up to rake my nails down Jassin's face. He hissed and released me. Just as I was about to launch at him again, the tip of Dad's knife pressed to my throat. I froze.

"Damon?"

Tears streamed down his cheeks. "I can't let you hurt him," he said.

Indifferent to our exchange, Jassin looked at Collith with glittering eyes. There were four angry marks down his skin, but his voice was unperturbed as he said, "Your mate just tried to take what is mine. I demand a tribunal."

That was when I knew; this was exactly what Jassin had wanted. He'd been steps ahead of me, probably from the moment I'd first embraced Damon. And whatever a tribunal was, it wasn't good.

Everyone waited for Collith's reply. Even now, he wouldn't acknowledge me. A few seconds ticked by. Finally he just nodded, brushed past, and walked back the way we'd come. Jassin snapped his fingers at Damon like a dog, then trailed after Collith without bothering to say another word. I almost launched myself at him then and there.

"Send word to the bloodlines," I heard my mate say. Who was he talking to?

Slowly, Damon lowered the knife. A single tear still hung off the edge of his jaw. Without a word or glance, he trailed after his lover and sovereign. He still clutched Dad's knife, and I wondered if he knew who it had once belonged to.

I watched them go, and it felt like I was on the verge of breaking. Somehow, this was worse than those three days in the goblins' cabin. There was more at stake, and I was losing. What would Oliver say if he was here?

You can do this, Fortuna. I know you can. You're a fighter... now fight.

Suddenly it occurred to me that there was no one in my way if I were to run. I had no intention of leaving Damon down here, but the tribunal sounded like something to be avoided. Maybe I could go for help, or at the very least run back to the house for more weapons. Just as I was about to bolt, I sensed a presence at my back. I moved to snatch the knife—my fingers grappled at empty air—and spun.

Two faeries stood there. One was massive, and the other was petite. Their features were plainer than those of Collith and Jassin. There were no imperfections, of course, but their coloring was duller. Like quails keeping company with peacocks. They were dressed in armor, of sorts, made of smooth wood and frayed rope. Each held a long, jagged weapon, and the blades looked like they were made of glass. I knew in an instant there would be no getting around them or fighting my way through; these were warriors. Collith's guards, probably.

How strange it was that I was now in a world where there was such a thing as guards.

Both regarded me with mild curiosity. "I'd tell you to take a picture, but then you'd probably just add it to your spank bank collections," I muttered.

Neither of them reacted. We kept staring at each other until the male indicated with his sword that I should walk. Feeling mutinous, I stayed where I was for a few more seconds. The male took a threatening step toward me. I was half-tempted to grab his arm and shatter his mind beyond all repair, but the female would be on me in an instant. So I gritted my teeth and turned. We started down the passageway, and my progress was less-than-graceful because of the dress. There was no sign of Damon or the bastards he'd gone with. I strained to hear the echo of footsteps or conversation, but there was just the scrape of my own slippers.

I was on my own.

The passages continued to branch off or end abruptly; it truly was a maze. Every now and then, the male spoke in a rumble, telling me which direction to go. We must've arrived at a more inhabited part of the Court—sounds came from behind the intricate doors now. A laugh. The strums of a harp. A rhythmic thumping. My grip tightened on the skirt involuntarily; I was in the heart of the lion's den.

The deeper we went, the higher the ceiling became. The stones along the floor and walls were smoother. They'd been placed carefully so there was no visible dirt. I could almost believe we were in a castle, were it not for the utter lack of windows. To make up for this, there were even more torches. Their soft crackling filled my ears. Then a new sound disturbed the stillness.

At first, I thought it was running water or a bee's nest. A few steps later the passage stopped, and I found myself in a huge room. On the other end was a doorway, open and beckoning. That was where the sound came from. Not streams or insects... voices. Hundreds of them. I could see faeries standing within, their backs to us. My stomach fluttered and sweat pooled beneath the stiff dress. "Keep moving," the female ordered. I shuffled forward reluctantly, feeling vulnerable without Dad's knife. And my powers hadn't exactly been helpful, either.

As we drew closer, I finally tore my gaze away from the faeries. There was a mural, of sorts, covering the wall all around the doors. Torches throughout the room gave the images an eerie movement. *It's a story*, I realized. While humanity evolved and fought and created, the fae had been making history of their own beneath the earth. Carved by different hands, each picture or figure depicted an event. A celebration, a battle, a birth. Centuries had passed in this small, dark world, and I knew practically nothing about these creatures my brother had fallen for.

We were at the threshold now, and I forgot about the mural. The female guard moved to my other side. They were finally in a position where I could grab them both, but it was too late. A purple-haired faerie at the back of the crowd took notice of us. She said something to her companion, who also turned. This happened again and again. Gradually, a hush fell, and soon everyone was looking at me. By some unspoken agreement, a path opened up in the middle of them.

We stepped into a cavernous room. It looked like the inside of a cathedral—columns lined the walls and a massive chandelier hung over the crowd. It was made of antlers and branches. But I couldn't stare at the ceiling the entire time; reluctantly I turned my attention to the massive crowd. *Send word to the blood-*

lines, Collith had said. There were hundreds of them. I had never felt so weak and small. To fight the feeling, I raised my head high.

The fae wore clothing of bark, leaves, furs. Some had jarring makeup like mine. Others wore modern clothing, clearly taken from the human world. I spotted a female in high heels and a male wearing a leather jacket. That one stared at me with obvious awe—so they weren't completely immune to my power.

There were also humans here. Many were hollow-cheeked and half-naked. One was a boy who couldn't be more than thirteen; he watched my progress with feverish eyes. Taking note of how his ribs stood out, my hatred for the fae grew. Farther on, my gaze met a woman's. She might have been my age, but the smudges beneath her eyes and the emptiness in her expression made her seem ancient. Someone had shaved her head, and remaining tufts of blond hair caught the light. At that moment, a faerie jabbed the woman in the ribs, and she lowered her eyes. I slowed, thinking to intervene, but the male guard growled in warning. I kept going.

At the far end of the room was a dais, and resting atop that was a throne. It was the biggest chair I'd ever seen. It had been carved from the roots of a great tree, which came down from the ceiling. Laurie stood near it, his shoulders hunched and head bowed. As I watched, Collith ascended the uneven stairs. I sent a prayer to whoever was listening that he would trip or fall. No such luck. He sat in the chair and looked out at his subjects. His scar shone in the light. In that moment, he truly did look like the Unseelie King. Like a dark fairy tale. Like a terrible dream.

Though he had to notice us making our way toward him, he still wouldn't look at me.

Moments later, we stopped at the base of the makeshift stage. Damon and Jassin stood to our left, but my brother was shielded from view. I shifted so I could see his face. He caught the movement, and when our eyes met, Damon's expression twisted with guilt and worry. Before I could do anything, he faced forward again. My father's knife was no longer in his possession.

There was a palpable sense of anticipation in the air. It occurred to me that many of these creatures probably passed their days and nights beneath the ground, without technology or a world to explore. Any break in routine must've been exhilarating.

"A tribunal has been requested," Collith called, lightly gripping the armrests. His voice echoed. "Who will stand as my council?"

One by one, three faeries detached from the throng. The first to approach was a reedy female with waist-length white hair. There was no way to know her age, but years hung around her like an invisible curtain. The second seemed younger, another warrior type with thick muscles and sharp eyes. The last was a dark-skinned male with delicate limbs and golden jewelry. He emanated a sort of… serenity.

They approached the dais. The warrior hopped up nimbly, and the rest followed more demurely. They stood around the throne like shadows, and I felt the last male studying me. "Why have you asked for this gathering? In English, please, so the Nightmare can understand," Collith commanded.

At this, Jassin arched an eyebrow. *The Nightmare.* I could practically hear the wheels turning in his head, wondering if he should reveal who I really was to the king. That I was his mate and not just a Nightmare come to save her brother. I had no idea whether it would make things better or worse for me. I was also regretful to see that the scratches I'd bestowed upon him were already healing. "Balance must be restored," Jassin said instead, almost absent-mindedly, as he wrapped one of my brother's curls around his finger. Collith leveled a look at him, and the copper-haired faerie rolled his eyes. "Very well, I found the Nightmare outside my chambers. She made efforts to steal my slave. Is that specific enough, Your Majesty?"

Mutters erupted through the crowd. I opened my mouth to say something—point out that Damon wasn't a slave, that I didn't abide by faerie laws, that *Jassin* had been the thief—but Laurie shook his head in a silent warning. Fury made the blood in my veins boil. *Why should I trust you?* I wanted to spit. Maybe I was a fool, though, because part of me still wanted to. So I gritted my teeth and stayed silent.

As if he sensed the danger, Collith chose that moment to finally address me. "You attempted to steal something that was already claimed. In return, the lord you offended will be allowed to take something of yours," he explained. His tone was polite and distant.

Just then, there was movement out of the corner of my eye. Damon was saying something in Jassin's ear, low and urgent. Whatever he said piqued the faerie's interest, and he turned his head. While they spoke, Laurie sidled up next to me. No one seemed to notice him. "They can't take your life," he murmured. "Because it was just a slave you tried to steal, the balance only demands something equal to a belonging or object."

Something in my chest loosened, and I breathed easier. "Oh, well, that's great. I'm so glad it was *just a slave* I set my sights on. Also, remind me why I can't defend myself?"

"Because punishment is inevitable. Speaking now will only amuse or piss them off, depending on their moods. Either way, you just prolong the process."

"I'm already bored with this," Jassin droned suddenly, pulling away from Damon. "Take the flesh from her back and be done with it."

A hysterical laugh burst from me. Laurie grasped my shoulder, giving it a squeeze of warning, but I shook him off. I spun to face our vibrant onlookers. *Don't you want to know who let me in?* I tried to say—if I was going down, I was taking Collith with me

—but all that emerged was a weak croak. A second ticked past, and I tried again. Nothing. Time seemed to slow as I realized why.

Collith had taken my voice.

Slowly, I turned again. For a minute, the rest of the room faded away. I stared up at the faerie I'd married, sitting on his pretty throne, and thought about punishments of my own. Ignoring me, the Unseelie King looked to the solemn-faced faeries standing around him. "Does the council find this fair?" he asked. The only indication that he was affected by my plight was his long fingers, which tapped an erratic beat. His ring flashed.

The guards closest to the dais came forward. They formed a tight circle around the three faeries. I strained to hear what they were saying. Their voices were too low, but each of them made slight movements that indicated a conversation was happening. My pulse was thunderous.

Apparently the tall female was their spokesperson; in less than a minute she straightened and gave a single nod. Her voice rang into the stillness, cool and refined. "It's a sound judgment."

At this, Collith signaled to the guards, and the female took hold of my arm. I jerked away and spit in her face. She responded with a blow that sent me to the ground—there was nothing human in the strength behind it. Spots of color filled my sight. The inside of my mouth tasted like salt and metal. The guard grabbed hold again, hauled me up, and moved toward another tangle of roots. It stood to the right of the dais, within everyone's line of sight but slightly removed from everything. My heart, which had already been pounding hard and fast, picked up speed. Was this really happening? Wasn't anyone going to stop it?

As though she could hear the panicked spiral of my thoughts, the guard produced a rope and secured my wrists to one of the thicker branches. I was still swaying on my feet, and there was no chance to react or decide. The instant she was finished, the guard turned away. I couldn't even snap an insult at her retreating back.

My breathing was loud and ragged. I tested the strength of the ropes and knew straight away there would be no escaping this. The prospect of pain didn't terrify me so much as an entire court of fae taking enjoyment of it. While I weighed my options, Jassin raised his voice, shouting in his own tongue. He seemed to be searching the assemblage.

Conversations halted.

For a few seconds, I had no idea why they'd gone silent. I craned my neck to see the room. Then there was movement along the back wall, and my gaze snapped toward it. Faeries were parting with obvious wariness as a creature slowly made its way toward the dais. It towered above all the rest and wore a cloth around its face. The brown material was covered in dark stains.

Jassin sauntered over to me. I yanked against the ropes in a futile effort to get away, which only seemed to give him more pleasure. He leaned close and whispered in a conspiratorial tone, "The children call him *druindar northana*. Roughly translated to Death Bringer, in your crude tongue."

He licked my earlobe, and I jerked back too late. Fresh hatred mixed with the terror, and my trembling intensified. With a smirk, Jassin returned to my brother's side. This time I didn't even glance at Damon; the huge faerie had arrived. He stood behind me, and the air felt colder than normal. I couldn't suppress a shiver. I kept twisting to keep my eyes on him, trying to see any hint of a face through those stiff folds. Then the creature's hand appeared. The first detail I noticed was his dark, splintered nails, even more distasteful than Jassin's. The second was the thing they were clutched around.

It was the handle of a cat o' nine tails.

"Fortuna Sworn," Collith called, "you have committed a crime according to the old laws. Balance must be restored. You have been sentenced to twenty lashes—an amount we've found even lesser creatures can survive—at the end of which your debt will be paid."

There was a moment of utter silence, and I turned to fix my stare resolutely on the floor. In doing so, I caught a glimpse of the crowd. Some looked on with obvious distaste, while others grinned or giggled. The male who had been staring at me with such reverence tried to come forward, but there was a brief scuffle and another faerie dragged him from the room.

Then the creature swung his gigantic arm. Though I was anticipating it, the blow was so shocking that I couldn't hold back a scream. Apparently Collith had returned the use of my voice. He wanted me to cry out. He wanted the Court to take enjoyment in the Nightmare's pain. My skin burned white-hot where the whip had struck. I held back a whimper, resolving to make no more sound. I was also determined to stay standing. But the cat o' nine tails came down again and it was no use. I buckled. My knees hit the ground with a jarring thud. I bit my lip so hard I tasted more blood. There was no thought, no sense of self.

Just the fire.

The whip kept raining down, tearing me from shoulder blades to calves. As it went on, I turned to look at Collith. To make sure he was watching every second. Missing nothing. Not the suffering in my expression, not the rope tearing my wrists, not the leather bearing down on me. With every lash, I lost more than skin and blood.

I lost the potential to someday love my mate.

The agony worsened with every blow. Eventually it was too much. Collith's inscrutable face became hazy, and I broke our stare to sag against the roots. The lashes didn't stop. I'd lost count of them. They just came again, and again, and again. Tears and snot ran down my face. I didn't care.

Someone spoke from a vast distance, and the whip finally stopped. The ropes around my wrists went slack. I slid to the floor, hovering on the edge of consciousness. The coldness that surrounded Death Bringer retreated, but I couldn't form a coherent thought. There was only the pain.

All at once, music began to play, whistles and fiddles that filled the air with merriment. Conversations came back to life. "Get that out of the way," I heard Jassin order. I opened my eyes —the world was a crooked blend of colors and movement—and watched as he pulled my brother into his arms. Damon glanced down at me, his face anguished. An instant later, he moved out of my view. A female's skirt swirled as the dancing started. Someone laughed.

Rough fingers wrapped around my arms and dragged me through the crowd of revelers. My destroyed back scraped along the stones, which should have been torture. Everything felt muted, though. I was distantly aware that our progress left a trail of blood. My gown was soaked through and parts of it were in tatters. We were heading for a small doorway. If they meant to kill me, I wouldn't be able to fight back.

Beneath heavy lids, I spotted Collith. He still sat on his throne, and his gaze met mine. In that moment, his mask seemed to slip, revealing something besides the cold creature that had been sitting in that chair all this time. I knew it was wishful thinking, a pathetic hope that I hadn't married a monster. I squeezed my eyes shut and willed darkness to swallow me. It didn't.

The sounds from the throne room faded. There was just my breathing, the dragging, and the guards' footsteps. A mental image came in and out of focus, a meadow covered in bright wildflowers. A familiar figure sat with his back to me. "Oliver?" I whispered. Just as he turned, the image slipped away. I moaned with frustration. A moment later, one of the guards stopped and lifted me. The male, I realized when I felt his flat chest against my shoulder. He smelled like he hadn't washed himself in weeks. He said something to his companion, and she replied in a bored tone. Probably discussing whether I'd last the night.

We were going down a set of stairs; the temperature dropped and the space felt narrower. Hinges squealed. A few steps farther, the guard threw me down like a sack of flour. I hit the hard ground and moaned again. Then a lock clicked.

The sound made my eyes fly open. The second I'd registered what was happening—they had put me in a cell—panic shattered through the wall of pain around me. "No!" I screamed. Apparently I did have some strength left after all; I flung myself at the bars in a futile effort to get out. The guards were already gone. I screamed after them, every obscenity and threat I could think of.

Silence answered me. Still gripping the bars, I sank to the ground. A single torch burned nearby, and its light was feeble. There was nothing kind about the resulting darkness. Though I hated myself for giving in, for letting them break me, I couldn't stop the sobs that wracked my body. The side of my face throbbed and the rest of me hurt so badly, I could hardly think straight. I'd never known pain like this. I'd already been punished, hadn't I? Why was I down here?

"Would you stop that wailing? Some of us are trying to sleep."

The voice came from all around, echoing off the cold, dripping walls. I jerked upright. The movement sent a lightning bolt through me, and it took a few attempts to speak. "Who are you?" I rasped.

"Just another fool they threw down here and forgot about," the voice replied. *Female*, I thought.

It made me wonder who else occupied the cells down here.

But if there were others, they were dead or asleep—the only sound in the vicinity was that small, struggling flame. I leaned my temple against the stone and fought another wave of dizziness. "What was your crime?"

The stranger sighed. "I gave my allegiance to the king, then promptly tried to assassinate him."

"But I thought faeries couldn't lie," I whispered. My mind raced.

This earned a derisive snort. "Oh, you poor, stupid creature. Of course we can. We lie about everything. That rumor was established millennia ago. Some clever faerie thought it would be advantageous if the rest of the world thought we could be trusted."

The revelation was too large, too heavy, and I couldn't begin to think about the implications of it. Once again, darkness hovered at the edges of my vision.

And there, wearing a ruined faerie gown, sitting in a pool of my own blood, I succumbed to it.

CHAPTER EIGHT

*T*here was no sign of Oliver when I arrived at our dreamscape.

I scanned the horizon, searching for his easel. A breeze stirred the ends of my hair. In the distance, the door to the house was wide open, like a beckoning hand. I snatched up the gown and started to run, but quickly realized that I'd brought my wounds into the dream—the lash marks throbbed. My pace slowed to a stiff walk. The tall grass tickled my knees and butterflies launched into the air, the picture of serenity. With every step, it became easier to leave reality behind.

At the threshold, I paused. The lamps were off, leaving only natural light. Oliver had his back to me. His hair glowed in the dusk. He'd set his easel up in front of the window, and the floor around his feet was littered with crushed flowers, bowls of paint, unused brushes. In the corner, there was an old record player. The familiar notes of "Moon River" drifted through the sun-dappled air—somehow Oliver had developed a taste for older music. I preferred the record player simply for the crackling sound it made when the disc had finished; it was oddly soothing.

I could have stood there for hours. Muscles shifted beneath Oliver's shirt as he moved the brush up and down. On the canvas, an image was just beginning to come together, a gentle union of grays and whites. A cloud-filled sky, maybe, or hills shrouded in mist. I longed to watch some more, but the fading sunlight reminded me that time was against us. Reluctantly I moved forward. The floorboards creaked beneath my weight, and Oliver turned. At the sight of me, he frowned and set his paintbrush down. "What's wrong? What are you wearing?"

My first instinct was to rush into his arms. Just as I started to, I remembered Collith. My mind flashed back to that shadowy ceremony in the woods, to the whispered words we'd exchanged. *I promise to be faithful.*

The faerie may have betrayed me, but that didn't negate my vows; Dad's teachings ran deep as ancient tree roots. My throat swelled with remorse and regret. I stood there, clenching and unclenching my fists. Oliver closed the distance between us in two long strides. He bent to kiss me, but I turned my face away. His brows drew together. "Fortuna?"

I didn't want to tell him. I couldn't tell him. Feeling like a coward, I mustered a weak smile. "I need to get out of this dress."

Oliver appraised me. Whatever he saw made him decide not to press the matter. For now, at least. He turned to clear away his supplies. After a moment, I moved to the dresser, trying not to show how much every step hurt. The top drawer held clothing that I still had no idea how Oliver had managed to conjure. Whenever I asked, he gave a flippant answer or just smiled mysteriously. I pulled out a pair of leggings and a soft sweater. After a few seconds of struggling, the dress settled onto the floor in a stiff, blood-soaked pile. The sweater settled against my back. I bit my lip to hold back a gasp.

Hoping he hadn't noticed, I faced Oliver again. He was just straightening, paintbrushes in hand. He dropped them into a color-stained cup and raised his brows. "Now will you tell me what's going on?" he asked.

I wasn't even sure where to begin. There was a loud, childish part of me that wanted things to stay as they were. It also wanted to avoid talking about the events of the past twenty-four hours. Stalling, I walked to the other side of the room and ran the tip of my finger along the bookshelf. It was utterly devoid of dust. Did he clean? Or was there no such thing as dust here? There were so many questions I'd never thought to ask.

When I turned around a second time, Oliver was leaning against the edge of the writing desk, still waiting for a response. He wore an expression that told me he would wait all night if he had to. *Stop being a coward,* I ordered myself. It wasn't fair to him. But there weren't any right words or a right way to say them. Haltingly I said, "The faerie came back. His name is Collith, by the way, don't know if I mentioned that before. Turns out he wasn't Damon's kidnapper, but he knew who was. We made a deal. In return for something he wanted, the faerie agreed to help me get my brother back."

"A deal," Oliver stated. Icicles hung off the words; he knew he wouldn't like what I was about to say next. He pushed off the desk and crossed the room. I stayed where I was, arching my neck to look up at him. Our chests nearly touched. The familiar scent of paint surrounded us. Oliver bit out the question we both knew was coming. "What did he want, Fortuna? What did you do?"

"I married him."

Silence met my words. Oliver stared at me, his eyes so cold that they burned. Like holding a handful of snow without a glove. Just as I opened my mouth again, he stepped away. I made a strangled sound and grabbed at him, but he evaded the touch.

Like normal children, then teenagers, we'd had our share of

fights. In all our years of friendship, though, he had never pulled away from me.

Oliver sat on the stool and faced his painting. A single ray of sunlight remained, and it reached through the window, settling onto my friend. He didn't seem to notice or care. The line of his shoulders was tense and hard. As I stared at him, sorrow fluttered in my chest like a butterfly caught in a jar. The significance of what we'd lost was obvious to both of us. I swallowed. "I'm sorry that I've caused you pain. But I'm not sorry for doing everything in my power to save Damon."

I waited. When he still didn't spare me a glance, I nodded and turned toward the door. Seconds later, Oliver's voice stopped me. "Fortuna, you're bleeding. What—" The floor creaked. Before I could react, he was there, lifting my shirt. I heard a sharp intake. I'd stopped, but I didn't turn. It felt like I was seconds away from cracking.

Outside, a bird began to sing. I kept my eyes on the doorway, hoping for a glimpse of it. "Collith brought me to the Unseelie Court," I said distantly. The memory of what happened in the throne room hovered, creeping closer, but I kept it at bay. "His people gave me an enthusiastic welcome."

"We need to clean these," I heard Oliver say. He took my hand.

I sighed as we walked toward the bed. "You know nothing you do here will have an effect after I wake."

"Then shut up and let me do this for my own sanity." He gently pushed down on my shoulders. Even that caused discomfort. Once I was sitting, Oliver strode to the bathroom. The faucet squeaked. He returned with a damp washcloth and a small tube. Despite how angry he'd been only seconds ago, his touch was gentle. He lifted the sweater again and began to dab with the washcloth. It took all my willpower not to jerk away. To distract myself, I read the label on the tube. Oliver hadn't opened it yet, but I knew he would in a few minutes.

"Why do you have antibiotic cream?" I asked through my teeth.

"I didn't until thirty seconds ago."

I was about to ask him how he knew what antibiotic cream was. Then I remembered. Everything I knew, he knew. *Because he's not real*, that inner voice whispered.

No. That was something else I didn't want to think about now. In search of another distraction, I looked over my shoulder to see what Oliver was doing. There was a mirror on the wall opposite the bed. What I saw almost made me gasp.

My back was unrecognizable.

The skin that wasn't marred by cuts and welts was blue and black, surrounded by yellow swellings. I would bear the scars for the rest of my life. I blinked rapidly and the reflection staring back at me blurred.

The mirror also brought someone else to mind. "He wouldn't come back with me," I whispered, watching my mouth form the words.

Oliver's hand stilled. "Damon?"

Hearing his name out loud was my undoing. I nodded, trying to keep the tears away yet again, but it was no use. Suddenly every second of pain and terror washed over me. Damon's refusal to leave, the encounter with Jassin in the passageway, being whipped, finding myself in yet another cage. Mute sobs shook my body. Oliver instantly put the washcloth down and tugged me back into his arms.

Being careful not to touch my injuries, he leaned back so his spine was against the headboard. As I wept, he rocked me back and forth. It should've been humiliating or strange. Instead, the motion was calming. My sobbing began to slow. Unconsciousness returned to claim me, but the darkness was only a reminder of what awaited in the real world. I came awake with a violent gasp.

I bunched Oliver's shirt in my fists and said frantically,

"There's too many of them. They're stronger than me, Ollie. I can't win." The admission left a sour taste in my mouth.

There were gaps in his knowledge—I'd barely told him anything—but Oliver didn't falter. He calmly tucked a wild curl behind my ear. "Sometimes it's not about being stronger. It's about being smarter," he told me.

"You don't understand. They've been alive for millennia."

"Which means they've gotten complacent," he countered. "Be patient. Learn their weaknesses."

It was difficult to imagine retaliation when my broken body was trapped in a cell. Even so, his words helped. It meant that some part of me was still hopeful, still clinging to strength. I wiped the tears off my cheeks and leaned back to see Oliver's face better. "When did you become so devious?" I asked, only partly joking.

At this, Oliver's eyes dimmed. He looked away, toward the window. The sun was gone, leaving only moonlight and shadows in its wake. "You created me. I am whatever you need me to be," he murmured.

I knew I wasn't imagining the faint touch of bitterness in his voice. Guilt curled in my stomach like a venomous snake. I cupped his cheek and turned him back to me. "Thank you," I said, letting everything I felt surge into the open. It went against all my instincts, but I fought them. For him.

It was worth it. A glorious smile stretched across his face, and just like that, Oliver was the person I'd always known. He kissed the top of my head, slow and tender. "Just remember one thing, okay? You're Fortuna Sworn, baby."

Now I laughed, a watery sound. Oliver's grip tightened, obvious affection in his expression, and he looked up. After a moment, I followed his gaze. The roof came apart, boards and shingles flying off into the night, until there was nothing between us and sky. One by one, the lights far above us started to fall. It was a trick Oliver had performed many times, but I never tired of it.

Something about tonight was different, though. I didn't care about what was happening overhead; Oliver watched the stars and I found myself watching him. Minutes ticked by, and the pain in my back was hardly noticeable anymore. Whether it was Oliver's doing—another ability he'd kept hidden from me—or because I was more absorbed in admiring him, I didn't know. As more time passed, tears glistened on his cheeks. Because of me, I knew. Because of the choice I'd made. And it hadn't been him.

I closed my eyes and pretended not to notice.

A sound. Hushed. Familiar.

Voices, I thought. They came from a distance, like one of those faraway stars. I wasn't fully conscious yet and I resisted the pull. I didn't want to return to that cell, to that broken body. But the voices drew closer. The blend of sound became words. "...has already treated her," someone was whispering.

"Impossible," another responded. "No one has been down here but the guard."

"See for yourself. The wounds are cleaned and covered in a salve of some kind."

My back was to them. Before I could decide whether to reveal I was awake, one of the speakers touched a lash mark. My eyes snapped open and I let out an involuntary gasp. I recoiled from the shadowy figures, ignoring the lightning bolts that burned through me at the movement. I slammed into the hard, wet wall.

"Who are you?" I demanded. Or tried to, anyway; the question was tremulous and faint. Their faces were obscured by darkness. One squatted nearby and one stood in the doorway. The faerie who'd touched me didn't respond, but the other did. I recognized his voice instantly. "This is Zara," Collith said. "She can't completely heal you, or they'll suspect her involvement, but she's here to relieve some of the pain. I apologize for your time down here; the guards weren't aware you had a room. They didn't know where else to take you. I've corrected this oversight."

He was calling my imprisonment an... oversight?

Rage gripped my throat and I didn't respond. Zara fiddled with something and there was a faint squeaking sound. Then, a moment later, a lantern came to life and illuminated the small space around us. I made a point of fixing my gaze on the female. The light revealed the curve of her cheek and long, dark eyelashes. She wore a beige abaya and a matching hijab.

As the two of them waited for me to say something, the silence was so prominent it felt like another presence in the room. "Who helped you?" Zara asked when it became too long.

"*Helped* me? Are you kidding? I have no idea what you're—" Realization roared through me and tore everything apart. In my mind's eye, I saw the house and the stars. The antibiotic cream in Oliver's hand. It couldn't be. Whatever he did in our dreamscape was confined there. That's how it had always been. How it always would be. Someone else must've snuck into the cell and helped me. Damon or Laurie, most likely.

"You know something," the female commented. With a start, I comprehended that I'd said something out loud.

My defenses rose. I looked directly at her and sneered. A spark of my old self flickered. "You've wasted your time. I don't want or need your help."

There was a pause, and I felt the two of them considering me. Then, breaking our stare, Zara glanced toward Collith. He gave a barely perceptible nod. She stepped past him and left us. Her footsteps echoed off the walls. Door hinges squealed. It slammed shut.

Leaving me and Collith alone.

I didn't look at him. I didn't speak to him. But the King of the Unseelie Court was no fool; he knew questions were ricocheting off the inside of my skull. He stepped closer. I could see his boot in my peripheral vision. "I know I owe you several apologies. Firstly, I'm sorry I didn't tell you who I was," he said quietly, as though someone might be listening, even down here. Somehow I didn't think the faerie in the cell next to mine counted. "I wish I had."

Eat shit and die, I wanted to say. Instead, entirely different words left my mouth. "Why didn't you?" I asked, hating how betrayed it sounded.

Collith didn't hesitate. "Cowardice," he answered bluntly. He still hadn't moved, but there was such a wealth of feeling in his voice, it felt like he was right there. "I thought if you knew the extent of how much your life would change, being my mate, you wouldn't agree to it."

"Now we'll never know. You didn't let me make that choice for myself."

I felt his eyes on me. "I know."

Somewhere in this dark place, a single drop of water fell. It made a hollow, lingering sound. As it faded, I finally turned to Collith. Though I couldn't see his expression, I imagined it. That stoic, regal look from the day before while my screams rang through the throne room. "There's so much I don't understand," I said at last. "Why couldn't you take Damon from Jassin? Why are you hiding our marriage from everyone? Why did you let another faerie whip your mate? Shouldn't an all-powerful king be able to—"

"I'm not all-powerful, Fortuna." His tone was imploring. When I said nothing, Collith finally approached. He ignored the damp and filth as he knelt beside me. He didn't dare reach out, but that didn't stop him from going on. "My position is precarious. History has already proven that ruling with fear leads to discord and treason. When I took the throne, I sought to rule with law and objectivity instead."

"And how well has that worked for you?" my neighbor called, startling me.

"Quiet," Collith replied, his voice sharper than I'd ever heard it. The line of his body was rigid. I observed all this thoughtfully, then schooled my features back into its cold expression as he turned in my direction once more. "And I stopped you from announcing who you were—taking your voice—at the tribunal because the fae have long memories. I wanted to introduce you at a moment of our choosing. Not Jassin's."

Out of everything he'd just told me, only a small part of it mattered. My heart pounded harder and faster. Menace dripped from every word as I asked, "What law allowed Damon to be kept captive for two years, tortured for so long that his mind broke from the brutality of it?"

And who knows what else Jassin has done to him? The thought made my stomach roll.

"Some traditions are ancient. Like the black market, for instance. If I tried to change them, I would have an uprising before I could blink. The fae are fond of their slaves and playthings." Collith's hand, which had been resting on his knee, became a fist. His ring glinted in the light, and I realized, then, that it was yet another thing I knew nothing about. "Why do you think I sought you out, Fortuna? I'm just as dismayed as you are by the things happening here. My feeble efforts to keep them occupied—carving doors, placing stones in the ground—aren't enough. I want to make a change. My power alone isn't enough to hold them at bay."

"I thought you didn't want to rule with fear," I retorted.

"That's still true. I simply want to survive the backlash when I create the kingdom I see in my dreams."

His expression was so earnest. If we weren't surrounded by damp air, if there weren't twinges of pain with each breath I took, it would be easy to believe him. Which made me even angrier. Before I could reply with something else thoughtless and furious, Oliver's voice stopped me. *Sometimes it's not about being stronger. It's about being smarter.* I swallowed the razor-edged words in my throat and studied Collith's face instead, the sharp lines and smooth planes. One of our first conversations echoed through my memory.

What do you want?

You.

He'd made it no secret. But that was before he'd shattered any fragile hope or possibility between us. This creature had no chance with me.

He didn't need to know that, though.

"Let's see it," I said. Collith frowned with obvious confusion, and I made an impatient gesture. The movement sent yet another jolt of pain through my back. "You crave my trust so badly; show me a glimpse of this supposed dream."

His eyes cleared. "There are things in my head that you wouldn't—"

"You trade in edicts and secrets; mine is nightmares and terror. Nothing I see will give me a second's pause, faerie." I couldn't hide my disdain.

"Will you ever say my name again?" Collith whispered, looking pained.

I didn't grace this with a response. That distant dripping continued while I waited for his decision. Within seconds Collith shifted closer and inclined his head. At first, I wasn't sure what the gesture meant. When he didn't move, I realized he meant for me to touch him. Hesitantly, I reached up. My fingers settled on his temples in the lightest of contacts. I'd never been so deliberate in searching through someone's psyche.

I tried not to remember the last time I'd put my hands on him, but images slipped through the cracks of my mental wall.

Ridges of bark. Light filtering through treetops. Collith's silky hair between my fingers. Now something stirred in me, low and hot. I gritted my teeth and pushed on.

There was a moment of slight resistance, but this time, Collith let me inside.

Going into someone else's mind usually felt like being underwater. Everything was slower, thicker, colder. But this time was entirely different. I stood in Collith's consciousness and absorbed the sensation of it. Where before there had been blankness, a careful nothingness, there were now hints of more. A subtle, sweet taste. Movement and light. I frowned and delved deeper. I felt Collith flinch, but he still offered no resistance.

At last, I found something. Not his fears, but exactly what he intended for me to see—his dreams. I stood on a hill, surrounded by blue sky and green grass. The colors and details were more vivid than any other I'd experienced. Nearby, nestled beneath some shade, a group of faeries sat around a picnic table. Laughter rang through the air. I crept closer, curious in spite of myself. The faeries were making no effort to hide their pointed ears while a pair of mortal children flew a kite a few yards away. There was no sign of dirt or darkness. Instead, it was clear his people lived above, among humankind.

There was a line of trees behind them. The foliage and shadows were disrupted by a round opening, a tunnel of sorts that traveled through. I knew Collith was guiding me, trying to influence where I went next. I decided to play along... for now. I left the merry scene behind and walked toward the opening.

Inside, there was nothing sinister or dark about the path; birdsong filled the air and a fragrant breeze slipped past. Since I didn't want to be here any longer than necessary, I didn't linger to admire the way sunlight filtered through the canopy above.

Up ahead, the tunnel ended in darkness. The air cooled. Wary of what I would find—the possibility of Oliver's efforts following me in the real world had changed everything—I slowed. The dirt beneath my feet became ice. I stepped into the open and realized why it was so cold.

Snow.

It floated down serenely, like nothing bad existed in the world. I was on a residential street, and the trees had given way to stars. Streetlights appeared every few feet, making everything soft and glowing. The houses weren't grand, but bright windows gave the neighborhood a welcoming feel. My boots crunched in the snow. I looked left and right, catching snapshots of scenes. Faeries were everywhere. They sat around Christmas trees and dinner tables. All of them wore modern clothing. I kept expecting to see some kind of violence, or a glimpse of their slaves, but there was nothing. Nothing but this bizarre content-edness and sense of belonging. This was Collith's hope for his people? I wanted to laugh or call him every kind of fool. For some reason, though, I couldn't.

Collith led me on. The road ended eventually, transforming into more beautiful places inhabited by the Fair Folk. They danced at weddings. They lay on beaches. They climbed mountains. All the while, they wore no glamour. There was no tension between races and no fear from humans. Everyone lived in unity.

But the beautiful dreams weren't all I had access to.

In one of them, I noticed a ripple in the air. Something was at the back of Collith's mind, so powerful that it was affecting everything else, and my instincts were drawn to it. I reached toward the disturbance. It had an old and worn feeling, like a picture that had been handled countless times. A memory.

Collith was holding it back, trying to hide this piece of his past, but it was useless to lock the door once someone had already entered. Now I put my arm into the ripple. Collith's panic made the ground tremble. Thunder sounded in the distance. I felt him try to throw me out, banish me from his mind entirely. *Too late*, I thought with vicious satisfaction. Smiling, I stepped closer.

"No!" Collith's voice cried from the heavens. It followed me through to the other side.

My foot landed on something soft and plush. A rug. I pulled free from the gap in Collith's consciousness, completely leaving the dream behind for reality. The disturbance in the wall solidified an instant later. I straightened and looked around, eager to see what Collith had been so desperate to keep a secret. My eyes adjusted to the abrupt change in lighting and sound. Compared to the din of moments before, the sudden silence was also jarring.

The female was the first thing to catch my attention. She lay in an enormous bed, one bare breast peeking out from the velvet covers. She had tumbling red hair and a sly smile. Oh, how Collith loved her. It filled the air, more powerful than freshly-sprayed perfume. He rested beside her, also naked, looking at her with tenderness in his eyes. The silky sheets were rumpled and slightly damp with sweat.

Just as it had been with the picnickers, neither of them seemed aware of my presence. They were wholly immersed in each other, and as I watched them, I felt a pang of something sharp and undefined. The female's name formed on Collith's lips like a song. "Viessa…"

Just as she opened her lovely mouth to reply, an invisible force struck me in the chest. Air left my lungs in a whoosh, and I was hurled backward.

I crashed through the wall and plummeted into unending darkness.

CHAPTER NINE

*M*y eyes flew open.

I gasped and shot upright. For a few seconds, I was wildly disoriented, trapped in that black freefall and my wet cell. The lantern Zara had brought burned steadily from its place on the floor. I focused on it, and the small flame became my anchor, keeping me here. Apparently going so deep into someone's mind had consequences—my head pounded.

I was dimly aware of Collith. He still knelt beside me, and his voice was uneven as he said, "I suppose I deserved that."

The pain wasn't going away. I closed my eyes against it, worried that I might vomit. "Just tell me why you're here."

But he didn't respond. Silence hovered in the tiny cell. Wanting to see Collith's face, I dared to open my eyes again. He was staring straight ahead. His long fingers twisted that strange ring. It seemed like an absent gesture, the movement of someone deep in thought. My patience was a thread swiftly unraveling, and just as I was about to snap, he spoke. "I'd like to reintroduce you to my people. On our terms, this time."

After a beat, I snorted. "They'll never accept me. I'm not fae."

"No," Collith agreed, meeting my gaze. His looked black in the gloom. "You're not. But you are Fallen."

Now it was Collith's turn to wait for a response. It was difficult to think when everything hurt. If he were here, Oliver would urge me to comply. Play the part. Use Collith's desire. But what about what I wanted? In this moment, it wasn't even Damon's freedom... it was mine. I shifted, as though to move away from the thought. The hard wall scraped against my injuries. I'd thought I was getting used to it, but when another wave of pain crashed over me, I nearly passed out. With that, the last of my endurance evaporated.

"Fine. Whatever. Just please... let me out," I whispered. My voice broke at the end; never had I felt so weak. In an instant, Collith appeared in front of me. Without a word, he lifted me into his arms. His touch was slow and cautious, but it was impossible not to brush the lash marks. I moaned. The sound echoed off the walls. More colorful spots marred my vision and everything tilted. I drifted in and out of consciousness as Collith walked down the passageway and up the stairs. "No, wait. Free the others, too," I tried to say. Nothing emerged.

Minutes or hours passed; it was impossible to discern which. At some point, door hinges whined. The sound roused me and I opened eyes that felt weighted down. We were in a bedroom. A massive bed took up most of the space, complete with a canopy. The floor was covered in ornate rugs. There were even human-made furnishings, like a dresser and a desk. Lanterns glowed from every flat surface, making the space seem inviting.

There was a second doorway that led to an adjoining room. We walked past and I caught a glimpse of bookshelves. One of the spines read *And Then There Were None*. So Collith was an Agatha Christie fan.

Not what I expected from a faerie king, I thought dimly.

Then there were no more thoughts.

A crackling, merry fire filled my vision.

Relief expanded within me, making it difficult to breathe. "Ollie?" I croaked. He didn't answer. I didn't want to risk sitting up or even turning my head; I'd had enough pain to last a lifetime. Seconds ticked past, marked only by the hiss and spit of flames. A frown tugged down the corners of my mouth. It wasn't just that Oliver hadn't made an appearance yet—something wasn't right about the dreamscape. It felt cold and unfamiliar. Nothing like the haven Oliver had created for us.

This isn't a dream, I realized.

Apparently I'd slept so hard that not even my best friend could reach me. Slowly, I became aware of other things. I was on my stomach, and the bed beneath me was soft and foreign. A faintly male smell emanated from the red sheets. My face no longer felt stiff and crusty, so someone must've removed the makeup Laurie had so painstakingly applied. The faerie dress was also gone, but it hadn't been replaced with anything. My back was exposed to the chilly air, with what felt like fur to cover the rest. Who'd undressed me? I strained to hear a sound besides the fire, to discern whether there was someone else in the room. Nothing.

Dissatisfied, I dared to shift my head so I was facing the other side. Instantly I saw the tray of food next to the bed, and I was reminded that I hadn't eaten since my last shift at Bea's. The meal had been delivered recently, because wafts of steam still rose from the white meat. Some kind of bird, I guessed. There was also a chalice near the platter, with drops of condensation rolling down the sides. Maybe there was an underground spring somewhere in these tunnels.

My stomach chose that moment to rumble. I was starving.

Just then, something moved. I jerked my head so hard that it should've hurt. It was Collith. The sight of him made my appetite vanish. He'd removed his shirt and his bare back shone in the light. Defined muscles moved beneath the skin. That wasn't what drew my gaze, however—it was the scars. There were two of them, and they traveled from his shoulder blades to his waist. Exactly where his wings should have been.

Collith turned and caught me staring. Our last conversation was still fresh in my mind, and there were still so many questions I wanted to ask, so many things I wanted to say. "Do they hurt?" I heard myself ask instead.

The faerie didn't pretend to misunderstand. He pulled another shirt over his head and shrugged it into place, effectively covering the marks. "Yes, but not in the way you mean. It's like a missing limb. Sometimes I can still feel them. Also, be sure to drink that. Don't worry, you can move."

A lock of hair fell into his eyes as he nodded at the tray. Holding the fur to my chest, I rolled onto my side to follow his gaze, and once again, the movement didn't hurt as much as it should've. *Zara*, I thought sourly. Doubtless she'd come while I was sleeping and healed some of the damage. I didn't like owing debts to anyone, especially a faerie.

Hopefully she was the one that took off the dress, though.

There were too many hours I couldn't account for. Thinking this, I frowned at Collith. "Why am I in here? Why didn't you take me to my room?"

"Thanks to the tribunal, my Court is now aware of your presence. Your room is no longer safe." Collith's tone was distracted. He looped a belt around his waist, and I deliberately focused on the objects in front of me. Beside the chalice was a wooden cup. I leaned forward to pick it up, thinking it would be water, but the liquid inside was opalescent. Was he trying to enchant me?

Still moving cautiously, I sat up and rested my back against the headboard. Hardly even a twinge. Glowering, I watched the contents of the cup glimmer and slosh. Mom's voice whispered in my ear. *It's been said that if you consume faerie food or drink, you'll go mad.* Which meant the delicious-looking meat was off limits, too. I rested the cup against my stomach and met Collith's gaze. The image of his back lingered on my mind, though. "You were there, then? At the beginning?" I asked next. I told myself I wanted to know more because information was power.

I watched him take note of the untouched drink and food. Apparently Collith decided not to comment. He raked his hair away from his face and that stubborn lock fell right back. "No. I was born in this world. Second generation. But we still form with wings; they fall off within a few years. God's reminder to us, I suppose, of what we lost in the uprising."

Though his demeanor was casual, his eyes betrayed a pain he still felt. Whether it was from the loss of his wings or because of a failed rebellion, I didn't know. Unsure what to say, my own eyes drifted. They landed on a coat draped over the back of a chair. It was black and embroidered with what I assumed to be the written language of the fae. The words were in golden thread, traveling along the hem and sleeves. It was a coat fit for a king. "Are you going to a party?" I blurted.

The question seemed to remind him of it. Collith retrieved the coat and pulled it on. The material made his shoulders look broader. "Yes," he answered, tugging at the sleeves with his long fingers. "I had hoped you'd like to accompany me. It's a three-day feast called *Olorel.* Like a human holiday, perhaps. It's why the throne room was so full when you arrived."

I made a sound that was halfway between an incredulous laugh and a disdainful scoff. "No, thanks."

"It's not like the… gathering you witnessed," he said with a grimace. "This celebrates one of our most important anniversaries."

At this, I quirked a brow. "You have anniversaries? No, wait, let me guess. It's for the day faeries discovered how to get off."

Collith laughed. It was the first time I'd heard the sound. It was deep and rich and vibrated through me. "Not quite," he replied. "It marks a day shortly after the Dark Prince was thrown into the pit. His followers were cast out with him, of course, and many angels were separated during the fall. This is how the separate species came to be. One group found themselves in the wilderness; they would eventually become known as fae. Most were drained or injured after the Battle of Red Pearls. For the first time, they were vulnerable against beasts, humans, and elements.

"There was one among them named Olorel. He had the ability to create openings to dimensions alongside this one. When he realized their survival was unlikely, he gave his life to create a place his companions would be safe. None of us would exist without him, which is why it's a sacred memory for our kind. You already missed the first night, but the second will be just as significant."

"Will the Seelie Court be there, too, then?" I asked, once again intrigued despite myself.

"They celebrate in their own domain." Collith inclined his head and appraised me. "Are you feeling well enough to go this evening?"

There were few times in my life I'd experienced fear, but now was one of them. The prospect of standing among the Court again—after they'd all watched my humiliation like it was a Broadway show—was terrifying. But I also didn't want to remain here, alone in a bed that smelled like him. Stalling, I ran my hand over the fur. It was white and soft. "You want me to accompany you, huh? As what, your plaything?"

"As my mate," Collith answered firmly. Without waiting for my reaction, he turned away. There was a wooden trunk set against one wall. He lifted the lid and began rummaging. After a few seconds, he faced me again. There was something in his hand. "Fae don't wear wedding rings, as you're probably accustomed to. Instead, we wear these."

He drew closer and opened his fingers. It was a necklace. The chain was long and silver, and dangling at the end of it was a sapphire. "It's beautiful," I admitted. I immediately hated myself for the compliment. I imagined stomping the jewel into dust and watching Collith's eyes widen with horror.

Oblivious to my dark thoughts, Collith's lips tilted upward in a half-smile. "When we began our lives here, every bloodline was given a handful of unique minerals or gems. Each one was found in the earth, as we worked to expand the passageways, and honed into perfection. My mother wore this."

His mother. For some reason, it was difficult to imagine Collith having one like everyone else. I'd been thinking of him as someone that had always been, rather than someone with a beginning. The realization that even an Unseelie King had parents was unsettling.

He was still waiting for me to accept. *Say you don't want it. Throw it back in his face,* an inner voice urged. Instead, without exactly knowing why, I took the proffered necklace. The silver chain pooled in the center of my palm, glinting like a snake in the sun. "Will I be meeting her?" I asked without looking up.

Collith acted as though he hadn't heard. He gave his attention to a mirror that stood in a nearby corner. "There are a few rules during the feast," he said, fussing with a nonexistent piece of lint. "Even the fae adhere to them. No killing and no stealing. To do so invokes another tribunal. You will be safe there. Well, safe enough."

He could evade and ignore all the questions he wanted. I had plenty more. "What happened to them? The first of the bloodlines? Faeries don't die of old age," I pressed. If someone had killed these ancient, powerful beings, I wanted to know how they did it.

As though he guessed my motives, Collith's eyes glinted with amusement. He answered easily enough. "Four of them were in the throne room yesterday. One chooses to stay apart from the intrigues of Court, and only those of his blood are permitted to see him. There was Olorel, who died, as you know. He didn't have a chance to father any offspring. Three live amongst humans. Another was murdered by his mate decades ago, but his descendants live on. The other ten reside at the Seelie Court, as far as I know."

"Nineteen living bloodlines, then," I murmured thoughtfully. So many. Were they all enemies? Or could I find an ally hidden amongst their ranks?

While I attempted to think of leverage I could present to a potential supporter—strategy had never been my strong suit— Collith took something out of a drawer. He turned slightly and I saw there was a crown in his hands. It glinted in the soft light. Like the swords his guards carried, it seemed to be made of glass, all jagged edges and sharp ends. Deadly and beautiful. To my surprise, Collith placed it on his head without any ceremony. I hadn't forgotten for a second who and what he was, but a flash of memory slammed into me. That cold, elegant stranger seated on his twisted throne.

Collith looked down, utterly unaware of the crown's effect, and smiled. "Well?" he said. "May I count on your presence tonight?"

This is for you, Damon, I thought. I tucked my hands under the blankets to hide how they trembled. The necklace warmed in the middle of my fist. "I need to get ready," I said.

The Unseelie King flashed me a rare, full smile, showing his perfect teeth. "Very well. I'll leave you to it."

I didn't smile back. Unperturbed, Collith bowed—the fluid movement revealed how many times he'd done it before. Then he straightened and stepped away, clearly intending to go toward the door. Something made him hesitate, though. The fire crackled as he drew near again. He extended a single finger and touched my cheek. The touch was so brief and simple, but it ignited something in me, however much I tried to deny it. "I shall wait for you at the throne room doors," he said. His voice was soft, as if he was affected by it, too.

My first instinct was to jerk away. But there was also a small, quiet part of me that wanted to lean in. I hated myself for the weakness. Was it because I felt so alone here, far beneath the ground, surrounded by creatures that enjoyed pain and spectacle? Or was I just attracted to darkness?

Maybe some of my thoughts showed; Collith's expression was thoughtful as he pulled back a second time. He went to the door, his boots making hardly a sound on the floor. With one hand on the knob, Collith nodded in my direction. I didn't react. After another moment, the king disappeared into the passageway.

Leaving me alone with the food. I fidgeted and tried not to look at it. I willed myself to fall back asleep and talk to Oliver. But my stomach was moaning again and my mouth had started watering. "Fuck it," I muttered. Better to be enchanted than dead from starvation. I dropped the necklace on the mattress beside me and grabbed the tray handles. I put it none-too-gently on my lap.

The meat had cooled, but I ripped into it with my teeth like a wolf devouring a carcass. Whoever had sprinkled it with spices had wasted their time; I barely tasted the food as it went down. Between bites I gulped water straight from the chalice. Some of it dripped off the edge of my chin. I swiped at it roughly and kept eating.

I only stopped when there was nothing left. I sat back, painfully full, and sighed. *You are so weak, Fortuna.* What would my parents think, if they could see me in this moment? Dad may have believed in equality between the species, but it couldn't be a coincidence he'd married the only other Nightmare alive. He'd also taught us how to fight. Yet here I was, mated to a faerie and permanently scarred by another. They'd warped and broken Damon. If our parents were to meet us now, they probably wouldn't recognize their own children.

The thought gave me a surge of fresh motivation. I tossed the fur aside and swung my legs to the side. The movement was too quick. For a few seconds, all I could do was hold my pounding head.

Once the room was still again, I straightened. As I'd feared, I was completely naked. The faerie gown was nowhere to be seen, but after a moment, I spotted my backpack in a corner. I rushed to it. Everything was still inside, seemingly untouched. I yanked on a pair of jeans and a wrinkled plaid shirt. It was the first time in my life that clothing felt like armor. Another battle was coming, and the first one had proven that I needed all the help I could get.

Wearing pants made me feel like myself again. Combined with Zara's recent healing, a spark flickered in my chest. It sent light through the dark place I'd been hiding since the moment that whip came down. I looked around with renewed interest, and the open doorway to my left beckoned. After a brief hesitation, I gave in to the urge.

It was a small space, not much bigger than my bedroom at home. But Collith had used every inch of it. There were even more books along the other three walls. I'd never been much of a reader —not even my ever-patient father could get me to sit still long enough for a single page—but I couldn't resist the chance to know more about the one I'd married. My fingers trailed along the books' spines as I walked the perimeter of the room. Soon I realized the collection was in alphabetical order. *So he likes things organized.*

There was more to Collith's library than mystery novels. Some of the books were so old, it looked as if a single touch would make them crumble. Many were in a language I didn't recognize—Enochian, I supposed. There were piles of paper tucked in the spaces above the books. I tugged at one, pulling it free. It was a hand-drawn map of Europe. The ink was fading and the paper was soft from countless handlings. Many of the lines forming countries weren't accurate.

Or maybe they are, I thought. There was still so much I didn't know about these creatures. If there could be an entire court beneath the ground, why not entire nations?

"You look well."

The voice came from behind. I spun around, my hand flying again for a knife that wasn't there. Laurie stood in the doorway with another gown draped over his arms. It was disturbingly similar to a wedding dress. "I'm not wearing that," I said flatly. The words belied the way my heart still raced. Casually, I lowered my hand.

Laurie didn't seem to notice the small movement. He rolled his eyes. "That's what you said last time. Can we skip the part where I point out all the reasons you should wear it and you realize I'm right?"

"Can we skip the part where I trust anything that comes out of a faerie's mouth?" I retorted. My hands had become involuntary fists again, and now I saw Laurie's eyes flick down. He raised his gaze back to mine. Those silvery irises looked darker, like a slate roof after rain. As we stared at each other, I knew we were both thinking of the tribunal. Screams echoed through my memory, and I couldn't hold back a flinch.

As though he could hear it, too, Laurie's voice softened. "I'm not your enemy, Fortuna."

I searched his expression, wishing I could believe him. It was more apparent than ever that I needed help. Not just in getting Damon back, but for my very survival.

The firelight made Laurie's hair look auburn. Shadows played on the sharp angles of his face and made his skin even smoother. I hadn't truly looked at him since we first met—I never seemed to notice anyone else when Collith was around. Laurie's presence wasn't as commanding as the Unseelie King, but there was still an allure about him. If Collith was a star-filled sky, Laurie was the breeze whispering past as you gazed upward. *Beautiful*, I thought. Like all the rest of them.

Now I knew what it felt like for others when they looked at my face. To lose sight of everything else and to forget what I'd been feeling just moments ago.

The sensation was infuriating. Scowling, I snatched the gown from his arms. The action revealed a basket in one of Laurie's hands. He wisely remained silent, and after tossing the thing onto the reading chair, I began to undo my buttons. Just like last time, the faerie turned his back.

Seconds later there came a sudden burst of light from the other room. I froze. "One of the logs shifted," Laurie said without turning. But my fingers had faltered on their downward progress, and I couldn't get them to start again. It went against my instincts to take the clothes back off. I would be facing the monsters without any armor. Vulnerable. Weak. Alone.

"Why am I doing this again?"

My soft words felt like a shout in the stillness. I'd been asking myself, mostly, but Laurie answered anyway. He turned his head to the side, as though he were addressing the books. "I'll admit that I haven't known you very long, Lady Sworn. Even so, you strike me as the kind who doesn't like others getting the last word."

I was about to agree when another flash of memory went off, like the click of a camera shutter. Crying in the dark. Huddling in that dank dungeon. A stream of blood running through the spaces between stones. "I didn't used to be," I said faintly. Pain whispered through the freshly-healed marks on my back.

Laurie turned even more. He still didn't look in my direction, but his pale eyes fixed on a point next to my head. "They tell me it's a full moon tonight. Isn't that interesting?" he mused. After a significant pause, Laurie faced forward again.

A full moon. The fae would be stronger... but so would I. An opportunity to save Damon might present itself, and there was no way in hell I'd miss that.

I also really, really wanted to kick a faerie's ass.

It felt like he'd given me a shot of adrenaline; suddenly I was eager to move. Clad in only a bra and underwear, I turned my attention to the gown. It was strapless. Delicate. The bodice was intricately beaded, but as it traveled downward, the skirt became a material similar to tulle. The white deepened into red, as if someone had dipped the hem in blood. There were two extra pieces, so long they almost touched the floor when I held them aloft. Metal encircled the end of each. Were these sleeves? Thinking to ask Laurie, I glanced toward him.

To my surprise, he was gazing back at me. No, not quite at me; his eyes lingered on my body instead. "You're looking!" I accused.

Before the words completely left my mouth, Laurie was already facing the wall again. As he spoke, I could only see the back of his head, but somehow I knew he was smirking. "I did no such thing. You're hardly my type."

I hurriedly stepped into the dress and pulled it up—at least it was lighter than it looked. My bra straps were at odds with the ensemble, so I bent my arms at an awkward angle to undo the clasps. "Just what is your type?" I asked crossly, tossing the bra onto the cushion, where the dress had been.

"Dull and compliant, of course."

In spite of myself, a smile tugged at my lips. Hoping Laurie hadn't seen it, I reached for the two extra pieces and fit the metal rings around my upper arms. They actually did trail along the rug. I took a soundless breath, remembering the last dress and what had happened while I was in it. "Okay, you can look now. Not that my permission stopped you before."

Ignoring this, Laurie turned and regarded me thoughtfully. A line deepened on the left side of his mouth. There was no trace of admiration or desire in his gaze. It was so expertly hidden, in fact, that I wondered if I'd imagined it. "Perhaps we should skip the makeup this time," he suggested.

"Why?"

"You're being presented as the King's mate. Everyone knows you're not fae. Why act like you're trying to blend in? Embrace what you are. Display it like a badge of honor." Laurie stopped, waiting for my reaction, but I said nothing. After a moment, he nodded at my hair. "May I?"

I nodded. With feather-light fingers, Laurie guided me to the chair. I was overwhelmed with a sense of déjà vu as he began. More images of the Death Bringer assaulted me; I gripped the armrests to keep myself from bolting. Meanwhile, Laurie twisted and teased the long strands. Every movement was deft and painless, making me wonder how many times he'd done this. How long had he been alive and serving the royals? Would there be any point in asking?

Laurie secured whatever he'd created against the back of my neck. He reached for something—probably the basket—and soon a floral fragrance teased my senses. I focused on that rather than the dread piling up against the mental wall I'd built. *Full moon. It's a full moon*, I thought over and over.

"What I would do for a curling iron in this hellhole," I heard Laurie mutter. He circled the chair and knelt. His fingers plucked and arranged, and wisps of hair tickled my cheeks as he worked. At last Laurie drew away. I stood and lifted the dress, intending to go to the door.

Suddenly a small, handheld mirror appeared. My own reflection confronted me, and I stared at it. The girl staring back was pale. Her eyes seemed too big for her face. Laurie had put tiny, white flowers throughout her hair. Going a couple days without washing it hadn't done much to its volume; Mom used to braid it back just so I could see. "I was starting to think faeries didn't believe in mirrors," was all I said.

If Laurie was disappointed, he didn't show it. "For the old

ones, they're a painful reminder," he answered. He didn't put down the mirror. "They were once beings of light. To look into a glass and see what they've become... it's unbearable."

My gaze returned to the thing he held. Dissatisfaction filled the girl's expression. "I'd like the makeup, please," she said.

Now Laurie did look displeased, but he said nothing. He simply nodded and, at last, lowered the glass. Moving with the grace of the fae, he bent and rummaged through his basket. The wicker made a sound of protest. Once again, he picked up a small brush and moved the bristles over my skin. For some reason, this particular silence felt stilted, but Laurie either didn't notice or pretended not to. I resumed the mental chant to block out everything else. *Full moon. It's a full moon.*

Some time later, Laurie's musical voice penetrated my thoughts. "Shall I accompany you to the throne room?" he asked. I opened my eyes. He was offering his arm, looking every inch like a prince rather than a slave. It struck me, then, that I had never expected to find kindness in the Unseelie Court. I allowed him to pull me up and, after a loaded pause, I rested my hand in the crook of his elbow. Laurie beamed as though I'd given him a gift, and we walked toward the doorway.

On our way out, I spotted the mirror—it lay abandoned on the floor. This time, I was the one to pick it up. My skirt rustled gently, like whispers in a church.

Gripping the handle with white fingers, I lifted it. To my relief, the girl from before was gone. Someone mysterious and aloof had taken her place. A dusting of white powder coated half of her face, glittering in the faint light. Gold lined her eyes. Her lips had been painted the brightest of reds, matching the hem of her gown. She looked ready for a battle or a crown.

Something was missing, though.

I knew instantly what it was. Without a word, I set the mirror on one of the shelves. In my peripheral vision, I saw Laurie appraising me. He didn't speak, but his condemnation surrounded us anyway. I walked past him, heading for the bed. There, still nestled in the covers, was the necklace Collith had given me. The jewel flickered like a blue flame. After an instant of hesitation, I placed it around my neck and secured the clasp. It rested against my chest, a spot of cold that didn't belong.

"Are you ready, my lady?" Laurie asked.

"Of course not," I answered. But I went to him anyway and accepted his arm a second time.

With a dramatic flourish, Laurie opened the door. He didn't give me a chance to reconsider; we stepped into the passageway and left safety and warmth behind. I tried not to let myself wonder if I'd be returning. Cool air moved past us, carrying snatches of distant sound. My throat filled with dread. I couldn't tell Laurie that he was wrong; I wasn't ashamed of what I was.

I simply wanted a mask to hide my fear.

CHAPTER TEN

*A*s we drew closer to the throne room, I thought of
Oliver.

We'd never gone so long without speaking, and I felt his
absence keenly. As a child, he was part of everything I did,
waking or asleep. My foster parents had dismissed this strange
behavior, labeling Oliver an 'imaginary friend.' I'd grow out of it,
they told themselves. But every night I rushed to bed, eager to
tell the very real friend—well, real to me, at least—about what
I'd done and seen that day.

There were only two occasions a night passed without us
seeing each other. Once was when I was fourteen and my
appendix burst. I woke in the hospital, groggy and disoriented.
The drugs they'd given me had been so powerful that all I
remembered between that vivid burst of pain to awakening was
darkness.

The second occasion was years later. I was seventeen and it
was the anniversary of my parents' murders. In the basement of
a boy I barely knew, I tried cocaine for the first time. I fell asleep
on his stained, scratchy couch, and my slumber was restless and
sporadic. Whatever dreams I had were brief and fragmented; I

didn't even remember them when I woke up. The cushions were covered in sweat. Soon after that my brother burst into the room, declaring that he was taking me home.

He'd missed his prom to spend the night looking for me.

It was after this incident that I had the courage to ask Oliver how it worked. Our meetings, that was. Did he summon me? Did I just appear?

"I wait for you," he'd said simply, turning his head to meet my gaze. A blade of grass tickled his cheek. "I'm always waiting for you."

Suddenly a scream echoed through the tunnels.

It jarred me from the bittersweet memory, and I forced my mind back to the present. I faltered, looking around, but there was only dirt walls and flickering torches. Laurie still walked beside me, and he seemed unconcerned by the sound. I remembered this was the Unseelie Court, the place where screams and pain thrived. Slowly, I resumed walking again. I thought of Damon in the mirror and how the scene had looked like he was being held unwillingly. Nothing was what it seemed here. I could very well run to save whoever it was making that sound, only to find that my attempts at rescue weren't welcome.

But what if, this time, they were?

The thought caused knots in my stomach. I longed for a distraction. Laurie hadn't attempted any conversation during our trek, though, so I decided to familiarize myself with the passages instead. As I noted yesterday, there was no pattern or reason to them. I was about to ask Laurie how he could possibly know the way when a tall figure appeared up ahead.

My thoughts dissipated like smoke. As promised, the king stood near the doors. Sound poured from the wide opening, a cacophony of voices and laughter. Collith was deep in conversation with a guard. The uniformed faerie was not the one who'd struck me or dragged me into the darkness, but the sight of him still made my anxiety leap. Collith must have sensed this through the bond, because he turned his head and spotted me. His gaze softened.

I began to walk toward him, but Laurie stopped at the mouth of the passageway. Gently, he extracted his arm from mine. Half his face was hidden in shadow and I couldn't see his eyes. "Aren't you coming?" I asked, frowning.

The faerie shook his bright head. "No, but I'll be nearby. If you'd like, we can come up with a signal. I'll see it and assist in whatever way I can."

"Oh, yeah? Like what?"

He grinned, revealing perfect teeth. "You could pick your nose. Or start shrieking."

"We might need something more subtle," I replied dryly.

Laurie chuckled and melted into the darkness.

Butterflies rioted in my stomach. I took a breath and faced Collith again. He stood very, very still, as though I were a wild horse that could spook at any moment. For what felt like the millionth time, we studied each other. The golden threads of his coat glimmered. His back was straight. His boots were shining leather. The crown rested on his curls as though it had always been there. Every inch of him was regal… except for that single, stubborn lock of hair.

For some reason, this small detail was comforting. I forced myself to approach. Once I was close enough Collith opened his mouth, probably to tell me how beautiful I looked, but I felt like I was about to vomit. "Let's get this over with," I muttered, snatching hold of his arm. The guard fell into step behind us. Collith offered no protests, and a second later, we walked over the threshold. I almost gasped at the sight that greeted us.

The room was transformed.

Drapes of red silk entwined the columns. There were flowers everywhere—splashes of vibrant color in the corners, on the floor, hanging overhead. Over a dozen long tables stretched across the open space. It had been dim before, but now it was ablaze with light. Braziers made of black bronze stood at the end of each table. The legs were three sculpted males holding the coals aloft. Bowls of incense also burned on every surface, creating thin columns of smoke that rose toward the ceiling.

The fae had dressed for the occasion. Like the last time I'd seen them, their styles were a bizarre combination of modern, archaic, and created from nature. A faerie that reached my stomach in height wore a mask of green leaves. One female looked like she was ready to see a heavy metal concert. Even more cultures were present than there'd been at the tribunal. I spotted clothing and faces that were Mexican, Indian, Chinese.

Humans were scattered throughout the crowd, carrying over-flowing pitchers of wine. They were easily discernible from their ragged clothing or expressions. While several looked dreamy—content to waste their too-short lives down here—many were clearly terrified.

Rich scents filled the air, making my mouth water. Heaps of food littered the wide surfaces. Fresh bread with honey rolling down the sides. Platters of roasted pig resting atop beds of sprigs and nuts. Steaming vegetables. Ripe fruit. As I watched, a female sucked grease off her fingers and let out a long belch. Suddenly the tray of food I'd eaten wasn't enough. Collith allowed me to gape for a minute before tugging me forward.

It didn't take long for our arrival to be noticed. Gazes swung our way and conversations halted. Many hurried to clear the path. I didn't know where to look; I was avoiding that gnarled tree and the crowd. Eventually my eyes settled on the throne. It loomed ancient and large. I wondered how high a price each king had paid to sit in it. How high a price Collith had paid.

My anxiety was so overwhelming that, for a moment or two, I'd forgotten why Collith wanted me to come in the first place. The reminder came in the form of a faerie whose blond hair nearly touched the floor. I knew the exact moment she spotted the necklace I wore; her pale eyes widened. She leaned over to whisper to the blue-skinned nymph beside her, who in turn, whispered to someone at her left.

Shock rippled through the room. Murmurs and stares began to follow us. Gazes zeroed in on the sapphire. Collith's expression remained as neutral as ever, and I wished I had his composure. My insides felt jittery. Every instinct screamed to run. The marks they'd bestowed upon me came alive, aching with remembered pain. Would my newly-revealed position as Collith's mate offer some protection? Or would it just put me in more danger?

After an eternity, we reached the dais. I waited for Collith to approach the great chair, but he remained by my side. He faced the crowd and spoke in Enochian. The cadence of his voice rose and fell dramatically. He gestured toward the grand doors—no, the drawings on the wall beyond them—and said a name. *Olorel.*

Moments after he finished, the entire Court spoke in unison. Their words had the feel of something that had been said countless times before. It was rhythmic and, however much I hated to admit it, beautiful. Then a brief silence fell.

Once more, Collith was the one to breach the stillness. He launched into a second speech, and this time, he gestured to me. Was he introducing me as his mate? Whatever he said, it was brief and final. As if they'd been under a spell, everyone moved all at once. Their conversations resumed and most turned away. Music weaved through the tables. The tight sensation in my chest loosened and breathing became easier.

"Well met, Fortuna Sworn."

Tensing again, I turned toward the new voice. It was the dark-skinned male that had been part of the council. One of the faeries that had deemed it fitting to whip me until I was half-dead. He bowed, his bald head gleaming from the nearby candles. At this proximity, I could see that every inch of his skin was covered in intricate tattoos. The lines were so fine that they were easy to miss. He wore the same expression he had when they'd declared their judgment. Polite. Interested. As though my whipping had been a conversation with a stranger. Just like that, I was tied to the tree again, biting my lip so hard that I could taste blood.

When I said nothing, the faerie spoke again. The deep timbre of his voice wrapped around me. "I am Tarragon of the bloodline Ettrian."

Collith inclined his head. "Well met, Tarragon."

It felt like he was speaking on my behalf, and if I'd had hackles, they would be standing on end. All at once I found my voice. "What the hell do you want?" I snarled. Fear gave way to fury. New visions swam before me—a whip in my own hand, the lashes striking out like a dozen snakes, tearing into this creature's flesh as it had torn mine.

If the faerie was offended by this, he didn't show it. He refocused his gold-lined eyes on my face. "You did well during the tribunal," he commented.

My lip curled. "How so? By not dying?"

"You did not allow us to break you. We do so love our broken things."

"Thank you for your kind words, Tarragon," Collith interjected. He turned to me, effectively ending the conversation. "May I have this dance?"

Tarragon bowed to the king and nodded at me. I stared back, longing to know what fears lurked beneath his skin. The faerie's eyes gleamed as if he could hear my thoughts. With another graceful bow, he retreated. The jewelry around his ankles jangled. *I'll remember you*, I thought.

Collith untangled our arms and put some space between us. He held out his hand. "Shall we?"

Just as I was about to respond, a female walked past us. Her glance raked over the king with undeniable lust. A moment later, she fixed it on me. The lust didn't fade. A wolf followed close behind her, its ribs poking out beneath ragged, gray fur. It was connected to the female by a chain, which clinked against the flagstones. A werewolf, judging from its size. Somehow they'd forced it to remain in animal form. If too much time passed, it wouldn't be able to change back. It would forget who it had been.

My fingers flexed, tempted to reach out and touch the female who held it prisoner. This one was actually within reach...

Suddenly Collith pulled me close. It was obvious what he was doing; I didn't even bother to look at him. Did he truly think I would be so easily distracted? I watched the female go with narrowed eyes. *I'll remember you, too,* I thought. Only when she was swallowed up by the crowd did I turn my attention to Collith. I waited for a reprimand or a warning.

But he didn't say a word. Instead, he continued to wait for my response. His grip was so loose, I could pull away without any effort. He was giving me a choice.

Instinct urged me to reject him, embarrass him in front of everyone in this Court. But there was also... curiosity. I'd been in a pattern for years, going to the same places, saying the same words, making the same choices. So I allowed myself to remain there, in the circle of his arms. Thankfully Collith accepted this as an answer, because I couldn't seem to give him one.

Maybe he gave the players some kind of cue; the music suddenly intensified. Collith gave me no chance to hesitate or feel uncertain. His grip tightened and he went through the steps artlessly, somehow making it feel like a joint effort. The classical instruments were accompanied by an eerie—but lovely—chorus. I craned my neck to find the source of the voices. Three females stood higher than the rest, standing on a small platform. Their bare toes peeked out from gowns so translucent I could see the outline of their breasts. But I hardly noticed this; their song seemed to fill every part of the room, like water.

I was so intent on them that I stumbled. Collith righted me and moved into the next step without missing a beat. At first, I watched his feet, captivated by the way they didn't seem to touch the floor. But the dance was simple, and soon, I began to see a pattern. My heart hammered as I attempted to imitate him. I glanced up for a moment, wondering if Collith had noticed. A faint smile lit his dark eyes. "Very good," he murmured.

Now I arched my head back completely, searching his gaze, though I didn't know what I was looking for. Against my better judgment, I found myself moving with him. Matching him step for step, enjoying the music sliding through me. We clasped hands, let go, locked eyes. Did it all over again. There were so many colors, so many other creatures surrounding us, but for the first time in my life I understood what it felt like to feel the rest of the world fade. Overhead, small lights bobbed, unattached to wires or walls. Magic.

Once more, the music changed without warning. The gentle strums of a harp drifted through the room. A young boy stepped forward and raised a penny whistle to his mouth. It didn't seem possible that such a tiny instrument should echo through the entire room. There was something ethereal about the sound. I tore my attention from the small figure and looked up at Collith, certain of what I was about to say next.

"This is why you were in such a rush to bring me to Court," I murmured. "You wanted me to feel this. Before I found out the truth."

"It's like a flower growing amongst the wreckage. Something beautiful hidden in the ugliness." His voice lowered. "Worth saving, don't you think?"

An automatic, scornful reply rose to my lips. For the umpteenth time, Oliver's voice in my head stopped me. *Be patient. Learn their weaknesses*, he'd said. Collith cared about these creatures. That was his vulnerability. I tucked the information away for later contemplation. "Maybe," I allowed. For a time, we danced in silence. There was so much to look at, so much to learn, but I saw none of it. I seemed only capable of staring at our clasped hands, wondering at the warmth. Trying so hard not to acknowledge the desire crackling between us like invisible lightning.

"Who is Ollie?"

The question made my gaze snap back to Collith's. I hadn't heard someone speak that name out loud in years. It felt as though my deepest secret had been exposed—I must've spoken in my sleep. The only emotion I could detect in Collith's expression was curiosity, but I knew better. He was searching for any cracks, any weaknesses he could exploit, same as I had been. Between us, he was the better opponent; I knew so little about him.

Unbidden, I thought of that bookshelf in his room, heavy with mystery novels. Maybe I was learning some things after all.

"I'm thirsty," I said stiffly, pulling my hands from his. "Is there anything here that's safe to drink?"

"Allow me," the king replied with a bow. A nearby female dressed entirely in ivy stared, open-mouthed, as if she'd never seen him do this before. Either oblivious to her or adept at ignoring others, Collith nodded at someone behind me. I turned and discovered the guard he'd been speaking to earlier. He wore heavy-looking furs around his shoulders, claws dangling off its edges. His face would be considered pretty—flawless skin, rosebud lips, blue eyes—were it not for a slightly aquiline nose. His hair was the color of sand, and in dreadlocks, though these were scraped back into a half ponytail. There was something familiar about him. Had he been at the tribunal?

"This is my Right Hand, Nuvian," Collith added, probably noticing my frown. "He commands the Guardians. He would also lead in my stead, if something were to prevent me from doing so. Come."

Still reeling from the mention of Oliver, I let him lead me to the edge of the dancing. The stoic-faced guard followed. A wordless communication passed between them, then Collith went off to get my drink. Nuvian rested his hands on the hilt of his sword and looked back at me. His skin was ruddy, as though he'd spent too much time beneath the sun. Unusual for a faerie. His eyes were a vivid blue, like ice at daybreak.

I was about to ask him whether we'd met before when there was a rush of cool air at my neck. I whipped around. A faerie drew back; she'd been blowing on me. "Do you need something?" I asked, hoping she didn't see the bumps rising along my skin.

The female had somehow secured feathers to her eyelids, giving them the appearance of lashes. She blinked, slow and deliberate. "So you're the one that finally snared our handsome king," she remarked. Her unnaturally white hair gleamed in the light from a nearby brazier.

We were being watched; some were subtle about eavesdropping, while others blatantly turned in our direction. I spotted an effeminate male dancing closer, closer, his expression sharp and curious. He caught me staring and grinned. The red lipstick he wore smeared on his slightly yellowed teeth. "I didn't tame anyone," I muttered, averting my gaze.

The female acted as though I hadn't spoken. "I wonder why he considered you significant enough to mate, but not to crown?" she mused. There was a faint bite in her dulcet tone.

Just like that, something in me snapped. I'd had enough of riddles, insults, games, and this time there was no one to intervene or reasonable voices in my head. And if it earned me another tribunal, then fuck it. I'd make tonight worth it. I smiled sweetly and stepped closer to the faerie. Unease flickered across her face. "There's a feather on your cheek. Here, let me."

Before she could recoil, I pretended to pluck something off her face. The faerie staggered back, but it was too late. I felt my nostrils flare as her fear rolled through me. She was terrified of drowning. "Enjoy your night," I purred. Water dribbled down her chin—or so she believed. The female watched me go with wild eyes. Unable to resist, I blew her a kiss, then turned my back. I'd find my own fucking drink.

Whatever had broken in me was like a dam. Recklessness poured through, submerging all the fear. I weaved through the crowd, touching anyone I could along the way. It was so light, so swift, that many of them had no idea. Flavors coated my tongue. One male thought he was surrounded by bees and actually ran from the room. Another faerie stared at an empty corner, his expression etched in horror. For the first time since escaping the goblins, I felt powerful. Decades ago, Nightmares were the most feared race. The fae had been unwise to forget.

If Nuvian disapproved of my behavior, he said nothing about it. He followed me like a spirit, soundless and unseen.

Collith had mentioned there were rules during their sacred holiday, but apparently restraint wasn't one of them—I skirted around two faeries having sex in the space between two tables. She was on her hands and knees, crying out again and again. Her breasts jiggled from the violence of the movements. Part of me wanted to linger, but I flushed and hurried past.

As I continued making my way toward the far wall, I realized Collith and I been dancing longer than it seemed; the food on the tables had been picked over. The floor was covered in scraps. The fae were wild and sloppy, as if they'd been drinking for hours. Laughter and music echoed in my ears. I reached for another faerie, intending to slide my fingers along her arm.

"Fortuna," someone said. It was almost lost in the din.

At the sound of that voice, I forgot about the faerie. I turned so quickly it was dizzying. Damon stood there, dressed in royal blue, his clothing like something from the Victorian era. His too-long hair had been brushed. He looked like a pretty doll. But his cheeks were still hollow, his skin too pale. There wasn't enough makeup in the world to hide it. I stood there, dumbfounded and brokenhearted, trying to reconcile this man to the boy who'd missed his prom to go searching for me.

As I stared, Damon pulled me into a rough hug. It was so unexpected that I froze. "I'm sorry," he whispered in my ear.

"For what?" I managed. Something was happening to me; the flavors from my victims were gone and my tongue felt thick and dry. It occurred between one breath and the next. Had I been poisoned? Bespelled?

"I couldn't stop it. The whipping was the best I could do. Jassin wanted to take your fingers." There was a note of pleading in my brother's voice. He stepped back and clutched my hands. "But I changed his mind. You see? There's some good in him."

Oh, Damon. How they've broken you. His logic was so twisted that I didn't know where to begin. Something else caught my attention, though; the fact that my brother had somehow changed Jassin's mind. I knew enough about how this world worked that suspicion took root. "What did you offer him in return?" I asked, struggling to keep my eyes on Damon's face, which was going hazy.

Air. I needed air.

He looked away. The movement revealed something peeking out from his collar, a spot of darkness. A bruise, I realized with a sinking stomach. "I have to go," Damon muttered. He took another step back. Someone screamed, distracting both of us. Back where the dancers were, the faerie I'd first touched was making a scene. She was on her knees, making frantic motions, as though she was trying to swim.

I turned back to Damon and dug my nails into his wrists to keep him there. He winced. "This is my vow," I said through my teeth. "I am going to save you."

"When will you understand? I don't *want* to be saved."

Normally I would've been able to stop him; I'd always been stronger than my thin-armed brother. But this time he pulled free like I was made of spider web. He hurried into the throng of revelers, and it was disconcerting how easily he disappeared among them.

There was a familiar flash of copper amidst the chaos. A moment later, I found myself glaring at Jassin. Though he didn't look in my direction, I sensed that he felt the heat of my focus. With one pale hand, he cupped the back of Damon's head—not tenderly, but aggressively, as one does a favorite toy—and kissed him. The sight filled me with such loathing that I didn't know whether to vomit or slit the faerie's throat.

"Are you all right?"

At long last, Collith had returned. A glass of water quivered in his hand, disturbed by every step and jostle around us. My gaze settled on his mouth. "Want to finish what we started in the woods?" I slurred.

Before he could respond, I grabbed his hand and dragged him through one of the smaller doorways. I didn't care if anyone noticed, and apparently neither did Collith, since he followed easily enough. My eyes adjusted to the abrupt change in light, and I saw that we'd stepped into another dim passageway. This one was narrower than the others; Collith's head almost brushed the ceiling. I kept going, seeking some kind of privacy. Some kind of escape from all those prying eyes I felt, even if I couldn't see them. The smooth stones around us gleamed, but farther along, there was nothing but darkness. Where the light ended, I stopped, shoving Collith against a wall. "Fortuna, what did you—" he started.

I grabbed the front of his shirt, bunching it in my fist. We were almost the same height, and I found Collith's chin instantly. As soon as our skin touched, however, the fervor eased a bit. Something mischievous and languid stole over me. I kissed that chin once, teasing, then made my way down. My progress was slow and sensuous. There was no taste to him, but he was a welcome coolness to my heat. I left a trail to the hollow of his throat, then traveled back up, eventually discovering what I'd been searching for all along.

As I claimed his mouth, Collith made a sound that opened a chasm in me. My body ached. I tried to deepen the kiss, but he resisted. Once again, he shifted as though to put some space between us. In a burst of frustration, I yanked his shirt free and sought what hid beneath. Smooth muscles greeted my fingertips. I slipped them into the waistband of his pants. What I wanted was just out of reach. I determinedly shoved my hand deeper and grasped the length of him.

At this, Collith's control slipped. He moaned and finally opened his mouth to mine. I'd never considered myself a petite girl, but he lifted me like I weighed no more than the feather I had pretended to pluck off that female's cheek. I linked my ankles at the base of his spine and, in response, Collith spun around until I was the one pressed to the wall. It gave me enough leverage to grind against him. He was so hard that it almost hurt to ride him through our clothing. I buried my fingers in his thick curls, and they were like silk.

Beneath the haze of desire, I was dimly aware of another sensation spreading through me that had nothing to do with the physical. There was that sense of rightness again. That feeling of being complete, as though I'd been half a person all this time. I fought it. I was Fortuna, whole and finished no matter what magic wanted me to believe. My defenses, which had been a pile of dust and rock around us, rebuilt themselves. I struggled to remember why I'd come in the first place. What I'd felt toward this faerie only an hour ago instead of the all-consuming passion driving me now.

Learn their weaknesses.

I almost gasped. Hearing Oliver's voice in my head helped me to think more clearly—Collith was the enemy. I was at this party to save my enchanted brother and here it was. The opportunity I'd come for. With effort, I pushed back the lust and coaxed rationality forward. Collith didn't sense the change in me. I kept kissing him while I reached toward his psyche. This time, I didn't tear through it. Instead I tiptoed in like someone in a dark room, trying not to wake the person still sleeping in the bed.

It worked.

My power was specific to fear, so that was all I expected to find. There was more, though. There were snatches of images I wasn't accustomed to finding in someone's mind. A curly-haired woman laughing. Dapples of sunlight hitting a forest floor. Colorful lights flashing over a crowd.

Maybe it was our mating bond that allowed me to see so much, and however much I tried to deny it, I was intrigued by the memories in Collith's head. Still, I forced myself to continue. I hadn't come for the beautiful things. More often than not, they were lies, anyway.

His nightmares were buried so far beneath, I almost missed them.

The first one was worn and familiar, like a beloved novel, which meant Collith visited it regularly. I found myself in a passageway so overpowered by roots that it seemed impossible to get through. There was something at the end of it; I detected movement in the dark. Collith dreaded whatever waited for him. Was that a voice? A moan? It was calling his name...

I took a step closer, hoping I couldn't be harmed by anything here. But suddenly the passage faded, giving way to the next of Collith's secrets. Surprisingly, I was in the open, the top of my head warmed by daylight. Flowers quivered in a breeze and someone had laid a path of bricks alongside them. It was a garden, I realized. A garden in the middle of a wood. A small house stood nearby, its walls made of gray stone. Smoke rose from the chimney. The scene looked like something out of a fairy tale.

I turned in a circle, wondering if I'd stumbled upon another happy place in Collith's mind. Just as I was about to retreat from the memory, I saw him. A male stood at the edge of the garden, an air of expectation hovering around him. His back was to me. He wore tight, black trousers and a billowy white shirt. His hair rivaled the sun above us in its brilliance. There was a delicate circlet on his head made of silver vines and sleeping buds.

The moment I saw him, a rush of feeling swept through me. The most powerful of all of them was pure, unadulterated terror. Whoever this male was, Collith was more afraid of him than any other creature on Earth.

Looks like I dug deep enough this time.

A moment too soon. Maybe he'd finally detected my lack of focus; before I could get a look at the distant figure's face, Collith pulled away from our kiss and effectively yanked me back to reality. His eyes were bright with hope—he had no idea what I'd discovered. It took several moments to reorient myself. Once I comprehended that I was still wrapped around him, I slid back to solid ground. "Fortuna?" Collith whispered. It trembled on his lips like a wish.

The noise from the festivities filled the silence between us. Only half of Collith's face was visible, and I stared up at the part I could see. Despite everything that had just transpired, my mind flashed back to the last time we'd been in that throne room. When he'd taken my voice. When he'd sat there as I screamed and bled.

A door inside me slammed shut.

"I hate you," I whispered back. I kept my gaze on Collith's long enough to see the light fade.

Then I bent and vomited all over his boots.

CHAPTER ELEVEN

I was back in the throne room.

For a few seconds I stood there, blinking in confusion, surrounded by too much movement and color. How did I get here? What happened after I threw up all over Collith? There was no sign of him now, but Nuvian was back, a solemn-faced presence behind me. My head was swimming. I had to get away. Get out. Get air.

Feeling as though I might vomit all over again, I jerked into motion and made a beeline for the closest doorway. Once again, I encountered the two faeries fucking between two tables. *Jesus, doesn't it get old?* I thought dizzily, stepping over the male's bare legs. As I hurried on, the female cried out, a piercing sound that hurt my eardrums. Nuvian kept up without any trouble. If I weren't so desperate to escape, I would turn around and scream at him to leave me the fuck alone.

The doorway was just a few yards away now, and I was tempted to break into a run. The combination of laughter and music was so loud. It felt like I was in a concert hall. Thankfully I was almost there, so close.

Then, as though it belonged to someone else, I watched my

hand reach for a faerie. Instinct, maybe, or just an overwhelming desire to see one of them pay. *No*, I thought. *Don't do that. Just go.*

Time slowed.

Before I could lay a finger on her, the creature turned a pale gaze on me. I froze, not from terror, but from the wave of power. It felt like a great weight pressed down on every part of my body.

"So foolish," the faerie breathed, studying me with those unnerving eyes. "You are a child among monsters. A worm beneath a flock of birds."

Her hair was long and dark. A loose-fitting white gown flowed around her. A male stood beside her who was just as eerily beautiful. I knew that most of the faeries here were ancient, but these were the first ones that *felt* old. I tried to find any evidence of their age—their faces were unlined and their backs straight.

Words stuck in my throat as I tried to give a mocking response. Magic clung to the air around us. In a burst of dismay, I realized the female was doing something. Desperately I searched the crowd around us for Collith or Nuvian. There was no sign of either of them, of course. *Now* they left me alone.

Her companion's expression was thoughtful, which was intensified by his long and elegant features. His hair fell to his waist in a straight, brown curtain. A golden band adorned his forehead. Like her, he wore entirely white. His skin almost matched it, and I wondered how long it had been since these two had seen the outside world. "I think you've underestimated this one, Arcaena. Power lurks in her depths," he remarked. His voice was polite and distant, as though they were talking about the selection of food or what everyone was wearing.

"Ah, yes, I see it now. She's bound." Arcaena's red lips tilted up. "Wrapped in chains of her own making. Shall we take them off?"

The male also smiled faintly. The effect was chilling, as

though his mouth weren't accustomed to it. In that instant, I realized they had to be twins. They weren't identical, but their expressions mirrored each other. "She would consider it a punishment, I think, rather than a kindness."

"Perfect," Arcaena purred. She stepped closer and cupped my cheek, and no matter how much I wanted to recoil, I still couldn't move. Under her breath, the faerie whispered something in a language I didn't recognize. After a few seconds of this, she let go and retreated.

At last, I was free of her—my knees buckled. Somehow I managed to remain standing, though I couldn't stop myself from using a nearby table for support. The faeries watched my face, their eyes gleaming. *What did you just do?* I tried to snap. But new sensations coursed through me, cackling and roaring like prisoners just let out of their cells. I wanted to find Dad's knife and jam it into Jassin's eye. I wanted to get so wasted that I forgot where I was. I wanted to dance in the middle of that crowd and enjoy being in my own skin. I wanted to find Collith and run my hands down his stomach again.

Some small, shrinking part of me clung to rationality. The seconds stretched into minutes as I struggled against the urges tearing my insides apart. Eventually Arcaena murmured something in the male's ear and they slipped away. Her comment replayed in my mind. *She's bound. Wrapped in chains of her own making. Shall we take them off?* My inner battle raged on and I finally realized what the faerie had done.

She'd lowered my inhibitions.

"Fortuna," someone said.

I know what's going to happen next, I thought dimly. It would be Damon standing behind me. He was going to hug me and apologize for what Jassin had done. After that, Collith would appear with a glass of water. I'd grab him and drag him off into some dark passageway, where I'd practically fuck him against the wall.

Slowly, feeling as though I were under water, I faced my

brother. He wore the exact clothes I remembered, the blue suit with too many frills. "This is a memory," I said. The voice didn't sound like my own.

Damon smiled. The shadow in his eyes made it mournful. "Is it?"

"Yes. That faerie messed with my head. She made me forget what she'd done."

"Then you probably shouldn't stay here. Wake up." Damon stepped closer and, instead of embracing me, kissed my forehead. His lips were so chapped that they felt like scabs. He moved away again, retreating into darkness that hadn't been there a moment ago. "Wake up, Fortuna."

My eyes flew open.

For the second time in twenty-four hours, I found myself in Collith's bed.

For the second time in twenty-four hours, someone had taken a dress off me.

This time, though, I wasn't naked. A quick glance showed that I was wearing what appeared to be yoga pants and a t-shirt. There was also no fire. Instead, a candle burned on the bedside table. The sapphire necklace had been painstakingly placed next to it. The light was small and, because of this, most of the room was obscured in darkness. I knew I wasn't alone, though—the bond was relaxed. The string wasn't being pulled taut between us. Soft sounds came from my left, and a moment later, Collith's unique scent teased my senses.

The sheets whispered as he slid beneath the blankets. The bed was so large that I hardly felt it. For a few seconds, I considered pretending I was still asleep, but it reminded me too much of my last conversation with Oliver. So I rolled over, putting my back to Collith, and stared into the tiny flame. "Tell me about the heavenly fire," I said.

The sound of my voice felt harsh in the stillness. Collith didn't seem startled; he'd probably known I was awake. His voice drifted to me, soft as a feather on the air. "Nuvian told me what happened at the feast," he murmured. "You were manipulated by one of the old ones and he didn't dare interfere. I'm sorry, Fortuna. I failed you."

My throat swelled. If we kept talking about that awful faerie and what she'd done to me, I knew I would cry. I never wanted to be that helpless again. "What matters to me, right now, is the fire," I said flatly. It was an image that had stayed with me—the blue tint on Collith's skin, the expression of concentration he'd worn, the elegance of his splayed fingers—and now was good as any time to ask.

I felt my mate hesitate. He was probably wondering if he should press the issue. "It's part of the reason they allow me to sit on the throne," Collith answered finally. "Some faeries have a... specialty. A certain power or ability unique from others. Usually the ability manifests during puberty, but in rare cases, it can arise through trauma. Arcaena, for instance, has the ability to reduce a creature to its basest instincts. Jassin is an incredible telepath, as I'm sure you've learned. He can even plant thoughts, in addition to hearing them."

"How did yours happen?" I asked, curious in spite of myself. Silence from the other side of the bed. Clearly I'd asked another question he was unwilling to answer. Feeling restless, I rolled onto my back. Shadows moved along the rocky ceiling. Exhaustion tugged at me. I was tempted to succumb, longing to see Oliver, but I worried about talking in my sleep. For a moment I considered returning to my old room, but the prospect of getting there felt daunting after all that had happened. So many passages to get lost in, so many opportunities for a faerie to prey on me again.

"You're safe here," Collith said without warning, clearly picking up on my emotions again. "Nuvian is posted outside the door and the other passages are guarded, as well. Also, the location of this room was spelled by a witch, so no one who means harm may enter. Get more sleep if you can."

His words did nothing to set me at ease; I was still surrounded on all sides by creatures more treacherous and powerful than I'd ever be. "Thanks," was all I could think to say.

"You're welcome."

The seconds ticked past, marked by flickers of the candle and the gentle sound of Collith's breathing. It was a strange development, sleeping in the same bed as him. I'd shared bedrooms with foster siblings, years ago, but this was different. More... intimate.

The thought sent a myriad of emotions through me, like colors on a carousel. Guilt, confusion, resentment. I went rigid as I tried to stop them. For a few minutes, I was actually successful. But then, in the stillness, flashes of the feast started coming to me. Strange braziers. Food on the flagstones. Sex. Then I saw a faerie with feathers for eyelashes and her syrupy voice filled my head. *I wonder why he considered you significant enough to mate, but not to crown?*

More riddles and games. I let out a frustrated breath. "Can you at least tell me how the Unseelie Court chooses its queen? Since apparently it isn't done by marriage, like the rest of the world?"

Once again, Collith was slow to reply. I could feel him looking my way as he spoke. "Obtaining a crown in the Unseelie Court is no easy feat. They won't simply give it to you; it must be earned. It's an... arduous process," he concluded. There was a heaviness in the way he said it.

"How so?"

The mattress shifted as the Unseelie King fully faced me. Wanting to see his expression, I turned onto my side again. We

---

were closer than I realized; Collith's breath tickled my cheek. His unique, intoxicating scent was everywhere. The flickering candle made his scar look deeper and more painful. "She undergoes a series of trials," he answered with obvious reluctance. "The first tests your strength. The next tests your cunning. The last tests your devotion. And once you begin the trials, you can't change your mind or stop halfway through. During my reign, no female has survived all of them."

"Lovely," I remarked. I wondered how many had attempted it. For some reason, I didn't want to know. "What happens if someone does survive?"

One of his bare shoulders lifted in a shrug, as though it was so simple. "Then she's Queen of the Unseelie Court. There are ancient rituals and traditions to make it official. After that, every bloodline is required to pay fealty. The Guardians pay theirs individually, of course, since their duties are different than a Court member's."

During all this, Collith seemed more interested in studying me. I stared right back—it was the first time I'd truly been able to. There was no black market to escape, no noisy bar to distract, no bargains to resist. In this faint lighting, the hills and planes of his face were even more pronounced. His full mouth was relaxed, inviting, and I tried not to remember what they felt like. I noticed there were no lines around those sensuous lips. *He doesn't smile often*, I thought.

At all once, though, his words registered. "Wait, they pay fealty?" I blurted. "What does that mean?"

Something shifted in Collith, but I wasn't sure exactly what. Without warning, he sat up, making that lock of hair fall over his eyebrow. The covers fell to reveal his stomach muscles. "It's a show of their loyalty," he clarified, seemingly oblivious to how my gaze darted downward. "Usually something small. A bit of symbolism more than anything else. But it's your right to ask for something more, such as a gift or a token."

His words echoed through me. *A gift or a token.* I forgot about my discomfort as an idea began to form. Suddenly very, very invested in our conversation, I propped my head up and met Collith's gaze. "Does it have to be an object? Or could it be... a person?"

"Yes." Collith's expression was neutral; he'd probably guessed where my mind was going. I was about to demand why he hadn't told me this before when he added, "But there's something else you should know. One of the rituals during the coronation might make you reconsider. After it's completed, in the same way you and I are bound, so you would be bound to them."

"Them?"

He nodded, a terse movement. His mouth had flattened into a thin line. "Every single faerie that resides in this Court."

Now I was the one to fall silent.

It was difficult to imagine. Even now, in a moment without strife or chaos, I could feel the bond between me and Collith. It wasn't painful, but I still hadn't gotten used to it. The sensation was like having an extra finger. Every time you looked down at it, the sight was startling. Strange. To have a bond with all the creatures of the Unseelie Court? My insides quaked at the thought.

An instant later, shame hit me. Damon would do it, if I were the one needing to be saved. He wouldn't even hesitate. But I'd already married a faerie and had the flesh taken from my back. If I did this... it could very well mean my sanity. Wasn't there a limit to the sacrifices? Was there any line I wouldn't cross for someone who didn't want to be saved?

Of course I already knew the answer. No. There were no limits to what I'd do for my brother's freedom.

Anguish ripped through me. My new future loomed and it was full of shackles, dirt, and darkness. Seeking some kind of comfort, or just the slightest reassurance, I lifted my gaze to Collith's again. "Did you go through these trials?"

A muscle moved in his jaw. He looked straight ahead, seeing something I couldn't. "I claimed my crown by other means," was all he said.

"We're supposed to be partners, right?" I challenged, exasperated at yet another avoidance. "I don't need to know everything, Collith. But maybe if you didn't have so many secrets, my blood wouldn't be all over the throne room floor right now."

His nostrils flared. He faced me again. His eyes looked nearly black in the guttering light. "Fine. I murdered the previous king. That, dear wife, is how I began my noble reign."

The words were so blunt, so flat, that it took a moment to comprehend them. I'd known Collith was powerful, but I had yet to see any sort of violence from him. Apparently I'd unwittingly started to believe he was different from the rest of his kind. Now I tried to picture it. Blood on his hands, a body at his feet. Surprisingly, it was an image that didn't seem like it could ever be reality.

I refocused on the present—there was a surge of fresh questions rushing up inside me—and realized I was staring at Collith's fingers. Normally they were splayed, relaxed, but at some point during our conversation they had clenched in his lap. I resisted the urge to reach over and uncurl them.

Collith watched me absorb the truth he'd just flung my way. Then he heaved a sigh, and in that single sound, I heard decades' worth of pain. "The trials are designed to break you, Fortuna," he said. "The chair beside me remains empty for good reason."

For the first time since we'd met, I didn't doubt the sincerity in his voice. I wasn't sure why, since he'd proven to be a good liar. Something about the sadness in his eyes—the same sadness that lived in mine.

"Why?" I asked finally. Collith frowned. A faint sense of

surprise vibrated down our bond. He hadn't expected me to give him a chance to explain. When he didn't answer, I kept going, refusing to let him evade yet another question. "Why did you kill him? There must've been a motive."

At this, Collith quirked a dark brow. "Maybe I just liked it. Maybe I just wanted the power."

If he had said that to me even a few hours earlier, I would've believed him. It was easy to think the worst of a faerie. But here, in this room and in this bed, everything was quiet and still. The agony in my back had faded. I had a spark of hope that my brother would survive this. And the bond, lying between us like a vein or a telephone line, continued emanating gentle sensations. Despite his harsh words and bemused expression, Collith regretted what he'd done.

"We have a lifetime ahead of us," I reminded him, raising my eyebrows right back in a silent challenge. I laid back down, making the bed frame creak. "Sooner or later, I'll learn the truth."

Collith didn't respond. Following suit, he stretched out beside me. This time he rested on his stomach, both of his hands tucked beneath the pillow. His biceps flexed, sharp and defined, like a paper cutout. The muscles in his back gleamed. Those long, jagged scars somehow seemed part of it, belonging on his skin like the small details in a distant horizon. *So beautiful*, I thought. *Too beautiful*.

As he got settled, Collith kept his face turned toward mine, making it all too easy for him to notice the direction of my focus. "I think you're beautiful, too," he murmured.

My gaze snapped back to his. When I realized I'd been caught, my cheeks caught on fire. Collith didn't smile, but his eyes smoldered in response to what they saw in mine. "Are you going to try for the crown?" he asked, deliberately changing the subject. I was so relieved I almost sagged; I wasn't ready to openly acknowledge the attraction hovering around us.

His question was a welcome distraction. An answer immediately rose to my lips, but at the last second, I wavered. If what Collith said was true and I began these trials, there was no going back. The fae would own me, body and soul. Fear lodged within my chest, spreading wide like some black, winged creature. Just as I started to tell Collith I would find another way, I felt Oliver tucking a curl of hair behind my ear. His voice drifted through me, a lullaby in the darkness. *Sometimes it's not about being stronger. It's about being smarter.*

There was no other way and I knew it. They'd whipped me. They'd used magic on me. Even on a full moon, they were stronger. I couldn't beat them as a Nightmare.

But maybe I could as a queen.

In my mind, I heard a door clicking shut. Closing on any chance at happiness, on separating myself from this marriage, on the hope that my brother and I could be a family again. "Yes," I answered, squeezing my eyes shut in a futile attempt to hide the sorrow crashing over me. He could feel it through the bond, anyway. Nothing was private anymore. "I have to. For Damon."

The candlewick popped, brightened, and faded. It was the only sound in the room. Collith didn't try to touch me or offer pretty lies. "Then we'll make the announcement in the morning. If you're certain this is truly what you want to do," he said.

His words burrowed into my heart like claws. *What I want? Since when do you care about what I want?* I nearly spat. It was late, though, and I needed to see Oliver. Fighting with Collith wasn't worth it. Instead, I twisted around in the sheets and put my back to him. Suddenly it didn't matter anymore whether he overheard something—I focused on the candle and waited for its flame to lull me to sleep. *I'm coming, Ollie.* Slowly, my anger simmered and cooled.

Just when the edges of everything were going dark, Collith

cleared his throat. The sound was oddly uncertain. "Is it my turn, then?" he ventured.

So close. I frowned in annoyance, keeping my eyes closed. "Your turn for what?"

"To ask a question."

"I'm tired, Your Majesty."

"Very well. I hope you have lovely dreams, Fortuna."

But now I was intrigued. I shifted and glared up at the ceiling, more irritated at myself than him. "What do you want to know?"

I could feel the weight of Collith's focus. His voice, already soft and soothing, became even gentler. Despite this, I wasn't prepared when he asked, "What happened to your parents?"

The words were a dash of cold water. I stiffened, knowing what was coming, but struggling against it anyway. Unbidden, inevitable, the images assaulted me. A blood-flecked chin. Glassy, vacant eyes. Curled fingers. It felt like there was a hand wrapped around my heart, squeezing tighter and tighter. I didn't look at Collith as I replied, "What makes you think anything did?"

"Regina mentioned something," he admitted.

Fucking Regina. I was going to spit in her drink next time I saw her. If I saw her. "Figures," I muttered. My muscles were still locked into place. A lifetime ago, the school counselor tried to teach me calming techniques. Something about breathing...

"You also talk in your sleep."

Just as I suspected. He hadn't thought to tell me, of course. But I wasn't able to muster any indignation; Collith's question still held me down, breathed tauntingly in my face. I stared upward so hard it felt like the lines in the ceiling would be permanently committed to memory. I hadn't told this story in a long, long time. Would I be able to without shattering?

Mom and Dad's faces swam before me. It had been years since that night and their features had gotten fuzzy. Back home, their pictures were in almost every room. It was my desperate attempt to cling, to remind, to reassure. *We haven't forgotten you,* I longed to say. *Never.*

For them. I'd relive it for them.

Collith had remained silent, compassion radiating down the bond. That made it worse, somehow. When I spoke, the words were distant and matter-of-fact. "No one knows what happened, exactly," I began. Everything came back in a rush, painfully vivid, as though it all happened yesterday. Rain pattering against the roof. Wind shaking the tree branches outside my window. Me awakening on sweat-dampened sheets. "I was eight years old. It was just another night—in the morning we'd go to school. Dad was a therapist and Mom was a professor. We always went to bed early, because everyone had to get up at the crack of dawn."

I was babbling. Realizing this, I stopped. My hands clenched where they gripped the blanket. Just as Collith's had earlier, I noted faintly.

"It sounds like a beautiful life," he said softly.

"It was." I blinked rapidly. Now that I'd started, need filled me like a balloon. I had to finish. "That night, I had a bad dream. I think that's why I didn't wake up at first. But eventually I did; there were noises coming from another part of the house. For some reason, I didn't want to move. Maybe some part of me knew. It took everything I had to stand."

Inhale through the nose, exhale through the mouth. That's what the counselor had said. I remembered now.

"I found Mom in the hallway. It was obvious that she was dead so I kept going. It wasn't because I hoped Dad had survived, though. Maybe I just had to see for myself. There was this... smell. God, this awful smell. Like old pennies. Dad was still in their room. There was no chance to hold his hand; he was already dead. He'd been killed right in the bed, actually.

Probably didn't even have a chance to open his eyes before it got him."

"It?" Collith repeated. His voice seemed to come from a vast distance.

I swallowed. My mouth was so dry. "No way a human did that. In the end, the police concluded an animal must've gotten in."

"But you don't believe them."

"No. I never did. Whatever it was, I think it was still in the house when I found the bodies. I remember a shadow..." More images flashed. Had it been standing in the hallway, staring at me? A silhouette against the window? The shape in my memory was unnatural. Monstrous. With bright, red eyes...

"Fortuna? Are you all right?"

Inhale through the nose, exhale through the mouth. I shook myself. "I don't want to talk about this anymore, okay?"

"Okay," Collith said instantly. Quiet descended on us, disturbed only by the sputtering of the dying candle, and I focused on banishing the memories. I tried to think of Damon, or the upcoming trials, or how I'd apologize to Bea and Cyrus when I got back. Nothing worked. Panic hurtled up my throat, making it difficult to breathe.

After another moment or two, Collith shifted. The movement seemed unthinking, casual, as if he were only trying to get more comfortable. I didn't miss that it brought him closer, though. "Where did you go after that? A relative?" he asked next.

It was like he'd thrown me a lifejacket—the gruesome memories made way for different ones. Still painful, but the sort of pain that was manageable, like a toothache or a paper cut. "We didn't have any relatives," I answered haltingly. My heart rate started to slow. "None that we knew about, anyway. Damon and I bounced around in foster homes for a while. Eventually we settled with a nice couple and they raised us until I turned eighteen. Dave and Maureen. I try to visit them every so often. Maureen calls once in a while." Those calls had been occurring less and less, though. To Maureen, I was probably just a painful reminder of the child she'd lost. The child she'd truly loved... Damon. Who had gone missing on my watch.

"Why did you leave?" There was no judgment in Collith's expression; just curiosity. I told myself that's why I was telling him all this.

At some point, I'd turned toward him again. We lay in the middle of that gigantic bed, facing each other but not quite touching. He was close enough that I would just have to tip my head forward to bring it against his. His scent, subtle and intoxicating, wrapped around me. Why did he have to smell so good?

Damn it. What had he asked again? Right, yes, why did I leave Dave and Maureen. I thought about this longer than I had with the other questions. It was a relief, having something to focus on. "I guess it was because I'd never felt... right. Like I belonged. Damon was so much better than I was at blending in. He had his girlfriend, the soccer team, drama club. He wanted to go to the University of Colorado and major in Psychology, like our dad.

"I mean, it's not like I didn't have friends or that Dave and Maureen weren't good parents. But it was never a question of whether I'd go—it was when. That week, once I was legally an adult, I knew it was time. I told Damon I was leaving. I didn't even invite him to come, since I'd never ask him to leave everything behind. But when I went to put my stuff in that shitty little car, he was there, sitting in the passenger seat. 'Don't bother,' he said. 'I'm going with you. We made a promise, remember?' So I shut my mouth and we just drove."

That was the happiest I'd been since our parents' deaths. I could still feel that sense of freedom. Music blaring from the speakers, wind combing through my hair. There was no one staring at me, seeing the face they wanted. There were no flavors on my tongue after I'd accidentally brushed up against someone in the hallway at school. Damon was there, a faint smile on his lips, looking more like our father every day.

I would never be that happy again.

The thought yanked me back to the present. I met Collith's gaze, knowing the bitterness I felt showed in mine. "I stopped in Granby for gas, and there was a bar with its door open. We could smell burgers. Damon was hungry, so we went in. That's when I met Bea."

"You love her very much," Collith commented. I must've given him a look, because he shrugged a shoulder. "I could hear it in your voice."

He wasn't wrong. It had taken me by surprise, my love for Bea. She felt more like a parent than my foster mother.

Growing up, Maureen had tried so hard. She pressured me to go to school dances, to go on a date with that nice boy from homeroom, to go shopping with her. All normal things that any daughter should want to do. I couldn't tell her how exhausting it was to be around the other kids. Their fears were even more potent than those of an adult, because the young weren't able to combat their phobias with logic or denial, a skill that was honed with age. Over time, it seemed like Maureen looked at me with frustration and exasperation more than anything else. Now, after so much time and distance, I knew it had been hurt and rejection.

But Bea hadn't tried to understand or shape me. She didn't ask questions. She observed with those sharp eyes of hers and just... accepted. The relationship with her was easy. Nice.

Collith was waiting for my response. Realizing this, I made a vague gesture. "There aren't a lot of—"

In that instant, the candle gasped and went out, shrouding Collith's room in darkness. I jumped and lost my train of thought. I stared up at nothing and saw myself as I'd been just a few years ago. Not much had changed, really, except for one thing. A small piece of myself that had fallen away, unnoticed by anyone but me. Sometimes I looked back at it. I hadn't told anyone it happened, hadn't allowed the pain to show.

Maybe that's why I did now... and to a faerie, no less. "I wanted to be a veterinarian," I murmured to the darkness. "Ever since I was little. Animals have always been peaceful to be around—their fears are so simple that touching them doesn't affect me. No images in my head, no horrible taste in my mouth. Helping something helpless, passing my days so simply and quietly? Yeah, I could live like that."

The faerie in question didn't laugh or talk about impossibilities. Instead, he replied softly, "It's not too late, you know."

I shook my head. "Going to school would mean leaving everyone. They're the only family I have."

"That's not true."

But I wasn't interested in arguing; I'd let go of that dream a long time ago. Once again we both lay there in utter silence, and this time, neither of us spoke. It was definitely my turn to ask a question—I'd lost count of how many he had asked—but suddenly it was difficult to form words. My eyelids felt weighted.

Once more, unconsciousness loomed. Collith moved again, just the slightest adjustment, and his forehead pressed against mine. The sudden contact should have been startling. This creature had become part of me, though. Truthfully, I'd known he was going to do it an instant beforehand.

I considered moving away but was strangely reluctant to follow through on it. *Don't be pathetic*, I told myself. In an effort to feel that earlier hatred for Collith, I recalled the cold figure he'd been, sitting on that throne as the cat o' nine tails came down. It worked, but only slightly. Hatred was overpowered by exhaustion and... something else.

It felt good to touch someone. I'd denied myself such a simple pleasure for so long. Usually, even the most fleeting of contacts brought terrifying images and unpleasant flavors. With Collith, there was only his cool skin and heady scent. *Just this once. It doesn't mean anything*, I thought. I had no idea who I was reassuring.

"Good night, Fortuna," Collith said. His voice was drowsy.

"Good night," I murmured back. Within minutes, the faerie's deep breathing told me that he was asleep. The warmth touched my cheek, again and again, oddly comforting. My own eyes drifted shut.

I would never love the Unseelie King. But maybe I didn't have to hate him, either.

CHAPTER TWELVE

*W*hen I opened my eyes again, I half-expected the scene I'd just fallen asleep to. Collith beside me, a burnt-out candle on the table, a looming earthen ceiling overhead. But this time it had been replaced by the familiar sight of rustling grass and a faraway sea. A content, gentle breeze whispered past. Fading light tinted the world red and yellow.

Finally.

It felt like I hadn't seen Oliver in weeks, and I didn't even glance down to see what I was wearing before searching for him. The first direction I looked, of course, was the house. Every window was dark. Since he didn't sleep, this had become our signal that he was somewhere else. I scanned the surrounding hills and dimming horizon. My gaze latched onto a slim figure standing off in the distance. As always, I broke into a run.

He heard me coming and turned. The moment I was within earshot I demanded, "How did you do it?"

Oliver frowned. The dying sun fell upon his eyes and hair, making strands of blond become glittering gold. "What are you—"

"When you treated my back, Ollie. What you did was still

there when I woke up. My blood had been cleaned off and the lashes were covered in ointment." I reached him then, and Oliver took my elbow to steady me. I wasn't in any danger of falling; I knew this spot better than any other in the dreamscapes. Oliver had spent so much time here that the ground was bare where he stood. Whenever I imagined him during our time apart, it was exactly as he appeared now.

"Fortuna, take a breath," Oliver ordered.

"How is that possible?" I insisted, ignoring him. The mystery had bothered me from the moment I woke up in that prison cell. The memory of Zara and Collith's voices was as clear as the ocean spray reaching toward us.

Someone has already treated her.

Impossible. No one has been down here but the guard.

See for yourself. The wounds are cleaned and covered in a salve of some kind.

I shied away from remembering more. The lingering horror of that cell made me speak without thinking. "Never mind, it had to be something else. You aren't... I mean, this isn't..."

Now Oliver gave me a sad, bitter smile. "How did I do it, since I'm not real?" he finished. I drew in a sharp breath. As I fumbled for the right response, my heart ached. *That's not what I meant*, I wanted to say, but it would be a lie. Waves pounded against the rocks far below, filling the painful silence between us. "Did you know you could do that?" I asked instead.

"No. I didn't." The words were clipped. "Would it be so terrible, Fortuna? If someday, somehow I was there when you woke up?"

"Ollie, no, of course not." He waited for more, but I was afraid of saying something else that would hurt him. I couldn't tell him that such a future was impossible or that this was all we'd have. Regardless of whatever new abilities he'd developed, in the other world, Oliver had no body.

It didn't mean he lacked significance. It didn't mean he was any less present to me than Damon, or Bea, or Cyrus. Thinking to show him how I felt, I cupped Oliver's face and kissed him. His reaction was stiff, unyielding, so I abandoned his mouth to make my way down his neck. This was a language we both spoke. It always brought us together, no matter how many differences or words unspoken.

Without warning, Oliver stepped back. It caught me so off guard that I just watched as he settled wordlessly on the ground. He faced the luminous skyline with a stony expression. Did he want me to leave? Had something between us changed? The thought threatened to break me. I'd already endured so much; I couldn't lose Oliver. Not now. Uncertain what came next, I shifted from foot to foot. After a moment, I sat down next to him. *This is Ollie*, I reminded myself. *Your best friend.*

My first instinct was to ask the questions piling up inside. My second was to let Oliver speak on his own time. I would simply listen.

It was the right choice. He didn't turn or look away from the brilliant sea, but after a few minutes, Oliver spoke.

"Right now, your main focus is Damon. I understand. He's your brother, your family. I was wrong before, when I told you to let him go." Oliver hesitated. Now he angled his body toward me and, a beat later, our gazes met. His was filled with a terrible sadness that I hadn't known he felt. "But I'm your family, too. I still feel what anyone else would, even if part of you believes I'm just a figment of your imagination. Try to remember that, even in times like this. Tell me the truth; don't try to distract me from it. I deserve some dignity."

My voice was soft. "I will. I'm sorry."

Sorry for more than he'd ever know. I'd created him. I'd made this gilded prison for him. It was a miracle he didn't despise me, really.

Now I mulled over my past few visits—no, the past few years—and realized how selfish I'd been. Giving him scraps of the outside world, keeping the pieces I deemed inconvenient for him to know. I had also kept to myself the fact that, in my mind, he was some imaginary friend or temporary insanity. I thought I'd done a good job hiding it, but of course he knew. Oliver constantly proved he was more intelligent than most of the people I considered real.

Unaware of the self-loathing coursing through me, Oliver merely kissed my cheek. Just like that, I was forgiven. "Now, tell me everything," he said.

I smiled reluctantly at these words. When we were children, they were always the first thing out of his mouth once I'd arrived at the dreamscape. Even now, I could see it. Young Oliver, his eyes too big for his face and his freckles pronounced, jumping up and down in the doorway of the house. His arms and legs had been so skinny.

The image brought back a rush of more light-filled memories, which I would need if I was going to relive my time in the Unseelie Court. Preparing myself, clinging to the happiness of days past, I took a breath. The events of the past twenty-four hours, if it had really only been that long, poured out. My introduction to the Court as Collith's mate, how Arcaena had used magic on me, what I'd seen in Collith's head, our conversation about the queendom and the consequences it would have.

I told him all of it. Even the kiss.

Oliver didn't interrupt or ask any questions. Throughout my account, his expression remained carefully neutral. I hadn't realized how much there was to say, how affected I'd been by it, because by the time I was finished it felt like someone had sucked poison out of me. Afterward, we just sat there, our legs dangling off the edge. Birds flew in the distance, small black dots that seemed to be heading straight for the sun.

Inevitably, my mind turned to the decision I'd made earlier, lying in that bed next to the Unseelie King.

Are you going to try for the crown?

I have to. For Damon.

"I think I know the answer to this," I said abruptly, shattering the peace like a hammer to glass. In my peripheral vision, I saw Oliver turn his head. Though I yearned to avoid him, shy from the truth, I met his gaze. "But I need to ask anyway. If I were to die—out there, I mean—you'd be gone, too. Right?"

My best friend tilted his head. The light touched his eyes again, even more intensely than before. "If you died, Fortuna, I'd follow you into whatever afterlife there is. The rest doesn't really matter, does it?"

Tears blurred everything. For once, I didn't hide or dash them away. "I don't deserve you," I told him.

A strange expression crossed his face. *Oh, shit, what did I say now?* I thought. Just as I started to ask him about it, Oliver nudged me with his shoulder. "Sure you do," he said. "But you must've done something very, very good in a past life."

I rolled my eyes and nudged him back. Daylight retreated fully then. It happened between one breath and the next, subject to Oliver's whim. At some point, without my noticing, the moon had emerged. The details of its rocky surface were sharp and detailed, like a painting. Nothing like the moon in my world.

Oliver's words chose that moment to replay in my head. *I'd follow you into whatever afterlife there is. The rest doesn't really matter, does it?* However much I appreciated them, the weight of another life settled on me. If I failed, not only would Damon remain in Jassin's clutches, but a creature capable of exquisite art and unconditional love would cease to exist.

Another silent minute passed. I stared down at the waves, their depths black in the moonlight, and swallowed. "Want to know a secret?" I asked. Might as well get it all out in the open, while we still could.

Oliver didn't hesitate. "Always."

I released a long, shaky breath. For as long as I could remember, it had been an instinct, a rule, a mantra. *Be the strong one.* At first, it had been for Damon. But once he was gone, it was for my own sake. If I wasn't hard, or closed off, the world would destroy me. Oliver had been the only exception. Now that death breathed down my neck, I couldn't face it like this.

"I'm terrified," I breathed. God, it felt liberating to say.

"Of what?"

"Some days it feels like I'm scared of everything. Losing another person in my life, disappointing Bea or Gretchen, or even just walking to my car alone. Right now, though? Whatever tomorrow is going to bring. There's a good chance I won't survive."

Oliver twisted his lips in thought. It was something else he'd done since we were children, and the familiar sight was enough to make me smile again, just a little. "Come on," he said. He jumped up, and in one quick motion, Oliver pulled his shirt off. Next came his jeans. The tendons in his arms flexed as he undid the button. Before I could look away, he stood naked before me.

I didn't have much to compare him to, but I suspected Oliver was exceptional in any reality. My core heated and clenched. He noticed my reaction and gave me a look that made it difficult to think.

Then, without another word, Oliver spun and leaped off the cliff. A splashing sound disturbed the stillness. Smiling fully now, I got up and quickly undressed—it was the first time I noticed that I was wearing the same sweater and leggings from the last visit. Air whispered over my bare skin. Nearly trembling with anticipation, I backed up a few feet and ran at the edge.

For a few brief moments, I was flying.

When I hit the water, it was warm and opalescent. For a few seconds I lingered in the depths, gazing up at the moon. It was so easy to forget about what awaited me once I emerged. But Oliver was waiting, too, and I thought of him as I kicked for the surface.

In the real world, a chill would've raced over my skin the moment I reached air. That didn't exist here. Content and drowsy, I closed my eyes to float there for a minute. To enjoy the sensation of being weightless. The seconds ticked past and I could sense Oliver watching—his desire floated to me like a scent on the wind. I tried not to smile. He drew near, a rush of water coming with him, and ran his palm down my stomach. The brief touch sent a shiver of pleasure through me.

"When we were young, do you want to know what I was afraid of?" he said. With that, all traces of yearning vanished. I jerked upright and looked at him. Oliver raised his brows at my reaction. "Yes, I noticed that you never asked. I didn't offer, either. I wanted this place, our place, to be different. Your life out there is hell, so I tried to make it the complete opposite here. But if I have to choose between preserving that illusion and your survival, it's no contest."

Too much was changing. I didn't know if I was strong enough to face this, too. "Ollie..."

"Ask me," he said. His tone said that he wouldn't let it rest until I did.

I swallowed. "Fine. What were you afraid of?"

Oliver swam even closer. The moonlight made his skin look smooth as glass. Unbidden, my mind conjured someone else's face, just as beautiful, just as pale, but with a jagged scar disrupting the perfection. *Good night, Fortuna.*

Get out of my head, Collith. Agitation surged through me like an electric charge, incinerating the image. Oliver didn't seem to notice anything amiss. With the tip of his finger, he traced the side of my face. I struggled to focus on our conversation. "I was terrified that you, Fortuna Sworn, would forget or outgrow me," he answered. "That someday, you wouldn't come back. I didn't care about fading into nothing or not existing. No, what haunted me most was the thought of losing you."

His words made me feel sick. To think, I had wondered

countless times whether I should do exactly that. Maureen had once suggested sleeping pills because she'd noticed how much I tossed and turned at night. "Why are you telling me this?" I managed, pretending that the sudden distance I put between us was for the sake of playing with the water.

Oliver's expression was knowing. He always knew. "Because of this next part," he said evenly. "I would've lost my mind if I'd let that fear live, Fortuna. So I started doing one thing, every single day, until I wasn't afraid anymore."

He was going to make me ask for this, too. My tone came out more exasperated than I meant it to when I said, "And what was that?"

"It's simple, really. Close your eyes. Picture the worst possible outcome. Be cruel to yourself. Spare no pain. Do this again, and again, and again. Until one day, you find yourself immune to it, and the fear no longer controls you."

I stared at him. He just stared back, unabashed and unapologetic. The ocean around us suddenly felt too quiet. "That's fucked up, Ollie," I said finally.

He shrugged his broad shoulders. The movement sent ripples through the water. "Everything is fucked up. If I found a way to cope with it, who cares how?"

"Most people suggest meditation," I quipped, hoping to lighten the mood. Then, before Oliver could protect himself, I splashed his face. He hardly reacted, his attention suddenly fixed downward. Water dripped from his hair and chin unheeded. Frowning, I followed his gaze. The swell of my breasts rose and fell with every breath.

That was all it took to send a blaze of heat through my lower belly. Oliver must've felt it, as well, because he reached for me. His voice was nearly a growl. "Well, I can give you something to meditate about."

I forced myself to pull away. Oliver stopped instantly, confusion replacing the hunger in his expression. "I made a promise," I whispered. "I shouldn't have kissed you before."

Pain filled his eyes and he lowered his hand. The sky above us dimmed. "A promise to the faerie, you mean."

"Yes. To the faerie."

I waited for Oliver's reaction, prepared for him to leave or start an argument. Instead, he made a visible effort to school his features. He reached under the water, seeking my hand, and held it as he rose to float on his back. Slowly, I did the same, though my entire body was still tense.

Preening like peacocks, the stars shone brighter at our attention. There were so many, every single one reflecting off the tranquil sea, and it felt like we swam among them instead of water. It only took a minute or two to forget my discomfort. Oliver and I drifted there, looking up at the sky as though we were so carefree, so young. My temple brushed against his.

With Oliver, the line between reality and pretend had always been blurred. I'd never been certain, especially now, if our time together was a crutch or it made me better. It didn't matter tonight, really. Not when I had no idea if we'd have another.

I let out a long sigh. Oliver sighed, too, teasing me. "Hey," I complained.

The corner of his mouth tilted up. He didn't look at me as he said, "I love you."

Normally it was hard to say it back. Not just to him, but to anyone. Now, though, I didn't hesitate. I caressed Oliver's profile with my eyes, that sprinkling of freckles over the bridge of his nose. "I love you, too."

His hand tightened around mine. A million more stars appeared. The horizon exploded with light.

And I woke up.

CHAPTER THIRTEEN

*O*nce my eyes adjusted to the sudden change in light, I instantly noticed the fresh clothing draped over a nearby chair.

It was something I'd wear to the gym. Without trying it on, I knew the tight pants would end at my calves and the tank top would crisscross my back. There were even tennis shoes on the floor.

A quick scan told me there was no one else in the room. Collith or a slave must have tended the fire recently, though, because it cheerily devoured a fresh log. I pushed the heavy covers aside, stood, and walked over to the chair. I didn't move to put anything on—my imagination fought to pinpoint what kind of fae trial would require an outfit like this. Anxiety began to consume me, like vines creeping over every inch of an old house. Oliver's advice didn't seem very solid right about now.

"Did I get the size right? I've never been very good at guessing feet."

I jumped so hard that my leg bumped into the chair. Laurie grinned at me from the doorway. "Jesus. How do you always do that?" I demanded.

Laurie closed the door behind him. "Your first trial is tonight," he remarked. The firelight danced over his ethereal features and pale hair, making him look more otherworldly than ever.

You don't say? I wanted to snap. The trials had been impossible to forget from the moment I agreed to them. But there was something about hearing the words said out loud. Full-blown fear rushed through me, and for a moment I couldn't breathe. In an effort to hide it, I put all my focus into getting dressed. I even forgot to care whether or not Laurie was looking.

Someone had moved my bag so that it rested next to the new clothing. As I pulled the top on, I caught sight of the mirror, which rested on top of everything else in the bag. It was a welcome distraction, however terrible the memory that came along with it. I bent to pick the mirror up, flashing back to the first time I did so. That faint image of Damon lingered in my mind. I ran a finger down the crack and asked, "How did he do it?"

Laurie turned—he'd put his back to me, apparently—and spotted the mirror in my hands. A fathomless expression crossed his face, there and gone before I could define it. "It was a witch's spell," he answered, coming closer. "She made it so the glass showed you whoever you loved most."

Just as he reached for the mirror's handle, there was a knock at the door. I didn't have to open it to know who stood on the other side; I could feel him. Laurie backed away, gluing his gaze to the floor, and I bent to put the mirror back. "Come in," I called, straightening.

The Unseelie King looked even grimmer than usual.

He was dressed in what I was beginning to recognize as his court attire. That lethal glass crown rested atop his head. His tunic was a dark, glittering material of some kind. The collar was high and stiff. And as for his pants... before Collith, I would've thought leather was impossible for anyone to pull off.

He did, though. His well-muscled thighs were evident through the clinging fabric. I knew his firm ass probably looked just as good, the bastard. Knee-high boots completed the formidable ensemble.

"You shouldn't have," I crooned. When Collith's brow crinkled with confusion, I gestured to his outfit. "You dressed up for my funeral. I'm so touched."

His expression cleared. I could tell from the tension coming down the bond that he didn't find me funny. "They're waiting," was all Collith said.

I didn't ask who he meant. It didn't matter, really. Hoping I didn't appear as nauseated as I felt, I sat to pull on the socks and tennis shoes. A brief silence fell. The fire crackled and hissed. Once again, Collith didn't grace Laurie with a single glance or word of acknowledgment. Did he think the silver-haired faerie was beneath him? Was that how he treated all his subjects?

Laurie caught my eye and, as if he knew what I was thinking, gave a subtle shake of his head. I scowled in return.

"Fortuna." The way Collith said my name caught at me. I finished tying the laces but gave him my full attention. He faltered, and as the seconds stretched and thinned, the entire scene felt like déjà vu. Collith's first warning echoed back to me. *Honesty isn't in my nature.*

I watched him wage an inner war, unable to detect what exactly was happening behind those hazel eyes—he kept the doors to his mind firmly closed. At last he asked, his voice strained, "Have I been clear enough?"

"Clear enough about what?"

He raked his hair back with long, pale fingers. He looked more agitated than I'd ever seen him. "The consequences of entering into these trials," he clarified. "Even if you win, you don't win."

I tilted my head, thinking about this. Though it was strange to have a conversation with Laurie there, acting like he wasn't, a curtain of desperation hung around Collith that I couldn't ignore. I got up and went to the door; I thought that would be answer enough. But Collith stayed where he was. We stood a foot away from each other now, and I couldn't help noticing the flecks of gold in his hazel eyes. "Do you have any siblings, Your Majesty?" I asked abruptly.

His face gave nothing away. "No."

"Okay. Do you have anyone?"

"I have you," Collith said simply. It was just as blunt, just as direct as the answer he'd given at Bea's when I asked what he wanted. *You.* The strangest part, though, was the sense of transparency traveling along that invisible string between us. He truly viewed me as someone important in his life.

How could one creature be so open and mystifying at the same time?

"That's not what I mean. I know you've loved someone," I reminded Collith. Her face flitted down the bond, every detail so defined, like a word freshly written in sand. I was careful not to react. Collith remained silent, his emotions still sealed away, but somehow I knew he was waiting for more. I tried to find the right words that would explain it. "They don't come along often. Those people who truly know you, who've seen the beautiful parts of you and the ugly ones, too, and stay anyway. Sometimes it's a romantic partner, like... like Viessa. Maybe it's a friend. But usually they come in the form of family. A parent, an aunt, a grandfather."

"A brother."

Sorrow dug into my heart, a sharp pain akin to a fingernail jabbing skin. I just nodded. "And wouldn't you do anything to protect a person like that? To keep them in your life?"

Once again, Collith gave no reply. I could sense my words had struck a chord, though. As the king opened the door for me, I glanced at Laurie, wondering what he thought of our exchange. He merely winked. Such a faerie.

Without another word, the three of us filed out of the room. Guards were waiting in the shadows, Nuvian and the long-haired female who'd struck me during the tribunal. She stared straight ahead and didn't acknowledge my hard stare. Collith inclined his head to the right and we all started down the passageway. It seemed quieter than usual; there were no agony-filled screams or cries of ecstasy. I hadn't quite given up on making sense of the maze, so noting the twists and turns took up most of my efforts. It still wasn't enough to distract me from the purpose of our journey; my heart pounded hard and fast.

Gradually, I noticed that Laurie walked on my left and Collith strode on my right. They were so different; even their steps were night and day. Laurie's was light, like a dancer's, while Collith's were filled with purpose. How had they come to know each other? Was there some kind of dynamic at play that I was completely missing?

Just then, a doorway appeared up ahead. All my thoughts about the faeries on either side of me vanished. It was more of an opening in the wall than a doorway. At a glance, it was obvious only one person at a time would be able to fit through. Somehow it looked older than anything I'd yet seen down here. *Please don't let that be where we're going,* I prayed.

Laurie ducked inside. I swallowed a curse.

Now it felt like there was a flock of birds trapped in my stomach. The rest of us paused at the jagged threshold. No sound came from the other side. I peered within, hoping to catch sight of anything that would alleviate a bit of the mystery. Ease my fear. Aside from the possible flicker of a distant flame, though, there was nothing.

I could feel Collith looking at me intently. "It's not too late to change your mind," he murmured. At some point the guards had stepped back to give us the illusion of privacy. "Walking away isn't an indication of weakness. Sometimes it's the harder choice."

Damon's face rose up, the gaunt-cheeked stranger he'd become. "The only place I'm walking to is that creepy hole," I said flatly.

It seemed to shrink the longer I stared at it. My mind conjured images of monsters and demons waiting in the depths. *Get a grip, Fortuna.* Steeling myself, I hurried into the darkness before I could reconsider.

Nothing lunged forward to eat me. Thank God for small favors. Once again my eyes had to adjust; the lighting in here was dimmer than any passage or room I'd seen at Court. The air was cold and dank. After a few seconds, I saw that it was another chamber made of rock and dirt. It was as long as the throne room, but with a much lower ceiling.

Fae awaited us, of course. They were crowded on a high, rocky ledge around the doorway. Surprisingly, little conversation passed among them. Their finery tinkled and flashed, but their expressions were wary, which sent alarms blaring through my head. Why should they be afraid, too?

Collith and his guards had entered close behind me. With gentle fingers, the Unseelie King took hold of my elbow—I still jumped—and steered us to the right. I noticed Laurie, then, standing separate from the throng. Collith and I stopped beside him. As more faeries came in, I turned to survey the rest of the space. Beyond the ledge, there was only water. Its surface was like black ice, not a ripple or wave in sight. Torches lined the walls, but the ones that hovered over the pool looked like they hadn't been lit in a long, long time. Moss covered several of them. My sense of unease heightened.

In the meantime, the crowd also continued to grow. I didn't pay attention to them until there was a flash of copper. Jassin, of course. As I had hoped, there was a smaller figure beside him. "Damon," I whispered. As though he'd heard the small sound, Damon spotted me. He took a step in my direction, looking desperately like he wanted to say something. Quick as a snake,

Jassin grabbed my brother's arm and hauled him back. He spoke in Damon's ear. Properly cowed, Damon fixed his gaze onto the floor.

It was just the motivation I needed—any trace of uncertainty about going through with the trial vanished.

"Here we go," Laurie muttered. I tore my attention away from Damon and followed his gaze.

The crowd was parting to reveal a heavyset male, and he was the most unattractive fae I'd ever seen. His head had been shaved, revealing a lumpy scalp. His forehead seemed overly large, protruding over his eyes. His lips gleamed like two flesh-toned slugs. His clothing, though, was another story. The robes he wore were silky and colorful. Earrings gleamed in his earlobes, bright and blue as sapphires. For all I knew, they probably were. Dozens of bead necklaces encircled his neck. They made a sound like rain as he shuffled forward.

Collith left my side to speak with him. The other faerie rumbled back. Their voices were so low I couldn't make out what they were saying.

"He's called the Tongue," Laurie informed me under his breath. "Faeries who are granted his position study magic for centuries. He is held in the highest regard, sort of like how the humans view their priests or popes."

Everyone was raptly watching the exchange between the king and the Tongue. No one paid any heed to me and Laurie. "What does he do?" I asked.

"In a nutshell, he performs spells for the crown."

"So he's a witch, then."

Laurie shook his pale head. "Not quite. Witches get their power from demonic sources or nature. The Tongue draws his from Fallen blood."

Before I could ask what the hell that meant, the large faerie stepped away from Collith. A collective hush fell. To my horror, he turned and began walking toward me, slow and steady. His feet were bare and made slapping sounds against the rock. Once he was close enough, he reached out without any explanation and wrapped his swollen fingers around my wrist. A lifetime of avoiding touch and the fear shrieking inside me wanted to immediately yank free. Just as I was about to give in to the urge, Collith caught my eye. He didn't say a word, but a soothing warmth traveled down the bond. I breathed hard but managed to stay still.

Using his free hand, the Tongue pulled a small object out from the folds of his robe. No, not just a small object—a knife. This time, I did try to jerk away, but he held me fast. In a swift, practiced movement, the Tongue opened a small cut across my palm. I didn't have a chance to react; at a signal from the big faerie, Collith moved to join us.

Speaking in the angelic language, the Tongue raised his voice so it boomed through the entire cavern. Words poured from him like water. Despite the dread curling in my stomach, I was mesmerized. His expression was a combination of gravity and concentration as he did to Collith what he had just done to me. The king didn't so much as flinch when the knife touched his skin. Once it was done, the Tongue brought our hands together, smearing our blood.

Magic prickled around us. Looking for more reassurance, I searched Collith's eyes. He gazed back for just a moment before giving his full attention to the faerie chanting to our left. Of course the Tongue was still speaking Enochian, so I had no way of knowing what was happening.

Once again, Laurie shifted closer. His breath tickled my neck as he translated. "The Queen of the Unseelie Court must possess extraordinary strength, for the crown is heavy. She must be as cunning as the Dark Prince, for she will defend our doors. She must be devoted to the people, for not all have power or wisdom to do so themselves. Fortuna Sworn has put herself forward to prove her worthiness. On this night, she shall undergo the first trial. If she should attempt to depart before the task is completed, she will be put to death by his Majesty, the King of the Unseelie Court. Do you accept this candidate, Collith of the bloodline Sylvyre?"

Collith didn't hesitate. Whatever reservations he'd had earlier were carefully locked away, where not even I could reach them. "I do," he answered in English, probably for my benefit. The sound echoed, and the dark room swallowed it, hunching over it like a beast over a carcass. I wanted to run so badly. Run away from all of this, hide in my little house, and never think of faeries again.

For the first time since his arrival, the Tongue fixed his disconcerting eyes on me. They were such a light blue they almost looked white. Laurie quickly made himself scarce. "For your first task, you will be given a single weapon," the faerie said, also in English. The abrupt shift startled me.

In response to this, Nuvian stepped closer. He held out his sword. It flashed in the weak light, sharp-edged and nearly transparent. Collith released me and stepped back. Trying not to appear tentative, I grasped the hilt firmly. I was still unprepared for the weight; it was heavier than it looked. "What am I supposed to do with this?" I demanded, sounding more composed than I felt.

No one said anything. I glanced toward the silent, glittering spectators. Most were staring my way, as expected, but some faces were turned to the water. It hit me, then—I was supposed to go in. Which probably meant something was down there. Waiting. Watching. I turned to Collith and knew I wasn't hiding anything now. The terror was so overwhelming that I felt seconds away from vomiting.

He shifted as though to grip my shoulders, but his hands fell back to his sides. We had to keep up appearances, after all. No favoritism. Not even toward his mate. "You will survive this, Fortuna. That I can promise," he said in a low voice.

"How? How can you promise me that?" I hissed, gripping the sword as though it were a lifeline. "Can you see the future?"

A muscle ticked in his jaw. Not from anger, the bond told me, but from an unwillingness to answer. More secrets, then. Fine. Fuming, I turned away and faced the eerily still water. "How the hell am I supposed to get down there?"

Polite as ever, Collith gestured to the ledge. "There are indents carved into the rock."

I stayed where I was, waiting for some kind of sign, a gong or an announcement from the Tongue. But stillness hovered through the underground cavern. Someone giggled. I allowed myself one last glimpse of Damon. *I love you,* I mouthed. His eyebrows knitted together. He looked surprised and pained all at once. Slowly, I faced the darkness.

Well, no time like the present.

Eyes bored into my back as I walked to the edge of the ledge and peered over. Just as Collith had said, there were gaps in the rock, clearly meant to be climbed. Though it was my first instinct to stall or delay the inevitable, I forced myself to turn around to start the descent. In doing so, my gaze clashed with Collith's again. However calm he appeared to be, worry vibrated up and down the bond. Not exactly encouraging.

My heart was beating so hard I was certain everyone could hear it. There were no handholds, so I grabbed the edge of each gap with my free hand as I went down. The sword scraped against the rock with each movement. As I fit my feet into each step of the rudimentary ladder, I kept expecting them to be slick, like it would be at a dock. But there were no waves down here and the steps were dry as bones. I reached the water too quickly. There at the bottom, I faltered. Now what?

I craned to see any sort of movement or path. There was a small rock at the center of the pool; it protruded from the surface like a frog's head. Unless I intended to linger here or in the water—something my instincts shied away from—it seemed to be the only other place to go. Rigid with fear, I lowered myself into the pool as quietly as possible. It was warmer than I thought it would be.

Dad's voice sounded in my head, remnants of long-ago swimming lessons. *Keep your palm flat, Fortuna. Point your fingertips down. Pull straight back as you roll your shoulder.*

You try swimming with a heavy sword, I thought at him. He didn't respond. God, what I would do just to talk to my father for a few seconds.

As I cut through the water, the watching faeries seemed to forget their apprehension. They filled the silence by calling out bets and jeers. I ignored them, which was easy to do in that moment, as I struggled not to drop the sword and get out of the water as soon as possible. I kept expecting something to grab my ankle and yank me under. Nothing happened. A few yards in, I started to think maybe I'd been wrong about the danger.

Halfway to the rock, though, the underground lake began to boil.

CHAPTER FOURTEEN

*S*team rose all around me. Of course I'd suspected, but the sudden change was confirmation; I wasn't alone down here.

Nearly choking on panic, I frantically closed the distance between me and the rock. I clambered onto it, wishing it were bigger and higher. The sword made a clinking sound as it hit the hard surface. I froze and held it up, worried it had broken, but the colorful glass seemed intact. I found secure footing and straightened.

As I searched the black depths, straining to catch a glimpse of whatever was making it simmer like that, I realized I had a decent view of the faeries. Laurie stood beside Collith and even he looked shaken. Damon was buried in shadow, but Jassin stood in plain sight, an anticipatory smile curving his thin lips. What could excite an ancient faerie who'd seen everything?

Trembling like a child after a bad dream, I turned in circles, still trying to find whatever was coming. The sword in my hand felt like a toy. "Come on, come on, come on," I muttered. It helped to speak out loud, for some reason. My breathing sounded too loud, too ragged.

Then it surfaced.

I caught a glimpse of yellow, reptilian eyes. They latched onto me and seemed to brighten. A snout appeared next, the nostrils flaring, covered in black scales. Terror turned the moisture in my mouth to chalk. With a huff that made the water lap against my rock, the giant head sank back into the darkness and disappeared.

"The Leviathan," I whispered. A dragon from ancient times, first mentioned in the bible. My mother had made sure I knew all the stories, since she'd viewed them as our heritage.

How had the fae captured it? How long had it been down here, confined and hungry?

All at once, I knew what the first trial was. Kill or be killed. And if the Leviathan was still down here, it meant no one had managed to survive yet. How many skeletons rested at the bottom of this lake, abandoned and forgotten? Horror rushed up and clogged my throat. I fought against the feeling, wanting to maintain some semblance of dignity in front of the fae. But I knew there was no way to beat that thing. Here, down in this wet darkness, I was going to join my parents in whatever afterlife awaited.

"Look out!" someone shouted.

An instant later, the water exploded and there was a burst of heat. I caught a glimpse of a long, serpent-like neck as I dove to the side—there wasn't even time to scream. The water closed around me and I felt my bladder release. Not even a second passed before my eyes snapped open. There in the deep, I strained to catch any sign of movement. Everything was so dark. The rock was at my back, leaving my sides exposed. Though I'd need air soon, I was paralyzed with fear.

Open jaws rushed at me.

Bubbles streamed everywhere as I screamed. My survival instincts kicked in, though, and I shot for the surface. The dragon thundered past without touching me. I reached air, gasping, and didn't waste any time getting back to the rock. All I wanted was to go for the ladder, return to safety, but I knew Collith would have to kill me if I did. With one hand, I clambered onto the rock again, barely managing to cling onto the now-slippery ridges.

I stood there, trying to see in every direction at once. There were no telltale ripples or waves, but that meant nothing. It could very well be just beneath the surface, watching me, gathering its strength to leap again. Somehow I was still holding the sword—small miracle I hadn't dropped the thing—and I held it out in a feeble threat. The blade visibly trembled. In the temporary calm, my mind raced. I had to be smart about this. There was no way I'd get close enough to stab it. What were its weaknesses? Had Mom ever covered that during our studies of the bible?

Suddenly there came the sound of something shifting and moaning; the Leviathan was on the move. I jerked to attention, hardly daring to draw breath now. In the tense seconds that followed, the strange noise occurred again. I frowned. What the hell was that? It almost resembled... metal?

Then, in a burst of clarity, I recognized it. A chain.

So that's how they kept it contained.

A frantic, sloppy idea took shape. If I led the dragon around the rock, again and again, eventually the chain would hold it in place... maybe just long enough for me to use Nuvian's sword.

It was a weak plan, but it was better than nothing.

It did mean going back into the water, though, and the thought made a whimper lodge at the back of my throat. I swallowed it and squared my shoulders. For a second, just a second, I let myself glance toward the watching crowd. Damon still wasn't visible, but I felt him there. I saw that hospital room and his small hand clutched in mine. I heard that earnest promise. *From now on, I'll be a better sister. I'll take care of you. Promise.*

"Okay, here I am. Come get me," I breathed, slowly lowering myself, then sitting. I gripped the slick ridges of the rock and slid down. The water had become uncomfortably hot. Once it reached my waist, I decided that was far enough—even this small movement sent ripples across the surface. Once again, I held the sword out. Maybe the Leviathan would do me a favor and throw itself onto the blade.

I'd expected the creature to launch itself at me instantly, but it still didn't make an appearance. I tried not to let myself succumb to the creeping sense of hysteria. *Just wait. It'll come. Watch the water.* I'd seen enough horror movies in my life to prioritize looking behind me, as well.

The seconds ticked past. Each one felt like an eon. It took all my self-control not to scramble out of the water; I felt the same sense of dread as a child in a lake, picturing a creature coming up from below to bite my foot off. I'd never been able to hear my heart to this extent—it was like a song playing from the radio, the bass knob cranked all the way up. I became intimately acquainted with every pulse, every thump. It beat so hard I wondered how my chest wasn't fracturing from the pressure. *Thud. Thud. Thud.*

The Leviathan came from the right.

I saw it from the corner of my eye. As the monster rocketed toward me, its eyes glowing yellow, I thought I was ready. But either it moved even faster than before or I was too slow. Something raked my side and I cried out from the pain of it. I'd tried to throw myself out of range and around the rock as planned. Instead, the force of the dragon's blow sent me into the water again. My scream was cut short and it turned into a wet gurgle. This time, I lost my grip on the sword. Darkness and bubbles filled my vision. A hint of red clouded the depths all around. Blood. I didn't care, though; I was already searching for the Leviathan. I spun and spun, ignoring the agony each movement caused. Where was it? Oh, God, what if it was already coming back? The sword was utterly gone now. There was no way I'd find it.

Get out of the water, instinct screamed. I had just enough reason left to heed it. Fire licked up and down my ribcage as I hurried back to the rock and scrabbled around its perimeter, intending to take a new position and continue on with the plan, regardless of whether I had a weapon or not. If the faeries were making any noise, I was deaf to it now.

I was so focused on not slipping, so busy flinching at every shadow that I almost missed it—a sensation in my mouth that didn't belong. I froze as I absorbed it. Not the coppery tang of blood or the bitterness of tears. It was impossible to describe but still distinctive.

Was that... a flavor?

Holy shit.

I was so desperate that I didn't question it. Water streamed down my face while I searched for the Leviathan, this time with my mind. No fucking way. There it was. A source of warmth, a spot of light. I must not have truly believed I'd succeed, because for an instant, I did nothing. Maybe I'd imagined it. No, it was still there. The sensation was fainter than normal, which was surprising for a creature so gigantic, but apparently it was still enough.

The Leviathan had fears.

Urgency made me clumsy in using my abilities. I hadn't been this sloppy in digging through a mind since I was a child. The dragon felt the invasion; the entire cavern rumbled. Someone shrieked. I clutched onto the rock so hard that lightning bolts of pain shot through my fingers. Somehow, though, I focused. The images I found were disjointed and random. I struggled to make sense of them, knowing the clock was working against me.

The Leviathan was coming this way again. This time, it created a stir in the water.

In the odd structure of its mind I saw dripping walls, stalac-tites, and a rusted chain. Just like that, I understood—this crea-ture was already surrounded by its fear. It lived the nightmare at every moment. Above all else, it loathed being trapped down here.

Pity swelled in me.

Stop that. This thing was just trying to eat you, I reminded myself. Even so, when I went to test the full effect of my abilities on it, I thought of a spring breeze instead of the cruel illusions I normally used. I couldn't tell if it was working, but the dragon hadn't emerged from the depths or dragged me down to a watery grave. Hopeful now, I added trees and a blue sky.

A burst of hot air stirred my hair.

I stopped breathing. It took every bit of self-control I'd built up over the years to maintain hold of the illusion. It wavered for a moment, then solidified again. I didn't dare turn, but I could sense the Leviathan there, in the water next to me. I'd been so focused on our mental connection that I hadn't seen it surface. With herculean effort, I swallowed the scream ricocheting up my throat. Seconds ticked by and nothing happened. I was afraid to even blink; there was an irrational idea in my head that if I stayed very, very still, the dragon wouldn't hurt me.

Waiting became agony. I knew it was still there, because every time it exhaled through its nostrils, the breath surrounded me. Like I was inside of a preheating oven. Finally, I couldn't stand it any longer. My heart hammered as I slowly turned.

The dragon floated beside the rock, so close I could reach out and touch it. It didn't move. Didn't open its eyes. A semblance of reason ebbed back. Experimentally, I inserted rolling hills to the illusion between us. The Leviathan immediately made a humming sound, almost like a cat's purr. Animals didn't respond to my power—their mind was either too simple or the machinations of a Nightmare too complex—which meant that this creature had a consciousness closer to that of a human.

And I was supposed to kill it.

There was no time to wrestle with my conscience; the rules of the trial hadn't changed. If I tried to walk away, I was dead. If I failed, Damon would remain in Jassin's grasp. It was either the Leviathan or us. *Forgive me,* I thought, uncertain who I was talking to.

Willing myself to feel nothing, I closed my eyes and delved into its mind even deeper. It didn't struggle. The dragon was firmly in my grasp now; it would do whatever I bid. For a wild moment, I thought about sending a burst of fire in the direction of those gawking faeries, thinking themselves so safe on that ledge. I could almost hear the music of their agonized shouts. But Damon stood among them. He would burn, too.

So I sent it careening against the wall.

The Leviathan saw freedom. A sudden opening to the world it had once known, made entirely of blinding daylight and distant mountains. It didn't even question it; the beast rammed into the unforgiving surface again and again. It screamed the entire time, a sound that was desperation, fury, and pain combined. Blood stained the rocks. Cracks formed. The whole thing seemed to go on forever, but I didn't relent, no matter how much I wanted to.

Tears streamed down my face as the great beast finally slumped. The front of its skull had caved in. Its snout was a destroyed mass of flesh. It slid into the water, leaving a scarlet trail down the wall. Wafts of steam were all it left behind.

A creature of myth and legend reduced to nothing.

Collith's words sounded in my head like a cruel taunt. *Even if you win, you don't win.*

Stillness reigned in the cavern. I lifted my wet face and turned toward the ledge. The fae stood in shocked silence. *You made me do this,* I thought dully, looking at them beneath lids that suddenly felt so, so heavy. The adrenaline had seeped from my veins, leaving sorrow and exhaustion in its wake. I barely had the energy to climb down the rock, sink into the water, and swim back to the stone ladder. It crossed my mind that I should try to retrieve the sword—it might be valuable or have significance to Nuvian—but the thought died before it truly began.

When I reached the top of the ladder, there were no cheers or congratulations. Collith probably sensed my mood through the bond; he placed a blanket around my shoulders but didn't try to touch me or speak. *Don't you dare collapse*, I ordered myself. Without any pomp or ceremony, Collith and I ducked back through the hole and left the gaping faeries behind. If the guards followed us, if Damon spoke, if Laurie tried to signal to me, I was oblivious to it all.

This time I paid no attention to the passages; it was all I could do to put one foot in front of the other. Collith didn't offer assistance, but I knew that if I so much as wobbled, he'd be there. Strange that the one I trusted least was now the one I could depend on most.

Minutes or hours later—both felt entirely plausible—a familiar door appeared on our left. A guard stood in front of it, and at the sight of us, he moved aside. His sword flashed. It was almost identical to the one lying at the bottom of the lake.

A cool hand cupped my elbow and steered me into the room. I was so tired, so ready to get away from the fae that once again I offered no resistance. I was distantly aware of the door closing gently behind me. I shuffled forward. In my mind's eye I saw that streak of blood on the rocks again and again. My grip on the blanket tightened. I started toward the bed, an automatic movement.

"I need to see your injuries."

I looked up at Collith, who'd somehow gotten in the way without my noticing. His cautious tone made it clear that he expected refusal, but my only response was to drop the blanket. A chill raced over my skin, which was a strange sensation for me. Without pausing, I pulled off the sopping tank top. It

187

dangled from my fingers, heavy and dripping. I stood there, utterly topless, unable to care. Collith didn't seem to care, either. He knelt beside me and scrutinized the wounds closely.

"These aren't from its claws," he commented. His breath warmed my skin, which was indicative of just how cold I was. "It must've scraped you with its scales in passing. You were fortunate."

My voice was flat. "That's an interesting word for it."

Collith sighed, flattened his palms against his thighs, and stood. He moved to the chest of drawers. Wood slid on wood. When he came back, there was a billowy white shirt in his hands. He gazed at me for a moment and seemed to arrive at some kind of decision. Briskly, he put the shirt over my head and helped me get my arms through the sleeves. "I don't suppose you'd let me summon Zara?" he asked.

"You suppose right. She already helped me once. I don't need to add to my tab."

"Not all faeries think like that, Fortuna," Collith countered. He appraised me as the shirt settled into place. It smelled so much like him that he may as well have been embracing me. "Would you like to take a bath?"

No. I wanted to go home. But the words stuck in my throat. "I wasn't prepared," I said instead.

Collith's brow creased. He didn't ask me what I meant. He didn't tell me that it would've been impossible to prepare for what happened. "What do you need?" was all he said.

I cast my gaze toward the room of books. "To understand. To have knowledge. To be one step ahead. Do any of those contain information on your kind?"

The Unseelie King didn't hesitate. "Yes, they do. Please, have a seat. You look like you're about to fall over."

He pulled out an antique-looking chair, its legs and edges made of wood, the cushions worn and patterned. I didn't try to hide my relief as I sank down. Collith vanished into the other room. I turned my head to stare at the fire, as something about its noises and movements was so soothing. I gradually became aware of a dampness around my legs, though. When I looked down, I noticed the bottom of my borrowed shirt was already wet. Suddenly I realized I was still wearing the pants.

"Oh," I said tonelessly, beginning to rise. "I'm sorry. Your chair..."

Collith returned with two books in hand and I sank back down. He knelt before me, setting the books on the ground. "I don't care about that. We do need to get those off you, however. May I?"

My old self stirred. "I can do it. But... thank you."

Mom's scholarly voice sounded like a trumpet. *Fortuna, could you pay attention, please? This is very important. I know it may not seem like it right now, but this could come in handy later, okay? Now, lore says to avoid expressing gratitude toward a faerie. They'll take advantage of it and claim you owe them a service or a debt. So don't ever say 'thank you' to one. Ever.*

But Collith said nothing in response to my blunder. He just nodded and left me to it, going to the desk on the other side of the room. I sat frozen for a few seconds, waiting for the other shoe to drop. Collith merely sat down and pulled out a sheaf of papers from the top drawer.

After another moment, I got up to peel the pants off. It took longer than usual because they'd become a second skin. Just as I started to wonder where to put them, Collith returned. He took the pants and nodded at the chair, a silent order. I sat more from curiosity than compliance. Collith retrieved the thick, fur blanket from the bed, tucked it around my bare legs, and handed me one of the leather volumes he'd fetched. Then, still not uttering a word, he went back to the desk and resumed his work. The only sound in the room was the scratching of his pen and the sporadic crackle of the flames.

I gave a mental shrug and opened the book. Its spine creaked.

Thankfully, Collith had selected one written in English. Even so, it was difficult to interpret the slapdash handwriting. He'd brought me a history book. The volume was insanely thick, rivaling the textbooks they'd given us in World History I and II. The content made me think of the bible, ironically enough. It was story after story of infamous faeries or deeds, events or choices. Over half of the pages depicted the dark, complex history between the two Courts. Apparently they'd begun as one, here beneath the ground, and the division occurred when technology began to enter the world. Some faeries believed it was time to integrate amongst them while others clung to old ways and ideologies. The dissension was made permanent when certain events transpired… events that immediately brought Romeo and Juliet to mind. Perhaps Shakespeare hadn't been entirely honest in the inspiration for his famous play.

A paper rustled in the stillness, and I looked toward Collith. His profile, or what I could see of it, was sharp angles and weary responsibility. He wanted to change things, he'd said. Maybe he was going about it much slower than I would've, but what did I know about ruling? About the fae?

Well, I was about to know more.

I forced myself to focus on the tome in my lap. If Dad could see me now, he'd probably be convinced I was bespelled or another creature was wearing my face. The thought made me smile faintly.

Since I wanted to get through as much as possible, I didn't allow myself to linger on the drawings I encountered, however fascinating they were. Soon I was putting the book aside and reaching for the next one. This was a volume entirely about the war tactics a fae general used in their first civil war. While I highly doubted I would ever find myself on a field facing a magical army, I scanned the information anyway.

As I read, Collith continued adding books to the stack. At one point, he also thought to bring me a notebook and pen. He moved so soundlessly that, as usual, I hardly noticed his comings and goings. Every time I lifted my head, there he was at the desk, a picture of the dutiful king.

As the hours ticked past, a total of six books were added to the finished pile. The pages of the notebook filled with my own handwriting. All the while, the edges of sleep drew nearer. At last, when the fire burned low, I sat back and rubbed my eyes. *Just a short break*, I thought, still clutching the pen.

I must've nodded off, though, because the next thing I knew Collith was lifting me into his arms. It felt like part of a dream. I'd been back at the pool, reliving that fear I'd tasted after touching the Leviathan. I said something to Collith—or at least I thought I did—as he lowered me onto the bed. His lips brushed my forehead. "You're safe here," I heard him say. "I won't let anyone hurt you. Not again."

I wasn't certain whether he was really saying those things, and my mouth wasn't working anyway, so I didn't reply. The bed was so soft, so warm. It wasn't until I was lying there, my mind utterly open, that I was finally able to place the clean, almost tasteless flavor I'd experienced from the Leviathan.

Wind. Open sky. Air high above. Sorrow curled around my heart as sleep claimed me.

It was snowing when I arrived at the dreamscape. I felt a snowflake first, a small spot of ice on my cheek, and opened my eyes. The sky was a mass of gray clouds. The moon was there, but it struggled to shine through. The only true source of light came from the house, its windows aglow. Oliver stood in the doorway, hands shoved in his jeans pockets. He wore a wool sweater and his hair was a bit longer than last time. A fire flickered in the room behind him.

Doubtless he would want to know what happened in the time we'd been apart. My stomach clenched at the thought of reliving the trial. But I'd decided not to keep things from him anymore, hadn't I? I started forward, trying to steel myself to say the truth aloud. *I killed a creature that was in the same circumstances as me. Trapped. Angry. Alone. It wasn't a clean death. If it weren't for you and these dreamscapes, I'd probably have nightmares about it for months.*

Halfway to the house, I saw something move in the distance. It was so out of place that I looked toward it immediately. My heart stumbled at the sight of the Leviathan and I jerked to a halt, staring and open-mouthed.

Its flying made me think of a child that had been cooped up inside too long—wild and joyous. The creature's wings, much like a bat's in their transparency, caught the fading moonlight.

It didn't come near me, seeming to prefer flying over the open sea, but the Leviathan was big enough that it was possible to make out details even so far away. I hadn't been able to notice much in the darkness, not to mention the fact I'd been fighting for my life, but now I could see that its scales weren't entirely black. Like a bolt of velvet, they had hints of green that glinted with every tilt and dip. Beautiful.

"Rest in peace," I whispered, my guilt abating somewhat. At least one of us was free.

With an echoing roar, the dragon soared into the churning horizon and vanished.

This time, when I awoke, I knew exactly where I was.

The dull, throbbing pain in my side was gone. I lifted the covers to investigate, part of me already suspecting what I'd find. Yes—the gouges had healed to the point where they were covered in scabs. Still tender, still noticeable with every movement, but I would be able to face the next trial without any difficulty.

I lowered the blanket and swore at Zara, who was walking toward the door. She must've just finished. The faerie turned at the sound of my voice, and at that moment, she was standing directly adjacent to the fire. The last time I'd seen her, we'd been in a dark cell. The light revealed more details of her face. There were slight indentations in her cheeks that might have been dimples, if she were to ever smile. Her eyebrows were thick. Her lips were perfect and pink.

Beautiful, of course, like all the rest.

"You're welcome," Zara said dryly. She pointed at something to my left. "His Majesty wanted to make sure you read that."

"Let's be clear. I don't owe you a thing," I told her, ignoring this. Guilt churned in my stomach—I knew I was being a bitch —but I reminded myself that she was a faerie. I sat up and moved my bare legs to the side. Cold air reached for them greedily. "I didn't ask you to heal me."

Zara didn't acknowledge she'd heard. She walked to the door, opened it, and slipped into the dark passageway beyond. There were guards immediately outside, I saw, but no one spoke as Zara moved past.

Once the door was closed, my gaze fell upon the side table. Instead of food, there was a note waiting on its surface. I picked it up. Collith's handwriting was neat and elegant. *Olorel continues. My presence is required.*

Well, he certainly didn't mince words.

I left the note on the bed and moved to get dressed. The backpack was in its usual spot. I stood over it, strangely reluctant to take off Collith's large shirt. A thoughtful frown pulled at the corners of my mouth as I forced myself to do exactly that. Then I pulled on the only clothes I'd packed—the jeans and plaid shirt I'd been wearing when Laurie arrived with that obscene wedding dress.

There was no way of knowing whether it was night or day aboveground, but I suspected the latter, because my powers were muted. Which meant I couldn't defend myself with them. However much I longed to seek out Damon, it was hard to forget just how badly I'd lost to Jassin in our last encounter. Which made my plan simple—knowledge first, action later.

I sat in the chair I'd been in last night. The fur blanket was neatly folded and draped over its back; it tickled my neck as I got comfortable. Collith must've fetched some books while I was sleeping, because a new stack was waiting for me. I lifted the top one and opened it. The spine let out a brittle sigh.

As with the rest of Collith's collection, the pages were yellowed with age. The words upon them were still faded, but actually typed this time, making it much easier to read. A quick glance revealed that this volume would be about magic. *Finally*, I thought. From the moment I'd met Collith, it had been painfully clear that I needed to know what the fae were capable of. Going off myths and lore had already cost me. So I started at the beginning and resolved to read every word.

Time felt like a dying creature, dragging itself torn and bleeding over the ground. Though there was no clock on the walls, I swore I could hear one of the hands ticking. The fire—who the hell kept tending to it?—crackled with a merriness that I found grating instead of soothing. I shifted restlessly. My attention kept wandering, unable to focus on the book. Again and again, I glanced at that piece of paper on the table.

The smartest course of action would be to stay right here, learn about the fae, and prepare for the next trial. Yes, that was the smartest course... but it wasn't what I wanted to do. No, my mind was in the throne room, where Collith was. I wanted to see him interact with his subjects. I wanted to watch him without him knowing I was watching. My mate was an enigma who was cold one moment and kind the next.

No, Fortuna. Be smart. Damon and survival first. How many times had I sat through movies where the main character acted like an imbecile? *This is what I would've done*, I said to Damon every time.

Without fail, I would proceed to list all the ways I would have acted differently and actually survived.

Well, I wasn't about to be one of those girls now.

Determined, I gripped the edge of the book. I scooted lower in the chair and made a valiant effort to immerse myself in the book again. But that invisible clock didn't stop. *Tick. Tick. Tick.*

In the end, curiosity got the better of me.

Moving in a burst of frustration, I abandoned the book and the chair. I yanked on my boots—the ones I'd worn during the trial were still wet—and started toward the door before remembering that, at the moment, I was virtually defenseless. There was still no sign of my father's knife, so I turned in a circle, searching for something else that could be a weapon. Once again, my eye fell upon the shattered mirror. Perfect.

I fetched one of the broken shards, wrapped most of it in a sock, and tucked it into the waistband of my pants. Once I was ready, though, I just stood there with my palm against the door. *Come on. Open it.* But I couldn't seem to push. It was self-preservation, I told myself. Not cowardice. I was that girl in the movie, about to do something completely asinine that would doubtless get me killed. *She'd deserved it*, the audience would say. *This is what I would have done differently...*

Right on cue, obstinance streaked through me, stronger than any bolt of electricity. The heat of it made me shove the door harder than I meant to. It slammed against the dirt wall and bounced back, closing in my face. My cheeks burned as I opened it again, a little more gently this time. The guards didn't so much as turn their heads. But the female's mouth—she was one I'd never seen before, with cropped red hair—curved slightly upwards.

"Thank you, I'll be here all week," I muttered, hurrying past.

They waited until there was a bit of distance between us before following; I could hear their leather armor creaking with every step. It took me exactly four steps to realize that I had no idea how to get to the throne room on my own. Normally that wouldn't stop me from blundering around, hoping for a clue or a streak of luck, but Jassin, Death Bringer, and the Leviathan were proof that monsters lived in these dark passages. I slowed, then stopped completely. I angled my body toward the two faeries, mulling over the best way to ask for assistance.

"Ach, just spit it out," the female said with a roll of her eyes. Her accent was thick but the words were swift. She was Scottish or Irish.

They both stood there and stared at me. Impatience emanated from the hard lines of their bodies. Despite this, I didn't rush to speak. I phrased the statement carefully. "Okay... I don't know the way to the throne room."

"And?" The female raised her brows and waited. She wanted me to ask for help. I knew better.

"The way I see it, you have two choices," I said, thinking quickly. The torch beside us quivered. It made the shadows on their smooth, pale faces look like living things. "You can follow me around all night—I'm betting you'd miss the shift change and be forced to stay on guard duty much longer than you should've—or you can lead the way. Which will it be?"

It was my turn to wait for a reply. In the silence that followed, I considered using my potential queenship as leverage, but the last thing I needed was another faerie who didn't want me surviving the trials. It was honestly surprising that there hadn't been any assassination attempts. Then again, no one probably thought I would pull it off.

The female was contemplating whether or not to do it; I could see it in the tilt of her head and the twist in her lips. "Úna," the male said beneath his breath. A warning.

"What's the harm?" she asked him, shrugging broad shoulders. "Like the Nightmare said, I'm not prepared to wander around all night. And if she gets killed, she won't say anythin', will she?"

The other guard's nostrils flared. "Who do you think will be blamed if she dies? Or what if His Majesty is displeased that we brought her?"

"He invited me to join him," I interjected. They both fixed dark gazes on me again. The trick to a good lie was to forget that it was, in fact, a lie. I put it in my mind that the scribbled message Collith had written contained longing and warmth. "If you don't believe me, read the note. He left it on the table next to our bed."

Our bed. I knew those were the words they heard most clearly. Neither of them spoke again. After another moment, thick with tension, Úna walked ahead of me and the male fell into step behind. I could practically feel the disapproval rolling off him—he *really* didn't want to help me—but the guard didn't say anything more as we made our way to the throne room.

"How is it that so many of the fae I've met come from different backgrounds?" I asked. "Since you all live here, away from human society?"

It was a question that had been hovering in my mind since meeting Zara. Surprisingly, the male answered me. "Most of us are nephilim," he said shortly.

Dad's lessons had been thorough; I didn't need to ask what a nephilim was. Half-breeds. Creatures with one human parent. Any caste of Fallen—faeries, goblins, shapeshifters, were-wolves—had difficulty reproducing offspring. Though there had to be a scientist or two among our midst, it seemed that no one knew the reasoning behind our infertility. Throw in some human genes, however, and the odds improved. So it wasn't strange that there would be nephilim at the Unseelie Court, really. I should've figured it out sooner.

It was as though Úna wanted to get away from my words; the pace she set was grueling. I didn't have a chance to ask any more questions, as I was too busy trying to catch my breath. We reached the mural room much sooner than I had with Laurie.

The male hung back at the mouth of the passageway, clearly not wanting to be spotted. I barely noticed; my focus was on that doorway at the far end. From here, I couldn't see a single faerie, though the doors were wide open. The air was so quiet and still. Was something wrong?

I took one step toward the doors before Úna seized my arm in a biting grip. "Mind this. Mind that I helped you," she whispered in my ear, her breath hot, her brogue even thicker now. I turned slightly to look at the guard, and I saw a light in her eyes that I'd seen in so many before. Want. Desire. Lust. These faeries were so accustomed to beauty, and their reactions to me so muted, I was already forgetting the effect a Nightmare had on most creatures. Up until now, this one had hidden it well.

I pulled away from her. There were angry marks on my skin where she'd touched me. "Oh, don't worry, I'll remember," I said coolly. Her hand formed into a fist and she watched me go with obvious reluctance. *Be wary of that one*, instinct whispered.

Wondering what he thought of his companion's comment, I glanced behind me, toward where the other guard should've been standing. He hadn't seen our brief exchange; he was already gone, hurrying back to his post, no doubt. Had Collith assigned them to protect me or his precious chambers? The latter, it seemed. I tried to ignore the odd sting this realization caused. The blood-filled mural loomed overhead as I finished crossing the room. I hesitated just outside the doorway. Then, erring on the side of caution, I peered around the corner rather than striding right in.

The scene was like something from a Shakespearean play.

I knew my eyes were huge as I stepped fully into view. The very air felt bloated with fae, like a tick swollen with blood. They covered the flagstones, the tables, the benches, the dais. Most were in various states of undress, their finery torn or discarded. Some were outright naked. Bare skin gleamed in the firelight.

And every single one of them was unconscious.

Even Collith.

I stared in his direction, my heart picking up speed. Had something happened? Was this some sort of sabotage or spell gone wrong? No, I concluded, it was more likely the fae had just consumed so much wine they'd been reduced to this.

The distance between me and Collith made it difficult to see much of his features, but from how he was slumped and still, he was obviously comatose like all the rest. Despite this, he was still apart. Other. Different. He sat on that twisted throne, the highest one in the room. Slowly, I started making my way toward him.

With every step, I took in the spectacle around me.

It was a sensation similar to being at the zoo, disconcertingly close to an animal that could easily kill you, and all that offered protection was a single sheet of glass. I stepped over faerie after faerie, half-expecting one of them to lurch awake, but my luck held. Chests rose and fell with the breathing of deep sleep. Not dead, then; they'd literally drunk themselves to sleep. I breathed a little easier. There were puddles everywhere, some dark-colored and others light. I didn't look any closer to figure out what they were. Food and bones also littered the flagstones.

After what felt like hours, I ascended the stairs—the soft sounds my shoes made were piercing—and stopped directly in front of the Unseelie King. Our toes nearly touched. I searched the area behind the chair, expecting to see stoic faces looking back at me. Where were his guards?

Collith's only protection seemed to be a faerie sleeping face-down nearby. The male's bottom half was draped down the stairs. His hand rested on a plate of food, as though he'd been reaching for one more chicken leg before succumbing to oblivion. Next to him was a bird-boned female, also asleep, wearing a brilliant gown of gold. One of the sleeves was covered in blood.

I quickly returned my gaze to Collith. He slept so deeply that the bond between us was dark. It occurred to me, suddenly, that this was an opportunity. The shard of mirror burned in its hiding place against my hip. It would be so easy. So quick. No one would be the wiser, either; who'd suspect the Nightmare that had been found asleep after the murder, anyway? Killing Collith would send a shockwave through the Court and Damon and I could make our escape during the chaos. It would also take care of the pesky mating bond, in the process.

Hell, I could kill all of them, while I was at it. It would probably save hundreds—if not thousands—of human lives. No one would mourn the Unseelie Court.

Never in my life had I thought so casually about ending another creature's life, and here I was, contemplating the benefits and consequences of eliminating every single one in this room. Was it the influence of living amongst fae? Or just what survival had forced me to become? Perturbed, I refocused on Collith, wishing I could ask him.

It struck me, then, that I'd never truly been able to stare at my mate. Knowing this chance might never reoccur, I studied him as though I'd never seen him before.

His eyelashes were so long that they feathered against his skin. *He has the nose of a king,* I thought, hating how ridiculous the thought felt. But he did. His mouth was, in a word, sensuous. His jaw was not quite square, yet it was pronounced and strong. The hollow of his throat, too, was exquisitely defined; I had a strange urge to bend down and press my lips against it. His hair gleamed from the flickering flames around us, not a simple shade of brown, but with strands of gold and red. That stubborn, thick lock was right back in its spot, now lodged beneath the crown. The crown itself had tilted, making Collith look like a boy playacting at being king.

It took a few seconds to realize that I hadn't even noticed the scar. It had become so much a part of him, in my mind, that I'd dismissed it entirely.

I wasn't sure what that meant, exactly, but it bothered me. My focus deliberately shifted to his arms, which swelled with muscle, down his straight torso, and to his firm thighs. The pants he wore were very, very tight, and I had no trouble examining the considerable bulge there. My core contracted in reaction. The rest of me tensed, too, as I waited for Collith to sense arousal through the bond and open his eyes. When he didn't, though, I relaxed again and returned to my examination.

Every part of this faerie emanated grace and power. If ever there was a time to kill him, it would be now, while he was vulnerable and unprepared. He'd have no chance to summon the heavenly fire or whatever other weapons he had in that mysterious arsenal.

And yet, despite every reason and logic, I couldn't bring myself to pull out the shard. Fear held me back, yes, but something else, too. A reluctance to end this creature that I was only just starting to know. An unwillingness to put an arrow through the magnificent stag's heart.

I glared at Collith and wondered if God had created his angels beautiful for practical reasons, rather than aesthetic ones. A beautiful thing was much harder to destroy than an ugly thing.

Growling in frustration, I swung away.

Laurie stood behind me.

I froze at the sight of him. My heart lurched into a panicked gallop. How much had he seen? Had my thoughts been at all obvious as I'd been standing there? Thank God I didn't reach for the mirror shard. *Say something, Fortuna!* instinct screamed. Striving to sound casual, I asked, "What happened here? Where are the guards?"

"This is usually how Olorel ends—not with a bang, but with collective snoring." Laurie shrugged, a liquid movement. "As for the guards, I'm not entirely certain. Maybe Collith sent them away."

K.J. SUTTON

"What? Why would he do that?"

He gave no answer. My instincts were shrieking like a smoke alarm. There was something different about him, I realized. It seemed like every time I encountered Laurie, another layer of him had fallen away, revealing an entirely new one.

This time, the layer had revealed a faerie. Somehow, at some point, I'd stopped thinking of him as one. That had been my first mistake. His t-shirt and jeans were gone, replaced by a crisp gray suit. The button-up shirt—so white that it had to be brand-new—strategically allowed a glimpse of his skin, which was smooth and golden.

"I don't like games, Laurie," I informed him, hoping he hadn't noticed the way my eyes had lingered in the direction of those undone buttons. There was a warning in the words. After killing the Leviathan, something within me had hardened. Or just broken.

Hearing it, he raised his pale brows. "Then why are you playing one?"

Conscious of Collith sitting a few feet behind us, I moved away from the dais. Laurie trailed after me, hands in his pockets, as though he didn't have a care in the world. His tan shoes looked like Italian leather. Who the hell was he? Because I was starting to think the browbeaten slave had all been an act. "I'm doing this for Damon," I hissed.

"Are you?"

His tone was polite, interested, but I sensed the challenge lurking beneath. My patience was a thread swiftly unraveling. "What's that supposed to mean?" I demanded, forgetting that we were surrounded by dozens of slumbering monsters. I darted a glance at the fae closest to us. Not a single one of them stirred.

Laurie didn't seem too concerned; he kept his gaze on mine as he said, "We should really stop answering questions with

202

questions. It makes everything so confusing. But I do appreciate how it prolongs our conversation."

He's flirting with me, I thought. This time it was unmistakable. What about his so-called loyalty to Collith?

Suddenly it occurred to me that I had no idea what Laurie's motives truly were. He'd pledged himself to Collith the night we met, but I didn't know then that faeries could lie. I'd also been desperate for an ally. If Laurie wasn't dedicated to Collith, what was his angle in helping all this time? In speaking to me now?

He was so fond of games. Fine, I'd play. "Well, you obviously have a theory," I said at last.

Before Laurie could respond, I made for the far doorway, gingerly stepping over bodies and trash. I didn't look behind to see if Laurie followed, but I strained to hear his footsteps. The only sound I could detect was that of a faerie violently snoring.

When I reached the doorway again, there was no sign of Úna and her companion. Well, here's to hoping Laurie took the bait, because otherwise I would probably get lost in the tunnels. I swallowed a flutter of nerves in my throat and marched into the darkness.

The first few forks and turns were easy. Once I ventured into the heart of the maze, though, I began to lose confidence. Most of the doors here hadn't been carved, so there was no discernible way to tell the difference between passages. It wasn't until I was starting to truly get nervous that Laurie fell into step beside me. As always, his appearance was sudden and soundless.

A sound of relief nearly escaped me. At the last second, I held it back, though. Couldn't have him thinking he'd gotten the upper hand. I felt my face settle into a dispassionate mask. Just then, however, I was hyper-aware of his hand, which swayed so close to mine.

How had I never realized before that Laurie had never touched me? Not even when he'd been applying makeup to my face; he'd used a brush every single time. He knew I was a Nightmare—doubtless it was why he'd been so careful to avoid physical contact. What secrets lurked beneath his skin? Would his fears show me what he was capable of?

It was this very thought that made me put some distance between us. Pissing Laurie off was too risky right now. Like it or not, I needed him.

We walked for a minute or two in silence. Thankfully, Laurie guided the way without forcing me to ask. It was time I learned more about this enigmatic faerie, but I refused to speak first. I'd discovered a long time ago that most people couldn't stand silence, and the words they chose said everything.

Yes, but you learned that from humans, reason pointed out.

Before I could form a counterargument—great, I was arguing with myself now—Laurie's voice penetrated the stillness. "Decades ago, I was an addict," he said, detached, as if he spoke of another person. "Meth, cocaine, heroin. If something new came onto the scene, no matter how little was known about it, I was the first in line to give it a try. A human would've died living the way I was."

I pretended to be uninterested, another tactic I hoped would encourage him to say more. "Fascinating story. Any chance you're getting close to the end?"

"There was one drug even more consuming than the rest," he continued, ignoring me in a manner much like Collith's. "One drug that I still crave, even after surviving withdrawals and attending all those meetings."

We'd reached the king's rooms already, and once again, there was no sign of the guards. Suddenly I couldn't wait to return to those books and gain some kind of advantage over these creatures. Or at least stop feeling like a child standing before a vast, unstoppable sea. *Your mask is slipping. The game isn't over,* that quiet voice reminded me. I halted in front of the door and contemplated it for a moment, as though I were debating whether to just go in. The carving looked alive in the firelight. "What drug is that?" I asked after a notable pause.

Laurie had stopped, too. He was standing closer than I'd realized. He didn't respond straight away; he studied me, his eyes bright and searching, as though he could see thoughts written there in ink or blood. He lifted his hand, as though to touch my cheek. Even though it was what I'd wanted a few minutes ago, I tensed, about to move away. He dropped his hand before I could. His expression was... troubled.

"Power," he answered finally. I blinked, struggling to remember the original question. *What drug is that?*

The trembling stillness between us shattered. I almost laughed in his face. He thought I wanted the throne?

A dozen retorts rose to my lips, but what would be the point in arguing? If I had my way, we would soon never see each other again. "Think what you want," I said, pushing the door open and effectively ending the game. *Unless the game never ends*, that voice whispered. I resisted the urge to snarl at it.

Hinges whined into the silence. I moved over the threshold and faced Laurie. Once again, he was studying me with those metallic eyes of his. It was unnerving, especially when I didn't know anything about his loyalties or abilities. Maybe he could influence emotions. Maybe he could take my life with a single kiss. Good grief, I'd even turned my back on him. Was I trying to get myself killed? My fingers twitched, yearning to reach for that shard of mirror still tucked away.

When I finally spoke, the air between us felt thick with words unsaid. "I'm here for my brother, and once he's free, we're walking out of here," I snapped. I felt betrayed, somehow. As though the friendship he'd lured me with should have been genuine. It was my fault, though; I'd forgotten what he was. "I'll leave the crown at the door."

Laurie's expression was a blank mask now. "Nothing is ever that simple," he remarked.

He was right and I knew it. But I couldn't stand letting him have the last word. I grasped the edge of the door and gazed up at him unflinchingly. Never again would I forget. "Well, it's like you said. I'm not a faerie."

Before he could respond, I shut the door in his face.

CHAPTER FIFTEEN

*I*t turned out that the conversation with Laurie was exactly what I needed.

After using the bucket—I cringed the entire time—and wolfing down one of the protein bars I'd brought, I went back to the stack of books with renewed vigor. For the first time, I was thankful there was no clock in here; I would've lost precious seconds glancing at it. Worrying. Dreading. The second trial loomed closer and closer. Collith had mentioned they would take place, one by one, at the same time over the next three days.

I finally learned a few things that might come to be useful. Some spells that could very well save not only me, but other humans, too. I turned on my phone and took a picture of the pages—data didn't work down here, of course, but that didn't affect the camera—since there was no way I was memorizing the complex words. Having them might come in handy, later.

Just as I started to put my phone down, an odd video in the photo albums caught my eye. The screen was entirely black. With a jolt, I suddenly remembered what it was—I had recorded

Collith's wedding vows. After everything that had happened, I'd completely forgotten about it.

My curiosity was piqued now. Just as I started to press the white circle that would play Collith's words, the door opened. I jumped and shoved my phone under the cushion, as though I'd been caught doing something forbidden. Three women came in, carrying a heavy-looking tub between them. Their clothing was ragged and their frames too thin. I rose, but none of them looked my way. They set the tub down in the middle of the room and walked out. *Okay,* I thought. *Thanks for the tub, I guess.*

Just as I moved to sit down again, the women reappeared. Now they each carried a wooden bucket. One by one, they dumped water into the tub. Steam rose toward the ceiling. I started to ask them if I could help, but once again, they all left. This time, I didn't sit. As I suspected, they returned a few minutes later, their buckets once again full to the brim. "Where is the water? I want to help," I insisted. It irked being waited on by humans who had no choice in the matter. But the women ignored me, and by the time I considered following them out, they were already gone. I poked my head into the passageway—there were two guards I'd never seen before—and there was no sign of them. Book forgotten, I paced in front of the fire.

The next time the women appeared, there was a finality in the way they poured the water. I'd missed the boat, apparently. "Wait," I said as they turned to go yet again. "When was the last time those assholes let you bathe? Stay. Use the tub."

The tallest woman paused. She wouldn't look me in the eye, forcing me to stare at the greasy part in her dark hair. "For you," she said in broken English, gesturing jerkily at the tub. One of the other women was draping clothes over a chair. It was nearly identical to the outfit I'd worn during the first trial. In the handful of seconds I took to notice this, they all hurried out and closed the door behind them.

The bucket in the corner had been replaced, too. That wasn't embarrassing at all.

I sighed and fully turned toward the bath they'd prepared. Petals floated on the water's surface, emitting a floral smell into the air. My muscles ached just imagining the heat, the momentary lapse from this underground chill. While I was Fallen, and therefore impervious to cold, it still wore on my psyche—the constant darkness and cold. It had begun to feel like I was trapped in some kind of purgatory. I shifted from foot to foot, eyeing the steam rising off that clear surface. I tried to think of any reason why using it would be like giving in or losing ground.

Oh, what the hell.

Moments later, my clothes were nothing more than an abandoned pile on the ground. With cautious movements, I stepped in. Dear God. I nearly melted the rest of the way down.

For a while, time lost meaning. My entire world narrowed down to the delicious warmth and the soothing sounds of the water lapping against the sides of the tub. It almost felt like every second of pain or horror seeped from me.

The next trial is in a few hours.

The thought came without warning. Though the words were quiet—nothing more than a whisper—my heart pounded fast and hard. I leaned forward to splash water on my face, willing the heat to wash everything away again. But it was no use; the thought had entered, unpacked its things, and made itself a permanent home inside me. Now it was all I could think about. What did the fae have in store tonight? What could be worse than an ancient beast that breathed fire?

Suddenly the door opened. I stiffened, torn between the urge to cover myself or dive for the shard of mirror. When I saw it was Collith, I relaxed somewhat. Before I could form some kind of greeting, he turned slightly to say something to Nuvian. Once again, I seized the chance to stare. I wondered where the king had changed; he looked more ordinary than when I'd seen him asleep on that throne.

This was the faerie that had visited me at Bea's. His hair was artfully tousled. Dark jeans hung low on his hips and a white button-up clung to his every muscle. Collith faced me and I instantly averted my gaze. "Where did you go today?" I asked. The question emerged faintly bitter, though I didn't mean it to be.

Voices sounded from the passage and boots crunched over dirt—it must've been a shift change. Ignoring the disturbance, Collith sat on the floor next to me and rested his forearms on the tops of his knees. All at once, I remembered I was naked. A furious blush crawled up my face as I hugged my knees against me. The water protested this abrupt movement, nearly sloshing over the sides.

"I went back to the bar," Collith answered. His hazel eyes darted down. He didn't try to hide it.

But I was too startled to care. At his response, I blinked. "Bea's? Why?"

"To check on the humans there; I know you care about them. They're doing fine, by the way. Worried about you, of course, but fine." Collith got onto his knees and gently took the sponge from my fingers. "May I?"

No, I said promptly. But nothing left my mouth. I sat there, being ripped in half by terror and desire. The real answer was that, yes, I wanted to feel his touch again. Our kiss in the woods was never far from my mind. Even after the truths Collith had withheld, the words he hadn't said, the battles he hadn't fought. How pathetic was that? Was it some kind of Stockholm Syndrome, or was I just that weak?

Collith was still waiting, his gaze steady, patient, as if he had all the time in the world. *Well, actually, he does*, that inner voice reminded dryly. I couldn't bring myself to give Collith permission, though. It felt like my mouth had been glued shut. It also felt like I would be betraying someone—Damon, probably, or myself.

Maybe Collith sensed this through the bond; he stopped waiting for me to say the words and began running the sponge over my skin. My core clenched and tingled. Without thinking, I leaned forward to give him better access. "When do Úna and the other guard come back?" I asked abruptly. Anything to keep from acknowledging what was happening between us. I allowed myself a single glance toward Collith.

A shadow passed over his lovely face. He focused on the motions of his hand. "They won't be returning, actually."

"Why not?"

Collith tilted his head in that way he always did. He avoided looking at me. Why? Was the almighty faerie king ashamed? "I am still a relatively new ruler," he said matter-of-factly. From his side of the bond, the darkness was very still, almost deliberately so. "I haven't earned much loyalty, and loyalty is difficult to find in a faerie, anyway. If some in the Court were to catch wind that I ordered my guards to protect you at the cost of a fae life, there would be rumblings of unrest. More than there already are, I should say. So I told those two to guard my rooms, instead, since that would be accepted. They knew what I really wanted, though; Úna and Abe aren't fools. So you can imagine my displeasure when I learned you'd been wandering the passages alone."

I hadn't been alone, really. Although, after our conversation last night, I wasn't sure whether Laurie would intervene if my life were in danger. But Collith was being surprisingly forthcoming, for once—it was the first time he'd readily answered one of my questions without any dodging or dancing—and I wasn't about to bypass this opportunity. "Why did you want to be king, again?" I asked, trying to hide a wince as the sponge pressed slightly on a bruise along my collarbone. I hadn't even known it was there; it must've happened during the battle with the Leviathan. "Honestly, it seems like a shitty gig."

Collith laughed. Strangely enough, the sound made my stomach flutter. "You have such a way with words. Yes, it is, indeed, a 'shitty gig.' Most days, I feel as though I've made no difference here. The fae loathe change and they resist it at every turn."

"Then why do it? Especially if there's a line of faeries just waiting for their chance?"

"That's exactly why," Collith said. He leaned closer to run the sponge along my chest. I tensed, but he didn't dip lower or make an advance. His scent teased me for the hundredth time, so subtle and appealing. Collith settled back again, not seeming to notice my reaction. "Given a chance, the faeries in that long line would be tyrants. They'd relish in the corruption. They'd nurture it. The human disappearances would increase. Down here, slaves would be treated even worse, if you can believe that. I may not do much, but I hold them at bay as much as I can."

I frowned at the water and considered this. His logic was twisted, yet noble, at the same time. What would I have turned out like, if I'd been raised amongst my species? If I hadn't been fortunate enough to learn countless lessons at my father's knee?

I could feel Collith watching my face. The silence had stretched too long as I'd been thinking. And those thoughts frightened me; they reeked too much of compassion. Feeling like a coward, I looked down as I spoke. "I won't pretend to know anything about politics or faeries. However, from my experience, loyalty is rarely something that's just handed over. You have to do something that inspires it."

"Spoken like a true queen," Collith said softly. My eyes darted to his, startled, and our gazes locked. *Hazel*, I decided. *His eyes are hazel, not gray.*

I was saved from having to respond—just then, the sponge finally touched one of the lash marks on my back. I made an odd, faint sound and stiffened. A strong burst of emotion vibrated down the bond, entirely unexpected after how quiet it had been all this time. Collith went still and stared at the network of scars. His dark brows drew together.

"I made sure to feel every single lash," he murmured.

I frowned in confusion. "What do you mean?"

Collith seemed to shake himself. He resumed his administrations, making them even gentler, somehow. "During times of heightened emotion, the bond is more... navigable, perhaps," he explained, his breath teasing my wet skin. "It's how I was able to take your voice. We're already able to feel what the other is feeling, but in circumstances like the tribunal, that can translate to the physical as well."

I didn't know what to say. My mind flashed back to his grip on those armrests. Back to his pale fingertips. That night, I'd assumed it was borne of excitement or habit. What if it had been something else, though? A voice in his head, screaming at Collith to do something?

I was beginning to understand this faerie king. He wasn't evil, or cruel, or selfish. He was someone with a cause and nothing would pull him away from it. Too often, though, someone with a cause lost sight of themselves. The lines between right and wrong blurred. Passion became fanaticism. Collith seemed precariously close. After all, he hadn't been deterred from his purpose even when it meant watching his mate being whipped within an inch of her life. I could hardly judge him for it. Look at the limits I was willing to go for my own cause—saving Damon.

If it meant sacrificing Collith, or myself, or anyone else, I'd probably do it. In this, Collith and I shared some similarities. The realization made me deeply uncomfortable, so I sought to change the subject. "How are you such an expert on mating bonds?" I questioned, saying the words too loudly.

At this, a faint smile touched Collith's lips. His eyes went hazy with remembrance. All the while, though, he didn't stop trailing the soapy sponge along my shoulders, chest, and arms. "Growing up, I pestered my mother with questions. I was enamored with the idea of a best friend and a lover tied into one. I couldn't wait to find her," he added.

We were back in dangerous territory. *Lover.* Something we were not, but something both of us were thinking of now. The ambiance didn't help. The crackling fire, the flickering lights and shadows, the steaming water. Once again, Collith's eyes caught and held mine.

I like that he can see my real face, I thought suddenly.

I tried to look away, but something inside me resisted. As we continued to stare at each other, I felt my nipples harden. Collith's gaze dropped, taking note of this fact. At a leisurely pace, his hand dipped into the water, where he abandoned the sponge, and then his fingers trailed back to the point they'd started at. They skimmed along my collarbone. Down the column of my throat.

A sensation spread through me, as though someone was running the tip of a feather over every inch of skin. There was no denying it—I wanted him. I would bear scars from his Court on my back for the rest of my life, but somehow this faerie still made me ache. When I offered no resistance, his bold fingers drifted down the middle of my chest, then over the curve of my breast. His thumb teased my nipple in slow circles. Bumps raced across my skin.

Still giving me a chance to protest, Collith slowly dipped his head and pressed his lips to my neck. The feel of his tongue made me clench and tingle. I bit my lip to hold back a sigh. He continued to kiss and suck while his hand finally slid down my stomach and back into the soapy water.

The moan burst from me.

His touch was... exploratory. Reverent. I rested my head against the ridge of the tub and couldn't stop myself from moving against his hand. Collith's fingers didn't dip inside, as I anticipated. Instead, they stayed on the surface, rubbing steadily at first. Then faster and faster. I bucked, helpless against the sensations coursing through me. He knew exactly where to keep his hand. Water splashed onto the floor.

I came in a smattering of seconds, the moment I reached that peak one of deafening and all-consuming pleasure.

Seconds passed. Everything felt slowed down. Heavy. I opened my eyes and Collith's face came into focus, as though I had adjusted a camera lens. His eyes were glittering. When he stood, I saw the bulge straining at his jeans. *Want*, the drowsy part of me whispered. I sat up a little, on the verge of saying something dangerous, foolish, and completely unlike myself. *Don't stop.*

"As much as I'd like to stay and admire, I'll leave you to dress," Collith said, the words thick. He cleared his throat. *So you do affect him*, that voice noted smugly. Holy shit, it was hot in here. I needed to get out of the water. "And someone will bring a tray of food—you haven't eaten much since you've been here."

It took another second for me to pay attention to what he was saying. The same instant I comprehended that he was actually leaving, he was already at the door. *Wait, seriously?* I nearly blurted. Collith nodded in farewell, wearing a half-smile that I'd never seen before, and allowed the darkness to swallow him.

In the minutes following his absence, my heartbeat slowed to its normal rhythm. Soon enough, self-loathing poisoned my insides. So I was no different from the rest of the females here that I'd seen draping themselves all over the fae. Groupies. Mindless. Morons. Collith hadn't even had to try, goddamn it. One touch and I'd practically dissolved. Had he known this feeling would hit me? Was that why he'd left so quickly?

Still berating myself, I finally got out of the tub. The cold air was a welcome slap to the face. After toweling dry, I dressed in the outfit the three women had brought. Next I contemplated the huge, tempting bed. That orgasm had left me drowsy, but I didn't want to sleep. Oliver knew me too well—one look and he'd be asking me what was wrong. That wasn't a conversation I was ready for. Eventually I'd tell him what Collith had done to me in that tub. What hot, slow, delicious things he'd done.

Get a grip, Fortuna. I swallowed and tried to ignore the part of my body that was throbbing again at the mere thought of Collith's fingers. Okay, so, there would definitely not be any sleeping.

A sigh left me, long and resigned. I picked up a new book from the pile, sat down, and went back to work.

The entire room was silent.

Even the sound of my gum chewing seemed obtrusive—I'd discovered the piece of Dubble Bubble in the bottom of my backpack. Feeling defiant, I chewed louder.

Once again, I found myself standing before the throne. This time, I stood alone. This time, I had slain a dragon. This time, I looked at Collith without expectation. He would not help me. He would not intervene if things took a turn for the worse. He was not an ally, but the Court's bitch.

I wasn't sure when it had happened, exactly—maybe during the long walk to the throne room, or the moment I'd looked at Jassin and Damon, or in the instant I lifted my face toward Collith and saw the detached king looking back—but at some point my fear had been overridden by anger. I was fucking *pissed.* These creatures had broken my brother, tried to break me, and kept the Leviathan in the dark for only God knew how long. Their reign of terror had to end.

Which, I supposed, sort of put me and Collith on the same side.

The Tongue had already performed most of his ritual. There

was a fresh cut across my palm that I hid by clenching it into a fist. He was wrapping up now, the lovely words rolling over me like waves along the ocean floor. There was nothing beautiful about this—these trials only brought death and pain.

Hundreds of eyes bored into my back. I didn't think it was my imagination that the room was even fuller than it had been the last time; word must have spread about the trial. No one had survived this long. They were curious. They were excited.

Jassin's comment slithered through my head. *Few things give me pleasure or reprieve from this endless boredom.*

"For this task, Nightmare, you will not be allowed to ask another creature for aid," the Tongue said in English. It was the first time he'd bothered looking at me since I'd entered the room.

I blew a bubble. It popped in a burst of pink. "Are you going to, like, tell me what I'm doing?"

The corners of his mouth turned down with disapproval. "Find the door that leads to your world."

That was it? I waited, certain there had to be more, but the Tongue just stared back. His eyes were black as oil. My gaze darted to Collith. As per usual, he wore that distant expression, the tips of his long fingers curled over the armrests. Resentment sprouted within me, but I didn't give it a chance to grow. I transferred my gaze to Laurie, who stood beside his sovereign. Gone was the cowering, subservient creature he'd shown me until now. He stood there, his posture relaxed and casual. His bright eyes regarded me with interest, as if curious to see what I'd do next. Once again, questions pounded at me. Had it all been an act? But what was the purpose?

Screw them both. I swung away and strode briskly down the center aisle.

The entire room watched me go, and snatches of whispers floated through the air. *Do you think that she... but what if it doesn't... well I heard... to the viewing room...*

I walked with purpose, every step firm and self-assured, as if I knew exactly where to go. It wasn't until I was out of sight, well into the shadows of the maze, that I stopped and let the panic creep in. I spit out the wad of gum, hoping childishly that one of the fae stepped on it. What now? Blundering around without a plan wasn't going to help me find the door. I pressed my back to the dirt wall and took a few deep breaths. If I was a faerie, where would I put a secret door?

The trial seemed a bit strange to me. Wouldn't the Court want to watch, as they did with the first one? How would they know whether I succeeded?

I could stand here for eons and never understand the way they thought. But I was going about this the wrong way—all I needed to do was stumble across a faerie and discover its fears. Once I had a hold of its mind, the faerie would lead me straight to the door in an attempt to survive whatever it believed was coming. The Tongue had said I couldn't ask for help; he never said I couldn't commandeer it. See, thinking like a faerie wasn't so hard. I just had to be willing to exercise cruelty and resort to trickery.

Having a plan felt like being back on solid ground after hours in the water. I straightened and reached out with every sense I had, hoping to hear footsteps or voices. The passageways were eerily still. This alone was a sign that something unusual was happening at Court; normally the air was filled with pain-filled echoes or sounds that had no name. Perturbed, I rushed down the tunnel and into another, wanting this to be over and done with. The Tongue hadn't mentioned any sort of time limit. If I didn't find the door soon, did they intend to watch me wander the maze until I died of dehydration?

Since I was Fallen, that would take a very, very long time.

Resolve quickened my pace. I turned into new tunnels, again and again, trying to find some pattern in the torches, shades of earth, the doors. Time passed slowly and in a blur. All I had for company was my own thoughts. As the seconds moved into minutes, and the minutes into hours, the edges of fear started to creep in. This was taking too long. Could I use the bond to communicate with Collith? But what if he told the others that I was asking for help?

I swore under my breath. All right, so I wouldn't be speaking to Collith. Where *was* everyone?

At long last, I heard something. I halted in the middle of the passage, hardly daring to breathe. What if I'd imagined it? What if it was an illusion of some kind? I tilted my head. Yes, there it was again. Against my better judgment, I followed the faint noises. Within moments I found their source. To the right, farther down the tunnel, was a doorway. There was no door attached to it, so shouts and clattering dishes poured from the opening. Ever cautious, I stuck to the shadows and peered in.

The smoke was so thick that it tickled the back of my throat and made my eyes sting—there seemed to be only one hole in the ceiling for it to filter through. It was the biggest, strangest kitchen I'd ever seen, comprised of several rooms with high ceilings. There was an open hearth in the middle of everything. Worktables and chopping blocks were scattered throughout. Every surface was littered with tools. A single glance showed knives, ladles, pottery, wooden bowls, forks, and scissors. There was a giant tub along the far wall. In the farthest corner, some kind of gutted animal rested in the dirt. Next to it was a long bench made of masonry stone that held several deep containers. They looked to be lined with ceramic. Charcoal had blackened most of them. A stove, maybe?

I turned my attention to the slaves in the room. Two children turned huge joints of meat on a metal rod. A boy who looked to be twelve or thirteen swept the floor, his motions aggressive and swift. A woman was frantically stirring several pans set over the flames, throwing in a dash of spice now and then. Yet another woman was adding firewood to the base of the hearth, her mouth pinched and weary. The tension in the air was palpable, as if there was a giant clock on the wall, ticking down to some terrible ending.

As I took it all in, thin-lipped with fury, a man rushed past. He didn't see me, as he was a bit preoccupied with the human-sized pot he was carrying.

I darted a glance at the woman who had to be the head cook —she was shrieking at a young girl, whose head was bowed in shame—and hurried after him. As I fully entered the kitchen, a mouth-watering smell assailed my senses. I'd wolfed down a bowl of stew and warm bread earlier, but apparently it hadn't been enough. My stomach rumbled as I forced myself back to the task at hand. I darted past a room full of barrels and another one glinting with wine bottles. The slaves noticed me, of course, but none of them said a word.

The man entered a pantry, of sorts, and didn't realize he'd been followed until he finished putting the pot in a haphazard stack that extended from floor to ceiling. He turned and spotted me. His eyes widened with recognition.

"What's your name?" I asked quickly, hoping to stop him from sounding an alarm.

He glanced toward the cook, though a wall stood between her and us. Shelves of food looked back. "Shameek," he mumbled, shifting as though to leave. The cook's tirade cut short and there was a cracking sound.

"It's nice to meet you. I'm Fortuna." I thrust out my hand and Shameek took it automatically. An instant later, he realized his mistake and jerked his hand back. Too late, of course—his fears coated my tongue. They tasted like wine and dirt. *Faeries.* The pointed-eared creatures were in his dreams and his waking thoughts. He could never escape them.

Another image slipped through. A flash of the human in front of me putting something into a drink. I frowned, wondering at this new development of my abilities, but there was no time to ponder on it. In that instant, the young girl hurried past. She was sporting a fresh cut on her lip. My sense of peril heightened; something told me I needed to avoid that cook. I leaned close to whisper in Shameek's ear. "I know your secret. You've been poisoning one of the faeries."

I didn't think it was possible, but at my words, the man went even paler. "What do you want?" he asked past trembling lips.

You will not be allowed to ask another creature for aid. Good thing I wasn't going to ask for it, then. Hating myself, I forced the next part out. "Take me to the door that leads back to the human realm."

"I don't know where—"

"There's no time for lies, Shameek. I know how they treat humans here; they barely notice you. Which makes it really easy to overhear things you shouldn't. And you have the look of someone that's been here for a few years."

His Adam's apple bobbed. Once again, his brown eyes darted in the direction of the heavyset woman, who was now shrieking at the boy who'd been sweeping. Something about leaving the animal in the corner too long. "I'll show you which passageway," Shameek whispered. The kitchen was so loud that I almost missed it. "But I won't go all the way to the door or they'll know."

Triumph blazed through me. I clamped down on it, instantly hating myself. "That's fine. Thank you."

Shameek didn't grace this with a response. He edged past me, then dared to poke his head out into the open. I tensed, anticipating shouts or sharp words. The only sound that came was the chopping of a knife. A second later, Shameek drew back, gestured that I should follow him, and slipped around the corner. I hurried after him.

The head cook was apparently not a very observant creature, or she was only capable of putting her focus on one unpleasant task at a time, because she didn't even pause as we rushed along the back wall and into the passageway.

For once, it was a relief when the darkness of the maze swallowed me.

Shameek didn't have a moment of hesitation or uncertainty as he brought us deeper into the passages. At one point, I noticed that we both walked on light feet. Me, because it was in my nature to creep silently, and he, because his very survival depended on it. He'd learned how to be silent because he'd had to.

A fresh surge of hatred shot through my veins, hot and thick. The fae had roamed our world for far too long, doing whatever they liked, taking whomever they pleased. I didn't have a mind for politics, but it still seemed that Collith's steps toward change were too slow going.

We had put a fair amount of distance between us and the kitchen, so it seemed safe to speak. "You should—" I started to whisper.

Before I could go on, the entire passage shuddered. Rivulets of dirt trickled down from the ceiling and one of them fell on Shameek's shoulder. He jerked out of the way. Another put out a torch, which extinguished with a hiss. I spun around, my heart going into overdrive. It was already over, though; the whole thing had only lasted two seconds. I stared into the darkness, alert for any sign of movement. "What was that?"

When I looked to Shameek, he shook his head, looking just as frightened as I probably did. My instincts insisted I should learn the source of the commotion. Swallowing, I cautiously retraced our steps.

I discovered it just a few yards down. There was a huge rock in the tunnel that most definitely hadn't been there before; it blocked the entire path. Where had it come from? I took two steps closer, my eyes on the ceiling. More torches had gone out, but there were enough left to make out some details. Yes, there was the hole, which meant it had fallen out of the ceiling. I felt a ripple of unease; was the tunnel about to collapse?

Shameek hadn't come with me. Now worried that he'd seized the opportunity to flee, I broke into a run. My pulse slowed somewhat when I saw he was right where I'd left him.

"Guess you're not getting back to the kitchen that way," I said by way of explanation. But Shameek must've put two and two together—he didn't ask for details. He didn't even bother responding, actually. Without a word, he turned and plunged into shadow. Cursing, I rushed after him.

We walked for a while. Nothing interfered or disturbed our progress, though I kept waiting for something to. This passage in particular seemed longer than the rest. It went on and on, showing no signs of ending, forking, or turning. The absolute silence was unnerving. Every inch of my body was rigid; it felt like a single touch was all it would take to make me shatter. I tried to stay close to Shameek, but every time I neared enough to feel his body heat, he'd quicken his pace to put distance between us. I could hardly blame him, really. I didn't comment, and eventually, I relied on the sound of his footsteps rather than proximity.

At long last, another noise tore through the stillness. Though I'd been half-expecting it, my stomach clenched with dread. This one came from up ahead and it was undeniably from something alive. Sort of a... rapid shuffling.

I didn't bother asking Shameek what we should do; in unison he and I turned around to run the other way. Then, again, we froze at the same time, realizing that we couldn't go back, of course. The cave-in had made sure of that.

Suddenly I realized what, exactly, that cave-in had been—a barricade. To keep me in a certain part of the passages. I was a mouse in a maze and they were playing with me, dropping walls into places that had been clear moments ago, enjoying the sight of my terror and confusion. It was my first instinct not to give them the satisfaction, but I kept grappling for a weapon that wasn't there.

Shameek had pressed himself to the wall. Whatever was coming toward us must've caught our scent or heard the movement, because it began making noises. Guttural, urgent, and... hungry. Hearing this, Shameek let out a sound that was meant to be a hysterical laugh, maybe, but sounded more like he was struggling to breathe. "Did you think they would make it so easy?" he asked. There was a manic glow in his eyes.

The question made me wonder whether he'd been part of their plan all along—it *had* been strange that all the passageways were so eerily silent and the kitchen was the only bright, loud place to be found. Maybe Shameek had been instructed to lead me here. My own eyes narrowed back. "Do you know what that is?" I asked sharply. Despite the barricade, we were both sliding along the wall, instinctively trying to put distance between us and the thing coming closer.

The human's nostrils flared, as though he could smell the creature, but all my nose detected was dirt and damp. "I think it's a wendigo," Shameek replied. "There's a rumor that one was shipped in last night."

Distrust shot through me; wendigos had been amongst my mother's list of myths and legends. Either Shameek had lost his touch with reality or he was making it up. Regardless, it meant I had no idea what was coming down that tunnel. No weapon to fight with, either. I couldn't count on this foe being like the dragon and falling susceptible to my power. And who knew if it was nighttime, anyway?

"Shit, shit, shit," I muttered to myself. We could hide in one of the many rooms, but I didn't know what senses this thing used to hunt. What if it found us within seconds, and we found ourselves backed into a corner?

You're already in a corner, reason reminded me. Right. I opened my mouth to tell Shameek the plan.

Before my brain was able to comprehend what was happening, there was a blur of movement. Shameek started screaming. He was on the ground somehow, and something writhed on top of him. The air was ripe with its smell now, a familiar and putrid scent. There weren't enough torches to truly make out its details, but I saw the thing's head jerk forward, over and over again. Its teeth clacked. Shameek was keeping it at bay, just barely, and he hadn't stopped filling the tunnel with his shrill sounds of terror.

For a black, terrible moment, I thought about running. Using the fact that the wendigo was distracted and I'd surely get a head start in getting far, far away from here. *Fortuna Sworn, that's not who you are*, I could practically hear Dad saying sternly, managing to shame me even after death.

But he was right.

I resisted the moronic instinct to throw myself at the wendigo—anything to get it off Shameek—and hesitated a few precious seconds to take in every detail around us. *The rocks, fuck yes, the rocks*, I thought, rushing forward. I snatched up the first one my hand found and spun around just in time for the wendigo to slam into me. The blow was so painful that, for an instant, I couldn't breathe. Then my back hit the pile of rocks, and I forgot all about needing to breathe as an even bigger pain ricocheted through me.

The wendigo wasn't fazed, not for a second. It reached for my throat, my face, doing everything it could to rip into me and take its first bite. We tumbled to the ground. Just as Shameek had, I planted my hand against whatever part of it I could get a secure hold on—which turned out to be the upper half of its face—to keep it away. My arm shook. Meanwhile, the other arm rose. *Not enough force*, I thought dimly. Somehow I found the strength to draw the rock back, putting more distance between that unforgiving surface and the wendigo's skull

Then I brought it down.

The wendigo must've been older or more fragile than it looked; the bone cracked and broke like a dead stick. Those grappling stumps for fingers went still. I didn't have enough left in me to heave the body to the side and free myself. The wendigo's vacant eyes drew nearer to mine as I slowly, slowly weakened.

Suddenly the weight lifted. A moment later, the wendigo was tossed to the side, and it made a dull sound as it hit the dirt. Shameek's face swam into view. The sight of him surprised me; I'd assumed he was dead or already in another part of the maze. "Thanks," I rasped. He gave a single nod, his lips pursed, his eyes dark. A steady stream of blood ran down his temple. He extended his hand, which I took without hesitation, and he hauled me up.

Pain whispered through the parts of me that had landed on rock. I closed my eyes and swayed. Shameek didn't say a word, and after a few seconds, the pain ebbed to something bearable. I focused on the human again. In that moment, I realized that I wouldn't be alive if it weren't for Shameek. After all, I'd only had the chance to get the rock while the wendigo was busy trying to eat him. I owed a debt, however much I loathed to admit it.

The moment I was able to, I took a few steps back, since I'd seen too many horror movies in which the thing that was supposed to be dead jolted awake for a final attack. Shameek and I both stared down at the wendigo, if that's really what it was. The creature lay on its back, and for the first time, I got a good look at its features. Its smooth, hairless skin was milky white. The hands and mouth were covered in what looked like old blood. The rest of its body was so thin that the creature shouldn't have been alive—maybe it hadn't been. All it wore for clothing was a pair of ragged, green shorts. There were slits in place of where nostrils should've been, and its gaping mouth was crowded with sharp, yellowed teeth. The wendigo's white eyes, which stared upward, still blazed with malice.

"How many more are there?" I asked, my imagination filling the tunnels with dozens of these horrific monsters.

Shameek's breathing quickened. "What makes you think there are more?"

"I think I fought one of these things already. My first night here, in the woods."

"Well, better the wendigos than *them*. They know I helped you now." Shameek cast a despairing, terrified glance around us. Dirt and torches stared back. I was about to ask him *how* they'd seen when he added, "I thought if we moved fast enough, the cameras wouldn't be able to catch my face."

Oh. Now that comment I'd overheard about a viewing room made more sense. My voice was barely a whisper as I asked, "Will you run, then? When we reach the door?"

It had been almost exactly what I'd started to tell him before, when we were interrupted by the cave-in. *You should keep going when we get to the surface.* "If I don't, I'm dead," Shameek answered flatly. He turned away from the wendigo and began walking again. "They'll kill me."

However sympathetic I was to his plight, I was ready for this trial to be over. I didn't respond to his dismal comments, and this time, I stayed alongside him. My pace forced Shameek to take bigger and swifter steps. The eternal passage finally ended at a crossroads, of sorts. The one directly in front of us slanted upward. I didn't need Shameek to tell me it was the right choice; without waiting for him to give an indication, I rushed forward. A few more minutes went by, tense and wordless. Our shoes made the ground crunch. "It shouldn't be much farther," Shameek finally muttered. "This is where they're always coming and going from."

Just as he finished speaking, a ring of light appeared. The breath caught in my throat and something in my chest fluttered as I realized what it was—daylight. But which place did it open to?

What was it Collith had said that first night? *The trick is to expect more.*

Home, home, home, I thought in time to the beating of my heart. "I bet your family will be ecstatic to see you," I said, trying not to leave Shameek behind in my eagerness. There was nothing standing in the way this time. No dragons, or wendigos, or copper-haired sadists. At the thought, I almost broke into a run.

"I won't get to see them. I'm going back," Shameek answered. Like before, he spoke these words without any outward sign of emotion. As though something inside his brain had fried and now lay blackened. And then he stopped, staring at the light as though it were his destruction instead of his salvation.

I frowned and reluctantly stopped, too. I faced him in the wide tunnel. "What? Why? You said they'd kill you."

Shameek didn't look at me; he kept his face turned toward that distant glow. "I wouldn't survive long out there, either. There are some fae who entertain themselves by hunting. Not animals, of course. They prefer more... intelligent game. Those are the ones that would come for me."

"So you're just going to give up?" I demanded.

"If I beg for forgiveness, they might be lenient. A beating or two. Sometimes that's more entertaining than outright killing us."

The trial wasn't over yet. All I had to do was get to that door. Torn, I looked from Shameek to the outside world. "I'll be right back," I snapped, frustrated by his cowardice and my own shortcomings. Damon would've befriended Shameek by now and been able to convince him to escape. "Don't you dare leave. We need to talk about this."

The human said nothing. I waited a moment more, hoping

for some kind of response. When he wouldn't meet my gaze, I growled and swung away. With every step, I felt hope push out the fear. One step closer to fresh air. One step closer to Damon's freedom. One step closer to ending the Unseelie Court's tyranny. I caught a flash of green. *Trees.* God, I hadn't realized how much I missed trees.

A few feet away from the door, I sensed movement behind me. *Shameek,* I thought with relief. "Did you change your—"

Pain shot through me. Shocked, I stumbled back and hit the jagged wall. Shameek came with me, failing to extract the knife he'd embedded in my shoulder. My instincts took over; Dad's lessons had become part of every limb and reaction. Using Shameek's proximity against him, I grabbed his shoulders and shoved backward, sweeping my leg around and behind his ankles at the same time. He hit the ground hard. I braced myself, expecting him to come at me again, but the human just curled into a ball.

"You had a knife this entire time?" I rasped.

Shameek's stoic mask was long gone. He pressed his wet face into the dirt and sobbed. "I j-just d-d-didn't want to b-be afraid a-a-anymore," I heard him say between heaves.

Understanding slammed home. My heart. He'd been after my heart.

I probably should've felt terror or outrage. Instead, compassion filled the very thing he'd been trying to steal. I knew what it was to hate the fear living in your head. I remembered how it felt to dread falling asleep at night, worrying about whatever dreams awaited you. Shameek didn't need another enemy—he needed help. For now, though, I had to finish this damn trial. I turned my attention to the knife jutting from my body. I'd never been stabbed before, but I'd watched enough TV to learn that it probably wasn't a good idea to pull it out. God, it hurt.

"Like I said before. You should take your chance now and go back to your family. If not, I'll be right back. Maybe I can pull some strings with the fae." I gritted my teeth and kept walking toward the ring of light. Fingers clamped around my ankle.

I turned back. Shameek was on his stomach, his tear-stained face twisted with desperation, blood, and dust. "Kill me," he begged. "You owe a debt."

Clever human. He must've seen something in my expression earlier, when I'd realized that he had saved my life.

"I'm sorry," I said. There was no delay in my answer; taking human life was one sin I wasn't willing to bear. Oliver was already keeping so much at bay as I slept. I avoided Shameek's pleading gaze and pulled free. He sank to the ground, his sobs echoing up and down the earthen corridor. They followed me all the way out the door.

All thoughts of Shameek, wendigos, faeries, and stab wounds left my mind.

Fading sunlight slanted over me. It was gently warm, like that brief and perfect time when your bedsheets started to become accustomed to your body heat. It felt as though I'd been underground for a year. I lifted my face toward the sky. My nostrils flared as I inhaled the scents of leaves and breezes. Everything was serene and inviting. Birdsong flitted through the air. Standing here, awash in twilight, it was all-too easy to believe the horrors beneath my feet didn't exist.

"Congratulations, Nightmare. You've passed the second test."

My heart reared. I whirled, knowing that if the owner of that voice wanted me dead, I would be. I'd let my guard down. I'd been wholly unprepared. The Tongue was right behind me, his expression that same grave mask. We had stood this close before, but never in the light of day. For the first time, I was able to make out the big pores in his skin. The blackheads on his nose. The lines in his forehead. It seemed there was a price for his abilities—the Tongue was aging. I tucked the information away. You never knew what might come in handy later.

I stared at him for a moment longer, then looked toward the mountains again. Home was so close. It would be easy to run.

The heavyset faerie just stood there and watched me. There was no doubt in my mind that he knew what I was thinking. Maybe this was a test, too. Because, without a word, he turned around and walked back into the darkness. The jangling of his beads faded away. I cast a final, wistful glance toward the mountains.

Then I followed him back into the earth.

CHAPTER SIXTEEN

*S*hameek was gone when I reentered the passageway.

In the exact place he'd been laying awaited Nuvian. The faerie stood straight and expressionless, every inch of him ready. For what, though, I couldn't say. "The human that was here," I demanded without preamble, approaching him. The wound in my shoulder throbbed. "Where is he now?"

Nuvian stared at the wall ahead of him. His blond braids gleamed. I'd never seen him in daylight before, and unlike the Tongue, the light just highlighted this faerie's perfection. His skin practically glittered. "He has been brought back to the kitchens," the Right Hand answered. I waited for more, but he didn't elaborate.

"And will he be harmed?" I prodded. As Shameek had pointed out, I owed him a debt. Torture by fae would be shitty payback.

"I don't know what his fate will be, my lady. I am merely a guard."

"No, you're the Right Hand," I retorted. I saw his humility for the lie it was; faeries were all arrogance and conceit. I had told Laurie I would play their game and I'd meant it. "You're a pretty useless one, from where I'm standing, though."

Those gray eyes flashed. Not so impassive after all, then. "What would you have me do, my lady?" Nuvian asked tightly. *Oh, look who doesn't like his own game.*

"Lead the way back to Collith's room, then find Shameek. Either bring him to me or offer your protection until I can figure out how to get him out of here. He shouldn't be punished for helping during the trial. Now *hurry*, please."

Nuvian inclined his head, a silent acknowledgment of my order, then gestured that I should walk in front of him. However much I disliked having him at my back, I didn't see a way around it, so I moved to comply. I was probably making another enemy, but I didn't care. What was one more on my rapidly growing list, anyway?

As the Unseelie Court swallowed us whole, I didn't let myself look back. Didn't let myself wonder if it would be the last time I saw the sun.

Just as it had after the last trial, exhaustion crashed over me in a merciless wave. The stab wound had stopped bleeding, at least. Maybe it would be safe to take the knife out soon. I struggled to remain alert on the way back, wary for any sign of the wendigo, Jassin, or some other foe that wanted to kill me, but it felt like everything was underwater.

Once we reached Collith's door—a guard stood there, another one I didn't recognize—Nuvian faced me. All I wanted was to go into that room, clean and wrap my shoulder, then collapse onto the king's colossal bed. But I didn't move; I needed to see him take those first steps toward the kitchen. To be reassured that my debt would be paid in full. Nuvian and I stared at each other for a moment. "Well? Shameek?" I reminded him finally, feeling like I'd lost, somehow.

The faerie blinked, slow and deliberate. The movement drew my gaze to his ridiculously long lashes. Did every faerie have them? "I told the king I would protect his rooms. I follow his orders... and the queen's. But I see no queen here," Nuvian added. He quirked a brow, as if to say, *What are you going to do about it?*

Just like that, I'd had enough.

A feral sound tore from my throat. However prepared he looked, Nuvian wasn't expecting me to launch forward and clap my hand on his forehead. The other guard wasn't, either. Nuvian instantly tried to recoil. I just went with him, and as the faerie slammed against the wall, I pressed my body to his. Nuvian's dick hardened, but the bursts of air coming out of him were borne of agitation, not arousal. The process wasn't painful —not this part, at least—so he had no idea that his fears were already mine. They filled me, more heady than any buzz or high. Nuvian, Right Hand of the Unseelie King, was deathly afraid of werewolves.

"Fortunately for me, you faeries keep forgetting what I am," I hissed. The other guard had started to move forward, his hand on his weapon, and I barely spared him a glance. "Interfere and I'll kill you where you stand."

He froze. A brief assessment showed that he was younger than most of the fae I'd met down here—he held his sword without confidence and regarded me with poorly concealed fear. Certain that he wouldn't intervene, I gave my full attention to Nuvian.

We stood in a forest now, surrounded by solemn trees and moving shadows. The moon was visible over our heads, and it was as round and full as one from a fairy tale. Before Nuvian could form a response, a chorus of howls rose all around. Echoing, multiplying, nearing. Any one of them could be the beast he was so tormented by.

Nuvian reached for a sword that was no longer there. His precious armor was gone, too. "Hear that?" I whispered, my lips moving against the tender skin of his ear. He shivered. "They sound hungry, don't they?"

To his credit, Nuvian didn't make a sound. Normally my victims were screaming or weeping within the first few seconds. I took a few steps back to enjoy my handiwork. Nuvian turned in circles, his chest heaving. Bright eyes peered out from the darkness. They varied in hues of blue, gold, and green. A deep growl rippled across the clearing. "How much do you know about wolves, Nuvian?" I wondered.

He glanced at me, and this time, there was the shine of hatred in his eyes. A vein stood out in his forehead. "Release me from this place, Nightmare."

I leaned against a tree and crossed my feet at the ankles, hiding a wince as a bolt of pain went through me. Even more eyes appeared around us. "Wolves typically feed upon the vulnerable ones. The weak ones. It's called 'culling.' You don't strike me as the weak type, but you don't have a herd or a pack, which makes you weak in their minds. Also, in case you're curious about the whole… I don't know, eating process? Between hunts, they go days without feeding, so when it does happen they tend to just *gorge*. Oh, fun fact, they're also not known for dispatching their victims quickly. Not exactly great for you, but it's fascinating, isn't it?"

A moment after I'd finished speaking, a werewolf stepped into the moonlight.

It was massive. Bigger than any werewolf I'd seen in real life. Its paws looked like they could kill with a single blow. Its fur was thick and shone like pure silver. The eyes that were so fixed on Nuvian gleamed with intelligence and ferocity. An odd, strangled sound left the Right Hand. His back was to me, so I couldn't see his expression, but the corners of my mouth tipped up as I imagined it. The beast bared its teeth. Its muscles visibly bunched, about to charge its golden-haired prey.

I expected Nuvian to move into a fighting stance. Instead, he dropped to his knees and covered his head, exactly as a child would from a monster in the closet. He said something, but the words were muffled. I thought I heard *stop* and *please*.

The werewolf bent its great head and sniffed Nuvian, who shuddered in response. To his intelligible plea I just shrugged; bark scraped against my back from the motion. "You can make this end any time you'd like. All I need is your vow to protect Shameek."

"You have it," Nuvian mumbled, still not lifting his head.

The werewolf dug its claws into the dirt. Any second now, it would leap. "Sorry, I need to hear you say the words."

Nuvian jerked toward me so violently a braid smacked him in the cheek. His eyes blazed as he spat, *"I vow to protect the human called Shameek."*

"Excellent." Though it was unnecessary to halt the illusion, I snapped my fingers. As easily as flipping a switch, we were back in the passageway outside Collith's rooms. Nuvian lurched away from me, his hand instantly going to that pretty sword. I raised my brows at him in a silent challenge. He barely kept his composure as he brushed past me. As promised, he hurried in the direction of the kitchens. His grip on the hilt was white.

Before Nuvian turned away, I saw the stark terror in his face. Terror... and maybe a little respect. *That's what I'll do about it, asshole,* I thought, watching him go. My veins hummed from using my abilities. I hardly felt the stab wound now. Guilt hovered nearby, waiting for its chance to consume me, but I refused to let it any closer. Our parents didn't raise us to be ashamed of what we were. They also taught us to use our powers only when necessary. I thought Dad would've been proud to know I was fighting for a human's survival.

The bed was calling to me again. God, every day down here was so long. Just as I began to push the door open, I belatedly remembered the other guard. Sighing, I turned to him. He stood in the shadows and the whites of his eyes glowed. "What's your name?" I asked wearily.

There was a tremble in his voice as he answered, "Omar, my lady."

He wouldn't make the mistake of forgetting what I was. Not again. Maybe I could use that to my advantage. "I'm here for my brother, Omar. He's my family. All I have left. And I will do anything to save him, which means I *am* going to be queen. You can invest in your future now, by serving me, or you can be just another faerie I destroy. Your choice."

He said nothing—just kept staring with that dumbfounded, deer-in-the-headlights expression. I swallowed another sigh and finally entered Collith's rooms.

As I kicked the door shut, I saw there was a bath waiting. Unlike last time, there was shampoo, body wash, and a wash-cloth on the floor beside it, arranged on a silver tray. Relief filled me. *Thank you*, I thought to the three women who'd undoubtedly filled it. Maybe they were responsible for the toiletries, too. I took off my sweaty clothes and climbed in. Then, without letting myself think about it, I pulled the knife out of me. I let out a hiss, throwing the small blade onto the floor, and staunched the bleeding with the washcloth.

After a minute, I sank deeper into the water. The heat was heaven for my aching back, which would definitely sport some bruises tomorrow from slamming into those rocks. I waited another minute, then gritted my teeth and peeked at the puck-ered flesh beneath the washcloth. It didn't look terrible. Hope-fully cleaning it would be enough to stop any infection.

Worried that a certain king would make an appearance, I didn't linger. My movements were rough and efficient as I got out and donned a lacy nightdress someone had left. Then, as I'd been daydreaming of doing for hours, I went to bed. The mattress welcomed me like an old friend. I nearly wept from the overwhelming realization that it was over; I'd survived the second trial.

Now I just had to survive the third.

Sometimes, if you wanted it too badly, sleep liked to play games. It eluded, teased, or disappeared entirely. *If you don't take me to Oliver,* I told it with gritted teeth, *I'll get to him by other means.*

I must've been on a roll today, because within minutes, welcome and blessed darkness closed in.

I opened my eyes, uncertain of what I would find. There had been times over the years when Oliver was able to sense what I was feeling, out there, in the world of the awake and real. Did he know what Collith had done to me in that bathtub? Had I felt my terror during the battle with a wendigo?

However worried he must've been, Oliver was feeling calm—the meadow was the picture of serenity. The horizon was alight in shades of pink. The gentlest of breezes whispered through the grass. Colorful wildflowers soaked up the final rays of light. My best friend sat with his back against a tree. A butterfly flitted past, unnoticed since he was intent on the drawing pad against his knees.

"Hey, stranger," I said softly.

Oliver lifted his head and a smile stretched across his beautiful face. Warmth spread through me at the sight of it. He closed the drawing pad, hiding its contents, and patted the spot beside him. "Hey yourself. What do you want to do tonight?"

Still smiling, I shook my head and held out a hand to him. Oliver took it and got to his feet. "Have I ever taught you how to waltz?" I asked. It was rhetorical, of course. If I knew how to waltz, the person living in my head certainly did.

"Actually... I prefer slow dancing." Oliver took hold of my wrists and put them behind his neck. Next, he folded his hands at the small of my back and pulled me close. We started to sway. There was no music, but neither of us mentioned it. I rested my cheek against Oliver's chest and watched the way the hair on his arm caught the sunlight. Like liquid gold. He smelled so different from other people, too. It wasn't perfume or cologne. No, Oliver's scent was long afternoons spent painting, or hours submerged in saltwater, or of someone who rode the wind. He smelled like freedom.

A moment later, the entire world darkened. Oliver and I shared the same adoration for nighttime—he'd pushed away all remnants of daylight and brought out the stars. I tilted my head back to look up.

After a few seconds, I felt Oliver focus on me. "Since you're here, I assume the second trial went well?"

As I watched, one of the stars loosened from its perch and plunged down. I pretended to be absorbed by its progress as I thought of the best way to tell him about the trial. *I forced a human to help me and almost got him killed. Now he might be tortured and killed anyway because of his involvement.* Too soon the brilliant light faded to nothing. "Well…" I hesitated. But before I could go on, the world shook. Someone was calling for me. I knew that voice, and judging from the look on Oliver's face, he'd guessed who it was too. "Ouch!"

Oliver frowned and stepped back. "What is it?"

"That damn butterfly bit me," I growled, glaring at the small creature flitting away.

"What? Are you sure?"

I showed him the red welt that was already appearing. Silence hovered around us as Oliver cradled my hand and examined it. After a moment, he bent to brush a feather-light kiss on the mark. And somehow, it felt better. Cooler.

Collith said my name again. *Fortuna, wake up.*

This time, the dream began to fade. I could resist to a certain extent, but reality always won. I smiled sadly at Oliver, wishing we'd had a longer dance. This could very well be the last time we'd see each other.

Not wanting to vanish from his arms—that was just too cruel—I forced myself to back away. My best friend stayed by that twisting tree, surrounded by stars that were bigger and brighter than the ones I knew. Yet the beauty of them did nothing to distract me from the longing in his gaze.

His whisper followed me as I went somewhere he couldn't follow. "Bye, Fortuna."

Collith was even more solemn than usual.

His explanation for waking me had been cryptic. Quite a feat, considering how little he shared as it was. But my curiosity was piqued, so I reluctantly peeled the covers off, rose, and dressed. Zara had tended to me while I was unconscious; the wound looked weeks old and the pain was gone. "How much does she charge for her healing?" I asked Collith as I followed him to the door. "Just trying to figure out how much I owe at this point."

"Don't worry about that. The crown keeps her on retainer."

"How much, Collith?"

Maybe it was my use of his name that coaxed the truth from this evasive faerie king. He stopped with his hand on the door. "Her fee is usually a priceless jewel or a favor of some kind," he admitted. I felt my jaw drop. Oh, God. I was never going to pay her back. I didn't exactly have any diamonds and I wasn't about to owe some faerie a favor.

Collith sighed at my expression and dared to cup my elbow. "That's the least of our worries right now, okay? If you insist on paying her fees, we'll figure something else out."

I allowed him to tug me into the passageway, and then Collith dropped his hand. Once again, the guards awaiting us were ones I hadn't encountered before. Two females, one heavily muscled with cropped, greasy hair, the other tall, willowy, and bald.

"How do the Guardians pass the time when they're not standing outside your door or following you around?" I asked grumpily. Their armor softly clinked behind us. Collith offered his arm in response. For some reason, the gesture surprised me. I regarded it for a moment, oddly uncertain, then accepted. He was so cool and solid.

Collith placed his other hand atop mine, ignoring how I started, and actually answered the question as we made our way through the passages of doors. "They operate much as police officers or detectives do in the human world," he said. We skirted around a group of tittering young faeries and he gave them a courteous nod. Down here, he'd probably been considered the most eligible bachelor on the planet. "Investigating crimes that appear to be committed by fae or settling disputes that take place outside of Court. Amongst many other things, of course."

I was going to ask another question when Collith turned right. It brought us past a door covered in wooden snakes. The design triggered my memory; this was the direction of the throne room. Dread gripped my stomach with its ragged fingernails. What could be so important that he'd bring me here, the night before the last trial?

Within minutes of the realization, we were there, tiny figures in the room full of murals. God, I hated this place. I gazed up at those pain-filled images as Collith led me through the double doors.

It wasn't as crowded as it'd been during my tribunal, but faeries milled about here and there. Laughter and conversation floated through the air. A group of redcaps—fae known for their fondness of raw meat, human or otherwise—surrounded a nearby table. Blood stained the wood, their fingers, the floor.

"Why are we here?" I asked under my breath, wanting nothing more than to return to bed.

The Unseelie King didn't answer. Annoyed, I glanced his way

and saw he was focused on that carnage-covered table. Clearly, he wanted me to notice something about the redcaps. Maybe if I cooperated, we could go back to his rooms, and I could snag more time with Oliver. With resignation I forced myself to examine every detail. The intestines spilling onto the flagstones, the redcaps' yellowed teeth glinting in firelight, the uneven edges of the ribcage they'd exposed.

Suddenly one of the redcaps shifted, allowing me a glimpse of the face that belonged to their victim. The human's eyeballs had been removed, but the rest of his features—twisted in horror though they were—were entirely distinguishable.

Oh, God. No. The acrid taste of bile assaulted my tastebuds. I held on tighter to Collith, knowing if I didn't, I was going to bend over and vomit all over the floor.

It was Shameek.

A crude wooden sign hung around his neck. Or what was left of it. Someone had carved a single word onto the small surface. *Traitor.*

Suddenly all I could hear was the smacking those greedy mouths made. The sound got louder and louder until it surrounded me. The redcaps were so focused that they weren't aware they had an audience. "Why w-would you show me this?" I croaked, still on the verge of vomiting. Some poor human would just end up cleaning my mess, so I kept forcing it back down. I had to be hurting Collith, but he didn't so much as wince.

"Because I know it will have the opposite effect they intend-ed," was all he said. Emotion radiated down the bond, but I was so distressed, I could barely absorb my own.

I couldn't bear to watch the scene anymore. "Why didn't you stop them?" I whispered, looking at Collith instead. He was still holding my hand, I noticed faintly.

I'd learned enough about the Unseelie King to know that his

careful, vacant expression meant it bothered him, too. Thank God for small favors. "Not here, Fortuna."

My eyes traced the length of his scar, over and over, needing something to focus on. All the while, I tried to make sense of the horror just a few yards away. Someone wanted to frighten me. They hoped I would lose my focus. Whether Shameek had died for poisoning fae or his part during the second trial, it didn't matter. His death wasn't my fault—it was theirs. I was going to obliterate this Court from the inside out. And I'd do it wearing the crown they put on me.

"He stayed alive far longer than I thought he would," a voice said. Feminine, familiar, and ancient.

Even before I turned, I knew Arcaena would be the one standing in the doorway.

Every inch of her crooned elegance, power, and composure. Her raven hair was swept back into a waist-length braid. She wore a voluminous gown that brushed the floor like a bell. It was the same color as the human blood staining the redcaps' mouths. Her dark eyes were fixed on my face and her perfect, lovely lips bore that same half-smile as the last time we'd met. Despite the number of years she'd doubtless spent on this earth, her skin was creamy and smooth. Now that I wasn't her puppet, I was able to notice more details, like the small birthmark just below her left eye.

It was eerily similar to mine.

Was she the one who orchestrated Shameek's murder? Or was her timing purely coincidental? I looked at the table, then back at her. There was no such thing as coincidence at the Unseelie Court. Pain radiated down my arms, and I realized I was clenching my fists so hard my nails had made bloody crescents. "Remember this moment. I know I will," I said thickly.

She smirked. "How quaint. You actually think you're going to survive."

I didn't bother responding; why argue with a sociopath? I

finally put my back to the grisly scene and started toward the gigantic doors. Collith followed. As we passed Arcaena, she didn't try to touch or enchant me, and I suspected it was due to the other faerie present. He'd stayed by my side throughout our exchange and remained within reach as I sought to leave the throne room behind. Arcaena's perfume trailed after us, combining with the stench of blood, and it was almost my undoing.

The journey back was lost to me. My mind was trapped within the memory of Shameek's broken, half-eaten body. Twice I took a wrong turn, not thinking, and Collith gently cupped my elbow to turn me in the right direction. At one point he said something to the guards. In the next moment, it seemed, I was standing in the middle of his chambers again.

The instant we were alone, Collith spoke. "Whoever gave that human to the redcaps—" he began.

"His name was Shameek."

"Whoever gave Shameek to the redcaps did so quietly. No one can tell my Guardians who was responsible. Every witness they questioned just recalls seeing him dragged into the throne room, wounded but alive, and the redcaps beginning their consumption." Collith's brows drew together. He started unbuttoning his tunic in abrupt, agitated movements. "No one interrupted, of course. As you know, that group is generally unintelligent and violent. By the time word reached me, Shameek was already dead."

I sank into the chair and watched the flames dance. It was no tender, slow thing like what Oliver and I had done. "Arcaena was involved."

Sitting on the bed, Collith pulled his boots off and sighed. I'd never heard him make that sound before. For the first time since I'd met him, he seemed more human than faerie. "You can't know that for certain, Fortuna," he said. He lifted his head and looked at me. His hair glinted in the firelight, revealing those bright strands.

"I do, actually. It just won't be proved tonight. I need to get some sleep before tomorrow." Even as I said it, I knew falling asleep would be impossible now.

Clad only in a thin, white shirt that revealed the smooth muscles beneath, Collith moved toward the bedside table. Someone had put a goblet there. But I was more fascinated with his bare feet, for some reason. Was this really the distant king who'd watched me get whipped just a few days ago?

"This will help," Collith murmured, crossing the room again.

He lowered the goblet and I saw it was full to the brim. He'd anticipated my reaction, then. A flicker of distrust went through me. Here Collith was, offering oblivion, a respite for my fracturing mind… which he'd caused. It was almost too convenient.

Despite these thoughts, though, I downed the contents in four deep gulps. Anything was better than sitting here, repeatedly assaulted by those images, and if the Unseelie King wanted to kill me he could've done it a dozen times over already. The taste was terrible, like dirt and leaves, but the effect was almost immediate. I slumped, feeling fuzzy and warm, a sensation similar to an entire night of drinking. I felt Collith take the goblet back, then the weight of a blanket settled on me. I was too tired to bother with the bed. "Thank you," I slurred, once again forgetting the rule Mom had taught me about expressing gratitude to faeries.

But Collith just touched my cheek. "You're welcome, Fortuna."

CHAPTER SEVENTEEN

*F*or the third and final time, I put on the black clothes someone had undoubtedly left as I slept. Laurie, probably. He didn't make an appearance for any snarky comments or words of wisdom, and despite our confusing inter-action after Olorel, I found I missed that. Even before Sorcha, making friends had been difficult for me; I'd let down my guard with Laurie, just a little.

Collith had stepped out to allow me privacy as I dressed. A few minutes later, I opened the door and our eyes met. The aloof, glittering king had taken place of the weary, barefooted male of last night. It felt like we were stuck in a loop, taking the same steps. Facing the same threats. Withholding the same truths. But this time, he didn't say that I could change my mind or warn me of the consequences. Maybe he'd learned the futility of it. I took Collith's arm without waiting for him to offer it and forced myself to take deep, even breaths. He appraised me as we walked. I determinedly stayed focused, reviewing everything I'd learned from those books and going through Dad's self-defense moves. The fae had thrown a whipping, an enchantment, a dragon, a wendigo, and murder my way. I couldn't even imagine what was next.

"Fortuna—" Collith began suddenly, his voice jarring in the stillness.

I swallowed and kept my eyes on the passage ahead. "Don't. Please. Whatever you're going to say... I'm barely holding it together right now. I just can't."

Those hazel eyes darkened, more with worry than anger, I thought. But Collith didn't argue; he just nodded, put his cold hand on top of mine, and continued our journey.

We arrived at the throne room all-too soon.

The space was the most crowded I'd ever seen it. Every table had been removed, but even that wasn't enough. Faeries were crammed against the farthest walls, wearing expressions of discomfort and annoyance. Children sat atop the twisted chandeliers. Others rested upon bigger faeries' shoulders, looking for all the world like innocent families attending a summer parade. Well, minus the pointed ears and strange clothing. And as per usual, they were all staring.

Nerves fluttered in my stomach. I saw the flash of jewels and heard the chink of coins—they were betting on this. How many of them had put money against my survival? I searched for Damon, hoping the sight of him would steady me. There he was, standing near the front, alongside Jassin. He didn't have any new bruises, from what I could tell, but my brother somehow looked thinner every time I saw him.

I also recognized Tarragon and the tall female who'd passed judgment during my tribunal—I heard someone whisper the name Chandrelle—amongst the figures up front. Arcaena, too, stood amongst the onlookers. Her pale-skinned twin was beside her. An involuntary shiver whispered up my spine and I quickly refocused on the path in front of us.

That was when I noticed the individual tied to a wooden chair.

It had been put before the dais for all to see. The person's head and neck were covered by a burlap sack. However much of a prisoner they seemed to be, though, there was no sign of struggle or attempts to speak. My mouth felt dry, my tongue thick. What was this?

Collith left me at the bottom of the stairs—the sudden absence of his hand felt strange—and went to the throne. I tried not to fidget or make some senseless comment that would bring about another tribunal. The Tongue waddled over and began his rituals and chanting. I was loathe to let his paper-dry skin touch mine and it took considerable effort not to yank free of his grasp.

Through it all, the captive in that chair still didn't move. I kept glancing over, my heart pounding so hard, I knew the faeries could probably hear it. The hood was oversized and their clothing baggy, making it impossible to know whether a man or a woman sat there. Had the fae sent someone to Granby and brought one of my loved ones back? The possibilities haunted me. *Bea. Gretchen. Cyrus.*

Finished with his posturing, the Tongue fixed his gaze on me again. "The final trial will challenge your devotion to this Court," he rumbled. Slowly, the faerie reached into the folds of his robe. "With ruling comes sacrifice. There can be no limit to your loyalty."

I was breathing as though I'd just run a mile. It was that word—*sacrifice*. In that instant, I knew they were going to make me pay for surviving the other trials. I couldn't stop myself from glancing toward Collith, fruitlessly hoping he would save me—never mind that I'd made every choice bringing me to this point. He gazed back, wearing his usual inscrutable expression, but gentle sensations traveled down the bond. Not emotions, exactly. Not his voice, either. Yet somehow I understood that he believed in me. He thought I would win.

This knowledge might have been comforting, but then the Tongue's hand reemerged holding my father's knife.

I stared, dumbfounded, as he held it out. "What the hell am I expected to do with that?"

My question echoed throughout the immense room. The Tongue just stood there, waiting for me to take Dad's knife from him. The entire Court had fallen silent. After a few seconds, I did, just to keep this thing moving. Satisfied, the Tongue turned and approached the chair, his big fingers reaching for the sack hiding the captive's face. *No, don't,* I wanted to shout. Some part of me knew this was a moment that, if I didn't die within the next hour, would haunt my thoughts as often as Mom and Dad's murders.

Without another speech or spell, the Tongue yanked that hood off and stepped aside. When I registered who was sitting there, it took every scrap of self-control not to scream or recoil.

Damon stared back at me.

Every detail was my brother. The long face, that mop of brown hair, our father's eyes. They bored into mine, silently pleading. He couldn't speak; his mouth was covered by a scrap of material tied around his head. I twisted, searching for Damon at the front of the crowd, where he'd been just minutes ago. But Jassin stood alone. Smiling. As I turned back, still gaping, a faerie came forward and tugged the gag down. "Fortuna," my brother rasped the moment the tie was gone. The voice was his, too.

Bile rose in my throat for what felt like the hundredth time that day. I staggered, the room tilting, and my gaze collided with Laurie's. He stood at the edge of the crowd, a light in the darkness. His hair shone like a halo. He hadn't been there before; I would've noticed him. "Is this real?" I managed.

His expression was grim. "I don't know."

For some reason, I'd expected more. When he didn't say anything else, when he merely stared back at me, I turned back to Damon. My mind spun. What should I do? How could I outsmart them? If I tried to walk away from the test, the fae would execute me.

But it wasn't Damon. It couldn't be. Jassin wouldn't let them kill his favorite plaything... would he?

I fought the urge to pace. I battled the instinct to look at Collith again. I was alone. Completely and irrevocably alone. Strangely enough, the thought made a strange calm settle over my being. *Have I finally gone insane?* I wondered distantly. Maybe. Or maybe feeling alone was familiar territory. It grounded me.

Slowly, I faced Damon again. I held our father's knife in my hand—cruel, so cruel that they would choose this as the weapon—and moved to stand before him.

"Remember your promise," Damon cried, finally wrenching at his bonds.

At this, I stopped breathing. Then relief swept through my body, so overwhelming, so profound, I almost sagged. *You're not my brother,* I realized. The faeries had been eavesdropping, yes, but they hadn't learned everything about us. Damon never would've used Mom against me, no matter how desperate or frightened. He'd even tried to release me from that promise when I first found him down here.

But... what if I was wrong?

No. If I allowed that fear in, it would lead back to the foggy place of despair and indecision. So, between one breath and the next, I jammed the knife—underhanded, just like our father taught us—into Damon's heart. To keep myself from reconsidering, I twisted it. Dad's voice filled my head. *You want to reach those large blood vessels hiding behind the organs. When the arteries break open, death occurs very quickly. Regardless of what the creature has done to you, Fortuna, it's wrong to make it suffer.*

Damon's achingly familiar eyes widened. First with disbelief, then with betrayal, then with pain.

Just as I'd hoped, it was a quick death. The muscles in

Damon's face slackened, and slowly, the tension went out of his body. The imposter wearing my brother's face slumped. His glassy gaze fixed on mine.

I waited for the hallucination to fade, or even for the body to vanish completely.

Nothing happened.

I looked down at the knife, which I must've pulled out automatically. It was red up to the hilt. My fingers opened, sending the precious blade to clatter against the flagstones. I'd never stabbed someone before. No one had told me how warm it would be. How quickly the blood would cool. How sticky it would feel on my skin. The illusion was thorough, I'd give it that. Nauseated, I turned to the Tongue. "What are you waiting for? It's over, right?"

Still he said nothing. I faced the masses, hoping to get any kind of response. Their eyes were bright and hungry. They were waiting for me to break. So patiently, so quietly. I wouldn't give them the gratification. Instead, I lifted my chin and faced Collith. My insides roiled. "Well? Have I passed your test?" I asked. No waver or wobble betrayed me. *Bring back Damon. Bring back Damon. Bring back Damon.*

His expression was unreadable as ever. His crown glinted. "You have."

"Then what is this?"

While my back was turned, the Tongue had made his way up the stairs. After I spoke, he bent to mutter something in Collith's ear. They both regarded me for a moment more. Collith nodded, but his eyes were focused on something beyond me.

"Fortuna."

That voice. I turned, not wanting to breathe or speak, for fear it wasn't real.

Damon stood at the edge of the crowd, whole and alive, exactly where he'd been when I entered the room. It must've been part of the Tongue's spell. His gaze darted from me to the abandoned knife. It hit me, then, that he'd just watched me kill a version of himself. Slowly, I turned back to the body. It was still there, but Damon's face was gone. A stranger slumped in his place. He had clearly been brought up from the dungeons; his beard was long and matted, his skin covered in grime. I really had killed someone, even if it hadn't been Damon.

None of it mattered.

In a haze, I closed the distance between us. As though they belonged to someone else, I watched my hands cup Damon's face. They trembled against his skin. "You are my weakness," I whispered. As long as he was alive, these creatures could control me. All this time I thought I'd been outsmarting them. Beating them at their own game. Really, I had been following every pattern and course they set before me.

For a terrible moment, I considered snapping my brother's neck.

I heard a swift intake of breath—my own—and I swiftly withdrew from him. My chest heaved. The instant remorse felt like acid. I wished I could crawl out of my skin. What was happening? The thought of killing Damon, even if it had only lasted an instant, went against every reason I'd come to the Unseelie Court and every war I'd fought. The fae were infecting me like a disease. We'd been here too long. Never mind that I was married or that I would be queen.

We had to leave this place.

Damon said something, a note of concern in his voice. *Don't feel anything for me. I don't deserve it,* I wanted to scream at him. My first instinct was to stumble toward the door, but just as I started to, I realized how it would look. What they would think. They'd say that I was cracking. They'd conclude that I wasn't strong enough. They'd believe that even if they hadn't beaten me, they'd still won.

Somehow I found the strength to stop. The Court waited for me to speak. There were so many of them. So many to kill.

"Where are the musicians?" I finally whispered. A one-eyed faerie in the front row stared blankly. Another frowned with incomprehension. I forced myself to speak louder. "Where are the musicians? Isn't this a party?"

Collith must've made a gesture; gazes flicked toward him. Within a handful of seconds, a lute began to play. It was joined by the hollow sound of a drum. I saw humans rush through every door, holding trays aloft that were laden with drinks. More still followed with fresh, hot food. At long last, the attention fell away from me. The pressure eased in my chest. Blindly I found a spot along the wall to observe the festivities. Several faeries tried to speak with me, probably attempting to earn favor, but I acknowledged no one. Not even Jassin, who winked as he and Damon swirled past.

I waited until the celebration was well underway before slipping out the closest door.

It took longer than it should have to notice that Laurie walked beside me. Though there was so much I could've said, we didn't speak. We reached Collith's rooms without incident. In a methodical movement, I opened the door. I slipped through and peered at Laurie through the crack. "Sweet dreams, Your Majesty," he said. Whether it was a barb or encouragement, I didn't care. I closed the door.

Once inside, I closed my eyes and leaned against the wood for a moment. A face started to fill the darkness, though, and I hurriedly opened them again.

The room was warm and inviting. A cheery fire burned, the bed was made, and a bath awaited. Nothing had changed since I left hours ago. It seemed bizarre, even wrong, because everything had changed.

Feeling hollow, I walked to the water basin and put my hands inside. Red instantly bloomed across the clear surface. As I watched it, a whimper escaped me. Suddenly I was frantic. I rubbed at my skin so violently that water sloshed over the sides of the bowl. Within seconds all the red was off, but it wasn't enough. I kept rubbing, scraping, splashing. I needed to feel clean. I kept seeing the glassy eyes of that man, that stranger, who'd done absolutely nothing to me. Whose blood had coated my fingers.

Only when my hands were pink and stinging did I realize the truth; I would never be clean again.

Breathing hard, I backed away from the basin. The room was too quiet, too still. Water dripped onto the dirt floor. Seconds or minutes ticked by; I wasn't certain which. Eventually I drifted to the fire, drawn to the life emanating from those bright flames. Slowly, I dropped to my knees. The warmth was comforting, almost a presence of its own. But, inevitably, the events that had just transpired came creeping back. What I had seen. What I had done.

Quietly, so no one would hear, I pressed my face against my hands and wept.

Once my tears ran dry, I did nothing.

I didn't read, I didn't dream, I didn't cry some more. I simply sat in front of that fire, staring down into the shifting logs and flickering embers. My hands rested palm-up in my lap, limp and red, smarting from all the scrubbing.

Eventually a laugh came from the passageway. The sound jarred me from my strange stupor. Blinking, I frowned and turned. There was more than one faerie out there; their conversation drifted through the thin door. Something about an arranged marriage between two of the wealthier bloodlines. Only half-listening, I pulled the ponytail out, allowing my thick waves to tumble free. It eased the pain in my head a bit.

The door creaked open and Collith stumbled through. The crown on his head was crooked. He collapsed into the chair nearest me. Now the crown slid to the floor with a dull sound. Oblivious, Collith leaned forward, planting his elbows on his knees, and peered at me intently. In this light, his eyes were greener than ever before. "You were incredible today," my mate said. There was a slight slur in his words.

I wasn't sure whether to laugh or cry. "Are you drunk, Collith?"

"A little. I'm tired, too, which doesn't help." Despite his words, Collith left the comfort of the chair and lowered himself to the floor. It went against all laws of nature that he should make the move look graceful, but he did. He sat so that our shoulders pressed together. I had the distant thought that, if someone had told me a week ago I would soon be sharing a companionable silence with the King of the Unseelie Court, I would've laughed in their face. Yet here we were.

In another life, I would've called him a friend.

As the hour wore on, Collith dared to touch the back of my hand. I looked at him. Firelight flickered against half of his face, the other hidden in shadow. Through the bond, there came an undeniable feeling of longing. Collith wanted more than some fleeting moments in a bathtub. Images traveled between us, flashes of bare skin and heads thrown back.

But I felt raw. Like someone had ripped off my skin and every draft, every breath hurt. Not even someone as alluring as Collith could affect me now. Wordlessly I stood up and moved away, out of his reach. He didn't say anything. Once again I stared into the fire. I saw myself in the flames, stabbing Damon over and over. It was a choice I could never unmake, a moment I could never forget.

I wanted Collith to be in as much pain as I was… and I knew just the words to do it.

"There can never be anything more between us, you know. I'm in love with someone else," I said. It was hard to reconcile the dull, empty voice as my own.

The king must've heard the truth in it, though, because the air itself seemed to thicken. *Danger*, instinct warned. "Why didn't you tell me?" he asked tightly.

A faint, bitter smile curved my lips. I gripped the mantle. The wood was warm and rough. "Do I need to remind you of the secrets you kept, *my liege*? The secrets you still keep? I don't make a habit of baring my soul to strangers, either. Especially ones that blackmailed me into marriage."

"I'm sorry, Fortuna."

It was so unexpected that I faced him. I had braced myself for anger or jealousy. Instead, Collith's haggard face held nothing but regret. "Sorry for what?" I demanded.

He got to his feet and stood a handbreadth away. If one of us took a step or a long breath, our chests would touch. "For my conduct when we first met," he answered. His voice was low, more of a dying flame than someone trying to avoid being over-heard, I thought. Pain simmered beneath his voice like embers. "For manipulating you. If you'd entered the Unseelie Court as an unclaimed creature, they would've killed, raped, or enslaved you within the first hour. My preference would've been to wait and begin a courtship, but circumstances wouldn't allow for that. There are too many lives at stake, your brother's included."

I stared at him for a moment. Then, just like that, my grief turned to rage, star-bright and fire-hot. Before I could recon-sider, my hands flew out to shove him. Collith caught them against his chest as if they were nothing more than butterflies. I instantly moved to yank free. "Let go! Let go of me!"

Collith kept his grip on my wrists—being as gentle as he could, I suspected—and waited for the storm to pass. It didn't take long; grief had left me drained. After a minute or two, I closed my eyes and tipped forward, resting against his chest. Now it was my turn to say the words. "Why didn't you just tell me any of that?" I whispered into his collarbone. What I would've done with such knowledge, I had no idea. But now I would never know. Now I would never have a chance to experience what could've been between us.

He swallowed audibly. Or maybe I was only able to hear it because I was pressed against him. Slowly, Collith loosened his iron grip. He bent his head and kissed the inside of my wrist. Something within me stirred. "There were a dozen reasons, really," I heard him say. "For one, I had already started to know you. It wouldn't have been enough incentive to agree—you would've opted to risk coming here without the protection of my name. Another reason is that it's simply my nature to withhold and distrust. I wasn't born with this scar; someone bestowed it upon me. And there's also the fact that… I just wanted you."

His honesty sent a bolt of panic through my heart. I pulled away and raked the hair out of my face. "What does any of this have to do with Oliver?" I asked, having trouble breathing normally. The fire had done its job too well; it felt like we were standing inside an oven.

Collith's eyes flickered, taking note of the name. Making the connection. *Ollie.* Collith stepped back. "Nothing. Absolutely nothing," he said.

A stiff silence reigned the room now. Collith returned to the chair, pulled his boots off, and rested his elbows atop his knees. A sigh left him. Once again, it struck me as an oddly human sound. He tilted his head and peered up at me. "I can't help thinking you would feel differently if I hadn't made certain choices at the beginning."

"You're probably right," I said bluntly. "But we can't go back in time, can we?"

He studied my expression for a long moment. "No, we can't."

I still hadn't acknowledged his admission. *I just wanted you.* It was as though Collith had knocked on a door that I stood on the other side of. Nothing good would come of me opening it. Instead, I flung myself into the chair next to him and said,

"Hand me one of those books. Might as well keep trying to gain an advantage."

"You're relentless," Collith remarked as he acquiesced. When he said it like that, it sounded like a compliment.

Our fingers brushed as I took the book from him. This one had a thick layer of dust on its cover. I brushed it off, sending particles dancing through the air, and smiled at him through the cloud. "Oh, you have no idea."

CHAPTER EIGHTEEN

I drank the sleep tonic again.

It didn't taste any better the second time around. If it had been up to me, I would've preferred to fall asleep naturally and talk to Oliver. But whenever I closed my eyes, I saw that knife sliding into Damon's chest.

Well, at least I wasn't picturing the Death Bringer or the Leviathan anymore.

For a time, the king tried to stay awake, too. He sprawled in his chair more casually than I'd ever seen him, reading a book that looked brand-new. *The Drowned Girls,* its title read in blocky white letters. Did he make trips to Barnes and Noble? It was an odd mental image, this beautiful faerie browsing the mystery section. More than once, I almost gave in to the urge to ask.

As Collith read, though, his eyes kept closing. Eventually he moved to the rope and asked someone to fetch the tonic. When it arrived, he gave it to me without a word.

The last thing I remembered was him carrying me to bed.

When I woke next, there was no way to tell what time it was. Voices came from the passageway, which is what must've pulled me from sleep—the guards were changing shifts. I rested there for another few minutes, trying to avoid thinking about Shameek, the third trial, and what Damon was doing right then. Or what someone was doing to Damon.

Restless, I rolled onto my side. There, so close that our noses were nearly touching, Collith was still unconscious.

He was a messy sleeper, I'd learned. The two nights with him had both ended with the covers tossed or tangled. He slept in briefs—a surprisingly modern choice, given the clothing he wore at Court—and nothing else. I allowed myself a long, leisurely exploration of his body. Dark hair traveled down the center of his flat stomach and disappeared into that waistband. His thighs were slender but firm. The rest of him...

I swiftly averted my gaze and turned to leave the bed.

Since they were the only clothes I had—and I refused to stay in the outfit I'd worn during the trial—I put the jeans and plaid shirt back on. They were wrinkled but clean. I also pulled on my hiking boots, since it felt strangely intimate to walk around Collith's rooms barefoot. Dressed and alert, I found myself with time to burn. The stack of books was right where I'd left it last night. Though the trials were behind me, the coronation lay straight ahead, which meant my education on the fae had only just begun. I felt jittery, though, and desperate to keep moving. The room seemed smaller, as if the walls had crept closer overnight.

It was probably more dangerous than ever to go for a stroll around the Unseelie Court; doubtless I had more enemies than supporters when it came to my looming queenship. But it felt like if I spent one more second in this room, with its low ceiling and never-dying flames, I was going to scream. In a burst of frustration I snatched the mirror shard from its hiding spot, shoved it into my boot, and hurried to the door.

Nuvian was waiting in the passageway, along with a guard I finally recognized. She'd been at the tribunal. A memory flashed—her fist coming at me and the taste of blood in my mouth. For a moment I glared at her. She just stared back impassively, looking so breakable in the firelight. I was tempted to do to her what I'd done to Nuvian.

Instead, I turned my back on them and walked away. I had no idea where I intended to go, but they didn't know that. Well, the female didn't know that. She was the only one who followed; Nuvian remained rooted outside Collith's door.

Almost immediately, I found myself drawn in a certain direction. It took me a few minutes to realize that, at long last, I had learned my way to the throne room. There was the door with the snakes. There was the violent mural. Why I'd wanted to come here, I couldn't say. Nothing good had ever come from this place. I stopped within the doorway. The long-haired female halted a few yards away. The fact that there was so much distance between us seemed odd for a faerie that had been instructed to guard me. Then I remembered she hadn't been given that directive, exactly. She was just here because they'd probably get in even more trouble if I died and they were back at Collith's rooms, disregarding the spirit of his order.

But none of that mattered. It was a waste of time to even think about the Guardians' motives. Sighing, I peered at the strange chandeliers, the vast ceilings, the twisting throne. It seemed cruel to the ones that designed such a beautiful place, having their legacy stained by death and darkness.

What was it Collith had said during our dance? I remembered his hazel eyes burning with an earnestness that I'd dismissed as a facade. *Something worth saving, don't you think?*

I shoved the thought into a dim, dusty corner of my mind; there was nothing worth saving in creatures like Jassin or Arcaena.

There were hardly any faeries to be seen in here now. Instead, slaves occupied most of the space. Their expressions varied from exhaustion to agitation. In that moment, I realized what these poor creatures were doing.

They were preparing for my coronation.

I stepped forward, thinking to stop them. "I wouldn't," Laurie said, materializing next to me. I jumped and scowled. "They'd be forced to listen to you, what with your new position, but then they'd be beaten for the unfinished work."

My hands clenched. Yes, some things definitely needed to change around here, and I wouldn't be as delicate as Collith in enforcing them. These creatures were in for a rude awakening.

Of their own volition, my eyes went to the spot where the redcaps had been feasting. Surprisingly, Shameek's body was gone. There were still bloody smears on the flagstones, but everything else had been removed. I pitied the ones who'd had to do it.

Laurie stood so close to me our elbows nearly touched. "His Majesty ordered him to be buried. Highly unusual."

"Unusual? Why?"

He raised his silvery brows. "Your friend died a traitor. Not only did he try to harm one of us, but he sided with a Nightmare instead of our superior race. I'm not saying that I share this way of thinking, of course, this is just how most of them view it. Normally the human would've been left to rot. Or, if he had perished another way, it would be customary to burn him, as is the fae tradition. Instead our king gave the fellow an honorable, human burial."

The revelation sent my mind back through the passageways, twisting and winding through the dirt, until it arrived at the bed Collith still slumbered in. I imagined myself looking down at him, seeing again the lines in his skin. The jagged scar. Imperfections that managed to be beautiful, despite what they indicated.

Damon's desperate, hope-tinged words echoed back to me. *There's some good in him.*

Was this how Jassin had brainwashed my brother? Was I walking the same path that had led him here?

Disturbed by the thought, I faced Laurie, effectively putting the entire room out of sight. Now it was my turn to raise a brow. "I thought our... association was over."

"Nothing ends, Fortuna Sworn," he responded airily. He kept his gaze on the humans making their harried arrangements. "There are only continuations and beginnings."

I couldn't resist the urge to roll my eyes. In the next instant, a girl—she couldn't be more than twelve or thirteen—dashed by. A woman standing in a distant doorway made a sharp gesture at her and said something in Russian. The girl reached her and, after the older slave snatched her arm in a rough grip, they vanished.

There were still others in the room, but watching those two leave was a reminder of the work I had to do, too. In my head, reading those books on the fae had become not just important, but necessary. Someday the knowledge they held would either save lives or bring about the end of this Court.

The two weren't mutually exclusive, actually.

With that, my sense of urgency was back. I started toward the double doors and Laurie fell into step beside me. Once again, the female guard kept her distance as she followed. "You know, I've been thinking about that night," I said to Laurie, keeping my voice low. The guard could probably hear every word, anyway. "It was you who sent Collith's guards away, didn't you? The whole thing was a test. You wanted to see what I'd do."

Laurie laughed. The sound was lovely, however loathe I was to admit it. "I'd love to pretend I have that much power," he answered.

Laugh all you want, I thought. *We should've known you could lie. You've had longer than anyone else to perfect it.*

Another silence came between us. As it became overlong, the throne filled my thoughts again. I tried to imagine myself sitting there, embraced by all those gnarled branches. Facing an entire court of monsters. I couldn't hide a note of apprehension as I asked, "What's it like? The ceremony?"

"Let me think. Ah, well, have you ever seen the coronation of a British monarch?"

"No."

"You haven't missed anything exciting, rest assured. One of their kings, Ecgfrith, was fae. That isn't common knowledge, by the way, so I wouldn't go sharing it. Anyhow, he borrowed most of our traditions for his shiny coronation. Really, though, I'd say the most significant part is the vows of fealty."

Those three words sent my heart sprinting. Collith had mentioned this already—it was the reason I'd put myself through those hellish trials to begin with—but here was a chance to know even more. "Does every member of the Court make one?" I ventured, trying to sound offhand. There was a thick root jutting from our path. As I stepped over it, Laurie shifted as though to hold out his hand, but he didn't. He hopped over the root, every movement fluid and deliberate as a rushing river. *What are you hiding, faerie?* I wondered.

"I admit, I'm tempted to say 'yes' just to see your face," Laurie said, ignoring the obvious lull. "But no. Just the heads of the bloodlines—or a descendant standing in for them—and the Guardians."

Collith's room loomed ahead. Nuvian was gone, which likely meant the king was, too. The realization sent a flood of... something through me. Not disappointment, of course. More like chagrin. I had hoped to hear how Damon was, or request more books, or ask where Shameek was buried. His family deserved to know what had happened to him. "What do rulers usually ask for? As proof of their loyalty, I mean?" I asked, acting as though I was unaffected by returning to an empty room.

We were almost to the door. To my question, Laurie shrugged. His expression didn't reveal how he felt about Collith's absence, either. "Usually a bit of blood."

A tiny, dark smile hovered at the edges of my mouth. Oh, there would be blood, all right.

"Now." At the door, Laurie turned and focused on me. His eyes seemed to glow in the dimness. "Would you like to see your dress?"

Laurie had outdone himself this time.

The dress was both bizarre and beautiful. Its bodice was hard and textured, a sort of exotic flowered pattern in hues of red, yellow, and black. The neckline was low and straight across, lined with faux fur—at least, I hoped it was faux fur. At my thighs, it ended in ragged strands, as though someone had torn the skirt off. This was where the tulle began. The length was long, dark, and dramatic. The sleeves, too, were made of this see-through material. I stood in front of the mirror Laurie must've had delivered, fingering the dress's texture.

"And one final touch." As was becoming his habit, Laurie popped into sight behind me. An irritated growl ripped from my throat. He acted like he hadn't heard and dropped a necklace around my neck. It took him a moment to secure the clasp, and when I saw it was the sapphire Collith had given me, I had an instant to reject it. A chance to deny it.

I didn't move. The chain settled into place, a cool spot against my skin. The jewel was a solid weight. Light flickered along the edges and facets. "Why does it matter so much what I'm wearing?" I asked, touching it.

"The more they care about your dress and how low your neckline is, the less they're going to care about what you're actually doing in it."

"Really?"

"No."

I couldn't hold back a laugh. Laurie was still behind me, his fingers making quick work of the buttons. In the mirror's reflection, I caught him smiling. His head was bent, and because he was taller, a silken strand of his hair brushed my bare shoulder. Somehow I didn't think it was accidental. An involuntary shiver whispered through me. *Jesus, what's wrong with you?* I thought, turning quickly. *Oliver, Collith, Laurie...*

"It's all right, you know," Laurie said suddenly. He saw the question in my expression and smiled again. There was no mockery in it, thankfully; I only saw kindness and a hint of sympathy. "Sex. Desire. Lust. These things are natural. Humans have taught themselves restraint—they believe to give in is to be wanting, somehow—but that's such small thinking. Why set limits when we are creatures of impulse?"

"Because there are always consequences," I countered, my cheeks hot. Our faces were a breath apart. It would take a single movement to close the distance. "Aren't fae all about balance, too?"

"Touché. But coming from someone who's been alive much, much longer than you, a word of advice. My biggest regrets over the centuries were not borne from 'consequences'; they were because I let pesky fears get in the way. Hey, you know a thing or two about fear, don't you?"

With a wink, the bright-headed faerie moved to the door. Once again, I rolled my eyes. Laurie didn't see it, though. "Any other words of wisdom before I go become Queen of the Unseelie Court?" I drawled after him, hoping he didn't sense the pang of apprehension within me.

He paused with one hand on the door. His expression sobered. "Don't thank them for their fealty. You've earned it. It's your right," he said.

"That's not arrogant at all."

The lovely faerie inclined his head. "Of course it is. We are Fallen. Arrogance is in our blood."

With that, he went through the door. The guards standing

outside startled at the suddenness of it. Laurie walked past, but they didn't spare him so much as a glance; instead, they both gave me odd looks. I frowned back. Was the dress ridiculous? Is that what had their panties in a bunch?

"Fortuna? Are you ready?" a familiar voice asked. A moment later, Collith appeared, and the sight of him made my stomach flutter. He was every inch the king of shadows and impulse. His legs were once again encased in black leather pants, and the tightness of them made his muscles more prominent. Over these he wore a long, red coat. Its trimming was also leather. The shoulders were made of a material that was hard and spiked. The shirt beneath was white and loose, but cut deeply, revealing the smooth planes of his chest.

And there, glinting against his skin, he wore a sapphire that matched mine. "I had it made," Collith murmured, noticing the direction of my gaze. "Fae males have never worn something to represent their mates, which seemed strange to me. Why wouldn't we want to announce it to the world? Why shouldn't our partners have the same expectations our customs expect of them?"

We hadn't spoken to each other since I'd said that I would never love him—it was baffling that these were the words he chose. Words that made it plain he thought we had a future. I didn't know how to respond. Strangely, I didn't have it in me to shatter his hopes again. I was also self-conscious that Nuvian and the other guard could hear our exchange. "We'd better go," was all I said.

Moving at the same time, he offered his arm just as I reached to take it. Collith smiled. It transformed his entire face, and I smiled back without thinking. Something soft and colorful flew down the bond. It took me several seconds to realize it was awe. For a disorienting moment, I saw myself through Collith's eyes. It was my face, but not the one I saw in any mirror or reflection. Collith thought I was beautiful. Not for my perfection, though... he admired my endurance. My devotion to Damon. My ferocity.

"It's not too late," Collith said quietly, unaware that I'd slipped inside his head.

I blinked in confusion. Oh. To change my mind, he meant. I'd thought we were done having this conversation. "One would think you're having regrets, Your Majesty," I retorted, tucking what just happened away for later contemplation.

"About you? Never."

Then what do you have regrets about? I wanted to ask. But we were being joined by more guards and, after the third trial, I was leery of having an audience. They walked ahead and behind us, creating a protective barrier, and we began the journey toward the throne room. With every step, my anxiety heightened. Clammy palms, shallow breaths, overwhelming urges. Collith sensed it—or maybe just saw it on my face—and threaded our fingers together in reassurance. I allowed the touch, because it felt like the only thing stopping me from bolting.

The passages weren't empty today; every few feet, there were clusters of fae. When they spotted us, they went silent. Once or twice, I thought I heard something muttered in my direction, but we walked too quickly to catch the words.

It felt like we arrived at the throne room in seconds instead of minutes. We halted beneath the mural, and I wasn't ready for the scene we came upon. Wasn't ready for any of it, period.

The entire Unseelie Court was waiting. It was more faeries than had attended the first, second, and third trial combined. I'd never seen such a huge gathering before. Like me, the fae were dressed to impress. Even from my limited vantage point, I could see there were hundreds of beautiful gowns and tailored suits. Countless voices floated toward the ceiling, sounding more like a great waterfall than separate conversations. Little by little, though, the crowd noticed our presence in the doorway. A hush fell.

The path to the throne—no, *thrones*, since there were two up there now—was so narrow that Collith and I had to walk with our shoulders pressed together. One of his spikes poked my skin, but they were more decorative than efficient, because it was merely uncomfortable instead of painful.

As we made our way to the dais, the assembled faeries started throwing tokens into our path. Roses, jewelry, letters. So many that I had to hide my surprise. Were they hoping to gain favor? Was it a tradition? Or was it just my effect as a Nightmare?

There were some that spit or sneered, of course. Those were the ones that I gave a serene smile, hoping they saw it for the silent taunt it was. It also held a promise; I hadn't even begun repaying them for what had been done to me and Damon.

Damon, who I had yet to find amongst the faces turned my way.

After we reached the front, Collith moved aside. Immediately over a dozen faeries moved to form a half-circle behind me. One of them wore beads in her hair; they made a tinkling sound every time she shifted. I glanced over the rest, curious if these were the heads of the bloodlines. Four of them were Tarragon, Chandrelle, and the twins. The dark-skinned male emanated tranquility, as he had every time I'd encountered him. Chandrelle's expression was carefully blank. And Arcaena watched me with glittering eyes that resembled a snake curled in sand. A snake that, by the look of it, anyone would think was drowsy or slow to react... and that would be the last mistake they ever made. It went against all my instincts to put my back to her.

The rest were strangers. I didn't know who was an enemy or an ally.

The Tongue was present, too, of course. His robes were of the brightest, purest white. The only jewelry he wore were several golden rings on his thick fingers. Once everyone was in place, he proceeded with his usual combination of gestures, ingredients, and incantations. His jowls jiggled. I paid attention with a dedication I'd never shown in school, hoping to recognize a ritual from Collith's books, but my attention kept wandering. Where was Damon? Had Jassin guessed at my plan and locked him away?

None of what followed felt real—it had the haziness of being trapped between a dream and coming awake. After a time, the Tongue told me to kneel. I was barely aware of obeying; my pulse was a herd of wild horses thundering over hills and rivers. "Are you willing to take the oath, Fortuna Sworn?" the faerie finally boomed in English.

I hesitated, and in the following silence, Collith's voice drifted through my mind as I remembered the consequences of this oath. *There's something else you should know. One of the rituals during the coronation might make you reconsider. After it's completed, in the same way you and I are bound, so you would be bound to them.*

Them?

Every single faerie that resides in this Court.

The Tongue was still waiting for an answer. I licked my lips. "Yes, I am."

He paused, as if he sensed my trepidation, and I stopped breathing. He regarded me with his beady, dark eyes. After a moment, the faerie started asked a series of questions. Though he still spoke in English, the language he used was convoluted. I still hardly understood what he was saying. Belying the riot happening inside me, though, I agreed to each without hesitation or waver. My voice echoed throughout the room.

At the end of it, the Tongue placed a crown made of twigs on my head. Leaves still dangled off the delicate branches. That was when everything became clear again, sharpening and brightening like an image in Photoshop. I arched my neck back to peer up at the Tongue, but he didn't pronounce me queen, as I thought he would. He gestured that I should stand, which I did. No one spoke or moved. I waited for their thoughts or desires to invade me. Nothing happened. Clearly, I was supposed to do something. I searched for Laurie, hoping he would offer guidance.

"Fortuna," Collith said from the throne. I turned quickly. He sat there, detached and unmoving. "Claim your place here."

For the first time, I truly looked at it. The new throne was not natural or worn, like the one Collith sat in. Instead, it was a formidable chair. The back of it was several feet tall. Its cushions were the color of blood. High above, in the place of wings, was an intricate design. There someone had recreated the Leviathan in gleaming silver. Its tail curved around one edge, and flames shot down the other.

Whether the choice was meant to be a jab or a symbol of strength, I had no idea, but it was a reminder of the blood on my hands because of these creatures. I gritted my teeth, ascended the stairs, and gathered my dress. The skirt flared around me dramatically as I sat. Hundreds of faces stared back at me. I tried to imitate Collith's expressionless countenance, but my blood burned too hot. I knew I was glaring.

After a stilted stillness, Nuvian stepped forward. He removed his sword from its sheath, knelt, and touched its tip to the floor. His armor looked as though it had been buffed with oil. "I am Nuvian of the bloodline Folduin," he said loudly enough to make his voice carry. "I pledge my life and loyalty to Queen Fortuna. What does she require?"

Remembering Laurie's comments, I gripped the armrests and answered, "I require a drop of blood."

Without hesitation, Nuvian sliced the fleshy part of his palm with that wicked-looking edge. Scarlet drops appeared. The faerie flipped his hand and the Court watched as they plummeted to the flagstones. After this, Nuvian got back to his feet. I was relieved there wasn't anything more to it, and it was on the tip of my tongue to thank him. Luckily, the Right Hand retreated before any words could escape.

Another faerie was already moving forward. We went through the same song and dance. She walked backward, melding into the crowd, and yet another occupied the spot. I tried to remember the names and faces, but there were too many. Úna made her vow, of course, her eyes burning with desire as she spoke the formal words. Instead I heard her saying, spittle flying from her mouth, *Remember that I helped you.* It was a relief when she completed the vows. Then it was Omar's turn; he trembled through every second.

Eventually I lost track of time. There were no clocks at the Unseelie Court. It was taking all my self-control not to fidget as I waited for Jassin to come forward. *Where is he, damn it?*

Apparently every Guardian had made their pledge and it was time for the bloodlines; a male separated from the throng that didn't carry a sword. When I noticed who he'd left behind, my spine straightened a bit. *Here we go,* I thought.

The faerie bent a knee. He was rather unremarkable, as faeries went, with a square chin and a blunt haircut. He wore gray slacks and a matching jacket. I sensed no power within him. In fact, were it not for his pointed ears, I would've assumed he was human. "I am Ilphas of the bloodline Daenan," the male announced. "I pledge my life and loyalty to Queen Fortuna. What does she require?"

I tilted my head. "Is that your mate, Ilphas?"

Surprise flickered in his eyes. I felt the shock of the onlookers, too; this was the first time I'd said anything beyond the request for a drop of blood. He glanced behind him and saw that I was, indeed, pointing to the female he'd been standing beside. The chain she held, which was attached to the emaciated werewolf, had been clinking throughout my ceremony. "She is, Your Majesty."

"Wonderful. For your fealty, I require the werewolf's freedom," I stated. Collith was staring, I could feel it. I was going off the script that had been written for me.

Clearly befuddled by this turn of events, Ilphas opened his mouth. "Unfortunately—"

I could already hear the words that would come out of it. Something along the lines of, *Unfortunately the wolf is not mine to give.* My nostrils flared. "Ah, don't lie to me, now. I believe the fae take 'what's yours is mine' even more seriously than humans when it comes to marriage. If the wolf is hers, you have a claim to it, as well. Please don't waste more of the Court's time."

His mouth tightened with displeasure. What bothered him more, I wondered? Taking orders from a female or taking orders from a Nightmare? Hell, probably both. But Ilphas was no fool; he stopped arguing. He bowed again—this one notably briefer—and walked back to his mate. They whispered furiously. At last, Ilphas yanked the end of the chain from her grasp. She turned her gaze on me, visibly simmering. The clear jewel resting against her forehead quivered. Ilphas returned to the base of the dais, yanking the werewolf along behind him. The creature didn't have enough spirit left to resist, and its nails clicked against the stones meekly. Ilphas thrust the end of the chain at me. "My fealty, Your Majesty."

"Take him to my room. Stay with him, if he reacts badly, but do not cause him any pain or harm. I'll come after the ceremony," I added. Ilphas bowed a third time, wisely keeping any remarks or reactions to himself, and walked toward the nearest exit.

Arcaena took his place.

The moment I caught sight of her, my blood went cold. All thoughts of the werewolf ran shrieking. Her eyes gleamed as our gazes met. There was no trace of fear in her; she thought me weak. *Bound in chains of her own making,* she'd said. Well, those chains were gone now.

A moment later, the ancient faerie's voice sliced through the silence, and I knew I wasn't imagining the trace of mockery in her tone. It felt grating to my ears. "I am Arcaena of the bloodline Tralee. I pledge my life and loyalty to Queen Fortuna of the Unseelie Court. What does she require?"

I'd been waiting for this moment since the night she used her power on me. I wanted to savor it. Memorize it. After she spoke, we stared at each other, the seconds ticking past. I knew we were both hearing the words I'd hissed at her only hours ago. *Remember this moment. I know I will.*

Just as Collith turned to me, probably to ask why I hadn't asked for fealty yet, I smiled at Arcaena of the bloodline Tralee. "Are you familiar with the Rites of Thogon?" I questioned.

Once more, I felt the force of the king's attention. Waves of alarm and surprise came through the bond. I ignored him. Arcaena was worried, too—though she wasn't moving, somehow the faerie had gone still. "I am," she said tightly.

"Excellent. Perform them on yourself. That is what I require."

The silence shattered. Hundreds of faeries began talking all at once. No one dared intervene or protest, but the Court's shock was palpable. They were probably wondering how I'd even come into possession of such knowledge.

The Rites of Thogon. Centuries ago, there had been an unusual faerie, known for his kindness and empathy. He was also famous for his eerie abilities; a single touch inflicted gruesome diseases upon his victims. When Thogon met and fell in love with a human, he decided to do whatever it took to free himself of this terrible power. He went to witches and spoke to demons. After years of failed attempts, he succeeded in stripping himself of his powers with what became known as the Rites of Thogon. But, as with most things fae, it had come at a terrible cost.

The rites made Thogon mortal.

Looking like a cornered rat, Arcaena glanced at the Guardians lining the walls and blocking the doorways. There was no pity in their faces or loosening of the grips on their hilts.

Next she looked to her twin, who was tight-lipped with fury, but clearly powerless to intervene. Her choice was as simple as mine had been when I'd faced Damon with our father's knife—obey or be killed.

I watched her come to this realization. At last, Arcaena faced me again. Her lip curled, hatred sparking from those eyes now, and I knew I'd made a true enemy. *Bring it on*, I thought at her, wishing Damon were here to see what was coming. This ancient faerie would be as powerless as I had been. As Damon had been. They weren't invincible. They weren't omnipotent.

Whatever her flaws, at least Arcaena didn't bother delaying the inevitable. Like a soufflé, she sank to the floor in a fluid motion. A Guardian removed a dagger from his boot and held it out to her. After a hesitation so short I wondered if I'd imagined it, she accepted the blade and pressed it to her palm. Then, using her own blood, Arcaena drew symbols on the flagstones. She couldn't hide the way her hands shook. Even this part of the spell was grueling; several times she had to make a new cut to get more blood. She must've made a mistake at one point, because the Tongue stepped forward and said something that sounded like a correction. Arcaena didn't acknowledge him.

Then she started the recitation.

Saying the words were easy, at first. But everyone knew the exact moment she began to feel it—Arcaena suddenly hunched. The jut of her spine was at odds with the graceful faerie I'd seen so far. Her voice became halting and guttural. From what I'd understood of the text, the spell was yanking her powers out like a tapeworm out of someone's intestines. Drool gleamed on the stones at Arcaena's knees. To her credit, she didn't stop... and it wasn't a short spell.

We watched her perform the rites for the better part of an hour.

At last, Arcaena's eyes rolled to the back of her head and she collapsed. Everyone in the room waited with bated breath, but she didn't regain consciousness. A trickle of blood came from her nose. I nodded at Nuvian, who gestured curtly to two of his Guardians. They hurried down the dais and took hold of Arcaena's arms. Just as I had been after my tribunal, they dragged her away. I didn't take my eyes off their progress for a single moment. Only until the three of them disappeared through a side door did I turn my focus back to those still waiting to make their vows.

"Shall we continue?" I asked. My entire body thrummed—I felt more alive than I ever had before. I looked for the Tongue and directed my next question at him. "How many do we have left?"

"There are two, Your Majesty."

Before he'd finished speaking, another Guardian stepped out of the crowd. Either there was no particular order to the vows or this one was late in coming forward. I suspected the latter—it was the faerie who'd struck me at the tribunal. She met my gaze unflinchingly, but we both knew that just as Arcaena was, this faerie was at my mercy. Even so, her voice rang into the stillness without wavering. "I am Lyari of the bloodline Paynore. I pledge my life and loyalty to Queen Fortuna. What does she require?"

Once again, I allowed silence to fill the space between us. Somewhere in the crowd, a human coughed. As my indecision stretched, I realized that something kept me from taking immediate retribution upon Lyari.

This faerie's beauty was more delicate than most. Her nose was small and slightly upturned. Her skin was as luminescent as a pearl. There was a tiny cleft in her chin that was more charming than rebellious. Her hair fell to her waist in rich, umber waves. Perhaps her violence came not from darkness, but from a fierce desire to prove herself.

"For your pledge of fealty, I require you to act as my personal guard," I pronounced.

Lyari's eyes widened before she caught herself and schooled

her expression. She nodded once, a jerky movement, and ascended the dais to stand at my right. My very own Right Hand. I waved at the crowd to continue, and the next faerie emerged.

Jassin smiled up at me.

I ordered my heart to calm. There stood Damon, just behind him. I scanned my brother's face, seeking any new cuts or bruises. Then, when he was certain I'd see it, Jassin grabbed Damon's chin and jerked his head to the right. He kissed him, a hard and wet claiming. His timing had been deliberate—now that Damon's head was turned, I saw the red handprint on his cheek. There was no doubt in my mind that it would match the shape of Jassin's.

"Your vow, faerie," I spat.

The creature lingered before releasing Damon. He faced me, every inch of him the picture of compliance. He stood with his hands folded behind his back, his long tresses straightened and shining. Not a single hair out of place. "I am Jassin of the blood-line Sarwraek," he purred. "I pledge my life and loyalty to Queen Fortuna. What does she require?"

There was a swarm of hornets in my stomach now. This was the question that had pounded at me from the moment Collith mentioned the vows of fealty. This was the question that had lived in every thought as I fought the Leviathan. This was the question that had given me hope in all this deep, endless darkness. "For your pledge, I require the release of Damon Sworn," I said.

However ingenious I'd thought my idea was, no one else seemed astonished. With an unhappy expression, Damon began to walk toward me. Once again I didn't dare to breathe, on the slight chance it would wake me up, and this ceremony turned out to be a dream. *I did it. I can't believe I did it,* I thought dazedly. Whatever else happened to me, at least Damon was safe. He would go on to have the life our parents envisioned for him.

He hadn't even made it to the dais when Jassin grabbed his arm and yanked him back.

My brother wasn't able to stifle a cry of pain. I leaped up, on the verge of calling for the guards. "You never specified the length of time, my lady," Jassin interjected. Damon kept his eyes on the ground, his face just low enough that I couldn't see it, and I wondered if he was trying to hide relief.

Rage boiled inside me, more at my own folly than Jassin's trickery. Collith said something then, his tone logical and soothing. But I couldn't make out the words past the roaring in my ears. The wrath spilled over. I looked at the Unseelie King and said, my voice strangely distant, "Someone has to stop him, Collith."

Terror shone in his eyes. "Fortuna, don't—"

I fixed my gaze on Jassin and breathed, "I challenge you."

Yet another ripple of shock went through the crowd. Challenges were a tradition they had ceased using centuries ago—even the fae thought it was archaic—but I'd stumbled across the information in one of Collith's books. The opponents were placed in a warded circle. The magic couldn't be broken until one of them was dead. The fights were usually bloody and brutal, but sometimes, they lasted days. In one circumstance, it went on for years.

The Tongue was already at our sides; he moved quickly for someone his size. As the crowd buzzed, he went about sprinkling a circle of white powder around us, leaving a small piece of the ground untouched. Salt. In a detached way, I wondered what he got out of all this, if using such power drained the very years from him. "As is custom, the challenged will be allowed to choose the weapon," the Tongue informed me, thankfully oblivious to my thoughts.

I shrugged. "Fine."

The heavyset faerie left to fetch some ingredients from an awaiting slave. Jassin fixed his emerald eyes on me. "Did you like my gift?" he whispered. "I would've used your brother, but they wanted him alive for the third trial, so I made do."

For a moment, I stared at him. *What the hell is he talking about?* It only took a few more seconds to put it together, though. The realization hit me like a highway collision. Shameek. His gift had been Shameek. On that table, being feasted on, more blood and bones than a body.

I was going to be sick.

The Tongue returned with a handful of odds and ends. His palm cupped a dead dragonfly, a rodent-sized heart, a blue flower, and a tusk of some sort. I breathed evenly and refused to let Jassin glimpse the fury coursing through me at his revelation. "Enough. Make your choice," I ordered. Surprisingly, nothing in my voice gave it away.

Jassin looked to the Tongue, who nodded to indicate, I assumed, that I was right. It was time to choose the weapon I was going to kill him with. My brother's tormentor smiled and said, "I choose… fear."

It was better than a soap opera; the Unseelie Court burst into sound again after Jassin spoke. The Tongue raised his voice over the masses, brandishing that trusty knife of his. He grasped Jassin's pale hand and cut it, then did the same to mine. I hardly registered the pain. He left the circle and closed it behind him.

"Our blood was once as bright as the sun. Did you know that?" Jassin asked, watching me instead of the bright beads swelling through our broken skin. Laurie had spoken the truth —their blood was blue. The vibrant drops fell into the fire with faint hisses. There was a tangible shift in the air, but I couldn't define what kind, exactly. The din happening outside the circle seemed muted, as well. I didn't reply, but I kept my eyes on Jassin's as the Tongue starting chanting rapidly in the language of angels.

Suddenly I felt a spot of warmth at my side. When I dared a glance, I was shocked to see Laurie. No one looked his way or questioned his presence right outside the circle. Just as the guards hadn't when he'd left Collith's rooms. Just as Collith himself hadn't on every occasion they occupied the same space.

In that instant, a puzzle piece clicked into place. Something I should've realized days ago. "They can't see you, can they?" I asked under my breath. Jassin quirked a brow, knowing I wasn't speaking to him, somehow.

"No," Laurie said simply.

He didn't offer any explanations. My mind raced. "Well, your secret will probably die with me in a few minutes."

"Are you broken?" Jassin asked, his tone mildly curious.

We both ignored him. Laurie moved into my line of vision. He was dressed in a royal blue tunic with gold trimming. Combined with his silver hair, he was devastating. Who the hell *was* this faerie? "I just wanted to say that you're the bravest creature I've ever met," he told me with undeniable sincerity. "Should've mentioned it earlier. You distracted me."

I choked on a hysterical laugh. "That's nice, but compliments won't help me terrify a faerie who gets off on fear."

"Don't you know what strengthens a Nightmare's power?" Laurie crooked his finger and leaned over the fire. His breath—which somehow smelled of wildflowers and green things—warmed my neck. "Unleashed fury. Pain. The things bad dreams are made of."

Before I could respond or react, he blew a kiss and retreated. Then I couldn't say anything even if I wanted to; the spell was taking hold of me and Jassin. It was a sensation akin to falling. Colors and snapshots blurred past. Eons later, the chaos screeched to a halt. I was still standing, I realized, and my eyes were closed.

Jassin had chosen fear, which meant I was about to get a taste of my own medicine. Except, in this case, one or both of us was definitely going to die from it. I wasn't off to a good start, either, seeing as dread was already trying to sink its claws into me. I reluctantly opened my eyes, prepared to see the garage where the goblins had kept me, or the Death Bringer, or that wet dungeon. Instead, I opened my eyes to a ceiling. It was night. Rain pattered against the window to my left. I was lying down. A small boy was tucked against my side, thumb lodged firmly in his mouth as he slept.

I recognized it all instantly. Panic burned through me like wildfire. *Oh, Fortuna, you fool.*

This was where my parents were killed.

Before Oliver had manifested, when I was a child, nightmares plagued me constantly. I always woke with my chest heaving, skin gleaming with sweat. On the night my parents died, I had another one. But that time, as my eyes opened, a roar shook the entire house.

It was inhuman, full of rage and hunger. I flew upright, still trapped halfway between nightmare and reality. Damon didn't stir. There came the sound of tearing flesh. A gurgle. I was frozen with terror. *Get out, get out, get out,* instinct screamed.

But I wasn't controlling this vision. Jassin was. He wasn't about to change history in my favor.

Against my will, I carefully peeled the covers aside. On eight-year-old legs I padded into the hallway, making sure to close the door behind me. Damon was my constant shadow, and if he woke up, he'd insist on following. I turned, thinking to check the living room in case the TV was on... and stopped short at the sight of a figure on the floor, slumped against the wall. A whimper left me. "Mommy?"

No answer.

Though the urge to run filled every fiber of my being, I approached the prone form. My mother had died with her mouth open, probably just as she'd been about to scream. Her eyes were wide and terrified. Her entire front had been torn open like it was paper and her insides spilled onto the carpet.

I felt my mind crack. It was close, so close to shattering. But

I was moving again, stepping over Mom. I knew where I was heading. Trapped inside this younger version of myself, I fought it. Pleas and sobs lodged in my throat. I imagined digging my heels in, grabbing hold of the doorway, anything to stay out of that room. Younger me was naive, though. She had hope that she'd find one of her parents still alive.

Dad hadn't even had a chance to get out of bed.

The only reason Mom had gotten so far was most likely because the killer had been busy eating her husband. I knew, beyond the shadow of a doubt, that she'd been trying to reach us. Protect us. On feet that didn't feel like mine, I drifted closer. Closer. The thing in the bed wasn't my father. Light from the hallway spilled over him, revealing every detail.

Insanity breathed down my neck. I tried to summon the fury Laurie had said to unleash, but all I could find was the pain. "No, no, no," younger me started to moan. "Daddy, wake up. Please. *Daddy.*"

The word ended on a scream.

Shuddering, I bunched the bedsheets in my fists. I fumbled for another way to combat the fear threatening to consume me. If not anger, then its opposite. What would that be?

As though he were there, hearing my desperate thoughts, the answer came. It was another memory of Dad. Not this one; a real one. When he was warm and alive. I'd just woken from yet another nightmare. He rushed into the room—one of them always did—and rocked me until my sobs quieted. *I'm going to tell you something very important, and you need to guard it like a secret, okay?* he'd said. *Our power is not inescapable. There is something stronger than fear.*

With that, he pressed a hand to my small chest. He told me what I felt for Damon, for my parents, was stronger than the quaking in my stomach and the sweat on my brow.

So now, years later, I finally took Dad's advice and thought of them. My mother and her soft hands. My father and the crow's feet at the corner of his eyes. Damon and his shy smile. Family. Joy. Love. I wrapped it around me like a blanket.

When I opened my eyes again, I was back in the throne room.

Jassin still stood across the fire, holding his fist up. A trail of dried blood coated the inside of his wrist. When he comprehended that I'd pulled out of the vision, very much intact, Jassin frowned. "My turn," I crooned. He blinked, but besides that single moment, there was no chance for him to react.

Like a tsunami, my will crashed over him. It turned out that the spell amplified my abilities—locating Jassin's biggest fear was easier than breathing. What I found made my brows rise with incredulity.

Despite my surprise, I didn't let that stop me from using it instantly. The next moment, we were surrounded by iridescent, ancient, incomprehensible light. Jassin cowered on his knees, holding that bloody hand up to shield his eyes. A voice came from the radiance. It was neither male nor female, young or old, angry or forgiving. My mind nearly broke from the power of it. *"I will repay each person according to what they have done,"* the voice said, reverberating all around us.

Someone was screaming.

The illusion faded. I staggered but managed to stay on my feet. It was a struggle to make my mind come to terms with reality.

When it did, my heart broke all over again. Damon was crouched over Jassin, who lay unmoving on the stones. Blood ran from the faerie's ears, nose, and eyes. The pain I felt wasn't for Jassin, of course—it was for my brother, who was wailing like I'd never heard him do before. Despite the awfulness of that sound, it confirmed that Jassin was well and truly dead. I was unable to stop a sigh of exhaustion and relief. My legs shook. Any second now I was going to pass out.

Belatedly, I noticed the crown, resting haphazardly and abandoned on the floor. Feeling like an old woman, I slowly bent to pick it up. That was when I noticed the stares.

Every faerie in the room waited for me to say something. As I put the crown back into place, I didn't let myself look toward the throne, where Collith had remained throughout the whole ordeal. His voice drifted through my memory. *History has already proven that ruling with fear leads to discord and treason. When I took the throne, I sought to rule with law and objectivity instead.*

Fear was all I knew.

"Let this be a lesson to all of you," I said, meeting as many gazes as I could. Damon kept crying. "If you fuck with me and mine, I will return the favor tenfold."

The statement had its intended effect; most in the Court regarded me with wariness now. Unable to resist, my eyes went to the figure sitting on that gnarled throne. His was full of admiration and something else I didn't expect.

Sorrow.

I raised my chin and—appearances be damned—swept out of the throne room.

CHAPTER NINETEEN

*T*his time, Lyari didn't follow at a distance. Apparently pledges were taken seriously, because she stayed right on my heels. No one was going to assassinate me today, that was for certain. Good thing, too, since all I wanted to do was take off the dress, lay down, and let sleep take me.

It wasn't until I was halfway back to Collith's rooms that I remembered the command I'd given. *Take him to my room. Stay with him, if he reacts badly, but do not cause him any pain or harm. I'll come after the ceremony.*

Shit. The werewolf.

Willing myself not to appear as broken as I felt, I approached Ilphas, who'd followed my commands to the letter. "How is he?" I asked. One of the torches flickered, so close to dying.

"He hasn't made a sound, Your Majesty," he said, keeping his gaze forward. Couldn't blame the guy, really. I'd humiliated him pretty thoroughly. I was glad the bonding spell between me and the entire Court hadn't seemed to kick in yet. Maybe, if I was really lucky, it never would.

As to Ilphas's answer, I wasn't sure quiet was a good thing or a bad thing. What if I opened the door and the werewolf attacked me?

Well, only one way to find out. I couldn't exactly ask someone else to risk their life. Brushing past Ilphas, giving myself no chances to reconsider, I slipped inside. The male didn't try to stop me, but Lyari did. "Your Majesty—" she started, her melodic voice at odds with the note of exasperation in it. Maybe she was just realizing that guarding me was not going to be an easy task.

The door closed in her face. I pressed my back against it and turned, steeling myself for a burst of claws and teeth. The mirror shard was tucked away, utterly out of reach. The only weapon at my disposal was fear. Hopefully there was enough of a person left in that damaged body to feel it.

In all the human legends and lore, werewolves were beasts of fury and bloodlust. They didn't feel things like distress or pain. They were driven by the hunt and nothing else.

But the creature on the other side of the room was not one from those stories. Yes, it was massive. Looking at it, I would guess it stood at six feet and weighed around one hundred and fifty pounds. Were it healthier, that number would be much higher. That was where the similarities ended, though. This beast cowered in the corner, as far from the door it could get, and stared at me with wide eyes. The terror was evident in every line of its furred body. Hair along its spine stood on end.

The crown probably made me look bigger and otherworldly —I removed it without any hesitation and set it on the ground. Next I removed the sapphire, which was flashing every time I shifted. Finished, I presented my hands to the werewolf, palms out. *See?* the gesture said. *Empty.*

The creature still wore the chain, but the end of it dragged through the dirt, unheeded. At this proximity I could see that there was a ring of scabs and bald patches where the links rested around its neck. Physical proof, as if I needed any, that the wretched female I'd taken him from had been yanking and pulling this wolf around for months. Did it worry that I'd saved it only to be another cruel master?

"You're safe now," I whispered, worried speaking any louder would frighten it into action. "You can change back."

The werewolf just kept staring at me. I knew that they had supernatural healing, but I wasn't sure whether he—or she—had been tortured or harmed with holy water. If that were the case, it would have wounds that were healing at a human rate, or even slower. I'd have to get closer to see. Maybe that's what had kept it from changing back all this time.

When I was a teenager, still dreaming of being a veterinarian, I had researched how to approach fearful dogs. Granted, this was no dog, but maybe the basic concepts still applied. I turned slightly so my side faced the wolf. Avoiding eye contact, I took a step toward it. The creature's lips curled, revealing two rows of sharp teeth.

Okay, then. Time for a new plan. Still moving at a cautious speed, I went to the rope hanging next to the door and pulled on it. The werewolf watched everything, its ears flattened against its head. Remembering how quickly Laurie had gone into the passageway, I only waited a few seconds before doing so myself.

When I opened the door, Lyari shoved past me with a muttered curse. I heard the word *moronic*. Her sword was drawn, and before I could give a sharp command, she was inside. The werewolf bristled even more but didn't move. My heartbeat slowed a bit.

Once Lyari was out of the way, I saw that a human girl stood in the shadows. The one I'd summoned, no doubt. Despite the dim, it was easy to see that she was young. Much younger than I wanted to acknowledge, even in my own mind. Probably ten, at the oldest, and that was pushing it. Her skin was covered in grime and her clothes were more tatters than a t-shirt and jeans.

Her shoes were gone, and the tips of dirt-covered toes peeked out.

The child kept her gaze fixed on those toes. Every few seconds, a tremor went through her. I couldn't discern whether it was from terror or cold. Probably both. "Could you bring some meat, please?" I asked, my voice kind.

Her gaze flicked to mine, just for an instant, but it was long enough to see that they were startlingly blue. She got a good look at my face and her own slackened with reverence. It took her a moment to recover, but when she did, the girl nodded and fled. I glanced up and down the passage, but there was no sign of Ilphas. Hopefully that meant he and his mate wouldn't cause the wolf any more trouble.

"Why are you doing this?" Lyari asked from behind me. She kept her tone flat, cold, but it still bordered on insolence.

I remained where I was, waiting for the girl to return. Without looking at her I answered, "It's called compassion. You should look it up sometime."

Lyari didn't reply. Within minutes, the child was back. She carried a plate in both hands, which was weighed down by a bloody, raw steak. "Perfect, thank you," I said, taking it. I approached the wolf again. This time it was too focused on what I held to lift its lips or growl.

When I put it down a few feet away, the wolf sprang. Lyari reacted too late, but it had no interest in me; the creature snatched the meat so violently that it upended the plate. It retreated into the corner again and began tearing the steak apart with razor-sharp teeth. *Poor thing is more feral than Fallen*, I thought, watching with discouragement. The food an adequate distraction, though—as I knelt to finally examine it for injuries, the werewolf didn't so much as glance at me. In doing so, I caught a peek of what was between its legs. Yes, definitely male.

Other than its obvious thinness, there weren't any injuries

that I could see. "I wish I knew your name," I said softly, leaning back on my haunches. "Can you understand me at all? Make some kind of signal, if you can."

The werewolf didn't move.

"Do you need anything else, Your Majesty?" the girl asked. Then she blanched, as though she'd said something forbidden. She'd probably been instructed to stay silent.

"Yes. Do you know where my clothes are kept? Not the ones in the backpack. The outfits and dresses I've been wearing during the trials and ceremonies."

The child's gaze darted to Lyari as though she feared punishment. "In that wardrobe, ma'am."

"Oh. Well, then. Go in there," I instructed, feeling dense. The wardrobe had been there since the moment I first stepped into this room—I'd just assumed it only held Collith's clothes. The girl scurried to obey. "Pick the most sensible pair of shoes you can find, then put them on. My feet are bigger than yours, but you'll grow into them. If anyone bothers you about it, tell them to talk to me."

Halfway through my short speech, the girl froze. Her wide eyes looked from me to the wardrobe, as though she didn't know which she found more treacherous. I knelt there, in front of the feasting werewolf, and waited. Lyari didn't say a word.

After seven seconds, the girl obeyed. The doors of the wardrobe opened to reveal a very full collection. Jeans, gowns, shirts, sweaters. A pair of shoes for every occasion lined the bottom two shelves. *That would've been handy to know about,* I thought with annoyance. The child pulled out a pair of tennis shoes that had probably never been worn; they had that crisp, white appearance. Holding them uncertainly, she faced again. I just mustered a smile and nodded.

"They say you hate the fae," the girl blurted instead of moving to leave. I looked at her and waited for more. She hesitated, glancing at Lyari. Whatever she saw there gave her courage. "Will you destroy them?"

All at once, the fatigue was back. "Not tonight," I answered on a sigh. "Thanks again for getting the steak."

She saw it for the dismissal it was. The girl's mouth clamped shut and she nearly ran out the door, clutching her new shoes. Lyari stood in the middle of the room, sword still drawn, her focus on the werewolf. "I'm going to sleep now," I told her pointedly. "Will you guard the door until Collith gets back?"

Lyari looked like she wanted to argue. I cocked a brow at her in a wordless challenge. With a mutinous expression, she stormed to the door. Fortuna, two. Lyari, one. I allowed myself a tiny, satisfied smile.

It was probably very, very stupid to lower my guard in the same room as a half-starved werewolf, but I couldn't bring myself to care. At least it would be a quick death. After an awkward struggle with the dress, I stripped down to my undergarments and climbed into bed. I tugged the covers over me and waited for sleep to come. It didn't take long. The edges went dark, creating a shrinking circle of light, like the end of an old movie. The last thing I saw was the wolf, curled into a ball, watching me with its glowing eyes.

The instant I slipped from the real world and into ours, Oliver was waiting.

The landscape had changed. Gone were the rolling meadows and open skies. In their place were damp sand and roiling clouds. Dark waves pounded against the shore, making me think of some monster from the deep, grasping at something alive on land.

Oliver was worried.

He sat on the beach, his back to the house and everything else. I plopped down beside him and squinted at the horizon. The sun was halfway consumed by ocean, its orange glow setting the water on fire. "Since I promised not to withhold information, you should know that my body is alone with a possibly rabid werewolf. But I don't want to talk about it. I also don't want to talk about my brother, or faeries, or trials. Is that okay?"

I could feel Oliver looking at me. A lump filled my throat, and I knew that if he pressed, I would break. "That's okay," he said. His voice was gentle. After a moment, I rested my head on his shoulder. It fit so perfectly. My arm went around his waist, and his went around mine.

That little voice in my head couldn't remain silent. *It will only get harder from here. Release him,* it urged. *He is a childhood imaginary friend. He is a wistful daydream. He is a sexual fantasy.*

I clung to Oliver even harder.

———

The morning after the bloody coronation, I went in search of my brother.

I was flanked by Lyari and Omar. The werewolf, too, accompanied me, to my surprise and the Guardians' displeasure. When I had tried to leave without him, he stood on the other side of the door and howled until I let him out. The sound was so loud that dirt trickled down from the ceiling.

Now he matched my pace, keeping so close that I could feel his ribcage brushing against my thigh now and then. He'd let me remove the chain, and it was good to see him walk unencumbered by its clunky weight. It felt like I had a deadly, unpredictable pet.

Today I wore the clothes I'd arrived in—I'd had enough of gowns to last me a lifetime. Despite my bland attire, faeries spotted me from afar and abruptly turned around or ducked into other passageways. After so many days feeling weak and small, their fear was heady. I relished it like an addict getting a fix.

At the threshold of Jassin's rooms, which Lyari had reluctantly led me to, I didn't let myself hesitate. Hesitation would bring unwanted memories. The door creaked open at my light touch.

I was greeted by the sight of my brother's delicate-looking spine. He was sitting on the bed, bare-chested, his skin pale as the moon. There was a shirt in his hands; I recognized it as something Jassin had worn.

Though he must've heard me enter, felt my presence, Damon said nothing. I couldn't bring myself to step into the room. "I'm sorry," I said. It was true; I was sorry for his pain. For the fact that I'd caused it.

Still, Damon didn't speak. Looking at him, a frail figure sitting on that great, empty bed, it was hard to believe he was in his twenties. In this moment, he looked like the boy who'd written his sister a note and gone out to garden at midnight. I shifted, about to go against my instincts and step over the invisible line that separated us, but at that moment Damon stood.

"This is my vow to you," he said. His body was angled toward me, but he kept staring down at the shirt as he spoke. His voice and eyes were dull. "For the rest of our lives, I will hate you."

The response didn't surprise me, exactly. Still, it felt like someone had buried their hand in my chest. The werewolf growled as if he sensed this. Without thinking, I rested my hand on his back. The rumbling instantly stopped. I steeled myself, but there was no hint of flavors or images from the contact between us. *Interesting,* I thought, then focused on my brother. "Damon, please, I didn't want—"

"Just go."

"I'm not going anywhere without you," I countered, willing my heart to harden. I had a sense of time running out and that left no room for hurt feelings. "Hate me all you want, but we're leaving the Unseelie Court, Damon. So start packing. If you won't listen to me, then take it as an order from your queen. I'll be back in an hour. Be ready or the Guardians will remove you by force. Got it?"

Silence filled the room. I turned to leave. "Wait," Damon said.

Hope was a cruel thing. Though I knew his mind was on Jassin, I still halted, yearning to hear words of forgiveness. "What?"

"Jassin." Damon said his name like a prayer. "What was he afraid of?"

For a few seconds, I debated whether or not to answer. There was no way of knowing if it would cause him more grief or bring some kind of healing. I could also feel Lyari and Omar listening; everything we said here would probably be public knowledge at the end of the day.

But I didn't have the strength to resist giving Damon what he wanted. "God. He was afraid of God," I said finally.

He said nothing as he absorbed this. I bit my tongue to hold back disparaging comments about the faerie he'd loved. Then, intending to spend the next hour writing letters—even if I couldn't stay with Damon once we got home, I had to do something to ease Bea, Gretchen, and Cyrus's worry—I headed back to Collith's rooms. Lyari and Omar took their positions, giving the werewolf a wide berth.

Upon our arrival, I saw that someone was waiting for me in the passageway. The male turned. I was surprised when the firelight touched Laurie's face; for some reason, I'd been expecting Collith, who had been mysteriously absent since my coronation. The faerie's expression was wary; he was waiting for me to ask questions. My epiphany in the throne room floated between us like an apparition. *They can't see you, can they?*

In all likelihood, the guards already thought I was insane. Most of them had seen me talking to myself at one time or another, since Laurie was hidden from their sight. Even so, I waited until we were inside and the door was shut before speaking. "I never thanked you," I said, going against every lesson Mom had taught me about the fae.

Laurie blinked. For once, I'd managed to startle him. He thought I would interrogate him straight away. "Thank me? Why?" he asked.

"For being my friend."

At this, the faerie hesitated. "Fortuna, I—"

His words cut short when I hugged him. He hesitated. Slowly, his arms went around me, too. His chin brushed my temple, and it was the first time we'd truly touched. Just as it had been with Collith, the brush of his skin revealed no fears. But power lurked there, such bright, crackling vitality that it made my teeth hurt. Power a lesser faerie shouldn't have had. I pulled back.

"What are you?" I demanded now, keeping my voice low.

He smiled faintly and pulled away. "Too dangerous. Nothing said in the Court of Shadows goes unheard, remember?"

"Fine. You don't have to tell me. But I still need your help, Laurie."

"So does he," my friend replied. The words were said so quietly, I almost didn't hear them. Before I could say anything else, Laurie was gone. *Son of a bitch*, I fumed silently. Guess I had finally learned who he was loyal to. Now what?

My mind was already flipping through other possibilities. I saw the face of every faerie I'd met since coming to the Unseelie Court. Their voices sounded like a podcast playing in my truck. Tarragon, maybe? He'd been impressed by the tribunal...

My progress screeched to a halt when I reached a certain memory. There was someone else who'd been willing to help me, once.

At the thought of going to see her, though, I hesitated. There was a chance it was entirely unnecessary to seek answers. For all I knew, the fae would let me leave Court without any interference. Call it a precaution, then. What if they hurt Damon out of spite? What if one of them kidnapped him again to gain control over the new queen? After the third trial, every faerie alive knew my vulnerability. I was still playing the game, and it never hurt to have a backup plan.

Once again, I left Collith's rooms with resolve, the werewolf in tow. Lyari was at her post, of course. She stared straight ahead, somehow managing to emanate resentment without an expression. "Lead me to the dungeons, please," I said. A frown tugged at the corners of her perfect mouth, but she complied without question.

It was a longer excursion than the ones to the throne room, Jassin's chambers, or the Leviathan's watery grave. Our small party wound through unfamiliar tunnels for at least a half hour. I was on the verge of asking how much farther when Lyari abruptly turned and vanished. Alarmed, I hurried after her, then realized she'd just gone down a set of stairs dug into the earth. Moans and sobs drifted to my ears. I really, really didn't want to see where they came from. Omar hovered nearby. I half-wished he would say something comforting. But he wasn't a friend; those were few and far between in this place.

The thought was just the push I needed. I allowed myself a short, fortifying breath, and plunged into the murky underbelly of the Unseelie Court. I could hear the werewolf's footsteps behind me, following without hesitation. The stairs felt endless. I was not gifted with being able to see in the dark, so I touched the walls on either side, fumbling with every step. They had not been carved the same height or length.

Lyari waited at the bottom, holding a torch aloft. *Why didn't you give that to me before I started coming down the staircase from hell?* I wanted to snarl. Fortuna, two. Lyari, two. I still had no idea why I'd assigned her as my guard instead of taking satisfying, swift vengeance.

Already, the smell of this place was getting to me. I just had to close my eyes and I was back in that cage. So much dampness, pain, and filth. Walking past the cells made my skin crawl. I couldn't remember which one the guards had thrown me in—I hadn't exactly been at my best. "Are you there?" I ventured, staring into the darkness of each reeking hole.

"So it's true. You survived the trials. I thought the guard was lying for sport," a voice rasped. It came from farther down the row.

Had I survived? It felt like part of me had died. I stopped in front of the cell and glanced at the guards, more aware of their presence than ever. "Lyari, Omar, please make sure we don't have an audience. Yes, it's true. The bloodlines already paid fealty."

"I would advise against speaking to this one alone, Your Majesty," Lyari said stiffly.

The looming sense of urgency almost made me snap. It occurred to me, though, that I may want to refrain from pissing off the faeries guarding me. "I appreciate your concern. Really. But this is something I have to do. Please," I added. No one could miss the sincerity in my voice. Lyari bit back a scowl, bowed, and made a sharp gesture at Omar. The two of them left.

The faerie in the cell waited until the sound of their footsteps retreated. "That's quite the entourage you have there," she observed. Her voice was a little stronger. "I haven't seen a werewolf in years. Forgive me for missing your coronation, Your Majesty. As you can see, I was otherwise detained. What brings you back to my humble home?"

Hoping to draw her out, I wrapped my fingers around the rusted bars. Collith's would-be assassin remained in the shadows. "I wanted to speak to the faerie who told me the truth, even when she had nothing to gain," I remarked. Her words from that day came back without any effort, as though they'd been branded on my brain. *Oh, you poor, stupid creature. Of course we can. We lie about everything. That rumor was established millennia ago. Some clever faerie thought it would be advantageous if the rest of the world thought we could be trusted.*

There was a long silence. "This is about Collith."

The familiarity with which she spoke his name caused an odd twinge of jealousy. "In part," I acknowledged. "I only put myself through those trials to get my brother back. Now that he's free from Jassin, he can go home. Someone is always watching or listening, though. I need an advantage... no, maybe 'insurance' is a better word. I don't want anyone to stop us, or take Damon again, or whatever else the fae have up their sleeves. So I guess I'm asking for information. I'd hoped you knew a way to stop any of it from happening."

"Why should I help you?" she asked.

I had expected this part. Unease still fluttered in my stomach. "I'll be in your debt. A boon from the Queen of the Unseelie Court must be worth something."

After another pause, there came a shuffling sound. The werewolf next to me went rigid and growled a warning. I dared to touch him again, but he wasn't comforted this time. His yellow eyes remained fastened on whatever he saw in the cell. Foreboding squeezed my throat, making it difficult to breathe, and I followed his gaze.

A beautiful corpse stepped into the light. When I saw her face, my heart picked up speed.

Collith's old lover.

What was her name... Viessa. Yes, that was it. She was nothing like the vibrant creature from Collith's memories. What could have possibly happened to her? Wait, he'd said something about this. I put myself back there, in his bed, next to that guttering candle. *Some faeries have a... specialty. A certain power or ability unique from others. Usually the ability manifests during puberty, but in rare cases, it can arise through trauma.*

Clearly it had been the latter for Viessa. Her red hair was frozen in place. A fine shimmer of frost coated part of her face.

Her irises were the brightest, most unnatural blue I'd ever seen. Ice clung to her lashes. Looking at her, I had a single thought.

She would've made an excellent queen.

Part of her mouth tilted up in a wry smile. Ignoring my obvious shock, Viessa gripped the bars with frost-blackened fingers. My feet itched to step back. "You could seek the Seelie King for assistance," she suggested. "The Court of Light is no less corrupt than this one, but their ruler is rumored to have a soft spot for pretty things. And he has a history with Collith; he might jump at the opportunity to humiliate or work against his Court."

If she touched my hands, would that horrible ice spread to me? I strove to sound normal as I replied, "And how do I find the Seelie King?"

"You could try calling for him." She lifted one shoulder in an indifferent shrug. "His name is Laurelis."

My instincts stirred. "Laurelis…"

"Yes." Viessa must've noticed my strange reaction, because she went on. "He does go by another; perhaps that's why you're confused. His mother's nickname for him, while she was still alive. Only his closest friends are permitted to use it."

"What is the name?" I asked, though I already knew the answer before the words completely left my mouth.

Viessa's eyes glittered. "Some call him Laurie."

END OF BOOK ONE

FORTUNA'S STORY
CONTINUES IN...

RESTLESS
SLUMBER

AVAILABLE NOW!

ACKNOWLEDGMENTS

With this project, I met so many new and wonderful friends. For that alone, I will always be glad I took the leap into self-publishing.

The first of these remarkable individuals is Sheila O'Connor, professor and reader extraordinaire. I will eternally be grateful for your insights. I'm not a person who believes in fate, but I look back at the moment I got the acceptance from Hamline University as the first step on a path that led me to your class. You've helped me grow as a writer and, despite those few months when I questioned my worth as one, you never doubted. That made all the difference.

Next, I must thank Emma Bull. I was so fortunate to end up with a mentor perfect for *Fortuna Sworn*. Your wisdom helped shaped this book to what it's become. Thank you for the time and thought you put into this new adventure of mine.

My gratitude also goes to Jessi Elliott. I can now look at all the hours I've spent on Instagram as an investment, as they are what led us to meet. Your enthusiasm for this story drove me to the finish line. I also might've lost my sanity were it not for those occasions when I texted you, needing another perspective, and you didn't hesitate to offer one. Here's to many more nights FaceTiming and, like, actually writing.

Indebtedness also to Kristen Williams, who was another friend to answer every text I sent asking her opinion, whether it was on marketing, or the cover, or my own doubts. (If you're an author who's looking for someone to host your Instagram cover reveal or book tour, Storygram Tours is the way to go. Seriously.)

Thank you to my agent, Beth Miller, for being so supportive when I told her that not only did I want to completely change genres, but I also wanted to self-publish. Then you selflessly offered to be a beta reader. I first queried you eight years ago and it's now difficult to imagine working with anyone else. It's been such a wild ride. I can't wait to see what else awaits us.

Adoration and appreciation to Gwenn Danae and Jesse Green, who made this book truly beautiful. I can't wait to see what the rest of the series will look like!

ABOUT THE AUTHOR

 K.J. Sutton lives in Minnesota with her two rescue dogs. She has received multiple awards for her work, and she graduated with a master's degree in Creative Writing from Hamline University.

When she's writing, K.J. always has a cup of Vanilla Chai in her hand and despises wearing anything besides pajamas. She adores interacting with fellow writers and readers. Until then, she's hard at work on her next book. K.J. Sutton also writes young adult novels as Kelsey Sutton.

Be friends with her on Instagram, Facebook, and Twitter. And don't forget to subscribe to her newsletter so you never miss an update!

Made in the USA
Columbia, SC
24 May 2021

38458147R00190